The Vogels: On All Fronts

The Half-Bloods Series Book 2

Jana Petken

ISBN: 9781729169698

The Vogels On All Fronts: The German Half-Bloods Series Book 2, is a work of fiction set against the backdrop of WWII. Its characters are purely fictional, as are their individual stories in this book.
For authenticity purposes, historical personages have been mentioned. A few have been integrated into the storyline, but without contradicting historical facts.
Cover design by Adriana Hanganu

The Vogels: On All Fronts

Readers' Favourite, 2018 Award-Winner

Book description

"The Vogels are fighting on all fronts in this compelling story of intrigue and betrayal in a world at war."

European citizens feel the full force of German injustice, but not all are willing to bend the knee. From France to Poland, Resistance groups fight from the shadows to thwart Nazi rule and hinder their goal to exterminate Jews.

In Russia, Wilmot Vogel struggles to survive the ravages of a frigid winter, compounded by the German army's lack of progress. Hit by a surprise Russian attack on the front lines, however, he finds himself facing an even greater challenge than the freezing weather and Soviet bullets.

In Łódź, Poland, an idealistic doctor is resolved to oppose the Third Reich, but is he willing to betray his country? Will a Gestapo major find the answers he's looking for? Does a ghetto Jew avoid transportation to a Nazi extermination camp?

Can two spies rekindle their relationship, or will past betrayals become hurdles too great to surmount? Can Britain's MI6 maintain the upper hand in a contest against the German Abwehr? Who wins when one man fights for British interests whilst the other seeks to undermine them?

In the darkest days of war, love flourishes. Two women with very different paths are led to one man who changes the course of their lives forever – but only one will win his heart.

More Jana Petken Titles

Multi Award Winning #1 Bestseller, *The Guardian of Secrets*
Screenplay, *The Guardian of Secrets*
Audio book, *The Guardian of Secrets, with Tantor Media*
#1 Bestselling Series: *The Mercy Carver Series:*
Award-Winning *Dark Shadows*
Audio Book, *Dark Shadows*
Award-Winning *Blood Moon*
Multi-Award-Winning #1 Bestseller, *The Errant Flock*
Audio Book, *The Errant Flock*
Award-Winning Bestseller, *The Scattered Flock*
Award Winning, *Flock, The Gathering of The Damned*
Multi-Award-Winning #1 Bestseller, *Swearing Allegiance*
Award-Winning #1 Bestseller, *The German Half-Bloods*
Coming Soon, *The Mercy Carver Series, The Flock Trilogy,
Swearing Allegiance, The German Half-Bloods on audio in
association with Cherry-Hill Audio Publishing*

Coming Spring 2019, *Before the Brightest Dawn, Book 3 of The
Half-Bloods Series*

Acknowledgements

Thank you to the following people:
Editor, Gabi Plumm
Proofreading, Caro Powney
Patricia Rose
Graphics and cover design, Adriana Hanganu,

A huge thank you to all my readers who keep the faith and tell me to hurry with the next book. Without you, my titles would lie on a shelf collecting dust.
My thanks also to friends who, every so often, dig me out of my hermit's hole to have some fun and to Robyne who kept a tight rein on my German. My thanks also to her grandfather for the absolutely coincidental sharing of his name; Dieter Vogel.

This book is dedicated to my darling mother, Rena, an avid reader in her time. Gone, never forgotten, always loved.

Author's Note

This book is written in UK English and all spelling, punctuation, and grammar adhere to UK English, World English, and Oxford English Dictionaries.
All German names and connotations have been written with German spellings.

I hope you enjoy *The Vogels: On all Fronts*

To be continued, Spring 2019

Prologue

Dieter Vogel

Berlin, Germany
April 1933

Dieter Vogel peeked at his watch. He was running late for his next appointment with his old friend, Freddie Biermann; however, his present luncheon host, Konstatin Hierl, the State Secretary in the Reich Ministry of Labour, was his priority. Prior to the Führer taking office, Hierl had been a high-ranking member of the NSDAP and head of the Party's labour organisation, the *Nationalsozialistischer Arbeitsdienst.* During that period, he had been instrumental in helping Dieter to acquire significant government contracts. He was not a man to walk out on.

Dieter held a hand over his crystal Scotch glass. "I really shouldn't, Konstantin. As good as it is, I think I've had quite enough."

"One more, Dieter. Now that those boring farts have left, we can have a real conversation. Besides, thanks to Herr Goebbels' boycott of Jewish businesses, Berlin is at a standstill today, and so are your factories. Ach, come on, you deserve a break."

"Oh, all right, you've twisted my arm."

The two men appeared relaxed in their chairs, sipping whiskies. But privately, Dieter was anxious about the damage the boycott was doing to his business, as well as the ticking off he'd get from Freddie for keeping him waiting. Biermann was a stickler for punctuality, always arriving at his destination ten minutes before time.

Konstantin swirled the ice around inside his glass. Dieter had also sensed unease in the Minister during the long lunch they'd just had with other prominent business owners.

"You seem quiet today, Konstantin. Is something bothering you?" Dieter asked, putting his own concerns aside.

As he set his glass on the table, Heirl scratched one side of the rather untidy moustache that encroached onto his chubby cheeks. Still silent, he picked up his silver cigarette case and clicked it open. From a line of ten, he slipped one cigarette through the elastic holding band and then tapped it upright on the table to loosen the tobacco before lighting it. "I'm quiet but always thinking, Dieter," he finally said. "You know, the Party needs industry giants like you. You donate money and employ more than a thousand workers in your haulage company, depots and factories, and whatever else you have up your sleeve, and you have great influence over the way your workers think politically. You're also in a unique position to have the ear of politicians like me, but without having to get entangled in a web of dirty politics. You're fortunate. There are times I think it's a curse having inside information on the men leading the country."

"Why?" Dieter's forehead wrinkled with surprise.

"I'm seeing things, hearing things I don't like, but I've got to keep my mouth shut no matter how much I might disapprove or want to change policies. That's my curse." Hierl exhaled a long plume of smoke. "Herr Hitler's sycophants – and I don't include myself in that bunch of power-crazed megalomaniacs – are squabbling amongst themselves for positions in the cabinet. The infighting is oblique, of course, never fully out in the open because Hitler detests discord amongst his ministers. But I swear, Dieter, Göring, Himmler, Goebbels, and Hess – yes, him too –

spend more time trying to sabotage each other than working together on policies that will benefit the country."

Dieter was engrossed. It was rare to get insights like these into Hitler's cabinet woes. "I see. I can understand why you feel frustrated. Tell me, Konstantin, are they all aligned with the Fürher's policies?"

"Mostly. The anti-Semites in Hitler's inner circle are resisting those who are more moderate towards the Jews. Personally, I don't see the Kikes as a threat to Germany, and neither does Herr Göring."

"He's an odd fish. He doesn't seem to fit the socialist profile at all," Dieter said.

"I agree, yet Hitler gave him Minister of the Interior for Prussia, the largest state in Germany. Ach, no one will ever change Göring. He'll always see himself as aristocratic, what with his ridiculous flamboyant outfits and living in his family's castles. But unlike Goebbels, he's not opposed to the inclusion of Jews in German life."

"I've always found Rudolph Hess to be a rather strange man as well," Dieter mused. "Just before the general election … yes, just weeks before, I was at a dinner party with Hess, and he said the most extraordinary thing. He mentioned at the table … in front of ten other men, mind you, that he didn't do anything until he'd consulted with the stars, the pendulum, and Nostradamus' works. He believes in telekinesis. Did you know?"

Hierl nodded. "Yes, unfortunately I did. He once vowed at a meeting that one day he would move objects with his mind, including a chair. God help Germany if Hitler were to die or be removed. Hess, as Deputy Chancellor, would take over and probably start a crazed religious cult."

Both men, unwinding with the aid of their whiskies, enjoyed a moment of silence until Hierl said, "Hess is not the only one with strange ideas, Dieter. Himmler also has an interest in the occult. He interprets Germanic neopagan and Völkisch beliefs, which he claims espouse the racial policy of Nazi Germany. He's already incorporated esoteric symbolism and rituals into the SS – now, that's a man who detests Jews."

Dieter, his head spinning with too much alcohol, was fascinated by the titbit about Himmler's hobby. "He's never hidden his hatred of the Jews, but you know, I think Goebbels…"

"I call him the Nazi spin-master."

Dieter chuckled. "I call him a man with a vitriolic, pathological hatred of the Jewish race, bordering on obsession. He's probably the most anti-Semitic member of Hitler's cabinet. What do you think?"

Hierl shrugged, "There's not much difference between him and Himmler to be honest, only their ideas on how to deal with the Jewish *problem.*"

Dieter placed his empty glass on the table in front of him and asked, "And what of our Führer? Is he really against the Jews?"

"Hmm. Yes, I believe so. But not to the same extent as Goebbels and Himmler. The thing is, Dieter, the economy is not doing as well as the Party is leading the country to believe. It hasn't pulled itself out of the depression yet, and as much as I hate to admit it, demonising the Jews is a clever move. It shifts the blame for the lack of economic progress onto them, and what's more, it casts them as the architects of Germany's woes."

******

Dieter zig-zagged through the crowded streets towards the beerhall he frequented once a week with Freddie Biermann. Although he was late for the meeting because of his lunch, street demonstrations, and picket lines, he halted for the third time when he reached a mob standing in front of a shop. One of Rohm's Stormtroopers was putting the finishing touches to a white Star of David that he'd painted on a grocer shop's window. Next to him, another Brownshirt was writing the word JUDE on the wall. He turned to glare at the bystanders, his face full of malice, the paint brush waving in his hand. "Jude – you see what that says? Look, everyone – *Jude* – he's not welcome here!"

Another *Sturmabteilung,* a pubescent-looking bully, blocked the shop's entrance and shouted out the written text on the wide placard he held flush against his chest, "Buy from real Germans! Don't buy anything from Jews. They are our downfall. Go back to Palestine, Jews! Get out!"

Dieter grumbled to himself as he bumped into people watching yet another ugly scene outside a Jewish jewellery store two doors along from the grocers. Hitler had won the Chancellorship in the most spectacular way, using a very simple slogan to convey his message: *Brot und Arbeit, Bread and Work,* yet he had chosen to begin his term in office under a banner of anti-Semitism in its rawest form. It was ironic and deeply troubling.

Dieter's factory had ground to a standstill that morning due to the senseless disruption caused by the nationwide boycott of Jewish businesses. The Brownshirts had formed a picket line outside his gates, preventing Jewish workers from entering. Deliveries of machinery parts and tools ordered weeks earlier couldn't get through. His suppliers, many of whom were Jewish, had telephoned to apologise for the inconvenience; truck loaders and drivers had been scared off by thugs who had destroyed merchandise and flattened truck tyres to stop them from leaving the depots. It was blatant hooliganism coming directly from Herr Goebbels' office. The Minister of Propaganda had been on the radio for days spurring the would-be protesters on. He'd gone beyond mere encouragement, insisting it was the *duty* of *all* Germans to deny Jews a living for the sake of the country. Dieter was furious. This carry-on wasn't why he'd voted for Hitler. This was not what he wanted for Germany.

As always on a Friday, the beerhall was full of men enjoying a few drinks before their wives grabbed their pay packets. Because of the mild spring weather, the owner had opened the French doors leading to the establishment's back garden, and drinkers were standing in groups discussing the day's events.

Dieter found Freddie reading a newspaper at a small round table near the garden's end wall. "Sorry, Freddie," he said, wiggling his backside into a hard wrought-iron chair without a cushion.

"It's not like you to be late." Freddie tapped his watch. "Sit, you look puffed out. I'll get the beers. I'm one ahead of you already."

When Freddie returned, Dieter took the tall, cold glass in both hands and drank the frothy golden liquid until he was breathless. He exhaled. "It's chaos out there, Freddie. I don't know what's come over people. How could they fall for Goebbels' fearmongering?" He banged the almost empty glass on the table. "Although, having said that, not everyone was obeying those browbeaters blocking shop doors. Some sensible people are barging their way inside and buying what they damn well please, as they should."

"They're curious, I suppose. Herr Goebbels instructed people to stay at home and not to go anywhere near Jewish shops or businesses, and what do the people do? They run from one Jewish establishment to the next to appease their curiosity. It's like a waiter saying in a restaurant, "Please don't touch the plate; it's hot," and the diner then burns his fingers because he just had to do it. Apparently, the word *don't* is a paradox, with *don't* meaning *do*."

Dieter grunted. "Can you blame them for wanting to see the boycott for themselves? I thought all this anti-Semitism was just an election stunt…"

"It wasn't a stunt, Dieter," Freddie interrupted. "It was a promise, and Herr Hitler's going to keep it. You should be pleased."

Dieter frowned. *Why should he be happy about businesses losing money?* The divisive rhetoric was tearing the seams of democracy apart. He took a more measured sip of his remaining beer and decided that getting even more drunk than he already was had lost its appeal somewhere between Wilhelmstraße and Brandenburg Gate. Drowning anger in alcohol wasn't going to work anymore. His guilty conscience for voting the Nazi Party into power wouldn't be assuaged by a few beers and a double Scotch, nor would his premonitions of doom. He'd made a monumental mistake, and so had every other fool who'd been swept away by Hitler's populist promises, including Freddie.

"You're not sticking up for the Jews, are you?" asked Freddie, breaking into Dieter's thoughts. "If you are, you're being unfair to Herr Hitler."

"Unfair?"

"Yes. He's got to take tactical considerations into account every time he makes a move. It can't be easy manoeuvring between the Party's radical inclinations and the need to satisfy the conservative German elites, not to mention international public opinion. I think he's getting it just right. The Jews need to go if we're to stand any chance of economic recovery. There's no other way of looking at it."

Shocked, Dieter played with his glass, turning it around in his fingers. *The Jews need to go. The Jews need to go.* The changes in Freddie's political attitudes were like fissures fracturing their friendship. He could no longer be honest with his opinions or thoughts. He was not even sure if he could trust his oldest friend anymore. Maybe *fissure* was the wrong word; it was more like a glacial crevasse, a minefield that would blow his head off if he said the wrong thing.

"Are you regretting your vote, Dieter?" Freddie asked outright.

"I regret what Goebbels is doing today. I don't like my businesses being hurt by his ludicrous propaganda campaigns. Half my workforce in Dresden and Berlin are Jewish, and this nonsense is damaging to Germany's growth."

"I asked if you regretted your vote."

Dieter flinched at Freddie's harsh tone. "No. I still think Hitler's the man for the job."

"I'm glad to hear it."

After their second beer, it seemed that Freddie's mood lightened. Dieter laughed at his joke directed at *the stupid Jews*, but he was heavy-hearted. Five years earlier, his and Freddie's principles had been aligned. They'd actively followed Adolf Hitler's rise to power, attending his rallies and meetings together and joining the Nazi Party on the same day. The Führer's promises to lift people out of poverty and to regain Europe's respect for Germany on the international stage had convinced both men that the country they'd fought for in the Great War would be returned to greatness under a new, dynamic leader. But unlike Freddie, Dieter's faith in that magnificent goal had waned.

"You're not yourself tonight, Dieter. Is everything all right at home?" Freddie asked.

"Yes, everything is fine. I caught Hannah wearing her mother's rouge lip balm. Wilmot's a handful, as always. Max is off to England for a spell, did I tell you? And Paul has decided not to follow me into the business. He's about to go into medicine at the Munich Medical Faculty." Dieter gave Freddie a weak smile. "Ach, I'm a bit hurt – I just don't like my children growing up and leaving me."

"Don't worry about them, Dieter." Freddie chuckled. "They'll come back to you like bad pfennigs. That's what children do."

"I know. But I hate seeing my Laura upset. Those children are her life." Dieter cleared his throat. "Right, that's enough of me. What's this wonderful news you wanted to tell me?"

Freddie took a furtive look around the garden. Only five people including he and Dieter remained. The sun was setting, it was growing cold, and men were going inside to continue drinking. "I haven't told Olga yet, so keep this to yourself."

"I will. Jesus, Freddie, what have you done? Tell me you haven't re-joined the army?"

"No, but I have got myself a new job. I was hand-picked by Göring himself." Freddie puffed his chest out like a turkey jake. "To say I'm delighted would be an understatement. Meet the new Kriminaldirektor of the *Geheime Staatspolizei*."

"The what?"

"The Gestapo, Dieter. The new Prussian Secret State Police. I'm leaving for Prussia on Tuesday, which is ironic, considering that's where I come from and where I began my police career."

"Hmm." Dieter hid his worried frown. The new Secret State Police in Prussia under Göring had already started to gather intelligence on people known to oppose the Nazi Party. Konstantin, during their earlier lunch, had predicted that Göring's Gestapo would eventually be a nationwide force. The Secret Police could quite possibly become an intelligence agency, which would keep dissenters at bay during this crucial time in Germany's resurgence. Apparently, Himmler wanted all the security forces under his command.

"Have you *nothing* to say about my news?" asked Freddie, breaking the long silence.

Dieter shrugged. "I'm pleased for you, Freddie. I can't say I'm happy about you going to Prussia, but I do congratulate you on your new appointment."

"I have a feeling I won't be gone for too long. I'm getting in on the ground with the promise of a transfer back to Berlin if the Gestapo becomes a national force."

Dieter ordered two double Scotches to celebrate and, despite the cold creeping into his bones, suggested that they remain in the garden. Desperate to save their friendship, he asked, "Are you sure you want to do this? Do you really want to lock people up for speaking their minds? Have you heard about the detention camp that's been opened near Munich? Is that where you'll put the people you arrest?"

"You mean Dachau?"

"Yes."

"Ach, c'mon, Dieter, don't be so bloody naïve. We're talking about Jews and Communists. You know as well as I do that they're Germany's biggest problem."

"No. I don't actually."

Freddie clicked his tongue, an annoying habit of his when he was angry. "But you did when you cheered Hitler on at his political rallies – what's got into you? Those people are never going to accept the Nazi Party. They're trying to sabotage everything we've achieved. You know that, so don't look at me with those outraged eyes of yours. Dachau is a stroke of genius. It'll get those troublemakers off the streets and shut them up for good." He swallowed half the amber liquid in his glass. "Dieter, if it comes down to it, I'll report my own mother for treason. I would, for the good of my country. We'll all have to step up, even you. No one should be above the law or allowed to derail the Führer's policies. You must see I'm right?"

With one finger to his lips, Dieter patted Freddie's arm. His friend was becoming increasingly agitated as the discussion continued.

"Don't you shush me, Dieter Vogel. I'm glad to have the chance to silence agitators. Real Germans are the victims of Jews who want to take over Europe, and if we have any chance of growing, we must expel the lot of them. I'm all for tough measures. What about you?"

"Well, I…"

"Ach, don't answer. You're one of those people who's willing to go halfway but doesn't want to jump in the mud and get dirty. Thank God, you're in the minority. Never in the history of Germany has there been such enthusiasm for its leader. You know, I truly believe that the Führer was sent by the Almighty to cleanse the Fatherland."

"And I truly believe you've had far too much to drink, old friend." Dieter didn't know if he should laugh or cry at Biermann's belief that destroying civil liberties and an entire religion was the path to glory. But as he watched his friend's mouth snarl with hatred, he was certain that their friendship in its previous form had ended. He was devastated.

Dieter politely refused a lift from Biermann and hailed a taxi, giving the driver his home address. Halfway there, however, he changed his mind and told the driver to take him to another part of the city. He pulled a folded piece of paper from his wallet and studied the address written on it.

For weeks, he'd been mulling over the meeting he'd attended in London, at times kicking himself for opening a can of maggots that were now eating his conscience alive. Every day since his return to Berlin, he'd gone through the questions posed by the man he'd met: did the prospect of becoming a British spy make him feel nervous, excited, guilty, or justified? Was he on his way to ruination or salvation, helping Germany or becoming a traitor? Only after he'd found answers to these questions and was happy with them, was he to contact the British Intelligence Service with his offer to serve.

The taxi dropped him off at the corner of a street of terraced houses. He lit a cigarette while walking towards house number 547 and pondered the questions again. He still didn't have all the answers, but he had instinct, principles, and enough trepidation for Germany's future to warrant attending this second meeting. That answer would have to do for whomever he was to be seeing now.

When he reached the door, he glanced over his shoulder; he'd become paranoid in the space of an hour. And that was another reason to continue to his destination.

He knocked three times. The door was opened almost immediately by an elderly man in a dressing gown and furry slippers who looked furtively over Dieter's shoulders.

"Yes?"

"I've come to visit a friend from my old stomping ground."

"A friend, eh?"

"Yes, the Englishman."

"Well, you'd better come in then." He held the door wide and Dieter entered, a sense of fate and destiny giving flight to the butterflies in his stomach.

In the living room, a middle-aged man lounged in a deep armchair reading the *Berliner Börsen-Courier,* a German newspaper. When Dieter entered the room, the man folded it in four, stood, and extended his hand. "I'm very glad you decided to come, Herr Vogel. My name is Jonathan Heller of His Majesty's Secret Intelligence Service."

The elderly man in his dressing gown and slippers left the living room, closing the door quietly behind him.

"To be honest, Mr Heller, when I woke up this morning I decided not to come here or have anything to do with your lot. At lunchtime, I changed my mind. An hour ago, I got in a taxi intending to head to this part of the city, but instead, I instructed the driver to take me home before changing my mind again halfway there. And this is how it has been ever since my meeting with your agent in London. I'm not glad to be here, but after the day I've had and the things I have learnt, I see it as my duty to at least try to halt my government's path to Germany's undoing. God and history will judge me, Mr Heller, so let's get to it, shall we?"

Heller gestured to an armchair and waited until Dieter was seated before he regained his own. "Herr Vogel, after you approached us in London – and we're very happy you did – we looked at your background … standard procedure, you understand?"

"Yes. I understand. And what did my personal history tell you about me?"

"You were a good soldier and an enthusiastic member of the Nazi Party in the late 20s. You're a family man who has allowed his wife and children to keep their ties with Britain. You now have concerns about where your country is heading, and you want to stop your Führer from crossing the boundaries of nationalism into a situation of outright aggression towards his neighbours to the East. My agent told me of your fears. Would you care to elaborate on them?"

Dieter deduced that the only way any association with the British would work was if he were completely honest, not only with the Englishman, but with himself. He knew what he wanted to achieve and could only hope that Jonathan Heller was of a like mind. He was tired of compromising *his* truth.

"Your agent has a good memory, but I would like to explain further. You see, I believe that the Nazi Party is becoming fanatical about certain policies that might damage the country's economy and relations with the rest of Europe," Dieter began. "I'm particularly concerned about Herr Goebbels' Propaganda Ministry. It's always a bad sign when a government exerts jurisdiction over journalism, the arts, and information, and calls such establishments the enemy of the people. For example, I believe that newspaper you were reading will be out of business by the end of the year because it's bold enough to criticise the Nazi Party. Of course, Goebbels' expression, *the enemy of the people,* has been used throughout history, back to Roman times, if I'm not mistaken, when the Senate declared Emperor Nero a *hostis publicus.* My point is, Mr Heller, I cannot allow such disregard for the truth to go unchecked."

"What do you think you can do about it?"

"I think I can help my country by providing you with facts that will counteract the lies that Hitler and Goebbels are spinning to the German people. Our European neighbours deserve to know the truth, so they can prepare themselves for whatever is to come."

"And what do you believe is coming? War?"

"I'm not sure. Any financial analyst would say that Germany is in no position to declare war on anyone, at least not in the foreseeable future. But we haven't seen anyone like Adolf Hitler and his Nationalist extremists before. Mr Heller, anything is possible and that is why I am here."

Dieter's mouth was as dry as cotton, despite the wine, beer, and Scotch he'd downed that day.

Six weeks earlier, while on a visit to Laura's family in Kent, an MI6 agent who he'd met once before in Hyde Park had given him a piece of paper with a date, an address, and instructions: he was to meet with a British Intelligence operative in Berlin before midnight on the specified date. Today. The London spy had also stipulated that he was never to contact MI6 again should he decide not to go ahead with the meeting in Berlin. Likewise, should he agree to join the British Secret Service, he would not be able to get out later. If he tried to leave or double-cross the British, *get out* would mean being permanently disposed of. An obvious and scary assumption, although the agent had declined to expand on the statement.

"It was today's events that swayed me," Dieter repeated. "Had I not witnessed Goebbels' monstrous abuse of power on the streets of Berlin, I probably wouldn't be here now. But I am here, and I'm willing to sacrifice everything to help Britain keep abreast of the Nazis' agenda and combat their propaganda. It's up to you whether you accept me."

Heller looked pleased. "We'd be delighted to have you on board, Herr Vogel."

The two men shook hands. Dieter was desperate for a drop of alcohol to settle his nerves, but Heller had already begun talking about what the job would entail.

"... and information, anything your new Chancellor and his Nazi Party does that might threaten Europe or give you cause to worry. Any troop movements, changes to military structures or German citizens' rights, chatter about neighbouring countries to the East and West and North. We'll also need a written assurance of loyalty."

"I'll give you my word," said Dieter, not entirely sure what was meant by an assurance.

"I'm afraid that won't be enough. You will be required to go to Britain to sign an agreement, in accordance with the Official Secrets Act, then attend a couple of training courses in communication and tactics. We would like you in London as soon as possible. Can you manage that?"

"Getting to London won't be a problem. I'll take my wife to visit her sister in Kent."

Heller left the room and returned a few minutes later with the man in the dressing gown.

"Let me introduce you to Ernst Brandt," Heller said. "He's joined us tonight from Munich."

Dieter shook Brandt's hand. "Is this your house, Herr Brandt?" Dieter asked, looking at the man's striped pyjamas under his robe.

"No. His Majesty's government owns the property, but Ernst's name is on the lease," Heller answered. "Ernst's wife is Jewish, making their children half-Jewish and his grandchildren a quarter Jewish. He's concerned, as he should be, and he's also one of the best forgers in the business. He's been with us for almost a year, and now he's going to work with you."

"Why did you get involved, Herr Brandt, apart from being concerned for your family?" Dieter asked.

"That's none of your business, and you can call me Romeo from now on," Ernst Brandt scowled.

Heller chuckled as he handed Dieter a piece of paper with a telephone number on it. "You'll warm to him, Dieter. Your code name is Big Bear, and tonight will be the last time you will communicate with us using your real name." He pointed to the telephone number. "You can contact me at this number when you arrive in London."

When Dieter finally got to bed that night, he kissed Laura, his wife of twenty-five years who was sound asleep beside him, then laid his head on the pillow thinking about the momentous decision he'd made. His chest felt as though it were being crushed by an anvil. It was hard to breathe, hard to think of anything but the lifetime of lies and subterfuge he would now have to create to survive, but he had no second thoughts or doubts, not one. The Nazi Party was the most dangerous con ever perpetrated against a country, and they needed to be reined in before they plunged the German people into an abyss.

Chapter One

Max Vogel

London, England
October 1941

The two women waved from the window as the train huffed, puffed, and jerked as it pulled away from the platform. Laura sniffed and blew her nose with Dieter's handkerchief. "I love you, darling," she squeaked, her normally strong voice snuffly with a blocked nose. Hannah's face, however, was lit up with excitement. She and her son were going home to Frank, she had informed them all the previous evening; she was never truly herself without him by her side.

When the last carriage had disappeared down the track, Max and Dieter fought their way through Euston Station's crowded platforms to the exit. Max, who despite his stiff leg, had insisted on accompanying his father to the emotional send-off for his mother's sake. "I'll be happier knowing your father won't be alone when I leave him." Laura had wept that morning, smiling weakly as she hugged her eldest son. "Make sure he eats properly, and don't let him get into any more trouble."

Both men were going in the same direction, but they would split up when they reached Oxford Circus. Dieter had a meeting at MI6 Headquarters with Heller, and Max was going back to the SOE offices in Baker Street. The previous evening, he had received a startling telephone call from his boss regarding Paul, and the news he'd received had shaken him to his core. He hadn't slept a wink, nor would he in the days to come, he suspected.

He shot a sideways glance at Dieter whose face was rarely a window to his feelings. The last-minute decision to send Laura to Scotland with Hannah had been taken after long discussions that had lasted until midnight. Dieter, who'd hated the idea, had eventually given in to his wife after she'd reminded him that he would be spending most of his time in London, and she would be alone in Kent, albeit surrounded by her extended family. Max, who was finding it hard to even like his father at present, had been impressed by his sacrifice. If there was anything he knew to be true, it was his father's love for his wife and his reluctance to be parted from her for any length of time. He was a difficult person at times, but when one peeled away the layers of deceit and stubborn pride, one found a man with a deep-seated devotion to his family. Max saw a glimmer of hope for a better relationship with his father, but it wouldn't happen until the secrets and lies between them had been aired and expunged.

"You did the right thing letting her go, Father. It might not feel like that to you now, but it will be best for Mother. You'll hardly find the time to get back to Kent once you start work." Max patted his father's shoulder.

"Do you really think so, Son? I hated sending her off like that. She's only just got me back, and she's still coming to terms with everything that happened in Germany. Ach, I know she'll be better off. I just don't want her to think I was lying again or trying to get rid of her because I'll be too busy to spend time with her. I won't know what to do with myself without her to keep me right. This whole business has floored me."

The corners of Max's mouth lifted in a tender smile. His father was behaving like a love-struck teenager; it was touching to listen to his concern for the woman he loved. "Papa, this was her decision. She rightly presumes you'll be working all the hours

God gave, and you wouldn't get home to Kent more than a couple of nights a week at best. I know all about the demands at MI6 headquarters. It was the gruelling days that forced me to rent the bedsit in Central London, which you can use whenever you want, by the way."

Dieter nodded. "I suppose you're right. Mother will be a lot happier in Scotland with Hannah and little Jack."

"Of course, she will. She'll have her grandson to spoil, a place where she can take long walks, and you know how much she loves hiking the moors. She'll get plenty of fresh air up there, and she'll mother Hannah and Frank to death."

"Hannah was over the moon. Having her mother's company when Frank is at work all day will be good for her as well. She was especially glad of the promise of help with the baby. Did I tell you I've sent Judith Weber up there to stay with Hannah? She's a nice girl, been through hell."

Max was surprised. "No. Mother never said a word about that."

"You'll like her when you meet her, Son. She's a courageous young woman, full of fire."

The conversation about Judith stopped there, but Dieter continued to talk about Laura until they reached Oxford Street. There, Dieter hugged Max in a rare public display of affection. "I'm sorry about all the lies, Max. I hope you'll forgive me one day. I love you, Son. I never meant to hurt you."

******

Max waited alone in his boss's office. Major Blackthorn, the head of the French F-Section at the SOE, had placed a call to

Hannah's house the previous night after he'd found out from Heller that Max was planning to stay with his sister and parents for a few days to recover from the injury he'd sustained in France. During the conversation, Blackthorn had offered to let Max return to Baker Street to hear Klara's testimony regarding Paul's alleged abduction. The brief conversation had been infuriatingly ambiguous. Blackthorn refused to give any details other than Klara's admission that she'd played a part in Paul's death. That, and her request for Max to be present at her debriefing, was all Blackthorn would say. It was going to be a hell of a day with more revelations to add to the previous day's shocks which had left his family reeling.

It was still hard for Max to believe that his father, the Nazi, was also Big Bear, the head of Berlin's British spy ring. Max had been shut in the living room with his father until the early hours of the morning, long after the women had gone to bed. It had been an eye-opening experience, one in which Dieter had been completely honest, no omissions regarding his life as a British agent in Germany. He had spoken about why he'd joined MI6 and, subsequently, his numerous meetings with Herr Brandt in a dingy working men's beerhall. Max had found the apparent friendship between the two men particularly interesting. He had tried but failed to picture the brash, downtrodden Brandt drinking a pitcher of beer with the autocratic, wealthy Dieter Vogel, the industrialist. It didn't make sense to him, yet Dieter was clearly fond of old Ernst.

The previous night, the family had eaten dinner together, and during coffee, Dieter had spoken about the explosions in his factory. He'd deliberately left out the part where he'd killed three SS guards in the basement, and that Kurt had been his sidekick.

After the women had retired, he'd remarked that Mother and Hannah didn't need to know that the soldiers had died at his hands. "Your mother now knows she is married to a spy, and she has accepted that. But being the wife of a murderer would be a hard pill for any woman to swallow. She won't hear about any ugly business from me or you, Max. I hope you agree?"

His mother was an inquisitive woman by nature, Max thought now, but strangely, she hadn't quizzed her husband further after Hannah had questioned him about who he'd been working with in Berlin. He'd been quick to tell her he'd operated entirely alone for years, and to his knowledge there were no other British secret agents in Germany. That might have been believable, had his mother not told Hannah that Kurt had been injured in the factory bomb blast. He'd been an innocent casualty in the wrong place at the wrong time, she'd asserted. She had then assured Hannah and Max that Kurt had been ignorant of Papa's antics, as she called them.

Max surmised that neither Hannah nor his mother wanted to know about the nitty-gritty details of Dieter's job, or who was involved with him. Women were not built to hear about the dirty, backstabbing world of espionage; yet, he had come across exceptional operatives like Klara in almost every country he'd been to. Those female spies seemed to thrive on danger and were extremely talented at subterfuge.

Pulled from his thoughts, he jumped to his feet as Major Blackthorn strode in. "Thank you for this, Major. Is it time?"

"Not yet. I want to have a word with you before you see her," said Blackthorn, sitting at his desk and motioning Max to be seated. "I know you, Max, you're wound up like a ticking time bomb. I need you to be calm when you go in there. Can you promise me you won't lose your head?"

"I've been sitting here for almost an hour twiddling my thumbs, Bernie. I am calm, but I want answers, and if you understand me as well as you say you do, you know I'll do whatever is necessary to get them."

Blackthorn's eyes narrowed. "How did your meeting go with your father yesterday?"

Max returned Blackthorn's gaze. "You know about that? What have you heard about him?"

"I know he blew up his factory, killing three SS soldiers. I also know he faked his own death and is now having to take on a new identity. He's one of us, Max, a brave man who has lost his position and country by going into voluntary exile. I heard you were less than generous to him when you found him at your sister's house."

Max snorted. "What is this? Are you and Heller discussing my personal relationships now? Christ, is nothing sacred?"

"Heller is concerned about you and so am I. Dieter Vogel is a fellow agent who is supposedly deceased. If the Germans get a whiff of him being alive, it'll be all over for your young brother in the Wehrmacht. So, to be clear, Max, your father's situation is not a personal matter at all. Did your dad tell you yesterday that he has to disappear?"

Max frowned. "No?"

"Well, he does. I hope you parted on good terms with him, because you won't be seeing him again for a while."

The memory of his father's embrace in the street left Max feeling numb. That moment of warmth between them had been his papa's goodbye, and he had shrugged him off. He was struck by another thought as his mind wound back to the previous night. Papa had seemingly fought against his mother's wish to go to Scotland, but on deeper reflection, he'd introduced the idea to her.

"Scottish air will do you good, Hannah. I'm sure your mother would love to be in your shoes." His father, crafty to the end, had planned mother's trip long before the conversation had taken place; he had manipulated her to perfection.

Furious with his father, he blurted out, "You seem to know everything about my father, but did you know that he produced gas that killed children and babies."

"I know…"

"Doesn't that concern you at all? Or was that just part of his job description?"

Blackthorn lit a cigarette, blew out the smoke and then threw the matchstick into the ashtray. "I'll let that go, Max. You're upset and angry, but don't overstep the mark with me. We might hold the same rank, but I am your superior officer in this section and I won't tolerate your disrespect, regardless of how highly I value you as an SOE agent." He leant across the desk and added, "Pull yourself together, or I'm not letting you anywhere near Marine."

Max's thoughts were careering between yet another of his father's manipulations and Paul's fate, and he was impatient to get the meeting with Klara over with. And he wished they'd stop calling her *Marine*. She wasn't in France anymore!

"Look, you sent me home on leave, Bernie. Now I'm here at your request, so let's cut the bullshit about my father and take me to Klara. You can lecture me on my attitude after we're done with her."

An uncomfortable silence ensued while Blackthorn made a telephone call. "Is she ready? Right, we're on our way." Then he stood. "You'll leave the questioning to me, Major Vogel. You're only here to observe, and I will throw you out of there if you stall the interview. Is that clear?"

Max nodded. "Understood – sir."

Klara was seated at a desk, head down in the debriefing room, writing something on a piece of paper. Opposite her sat Captain Morris, the officer who had conducted her debriefing the previous day. When Max and Blackthorn arrived, he stood to attention and saluted. "Agent Marine is ready for you, Majors."

Blackthorn parked himself next to Morris, but Max, warned to hang back, leant against the wall behind Blackthorn and watched the woman he had once loved scribbling on the page. She was afraid or unwilling to look up from her task, and he, who knew her better than anyone, felt her shame. He hated her for it.

Max, who had been stunned at news of her involvement in Paul's death, didn't know whether to pity, love, or despise her. He wanted to throttle the life out of her, that was clear, but violence was his temper talking, not his feelings.

Her face was obscured by a curtain of golden hair until she finally raised her head and tucked it behind her ears. Tears rolled down her cheeks as she wrote, misery in her eyes when they finally settled on Max's face. He glared at her, shocked at the contempt he felt, disappointment filling the void of loss. He didn't give a damn how hard this was for her, how forlorn she looked or how she felt; she'd be feeling a lot worse when he'd finished with her.

Blackthorn had informed Max on their walk to the interview room that Klara was still going to Scotland for SOE commando training. The needs of the country outweighed any personal feelings Max might harbour. She'd been reckless, had mishandled a situation that had led to tragic consequences, but, he'd added, inexperienced agents and those who had still to receive formal training often made errors in judgement, and most new spies could be redeemed. With those fatuous apologies, Max was supposed to come to terms with Paul's death and her part in it. But he hadn't, and he never would.

Klara handed the sheet of paper back to Captain Morris, then offered a weak smile to Blackthorn. "Major, thank you for letting me tell you and Major Vogel what happened in France."

Max frowned when he realised she now knew his name and rank. He'd been braced for her to look broken, vulnerable, and ashamed when he'd walked in there, but he was indifferent to her inner struggles. He only cared about his own.

The Vogels

Chapter Two

Klara Gabula

"Marine, start from the beginning, please. And for Major Vogel's sake, don't leave anything out," said Bernie Blackthorn.

Klara glanced at Max, saw disgust in his familiar turquoise eyes, and turned her head from his callous glare. It was too late to turn the clock back, to undo what she'd done. Much too late to say she was sorry or to tell him that she loved him. If she could, she'd stop the clock at the exact moment she had entered the Hotel Lutetia's lobby on the night she'd abducted Paul, and start it again when she had got into the back of the van where Max had been waiting for her. She had rejoiced in his love on that day. She had melted into a gooey mess of adoration in his arms in what had been a beautiful moment until they'd pulled away from each other and she'd seen Paul in Max's eyes. She looked again at the three men in the room. They already hated her, but she had yet to relate the full story.

"I met a man. He was a communist by the name of Florent Duguay," she began. "A Pole called Darek told me that the Duguay's communists had collaborated on occasion with Romek, my estranged husband, so I contacted the Frenchman hoping he could help me mount an operation to rescue Romek and his Resistance fighters. They were being held in Fresnes Prison, just south of Paris, and I suspected they were facing torture and execution. I was desperate – the horrors they were facing..."

"Who did this Duguay work for?" Blackthorn snapped.

"No one, at least not for any of the allied military or intelligence branches. He conducted unilateral operations:

decoupling train tracks, setting explosives, hitting weapons convoys, ambushing soldiers. He had at least a hundred men and women under his command, mostly communists, and he was obsessed with the idea of targeting individual German officers and planning assassinations."

She gulped as she glanced at Max's cold eyes, her own sorrow having no effect on him. "I was stupid enough to get involved with Duguay without knowing what I might be getting into. At the time, I didn't foresee what he was going to ask me to do for him … make me do. I was … I was vulnerable."

She threw daggers at Max. "Major Vogel hadn't made contact for weeks and I had no idea who to turn to for help. I was abandoned and alone, and I was afraid of being captured…"

"Did you come to fear this Duguay fellow before or after you met with Romek at the Partisans' base?" Blackthorn interrupted again, without an ounce of sympathy in his voice.

"Afterwards. As soon as Romek left, I found Duguay while his men were interrogating one of Romek's fighters. His name was Oscar, an agent that Major Vogel and Romek had recruited over a year earlier. He was the traitor who brought down Romek's Resistance group, and Duguay thought I should … well … he ordered me to kill Oscar. And I did with one shot to his head. It was all very quick." She heard Max gasp.

"Go on, Marine," Blackthorn said, shooting a warning glance at Max.

Klara took a sip of water, then cleared her throat. "Duguay asked for the names of high-ranking Germans that I came across at functions. He wanted to know their routines, where they were staying, how many men were guarding them, and where they were going when they left Paris. Most of those important commanders went through Paris on their way to somewhere else, you see.

"A few days later I attended a birthday party at the Hotel Lutetia. I was taking photographs of the German officers and saw Major Vogel at one of the tables ... well, I thought it was him. When I got the opportunity, I followed him into the foyer and passed him a note asking him to meet me in a street behind the hotel when the party was over."

"You wrote in your report that he didn't recognise you despite your best efforts to get his attention. Didn't you think that was strange at the time?" Blackthorn asked.

"Of course, I did. He stared right through me as if he'd never seen me before in his life, and as the night wore on I presumed he was undercover on a mission and I didn't want to blow it for him. But when he did meet me behind the Lutetia and still didn't acknowledge me, I used one of Duguay's men to help me get him into the back of a Post Office van to find out what he was playing at..."

"Into the back of a Post Office van? Without getting answers first?" said Blackthorn, raising a disapproving eyebrow.

"Yes," Klara retorted. "I thought it was the only way to get him to talk to me. You weren't there. The streets were full of Germans." She pointed to Max. "I believed I was talking to him!"

"I understand. Go on."

"I took him to Duguay's base. My plan was to introduce him to the Partisans with the view to getting MI6's help to supply Duguay with weapons. I also wanted to know why Major Vogel was in Paris..."

"Didn't you think to ask him why he was pretending not to know you, or what he was doing in France dressed in a German officer's uniform before you took him to Duguay?"

Klara's bottom lip trembled at Blackthorn's harsh words. They made all the sense in the world ... now. "I should have, but he was unconscious when we got him off the street. Claude, the man who accompanied me that night, hit him hard on the head. I suppose I just wanted to get him out of the city as quickly as possible."

She looked again at Blackthorn and found not a modicum of empathy. "Why are you sitting here judging me when you weren't there? You must understand, at that point I was worried Major Vogel might be a German double agent. I even suspected that he had recruited Oscar to spy on Romek. I thought my head was next for the chopping block."

She paused to settle her nerves. Max was still scowling at her, despite her valiant effort to tell the whole truth. He'd judged her guilty before walking into the room. He hadn't an ounce of understanding in him. "Major Vogel, you trained me to destroy the enemy before it destroyed me. You told me to trust my instincts, and that was what I was trying to do at the time with the information I had. You should take some of the blame for your brother's death. You lied to me. You are not an only child with British parents who work in a factory in England. You're German, and if I was blinded to the truth about your brother, Paul, it was because you didn't trust me enough to be sincere about who you really are!"

Klara choked on a sob, unable to continue. Max gulped back his tears, probably knowing what was to come next. She was angry with him, but she also wanted to get on her knees and beg his forgiveness. She did blame him in part, but only because her guilt needed company. In truth, she had taken every stupid step to get to this situation all on her own. She, and she alone, was responsible.

"What happened to my brother when you got him to this Duguay?" Max asked, breaking the silence.

"Please … I need a minute," Klara pleaded.

"No! You've had days … weeks. Answer the damn question!"

"That's enough, Major Vogel," Blackthorn snapped.

Klara slumped forward, her elbows on the desk, pulling her hair by the roots as if the physical pain would lessen her anguish. "You don't understand how hard it was."

She took a deep breath and then backtracked to Darek's involvement with Romek and Duguay before moving on to the moment she saw Paul awake in Duguay's basement. "… he was Major Vogel to me in every way … his gestures, his eyes pleading with me were yours, Max. Yet even as I threatened him with interrogation at Duguay's hands, he gave nothing away, so I concluded he had to be an enemy spy."

She finished the water in her glass. "When I removed his gag, he said, 'My name is Paul Vogel. I am a Wehrmacht doctor…'" Klara's words hung in the air. Her eyes drifted from Max's face to stare unseeingly at the wall behind him. She had relived those final moments with Paul in the basement many times, but the images had never been as clear as they were right now. When Paul had spoken to her, she'd heard a stranger's voice in a cold, unfamiliar tone. She'd seen terror in his eyes instead of Max's loving gaze. "… it was in that moment, I realised my terrible mistake."

Klara covered her face with her hands, allowing her tears to fall freely. Captain Morris, the only person in the room who had any compassion for her, patted her arm. She dropped her hands and accepted his folded handkerchief. She thanked him, then wanting to end Max's torment, continued her testimony. "I wanted to set Paul free, but Duguay wouldn't hear of it. He ordered me out of the basement, and we argued in the kitchen upstairs…"

"And what was the argument about, exactly?" Blackthorn interrupted.

"It doesn't matter," she mumbled. "I lost. Duguay had no intention of listening to anything I had to say. He was going to deal with Paul, and I was to go back to Paris." She looked at Blackthorn. "If you knew Duguay, you'd understand why I was too afraid to disobey him."

"You left Paul Vogel with Duguay, then?" Blackthorn asked.

She nodded. "I got my things and then went out to the waiting van. I was just about to get in it when I heard the gunshot coming from the basement. I ran back inside the house and tried to go down the stairs, but Claude forced me outside again, and pushed me into the vehicle. He said he hoped I had learnt an important lesson. There were rules in war, and I had broken one of them by taking an enemy soldier into the heart of a rebel camp."

Klara heard her heartbeat pounding in the silent room. She looked up to see Max wipe his eyes with the back of his hand. The muscles in his jaws danced under his skin, but he remained as quiet as the other two men. "Your brother Paul died because of my stupidity. I'm so very sorry, Max … Major. So sorry…"

"Did you see him die?" Max demanded to know.

"No, but I'm certain he's dead."

Max lurched towards Klara, but instead of going around the table, he tried to climb over it. "He was my brother. And you killed him you, fucking stupid bitch!"

"Stand down, Major Vogel," Blackthorn shouted, then he and Captain Morris pulled Max backwards and pinned him against the wall. "I said, stand down!"

Max glared at Klara over Blackthorn's shoulder. "He was a doctor. He was my brother, for Christ's sake. I'll never forgive you – ever!"

34

Klara glimpsed Max's eyes for just a couple of seconds, so full of hatred he looked like a stranger. She slumped forwards and rested her head on her arms, as the other two men frog-marched Max from the room. She had no defence, no response that would ease Max's pain, or hers, so she remained where she was, her own self-loathing clawing at her broken heart, and her mother tongue bringing her comfort. "*Mam nadzieję, że mi wybaczysz* – forgive me, Max – *przepraszam.* I'm sorry."

Chapter Three

Max Vogel

Max made for the nearest pub and downed two double Scotches in quick succession. Blackthorn had insisted Max continue his convalescent leave and forget the earlier encounter. He lit a cigarette and looked out at the street from his chair by the window. The rain was lashing down. Thunder rattled the pub's front doors, and lightning periodically lit up the slate-grey sky, making mid-afternoon appear as dark as night. A gloomy end to a gloomy day, Max thought, staring at a woman trying to keep her umbrella up against the wind. A day in which anger and grief were so tightly entwined he could not unravel them or know where one ended and the other began.

You must move on. Blackthorn had insisted before throwing him out of SOE headquarters. Move on to what? To thinking that Paul was in an unmarked grave, that he'd been dumped in a river, or perhaps, by some miracle, was still alive?

His fingers shook as he lifted the cigarette to his lips. He'd have no peace until he saw Paul's dead body with his own eyes. Only then could he share his twin's death with their family and purge the terrible secret that was destroying him inside. Klara didn't see Paul take his last breath, didn't hear his dying cries. She heard a gunshot that could have hit the damn wall for all she knew. How could he sit his father down and tell him unequivocally his son was gone if there might be a sliver of hope for his survival?

Max left the pub, went to a familiar café at the end of the street, and ordered a cup of tea. He'd changed his mind about drinking himself into a stupor in a bid to forget what he'd just witnessed. Cowards used alcohol to subdue pain and memories, and he was no coward.

When a friendly face appeared with a steaming cup of tea with just a smidgen of milk, he tried his luck. "Do you have any sugar?"

"Sorry, Major, we've run out again. Gawd only knows when we'll get more in."

"That's all right, Tilly." He paid her, giving her a tip despite his disappointment. There was no point complaining about not getting sugar if there was none to be had. He knew only too well why it and other commodities were unavailable, and he, like everyone else, had to shut up and put up with the shortages. They'd been inevitable from the outset of war. Less than a third of the food available in Britain at the start of the conflict had been produced at home. The German navy was also very successful in their targeting of incoming Allied merchant vessels, thus preventing vital supplies, including fruit, sugar, cereals, and meat from reaching British shores. What else could the government do to ensure the fair distribution of food but to issue ration books to every person, each connected to only one specific shop depending on where the person lived. He sipped the unsweetened tea and screwed up his face as its bitterness assaulted his taste buds.

Max pushed the unpalatable tea aside and cast his mind back an hour to Klara's testimony. She had been precise during the interview, which had given him valuable insights into the communist, Duguay. She'd been afraid of the Frenchman who had forced her to put a bullet in Oscar's head, but had she also wanted to get into his good graces by taking Paul to him, truly believing she was introducing a British Intelligence Officer?

Klara's biggest mistake had been to knock Paul unconscious in the street behind the Hotel Lutetia before confirming what or who he was. Had she only asked, he would have told her, then hopefully, walked away unscathed. He'd still be alive today had she thought with her head instead of her heart.

Klara had mentioned Darek, the Pole, a man Max had never met but whom Romek had once described as being trustworthy. Darek had introduced her to Duguay, which meant that he was still active even after Romek's group was wiped out. He was the key, the person who would know where Duguay was hiding, and more importantly, where he might have buried Paul.

Outside, the rain pounded the streets, but instead of waiting for a cab in the shelter of a doorway, Max began to walk towards his destination. He could manage. His leg still gave him trouble, dragging a bit behind the other like a wooden pole, but he was finally on the mend. A thoughtless cabbie driving too close to the kerb splashed the bottom of his greatcoat with filthy water. After shouting a few fervent expletives, he kept going until he managed to hail one that was letting off a passenger.

As always, MI6 headquarters was a flurry of activity. Max greeted people as he headed to Heller's office, stopping only once to shake a friend's hand and ask about his family. He had no time to chat or tell people what he was doing in the building. He'd abandoned MI6 for the SOE, a sore point for some of the intelligence officers he'd worked with in the past and still a small source of guilt to him. The fewer people that knew about his job and his plans, the better.

Marjory, Jonathan Heller's secretary, beamed at Max from her chair behind the oak desk upon which sat a shiny black typewriter and a neat pile of papers and files ranged in rows beside it, along with an empty cup and saucer with a silver spoon sticking out the top.

"You look like a drowned rat, Major Vogel," she declared.

"I feel like a drowned rat. Don't go out there, Marjory. If this rain keeps up, people will be swimming down the Mall. Is Mr Heller in?"

She nodded. "You're lucky to catch him. He's just come back from a meeting."

Five minutes later, Max sat in Heller's office. The latter sent for a pot of tea and, joy of joys, he had sugar tucked away in a desk drawer.

"I can't tell you how sorry I am, Max. Bernie Blackthorn and I have had our differences when it comes to operations, but we both think very highly of you. He told me about Paul. It explains why you were so down in the mouth the other day at your sister's house. You must be devastated."

"Thank you, Jonathan. I don't think there are any words to describe how I feel."

"I take it your father and mother don't know yet?"

"No, and I'd like to keep it that way for a few more days."

Heller raised his eyebrow. "I'm surprised you want to do that. It would be terrible if they were to find out from another source who let it slip that you already knew. Your family needs to heal with honesty, not more deceit."

Max lit a cigarette, blew out the smoke, and sat back in his chair. "Jonathan, I wasn't the one keeping secrets. Those belonged to you and my father. And by the way, he's supposed to be dead, so I hardly think the German High Command or anyone else will notify him of Paul's ... situation."

Max sipped his tea, savouring its warmth and sweetness as it slid down his throat. "Talking about letting something slip, Bernie told me that my father is leaving again. I was hoping he'd still be here."

"He left an hour ago. He's gone, Max. You must have known he couldn't stick around London. We've disposed of many of them, one way or another, but the city might still have a few operational German agents milling around."

Max's jaw tightened. "What do mean he's gone? Gone for good? I don't suppose you'll tell me where he's being sent?"

"No, best I don't, at least not yet, eh? Maybe when he's settled."

"Does my mother know her husband has disappeared again?"

"She will – tell you what, how about you tell her when the time is right?"

Max shook his head and muttered, "And the lies continue."

Heller pushed his tea aside, went into a desk drawer and brought out two glasses and a half-full bottle of Scotch. "I keep these for emergencies," he said, while pouring the drinks. "I'm sorry we've got off on the wrong foot, Max. Earlier, you mentioned Paul's situation? What did you mean?"

Max accepted the glass, tossing the whisky to the back of his mouth. "Marine didn't see Paul die, and she didn't see his dead body. She didn't see him, Jonathan, and I can't tell my family Paul's dead when I don't … can't believe it myself. I need proof … I have to have that."

Heller let out a sympathetic sigh. "Blackthorn sent me over a copy of Marine's official report yesterday. As far as he's concerned it was a tragic mistake, one she says she will never repeat – look, Max, I'm saying this as a friend – your brother has gone, and the sooner you deal with it, the quicker you'll move past your grief. I'll get word to your father, but you need to tell your mother and sister. They have a right to know."

41

"I know that!" Max snapped at Heller, then raised his hand in an apology. "Sorry ... sorry."

Max took the liberty of pouring himself another tot of whisky. He lifted the glass in a toast to Paul, drank the Scotch then banged the glass down on the desk. "I always went above and beyond for you, Jonathan. I conducted unsanctioned missions, knowing they were off the books. I've covered your arse on more than one occasion. I have never asked you for anything, not one favour or day's leave that wasn't owed to me. You hid Big Bear from me for years ... *years*, and you would have kept his identity hidden had my father not turned up here. You caused irreparable damage to Paul and my father's relationship, and you made me list Dieter Vogel as a Nazi collaborator in my reports – there's something I need to do, and I can't do it without your help – you owe me."

Heller's eyes narrowed as he glared at Max in the silence that ensued. Max held his ground. Heller already seemed to be considering the unspoken request.

"Blackthorn will cause a stink. It can't be done – Max, you cannot go back to France on a wild goose chase using this section's resources," Heller eventually said.

"I'll get to Paris under my own steam, and I'll be in and out before my leave is up and anyone is the wiser, but I will need a return lift on one of your courier planes. This won't come back to you." Max leant in. "Jonathan, I need to see Paul's grave, and the man who killed him."

"This could sink you ... both of us."

"I know."

Heller tapped his fingers on the desk and gazed out the window. Then he mumbled something and reached for a file on his desk. "I can't believe I'm even considering this. I have a Westland Lysander flying to the Dieppe area tomorrow night.

You can hitch a lift. One of your agents from Saint Quentin is supposed to meet the plane and take a couple of crates of rifles and correspondence off the pilot..."

"Pasqual? But he's SOE, not MI6."

"True, but this is a joint mission between Blackthorn and me. Agencies tripping over each other seem to be the norm nowadays, and sometimes operational parameters get blurred and we work together. Blackthorn asks me for favours, I do the same for him, and we're both happy. I suppose before long we'll all get used to who is supposed to be doing what and, more importantly, what we should keep our noses out of."

Max exhaled a long breath. "Thank you, Jonathan."

"Don't thank me yet. The Lizzie won't be returning to Dieppe for eight days. If you get caught, you'll be put through the ringer for piggy-backing a government operation without an official stamp. They'll crucify you for using their resources to look for a lost Wehrmacht soldier. And you can bet your life I will deny any knowledge of it."

"Understood, though to be clear, Paul wasn't a soldier, he was a doctor and an officer."

"Doctor, brother, or whomsoever he was to you, the bosses will see him as the enemy because that is what he was."

Max swallowed a retort. What he was asking for was beyond the pale, and he didn't want to get on the wrong side of Heller.

Jonathan shuffled some papers, his eyes losing focus for a moment. He went into another file and pushed it across his desk to Max. "If, and that's still a big *if,* I allow you to go, I will need something from you in return. You won't like it, but it will make your mission a tad more legitimate should I be forced to explain your actions to the top brass."

Max cocked his head to one side, hesitant to say yes to an order he might not like. "So, if I do this something for you, is it a go?"

Heller nodded. "Yes."

"And is your something going to step on Blackthorn's toes?" he asked.

Heller chuckled. He sat back, pointedly ignoring the question. "I was particularly interested in Marine's account of the *Francs-Tireurs et Partisans…*"

Max raised his chin. "The communist group that had Paul."

"The very same. I ordered Romek to reach out to a member of that group a couple of months ago. I wanted him to offer collaboration to the Partisan leader, which Romek managed to do. Unfortunately, he was taken down before we could get any further with the negotiations and I never got the leader's name."

"Romek didn't mention this to me."

"Why should he have? You were transitioning to SOE at the time, and Romek was still an MI6 asset."

Max would always feel guilty for switching to another agency and leaving Romek and Klara in the cold. It was during that short period that everything had gone to hell for the Paris Resistance group. "Romek should have been covered during my transition period to SOE."

"He was. He still had access to my radio operator, and to me. It was you who disappeared, not us."

Max nodded, acknowledging that Heller held the higher moral ground. "What do you need?"

"We don't know where the Communist group is based, but I'm guessing that the man who leads it could be this Florent Duguay that Marine spoke of. If it is, I want you to offer him a deal. They work with us and, in return, we'll supply them with weapons and other resources."

Max's calm exterior belied his true feelings. Duguay was the man he planned to kill, not to negotiate with. "Those Commies killed Paul, and you want me to make nice with them?"

"Your brother probably wasn't the only German officer they assassinated, Max," Heller said, emphasising that Paul had been an enemy soldier. "Put any thought of vengeance out of your mind. I want this man on board with us, not dead. So, you will conduct yourself as a liaison officer for MI6, or you will not go to France using my plane. That's the deal."

Max swallowed the hard lump of revenge. It tasted rotten, like a stinking cancer at the back of his throat. He had reservations. Providing he found Duguay, how was he to look the man in the eye as he begged to be taken to Paul's grave, and in the same breath offer to supply him with British resources? How would Duguay react when he met a carbon copy of a man he had shot? Heller was a hard bastard who never backed down, Max thought, both admiring and resenting his old boss. If he didn't comply with his demands, someone else would have the face to face with the Communists, and he wouldn't find out a damn thing about Paul's death, or final resting place.

"Duguay will be trouble, Jonathan. According to Marine, he's hell-bent on getting biblical pay back by killing high-ranking Germans. He's very dangerous," Max said.

"I agree. Last week, Karl Hotz, the commanding officer of the German occupation forces in Loire-Atlantique, was assassinated, and I suspect that Duguay and his communists had a hand in that. I've just heard that Pierre Pucheu, the Interior Minister of Marshal Pétain's government, chose upwards of thirty communist prisoners from various prisons and handed them over to the

Germans as hostages. I imagine he did that to avoid the executions of innocent French people. The communist hostages were shot in three groups in the town of..."

"And you want to work with that loose cannon?"

"I do, because you are going to convince him to stop the assassinations. Christ, that lot across the Atlantic are even getting involved in this now. I got a copy of President Roosevelt's formal statement yesterday condemning reprisal executions carried out by the Nazis in occupied Europe." Heller rummaged through a pile of papers and then picked one up. "Ah, here it is. '*The practice of executing scores of innocent hostages in reprisal for isolated attacks on Germans in countries temporarily under the Nazi heel disgusts a world already inured to suffering brutality.*'

"But while he sympathises in public with the men and women being slaughtered, he is spitting mad with the irresponsible tactics of the resistance groups who have no regard for the lives of their compatriots – I'm paraphrasing that part of the statement."

"So, you think if we work with the Communists, we might be able to control their missions?" Max shrugged. "All right. I don't believe they'll stop, but I'll do it."

"Good man. You'll leave from the usual place at 22:00 tomorrow. I'll make sure Blackthorn and your father are kept out of this."

"And you'll also make sure neither of my parents find out about Paul until I return with definitive answers."

"That seems fair."

"Then fair it is," said Max, finishing his Scotch.

Chapter Four

Wilmot Vogel

Leningrad, Russia.
1 November, 1941

The German Army Group North had already destroyed the North Western Front and had virtually eliminated two Russian armies. Wilmot, in the 18th Army had been fighting battles to the west of Leningrad in a place that had become known as the Oranienbaum Pocket, a strategically important semi-circle of land held by Russians units. The prize was the Russian naval base, which was still supplying the city's population with food, medicines and weapons. The mission, however, was not going well at all, for no matter how many times the German army tried to breach the target, they were repelled.

A week earlier, Wilmot's unit had been moved to the east of Leningrad. Tired of being held back by Russian soldiers at Oranienbaum – who on paper didn't stand a chance against the Wehrmacht – he'd been jubilant when his unit broke through the Russian lines at Schlusselburg, a town at the head of the Neva River on Lake Ladoga thirty-five kilometres east of Leningrad city. The battle had been relatively easy compared to previous fighting, but the Russians had apparently foreseen Schlusselburg's fall and had taken measures to deny the Germans any spoils of war. Thus, the German soldiers were weak with hunger and freezing in the icy tundra.

Wilmot was sitting with his back against a brick wall during a heavy snowfall, nibbling his measly five ounces of bread and gazing across the water to the island fortress of Orekhovets. He was wearing a heavy wool greatcoat painted green to provide camouflage with silver dimpled buttons that didn't reflect the light. But he was blue with cold despite the coat; his body from head to toes was ill-equipped to deal with the start of the Russian winter.

Like many of the soldiers serving with him, he was angry at Adolf Hitler's High Command, who were supposed to excel in organisation and logistics. But the hubristic German commissariat had not transported anything like enough woollen hats, gloves, long johns and overcoats to their position, leaving the men freezing to death with the promise of the full-blown winter to come.

Claus and Geert, Willie's closest friends, were huddled next to him, protecting their hands inside the folds of their coats, and tucking their chins into their collars. They were a miserable looking trio among the thousands of men scattered along the riverbank.

Wilmot picked up the last crumb of bread mingled with the snowflakes on his coat, shoved it in his mouth, and then blew on his gloveless fingers. One hundred metres behind the three men, a group of officers were snuggled up inside a heated wooden hut. They had been in there for over an hour, leaving their soldiers exposed to the frigid air with stiffening joints and no information or new orders to get their blood flowing.

"They're going to take their time," Wilmot said to Geert and Claus, putting his gloves back on. "They've got a wood-burning stove in there. Would you come out if you were them?"

"I just want to know if we're going to have another go at that fortress today, or not. We'll turn into ice statues if we don't move," Claus moaned.

Geert kicked the snow off his boot. "That's what they're probably talking about, but I don't think they'll do anything until it stops snowing."

"Which could be never by the looks of it. What do you think, Willie? Will we assault it today, or not?" Claus shivered and pulled his hood down over his face as far it could go.

Wilmot stood up. "I don't know, but I think I'm going to get off my backside and take a listen to what they're saying. Wait here, I'll be back in a minute."

The officers' garbled voices grew clearer as Willie neared the hut. This was no discussion. It was a full-blown argument with raised voices and insults being thrown in to boot. He listened for a good ten minutes, along with a handful of other men who were there trying to catch what was being said or using the hut's outer walls for shelter from the wind. When he'd heard enough, he returned to Claus and Geert in an even darker mood than he'd been in when he'd woken up that morning.

"Well, what's the latest?" Claus asked, before Willie had even sat down.

"I don't want to spook you two, but the fortress is a heavily fortified garrison. That's why we've not rushed across there."

"How many Russians?"

"I don't know, Claus, hundreds maybe? They're using the island to take supplies and ammunition to their frontline, and if we don't take it, we won't be able to cut the Russian's transit route from Leningrad to the mainland. That's what I heard the officers say."

Willie had stupidly believed that the North Army Group had Leningrad in a stranglehold. They'd already cut off rail transportation links and had the city surrounded on the east, west, and north where the Finnish troops were positioned. He'd felt sure the next phase of the battle would be a full-frontal attack on the beleaguered city despite the on-going rumours of the Führer's siege strategy.

"Do you remember a month ago when we could see across the river to the buildings right in the heart of Leningrad?" Wilmot said to no one in particular.

"We've bloody gone backwards," said a disgruntled Geert.

"And from what I overheard, we're not going to move forwards again, at least, not as an army."

"Why do you say that?" Claus perked up from his slouched position.

"We're losing the 4th Panzer division. They're leaving us to support the Battle Group South. One of the officers said we're no longer a mobile army and we'll be stuck here without the tanks."

"So, we're the poor relation now – fucking great," Geert grumbled.

For a while, the three men vented their anger with a colourful variety of expletives and crude gestures to describe the officers who knew much more than they were willing to tell their soldiers. Wilmot accepted a tin cup of steaming hot tea from Claus. They had become good friends despite Wilmot's initial dislike of Claus during the first days of the Leningrad campaign. He supposed sharing a harsh, dreary existence in a series of manholes with someone who had a similar character could only end in one of two ways; they would either kill each other or become good mates. Thankfully, it was the latter.

Claus filled another cup with black, sugarless tea for himself and then took a sneaky look around the area. "This is Hitler's fault. He wants us to be right here."

"What do you mean, he wants us right here?" Geert scoffed.

"It stands to reason, Geert. He wants Leningrad at any cost because of its name and political status."

"It's just a city. There's nothing political about it," Wilmot disagreed. "Politics ended when the war started. Okay, so it's called after Lenin, I get that, but it's not worth all this cat and mouse carry-on. We should have blown every building to smithereens when we first got here."

Claus shook his head. "Jesus, Willie, you'll never make an officer. There are such things as history and strategy. Leningrad used to be the capital of Russia…"

"And it was the symbolic capital of the Russian Revolution back in 1917," Geert piped up.

Claus carried on, "The city is full of arms factories. What would be the point of blowing them all up when we can use the weapons and explosives to our advantage later?"

"You two think you know everything."

"We know a hell of a lot more than you do, Willie Vogel," Claus laughed.

"Maybe. But can either of you tell me why we're even in the Soviet Union to begin with? I can't see any German person wanting to live here, can you?"

"It's rich," Geert said.

"What? Are you off your head?"

"No, my head is firmly on my shoulders. Look, Willie," Geert used his teacher voice, as if Willie were a backward student. "Russia makes up one sixth of the earth's land mass. Deep veins of gold and silver run through its mountains. Copper, manganese, magnesium, nickel, tin, and a lot of oil are in its lowlands. It's rich in raw materials. Its forests cover millions of acres, and it has a quarter of the world's lumber reserves…"

"All right … all right … Jesus, I only asked a simple question. How do you know all this stuff?"

Geert's animated face turned serious, almost mournful. "I just graduated a month before the war in Europe began. I obtained a Masters in International Relations and Diplomacy at Berlin University. I also spent a year in Boston, America. Did you know that? Ach, I don't suppose any of that matters now. This war has shot all my plans to hell."

Willie started laughing and had to hold his side when he got a painful stitch.

"What are you laughing at?" Geert demanded.

"Sorry … sorry, Geert. It's just the thought of you going all the way through university to learn diplomacy only to find yourself fighting all those countries you hoped to be diplomatic with … ach, I couldn't help it."

A while later, and after Willie had apologised a second time for laughing at Geert, the three men found out the rumours of the day's orders were true. They weren't going anywhere that day, or the next.

By late afternoon, the snowstorm had intensified, doubling its ground height during the morning. Wilmot, taking the initiative, suggested to Geert and Claus that they secure their dugout from the worst of the weather before the ground became too hard to dig out the new snow.

Claus foraged for tree branches which the men then positioned across three quarters of the trench's length. They covered them with wet sheeting, normally used to sit on, and a few rocks that Geert had collected to stop the sheeting from blowing away.

Wilmot built a campfire on the tiny open part of the trench despite the snow swirling in every possible direction. It was forbidden to build a fire, but the trench was deep, and the men were confident that the Russians wouldn't spot it. Besides, the officers did it as well.

When the fire was lit, Wilmot helped the flames along with the aid of a cupful of gasoline he had acquired from a truck driver in exchange for the rest of his bread allowance for that day. It was going to be a hard job keeping it going, but they'd all agreed that just the sight of the flames made them feel better.

The three had nothing to sit on, having used the rubber sheeting for the roof, but they were a damn site cosier than they'd been out in the open and were pleased with their innovation. Other soldiers who walked by also liked the idea and set off to make structures for themselves.

Willie, Geert, and Claus made a pact not to let the fire go out, and they established shifts so that they could stoke it and keep it going in any way they could until the kindling ran out. They had also arranged to periodically brush the snow off the branch and rubber sheeting roof in case the roof became too heavy and caved in.

Willie lay down against the trench wall in the foetus position with his head close to the fire. He shut his eyes, luxuriating in the heat warming his crown and the crude ceiling above him keeping out most of the snow. Clause snored, and Geert tutted his displeasure at the wailing wind. And in that relative peace, Willie thought about his family.

Since receiving the correspondence about his father's death and mother's abandonment, Willie had predicted that he wouldn't receive a single letter from anyone. Gestapo *Kriminaldirektor* Biermann had stated that his mother wouldn't be returning to the

Fatherland. He'd also informed Wilmot that Paul had been posted to Paris – lucky bastard. Hannah was living with Frank in Kent, and Max was probably in the British army knowing him and his love for all things English.

He had written four times in as many weeks to the Gestapo major whom he now regarded as a friend. He didn't have personal feelings or thoughts to share with a man he hardly knew, but he was the only bugger he could think of to write a letter to. All who remained to him in Germany were his aunt and uncle in Berlin, and he didn't feel like burdening them with soppy, depressing tales about his beleaguered existence on the Eastern Front when his cousins were in similar situations. Biermann was the only person he could connect with. He understood this life, and eventually he'd reply.

Wilmot's letters had been sent via the German Army's very large and complex Field Post system. Wilmot had enjoyed writing them. They were an escape from the bitter fighting and long days of drudgery and…

His eyes shot open. Geert held a stick in his outstretched hand, and it snaked past him on the way to poking the fire. "It's your turn in five minutes, Willie."

"Then tell me again in five minutes, dope," Willie snapped and turned to face the wall again.

The blasts came in quick succession. Three loud booms that shook the snow off the dug-out roof. A fourth explosion deafened the men and collapsed the roof with the weight of passing infantrymen who'd been knocked off their feet and then dropped onto the snow-covered branches and sheeting.

Geert and Claus had completely disappeared under the mess of snow, branches, sheeting, and three blood-soaked soldiers. Wilmot's body was only partially buried, but his head, having been near the fire, had been struck by a soldier's boot and was bleeding with a gash on his crown. The man's back was right on top of the flames, instantly smothering them. His ankle and foot, the one that had kicked Wilmot in the head, was hanging vertically and almost separately from the end of his leg. Wilmot tried to move but the ground was vibrating beneath him, and his body was trembling like an earthquake.

The explosions continued, and although he couldn't hear a thing. Fountains of crisp white snow rained down on his face. He was paralysed under the soldier's weight pressing on his torso and legs. He tried to lift his head but couldn't see anything of Geert or Claus. They hadn't struggled to the surface, and he couldn't help them – they were going to die, all of them – the man without his foot, his friends, the whole bloody lot of them, snuffed out by a sneak Russian attack that no one saw coming.

Chapter Five

Wilmot Vogel

After a monumental struggle, Wilmot managed to dislodge the rubble on top of him. The incoming explosions seemed to have stopped, but he still couldn't hear properly because of the blast waves, and now adding to this, the noise of the rocket launchers from his own lines returning fire on the Russians.

He scrambled to his knees, panting with exertion, while he studied the soldier lying across what had been their comforting camp fire. He was dead. Wilmot didn't need to feel for a pulse to confirm that; the foot that had hit him in the head, was hanging on by only a thread, and a thick pine branch was sticking out from his chest, having pierced his body from the back. One of his eyes was caked with blood from a deep gash just above his eyebrow and his mouth was wide open with no misty breath coming out of it.

In the confined, cluttered hole, Wilmot began to bawl, tears coursing down his filthy cheeks leaving clean streaks in their salty wake. He scrabbled about on his knees, howling for his friends and throwing away branches and rocks that had been jutting through the snow. He imagined Geert and Claus suffocating under the weight of dead men, buried alive with soundless screams for help inside their heads. The thought of them suffocating spurred him on, but time was running out; he couldn't get to them quickly enough.

Wilmot grunted as he hauled the second body from where his friends had lain, but he was having to lift rocks and branches before he could get to the third soldier, who was a mangled heap in the spot directly on top of where Geert and Claus had been lying. As he yelled for help, Wilmot was aware of men running across the ground slightly above him, but he continued to throw rocks and branches out of the hole, not giving a damn where they landed.

The second soldier who had been lying beside Wilmot suddenly came to and shook his head. He tentatively explored an egg-sized lump and open gash on his forehead, then rose, staggered past Wilmot and clawed his way on to the ground above.

"Hey, come back and help me! My friends were underneath your feet … bloody moron!" Wilmot screamed after the man.

"You! Get out of that hole and report to me."

Wilmot stopped digging in the snow with his hands to look up at his *Unteroffizier*. "Sergeant. Thank God. My friends are under here. I'm out of time … I can't get … help me."

"We can't do anything for them now, Schütze," said the Unteroffizier stretching his hand to Wilmot. "They're gone, come."

Wilmot reluctantly abandoned the dugout and followed the Unteroffizier, denial of Geert and Claus's deaths filling his head. His rifle and rucksack were lost to him in the hole he'd called home, so he picked up a weapon and the equipment he needed from the dead along the way. He felt like a scavenger, but guns were for the living; corpses had no further use for them.

At first, he experienced almost complete silence as he walked towards the lines of able-bodied men waiting for instructions. But as his auditory shock from the most recent blast dissipated, the stillness gave way to countless sounds, distinct and infinitely gentler than the rocket fire that had continued for what had seemed like hours. His breath was loud and rasping. Under his feet, snow crunched and squeaked. To his left, multiple fires crackled, and in the distance rifle bullets snapped and pinged in the air.

Dead Germans littered the pastel-pink, snowy ground like broken dolls with contorted limbs and wide staring eyes. The hut where the officers had held their meeting earlier that day had been destroyed, and the area in which it had stood was covered in flaming red timber, giving the frigid air a welcome warmth. And when he joined a platoon of infantrymen, he saw his own horror reflected in their eyes.

"Gather around!" the Unteroffizier shouted.

Wilmot counted forty-five men in his platoon. Most of them he knew, but some were missing, Geert and Claus included. Some distance away, other platoons were also assembling. He couldn't imagine how many men had been killed in the attack, but he saw hundreds of survivors preparing for what he guessed would be a quick and decisive counteroffensive. Minutes later, the Unteroffizier confirmed Wilmot's thoughts.

"There's a village about eight hundred metres from here. It's about three hundred metres behind the Leningrad Line."

"We broke though that last week," one of the men said.

"And we'll break through it again," said the Unteroffizier, without confirming that the Russians had probably retaken that section of the line and had been able to launch their *Katyusha* rockets from there. "Our job is to clear the houses."

A whistle blew, moving the men forwards en masse; the blind leading the blind into another fog of battle. Wilmot glanced over his shoulder and saw a few men in his platoon lagging behind with reluctant or painful steps. His injured head was pounding and bleeding anew. Beneath his helmet, he felt the metallic wetness of his blood dribbling down his face, but regardless of his pain, he surged to the front, unafraid and relieved that they were rushing to battle instead of cowering behind their lines waiting for the Russkies to attack again with their rockets … or as the Wehrmacht called them, Stalin's organs. Enraged, he was glad of the chance to kill as many Russians as he could as pay-back for his friends. He knew of no greater motivation than revenge.

In an exposed formation, the platoon reached the dreaded Leningrad Line and were met with rifle and machine gun fire. Wilmot's relief morphed into terror as one by one the infantrymen fell to the unseen enemy. He glanced to his left. Hundreds of men were still running forward across uneven ground pitted with burnt out craters. He couldn't stop, couldn't go back, so blindly followed the Unteroffizier until the latter suddenly slumped to the ground screaming, his thigh laid open to the bone.

Unaccustomed to taking charge but fuelled by his hatred of the enemy, Wilmot took a unilateral decision and headed to the treeline on his right. Others followed, desperate to get out of the line of Russian fire that was knocking them off one by one like tin soldiers at a fairground.

Twenty men in Wilmot's platoon made it as far as the trees, but more than double that number lay dead or wounded in the open field. The Germans had taken the line only one week earlier, but when Wilmot was running towards the trenches he saw Russian soldiers, not Germans.

"We took it last week … we took it. What happened … and where's the Unteroffizier?" a soldier gasped.

"I saw him drop. I don't know if he's dead. I was too busy running." Wilmot grabbed his water flask.

The noise of guns blazing in the clearing was intense, but the men didn't feel safe in their concealed position because of notorious Russian snipers that stalked the woods. Wilmot again took the initiative by leopard-crawling on his belly and aiming his rifle outwards towards the open field. "Keep your eyes peeled on the perimeter," he yelled to no one in particular. The others followed his example, spreading out, and lying on the ground in a circle with weapons trained in every direction.

"What do we do now? We're cut off. Snipers might be surrounding us. How are we going to get out of here?" The soldier closest to Wilmot panicked. "Jesus Christ, we're going to die in here! We're all going to be cut down. I don't want to die like this..."

"Shut up, Martin. I'll kill you myself if you don't stop wailing like a baby." Blood dripped into Wilmot's eye and he swiped it away with his sleeve before glancing around him. The remains of his platoon were looking outwards towards the line of trees. At least the branches were bare, making it easier to spot snipers had they been sitting on a bough waiting to pick off Germans.

"...we have to go back," one of the men suggested in a ferocious whisper.

Wilmot thought about that idea as a few men began to argue among themselves. They'd lost their sergeant and very soon someone would have to decide about what to do next.

"We can't go back to our lines. We haven't been given the order to retreat," Wilmot reminded him.

"Well, we can't bloody go forward, can we, Willie?" Martin retorted.

"We'll have to join the other platoons. If we retreat, we'll be shot for running away."

"Willie's right," another man said. "We wouldn't be the first to get executed for cowardice. We've all seen what happens to men trying to get away from this ... Mother of God, I'm freezing. We need to move, or we'll ice up. Think … think, one of you. There must be a way out of here."

A fierce fight was still going on in the open field. German shells were exploding, which meant that the Russian resistance had been much heavier than expected, and no unit or platoon had broken through.

"We'll stay here – unless any of you want to get blown up out there – well, do you?" Willie asked, butting into the ongoing debate about how it had been possible for the Russians to retake that section of the line from the Germans who had been manning it for the last six days.

The Leningrad Line was a formidable series of prepared Russian defences. Areas of importance were surrounded by heavy fortifications and German units had encountered some up to six miles in length.

Wilmot's platoon had been involved in the previous week's attack, which had put this section of the line squarely in German hands. Another platoon had been told to man it after the Russians retreated. The platoon commander had set the place up nicely as a forward outpost, making themselves at home, as though they'd thought it would be an utterly impossible feat for the Russians to take it off them again.

"I agree with Willie," said Martin, having calmed down. "But if we get caught in here, we'll need to be ready."

The men tightened their circle. Two soldiers volunteered to scout deeper into the woods to see if there was a safe exit. Rifles were still trained in every direction. It was evident that the Russians' tenacity to come back time and again to retake what they'd once lost was galling to the Germans who'd thought they were far superior in every way – at least, on paper.

Wilmot listened to one of the men say he was ashamed not to be out there kicking the Russkies' backsides and thought back to the times he'd remarked to Geert and Claus that the German army had always underestimated the Soviet troops.

He disagreed with the arrogant fools who thought that the Soviets were badly equipped, and second-rate soldiers. If he were to be asked by a general what he admired about this enemy, he'd have a long list at hand. The Russians were hard to kill, like cockroaches when one stamped on them. Their white-clad ski troops appeared to be defeated one day only to resurge the next with greater numbers. They used cows, and sometimes their own men to clear mine fields and their strategy was successful. They had an unnatural ability to hide under the snowy ground and suddenly appear only metres from German troops, anytime, anywhere. They could walk ten times further on ice-encrusted ground than any German, and still be energised to fight at the end of it. And they scared the living daylights out of him.

An hour later, Wilmot's platoon came out of hiding and joined a new surge led by Stormtroopers charging towards the Russian line. Wilmot glimpsed his dead comrades as he ran, and it struck him just how lucky he'd been earlier on. An inch to the left or right, a second later or earlier, a wrong zig-zag pattern, a trip, a fall, and he'd be dead too; his fighting days over and the long, never-ending sleep beginning.

A sharp pain and violent shaking in Wilmot's hand made him drop his rifle. He plastered his bloodied hand to his chest but kept on running until he skidded to a halt when a Russian's head and shoulders popped out of a manhole like a jack-in-the-box. Both men stared at each other, instincts and common sense replaced by the shock of their proximity.

Wilmot was frozen with fear, but fortunately the Russian also seemed incapable of making a move. With an overwhelming desire to live, Wilmot went for his gun holster with his injured hand. The excruciating pain when he tried to grip his pistol then forced him to go for his spade handle instead. The Russian, having his own troubles, was fumbling in the hole's confined space to hike his rifle to his shoulder. He'd either dropped it in fright when he'd seen Wilmot less than a metre from his position, or it had got wedged in the hole.

Wilmot wrenched the spade free and, swinging it with both hands, sliced into the Russian's neck, nearly taking his head off.

He stared at the grotesque, almost-decapitated man for only a second or two before looking down at his own wound. He gasped. His hand had a hole in the webbing between his thumb and forefinger. A bullet had gone right through it, but he could still move all his digits; thus, it hadn't hit any bones. The pain was making him feel sick. Would an injury like this get him sent back to Berlin?

Russian guns had grown silent, and German soldiers were crossing the line, shooting the enemy who were already lying on the ground beside the German soldiers who'd lost the outpost earlier. Wilmot wrapped a bandage around his hand, then trotted towards a squad of men. Although it had seemed like hours, the whole incident with the Russian in the manhole had taken no more than a minute. That tiny spec of time would live in his memory until the day he died. It had been his greatest victory in the war, thus far.

After a German reconnaissance unit confirmed that the Russian rocket launchers were disabled, the infantry moved forward towards a row of houses. The Russians had managed to hold on to the enclave during the previous German offensive one week earlier. The structures had been built as defence and observation posts with heavy guns and other weapons hidden inside them, and, being designed to repel German mobile units, they'd been extremely difficult to take. The task, like many other recent missions, had been compounded further by General von Leeb's gripe that he didn't have enough resources to capture the hundreds of fortified bunkers across the Stalingrad Line; a sentiment echoed by many of the officers in the Northern Army. *We are the poor relation, the last of the three Russian campaigns to get anything, the furthest away from supply lines, the forgotten, the abandoned,* they constantly whined.

Wilmot and the men with him reported to an Unteroffizier who ordered them to check the houses for booby-traps and Russians who might still be hiding there. They found the first one empty, but they also came across fresh bread, cheese, and drinking water in canisters.

Wilmot shovelled the bread into his mouth, his cheeks bulging like a squirrel's as he chewed. Then he yawned, relaxed by the heat coming from an iron stove with a flue that went through a hole in the roof. The Russians must have been confident that they'd hold on to this house, he thought. They'd brought a picnic that hadn't been eaten and had built a fire. Blankets were on the floor along with straw-filled pillows and a couple of torn mattresses. It was a home from home.

The construction had camouflaged gun ports almost flush with the floor. Its interior was reinforced with sandbags and earth. Observation slots were cut into the roof, and they'd uncovered bunkers built into the floor connected to adjacent houses. What must it be like to sleep in a place like this? Wilmot pondered. There was a raging fire and shutters on the windows to keep out the worst of the wind and freezing cold and a gas stove to boil water for tea or coffee, if one were lucky enough to get one's hands on a bag; what he wouldn't do to spend a single night there.

"The officers will probably barrack here," said Martin, reading Wilmot's mind.

"Lucky gits. Ach, never mind, Martin," Wilmot said, smiling for the first time that day, "at least we're a bit closer to the city than we were this morning. We'll drag the Russians out of their beds when we march into Leningrad."

Chapter Six

Wilmot had been given the unenviable job of burying the German dead in a mass grave; no easy task because of the icy ground. Minutes earlier, he'd been throwing dead Russians onto the backs of the trucks that were being used to transport the corpses to the nearby river, where they'd be tossed in and forgotten.

The bulk of the German army was moving forward to Wilmot's location later that day, and two platoons, a total of sixty-one men, had been ordered to mop up the blood and debris in the area surrounding the village. Within hours, the officers were going to barrack in the houses the Germans had just taken, and thus claim they'd moved even closer to Leningrad.

With the last of the German bodies interred, Wilmot sat on a patch of burnt grass and lit a cigarette. "It's at times like this I wish I'd gone to officers' academy," he remarked to a Schütze lying beside him. "I'm sick and tired of getting these dirty jobs. If I'd wanted to be a bloody gravedigger, I'd have stayed in Berlin. And look at the state of my hand – bloody disgusting, shovelling earth and getting it into an open wound like that. I've got a fucking hole the size of a grape next to my thumb – look at the filth on the bandage. You know, they never even gave me something for the pain…"

"Sod your hand, Willie. I'm freezing my balls off here…"

The private's voice died under the deafening noise of a shell hitting one of the houses a few metres from their position. Wilmot dropped his cigarette – the last one he had – leapt to his feet and sprinted away, but in blind panic got caught by another blast behind him. He fell. The world disintegrated and went black.

When he came to, he was lying on his stomach, peering through blurry eyes. The area was crawling with Russian soldiers; many hundreds of them – could be thousands – or was he seeing double? With ringing ears, he struggled to make sense of what had happened to him and what was going on now. He recalled the strange sensation of flying through the air in slow motion, loud bangs in his ears, feeling drunk and floating like a feather. He'd felt no pain or fear, couldn't remember landing, and didn't know how long he'd been unconscious.

As his vision cleared, he peered around his immediate area. He thought about sitting up to check if he'd been hurt. His body felt heavy and a bit numb. Jesus, had he lost a leg? He might be paralysed; he couldn't see or feel a thing below the waist.

His ears tuned in to the sound of gunfire, not from rifles but pistols. He squinted around again, lifting his head an inch off the ground and turning it from side to side. The Russians were shooting Germans who were moaning and groaning. His line of sight was limited, but the shouting, talking, laughing enemy voices were sharp enough.

He still had his 08-pistol with a couple of bullets left in the breech. A full magazine was also in his belt pouch. If he moved to get the gun or ammo, they'd shoot him. If he didn't move, they'd bury him alive or put a bullet in his head just for the hell of it. He'd seen plenty of Germans do that to Russians. Why had the German army not advanced again? They knew they'd left sixty-one men at this location, as they had done a week earlier. They must have heard the shells destroying the houses. Was the Wehrmacht bloody stupid? They were so very close yet seemed a hundred miles away. He felt as though he'd been ripped from his mother's womb and abandoned.

An anxiety attack took his breath away, leaving him gulping for air. Terrified, he feigned death. The soldier he'd been talking to earlier lay close by, flat on his back, his eyes wide open. "Are you alive, Jürgen?" Wilmot whispered, turning his head slightly.

Jürgen moaned, "Hard to believe, but yes, I think I am." He struggled to sit up and appeared to be in the same dazed state Wilmot had experienced minutes earlier.

Wilmot also sat up and expanded his lungs. "Thank God ... thank you, thank you ... am I wounded?" he mumbled. Then, he saw the Russians and froze.

"Put your hands behind your head, Jürgen," Wilmot said, seeing other Germans trying to surrender. "And don't talk."

Jürgen gasped when he finally looked around him. "How did the Russians get this back? What's going on, Willie?"

"Shut up, Jürgen – shut up."

Both men raised their arms and clasped their hands at the back of their heads. The small of Wilmot's back was struck by a rifle butt, and he groaned, more with fright than pain. The Russian soldiers who had surrounded them were shouting angrily, but since the two did not understand a word they were saying, they elected to remain on their knees.

"Nazi pigs. Get on your feet and keep your hands in the air," a Russian ordered in German.

Wilmot, with slow, cautious movements, leant forward whilst raising his eyes to the Russian who'd just given the order. He kept his gaze on the man, but when he raised his right knee to stand, someone kicked him in the back, laughing uproariously when Wilmot fell forward.

Winded, Wilmot gasped for breath, fighting the pain to his kidneys.

"I said, get up!" the German speaker ordered again.

This time, Wilmot moved quickly, getting to his feet as two of the Russians searched him for weapons or anything else he might have hidden. He couldn't blame them; he'd done the same and worse to plenty of Russian prisoners.

When the Russians eventually moved on to Jürgen, he followed Wilmot's example of rising quickly, but he had tears running down his face.

They haven't killed me yet, Wilmot thought as he moved forward to the universal command of a rifle butt in his back. He was still alive and could run. He was a fast runner; at least, he had been in school. His eyes darted left, right, and finally in front of him, searching for an escape route, but Russian soldiers were making a perimeter and training rifles on the corralled, outnumbered prisoners. Running would be suicide.

The two German platoons were completely cut off from the main force. *Would their commanders even order another attack today?* Wilmot wondered. No. They were probably ashamed of their poor strategies and huddling in this snowstorm, licking their paws and worrying about getting hammered in yet another defeat.

The prisoners with Wilmot and Jürgen trudged past the row of burning houses and then on to where about fifty Germans were gathered. Wilmot smacked the side of his head, trying to get some brain cells working, but nothing made sense. In the space of twenty-four hours, the Russians had pushed the Germans back. The Germans had retaliated, pushing the Russians into retreat. The line had been broken a second time with the Germans appearing to hold it, but within hours, the Russians had taken it back. It was all so bloody senseless. All this death for a few metres of ground, a row of trenches, and some wooden houses: back and forth, day after day, with bodies piling up and no significant advances made. And now he was either going to die like the Russian civilians who'd been forced to dig their own graves a month earlier or the Jews in that Baltic town who were killed for sport in a pogrom. What the hell was it all about? It seemed to him that this had nothing to do with giving Germans more living space and was all a game of annihilation, a race to inflict the most atrocious suffering on the enemy. Russians – Germans – Hitler – Stalin? Those two were a couple of bloody sadists!

******

That evening, Wilmot saw the full extent of the recent Russian campaigns. After walking for more hours and kilometres than he could count, he and his fellow captives joined hundreds more German prisoners who were being corralled on the tracks of a disused railway station. Jürgen, the teenage German who'd earlier trudged beside Wilmot, was gasping for breath.

"How long have you been here … as a prisoner?" Jürgen addressed a half-starved soldier.

"Two weeks. They just keep bringing more of you in … every day they bring more … every day. I think they're leaving us here to freeze to death."

Wilmot had no water and neither did anyone else as far as he could see. Hundreds, maybe a thousand men were gathered on the tracks. They looked ravenous, gaunt and grey faced, exhausted and dehydrated, with white crusted lips and bodies that shook with the cold and failing organs. Some were lying with their legs across other men's bodies because of the lack of space. They were sharing coats, hugging each other like lovers to keep warm. The stench of piss and shite was so strong, men were covering their mouths with scarves. And their moaning and mumbled pleas for help, although deafening at times, were being ignored by the Russian guards.

"Is this it?" Wilmot aired his thoughts. "Is this where we die, like this?" He slumped to the ground and covered his face with his hands, his eyes stinging. He didn't have enough water in his body for tears to form, much less fall down his dirty cheeks. He sniffed, embarrassed, but refused to look at the Russians, or the indignities thrust upon his countrymen. Instead, he curled into a ball, shielded his face with his arms and let the sobs wrack his freezing body. If he'd had a gun, he'd have shot himself then and there. He'd been through one devastating concentration camp before; he wouldn't survive a Russian-made one. He wanted it to end. Everything.

Despite the noise and discomfort, Wilmot managed to doze off for a few minutes until the shrill of multiple whistles startled him. He was as stiff as frosty grass and struggled to stand when ordered. His hand was stinging, but he was too afraid to look at the damage or remove the bandage; it was the only one he had. The hand was going to turn green and he'd lose it altogether unless he got treatment. He laughed at himself. Here he was worried about his hand when he should be concerned about not getting his head blown off. What were the Russians waiting for?

"Jürgen, what's going on?" Wilmot whispered.

"They're moving us ... don't know ... don't care where we're going. It has to be better than this place."

The German soldiers were paraded through Leningrad in lines stretching the width of the avenue, in full view of the civilian population who were crowding the pavements. The city's destruction was much more extensive than Wilmot had been led to believe. Every building was damaged, and the streets were littered with rubble.

The snow, coming down like pillow stuffing, was not settling on the well-trodden ground; a graveyard with dead bodies rotting where they lay. Wilmot's eyes grew round like saucers: a corpse with parts of its torso, arms and legs sliced off, had evidently been cannibalised with a butcher's knife. He wondered what human flesh might taste like, then gagged in disgust at his own thoughts.

Shops and houses were windowless. Front doors had been blown off and replaced with cardboard sheets, and the people looked just as starved and desperate as the German prisoners. Germany was obliterating not just the city, but the people in it, yet they still hadn't managed to occupy it.

Wilmot kept his head erect and his eyes focused on the shoulders of the man in front of him, as he was pelted by stones, spat on, and cursed in the common language of hatred.

He squealed when a jagged rock hit him just above the ear, and salty blood flowed onto his cheek and into his mouth. Stunned by the vitriol, he glanced in the direction from whence the rock had been thrown and saw a middle-aged woman pushing her way through the crowd, spitting and cursing at the bedraggled soldiers.

"Nazi scum! Nazi brutes! Fascist Nazis!" Nazi, Nazi, over and over until it sounded like a choir singing. Wilmot's eyes filled again. Where were they marching to? What was going to happen to them?

Chapter Seven

Florent Duguay

Paris, France
November 1941

The three men climbed the hill to the railway tracks. Duguay, leading the midnight attack, wormed his way to the top of the rise then raised a fist to halt the two behind him.

To his left, two German soldiers ambled down the line with their backs to him. To his right, two armed civilian guards stood watch on either side of the railway line. Duguay's lips curled; they were in position.

Without taking his eyes off the German soldiers, Duguay pried a small torch from his pocket, switched it on, and then flashed twice at the two civilians; in reply, he got a raised hand.

"Our men are ready," Duguay whispered over his shoulder "Remember, you two, no guns unless you muck up."

Claude and Pierre ran, heads down, along the side of the hill just below its crest. The Germans were still sauntering along the tracks deep in conversation, their backs to the Frenchmen. Claude halted, nodded to Pierre, then both men pounced on the soldiers from behind, plunging their knives deep into the unsuspecting Germans' necks. The soldiers slumped to the ground, carotid blood fountaining across the railway tracks, and, as they gurgled their last, Claude relieved them of their rifles.

Duguay saw Claude's raised arm and smiled with satisfaction. He'd noticed a six-man German patrol a kilometre from their position and had worried that gunfire would alert them, had the attack not gone to plan. The hardest part was over; his men had made it look easy.

He strode to the centre of the tracks and greeted Jean and Adrien, the two Frenchmen who had been seconded by the Germans to guard the area. "It's almost too easy when they use Resistance fighters to guard their train tracks. When will they ever learn?" he chuckled, shaking their hands.

"You're late, Florent," said Jean, a short, stocky little man with a tonsured pate.

"We came across a patrol not far from here," Duguay responded, gesturing to the woods from whence they'd come. "They were going in the opposite direction, but we had to wait until we were certain they wouldn't double back."

Duguay rummaged through his rucksack for the required materials. He took out a block of *explosif plastique,* put it in a napkin and handed it to Jean. "Hold this. Be careful, Jean. I don't know how stable it is."

"It smells like nuts," said Jean, sniffing it.

"Almonds, to be exact."

"Is this enough to do the job?"

"It's probably too much." Duguay took out another lump and turned it in his hand. "This won't just derail the train, it will blow the tanks and heavy weaponry to smithereens."

"If it's as good as they say it is," said Jean, looking sceptically at the green lump.

Claude and Pierre returned to Duguay once they had rolled the dead German soldiers to the bottom of the hill. They'd left the bodies concealed in bushes but had also taken their side pistols and knives.

"Waste not, want not," Claude said, putting the pistols and knives in their rucksacks. "How long until the train comes, Florent?"

"About ten minutes by my calculations."

Duguay ordered Jean, Adrien, and Pierre, who'd arrived with Claude, to descend to the bottom of the hill. The treeline to their left would be their cover. As soon as they saw Duguay and Claude running down the hill after igniting the fuses, they were to retreat further into the woods and wait. Duguay, although confident, wasn't sure how large the blast would be or how much damage it would cause.

After setting the thick, green, plasticine-like devices on two different spots on the tracks, Duguay inserted fuse wires and then backed away until the two metre wires were taut. Timing was everything. He'd estimated by the length of the wires how long it would take for the explosives to ignite from the moment they lit the fuses to the spark reaching the detonation points. His hope was that the blasts would occur about two seconds after the driver's carriage had passed the hot spot. He wanted the brunt of the explosion to hit the carriages carrying the tanks, heavy weaponry, and soldiers, sparing the driver and stokers at the front of the train; he never wanted to kill Frenchmen or women during their missions. The Germans murdered enough innocent people, and the British heavy-handed airstrikes caused horrific collateral damage.

Claude and Duguay lay once more on their bellies just below the tracks, their heads raised slightly so they could peep over the crest of the hill. Both held the ends of the fuse wires in one hand and their Zippo lighters in the other. Duguay also had a box of matches in his pocket just in case the unthinkable happened and the lighters didn't work.

Duguay stared long and hard down the length of the empty tracks until they were shrouded in darkness. This was the first time he had used *explosif plastique* for an operation, and he was unnerved by its mysteries. He had acquired the sophisticated materials from Romek via Darek. Romek, worried about being captured, had passed on the location of an abandoned hut in the forest close to the toy factory. According to the Pole, a weapons cache lay hidden under the floorboards; a gift from Romek to Duguay in the event of Romek's group being overrun by the Germans. After Romek's premonition had come to pass, and he and his thirty-odd fighters had been imprisoned, Darek had offered to take Duguay to the hut. Duguay had refused the generous gesture. "You were Romek's man, and the Gestapo are probably looking for you, too. You're a liability," he'd told the Pole. Two nights later, he had sent his own men to the abandoned hut, and they had successfully retrieved the weapons and materials. They had got the explosives just in time for this operation.

The sound of the steam train chugging down the track reached them just before the two men saw its lights. Duguay had calculated its speed beforehand based on previous surveillance of carriages carrying similar loads, but he'd been reminding himself all day that this attack was against no ordinary train. It was, according to his spies at the train depot, unlike anything the Resistance had seen so far; a mobile iron fortress hauling *Panzerkampfwagen III*, the lethal Tiger Tanks, anti-tank rocket launchers, crates of MG-34 Machine Guns, and thousands of small arms.

The two lumps of green plasticine began to tremble as the tracks vibrated with the oncoming train. One *explosif plastique* would probably be enough to do the job, Duguay thought again, but two lumps would impress upon the Germans that the Resistance not only had the means, but also the sophisticated weaponry to do real damage.

"If this stuff is as effective as I've been led to believe, I'll have wasted a full lump of it," Duguay mused aloud to Claude.

"And if it's not, you'll be glad you used two instead of one.

"I suppose – right, this is it. As soon as you light that fuse, get down the hill and behind the treeline. Don't wait for me."

At Duguay's nod, they each lit the ends of the wires, watching the sparks snake up their lengths for only a couple of seconds before they both ran for their lives.

From the bottom of the hill, Duguay saw the train coming closer – one hundred metres, then fifty. Mesmerised, he watched for a second longer until a massive explosion of metal and wood erupted into towering flames as the front of the train passed the spot where the *explosif* had been placed.

From inside the coppice, the men held their breaths as a scene from hell unfolded. Four carriages seemed to rise off the ground before toppling over, one after the other, onto their sides then rolling down the hill. Tanks, rocket launchers, and the soldiers who'd been on the roofs guarding the train were smashed to a smouldering pulp in the flying rubble. The night sky blazed red, while the cacophony of exploding ammunition battered the men's eardrums and the smell of cordite and burning flesh assaulted them. The ground shook beneath their feet, and as the destruction spread in what was like a surreal, slow-motion film, Duguay felt the exhilaration of victory rippling through him like raw power in his mind. This was but a miniscule win over a gargantuan enemy, but he felt as though he had single-handedly won the war.

The German soldiers who had been in the back carriage had been spared the devastation at the front. They appeared through the curtain of smoke, many injured, stumbling in the darkness, some rolling like boulders down the hillside. Men stood frozen to the spot as the thick grey smoke and white-hot flames still shooting skywards from the mangled train blocked their escape routes. They were defeated, devastated.

Duguay joined his fighters and grinned. "Those soldiers will eventually come after us when they regroup. Get to the van as fast as you can. We can bask in glory when we get back to the farm."

The din of destruction receded only slightly as they ran through the trees. Further explosions, presumably caused by more ammunition igniting, shook the bare tree branches. Even as he fled, Duguay maintained his grin. The damage had been even greater than he'd anticipated and would be more crushing to German morale than he'd dared hope.

There would be reprisals.

Out of breath, Duguay waited for his four men to catch up before stepping cautiously out of the treeline and onto the narrow lane where Claude's Post Office van had been parked. They were one kilometre from their mission objective, and the men were jubilant.

Claude slid open the van's side door, and had his hand on the driver's door handle as the first shots rang out from further down the lane.

Adrien was killed instantly by a shot to the head. Pierre had been getting into the van when he was shot in the leg. He fell backwards onto his back, howling in agony beside Duguay and Jean. "Get him in the van!" yelled Duguay, as he stepped in front of the injured Pierre.

Crouched at the rear end of the vehicle, Duguay saw a group of German soldiers running towards them; the patrol they'd spotted on their way to the railway tracks. They were about fifty metres from the van and had obviously been just as surprised to see the Resistance fighters as Duguay and his men had been to see the patrol.

Chaos ensued, with both sides firing haphazardly at each other from exposed positions. The Germans fired their rifles as they ran. One of their number was hit and dropped like a stone, then Jean hit another. The Germans were unprotected, and with no reasonable chance of advancing further without being shot at, they went to ground.

Duguay gave Claude cover fire while he jumped into the driver's seat and started the engine. The injured Pierre was already in the back and had been joined by Jean after Duguay had told him to go. Standing flush against the side of the van, Duguay was unable to move backwards or forwards. Trapped by German fire, he dug into his breast pocket and took out his weapon of last resort. He pulled the pin and lobbed his grenade as far as he could. In the ensuing explosion, he hauled himself into the passenger seat beside Claude.

"Go! Go!" he shrieked.

"That was far too close," Claude yelled, the tyres screeching as he lead-footed the pedal.

Duguay suddenly became aware of blood running down his sleeve. "*Merde*. I've been hit – bastards nicked me." He turned his head as far as he could and called over his shoulder, "How is Pierre?"

"I'll live," Pierre croaked.

Twenty minutes later, they arrived at the farmhouse. Two men carried Pierre to a downstairs bedroom while Duguay headed to the kitchen. There, he went for the brandy, glugging it straight from the bottle before stripping off his sodden jacket and pouring some into his wound.

"Stay here. I'll get the doctor to look at you both," said Claude, heading for the door.

"We've scored a victory tonight," Duguay said, wincing. "Tell the doctor to see to Pierre first. He can take the bullet out of my shoulder when he's finished."

Chapter Eight

Max Vogel

Paris, France
November 1941

The Lizzie landed on a grass airstrip just south of Dieppe. The pilot did a one hundred and eighty-degree turn, stopped, but didn't cut the engine while Max and the crates were unloaded. Then, the hatch was closed and within a couple of minutes it took to the sky again.

Marcel, the leader of the Resistance group, drove Max to Saint Quentin in a food delivery van, and during the journey Max explained why he had returned.

"It's like coming home," Max joked to Marcel when they arrived at the farmhouse on the hill. "It seems much longer than three weeks since I was here learning to walk again after my parachute injury. I don't think I ever thanked you properly."

"You did, Englishman," Marcel said. "You did. Many times."

For an hour, Max discussed the group's progress with Marcel and Pascual. The pair had been busy in his absence, spreading the word about the group via contacts in Paris. The number of fighters in Saint Quentin had more than doubled, with most of the recruits being Dieppe, Saint Quentin and Paris natives.

Marcel refilled Max's coffee cup. "And now I'm going to do you another favour. There's a Polish man here. He came to me a week ago from Paris. He's the only surviving Resistance fighter from Romek's group, but more importantly, he knows the communist you're looking for."

Max raised his eyebrows at Marcel. "He's here? This is good."
Marcel then bid the Pole to enter the kitchen.

Max studied the man that Klara had spoken about at her
debriefing in London. Over six feet tall, of medium build, and
with a full head of blond hair, Darek Lukaszewicz was an
arresting figure. His most interesting features, however, were not
his height or build but the contrasts in his colouring: white, almost
translucent skin covered in freckles, so very copious that one
would have a hard job sticking a pin in between them. But
seeming to go against the laws of nature, his eyes were dark
brown and surrounded by thick, black eyelashes beneath equally
dark eyebrows. Max could understand the man wanting to get out
of Paris; that face would stick out in any crowd.

"Marcel tells me you were afraid to remain in Paris," Max
began the conversation.

"That's correct. I was desperate to carry on the fight against
the Germans but didn't want to stay in the capital after the
Gestapo and SS rounded up Romek's people. I heard about
Marcel and Saint Quentin, and I knew I had to get here."

"I'm glad you did. You've made my job much easier. I was
planning to look for you in Paris."

"You wouldn't have found me." Darek frowned. "I didn't sleep
in the same place two nights in a row."

Because of Romek and Klara's trust in the Pole, Max had no
reason to suspect him of colluding with the Germans.
Nevertheless, he had a few niggling questions that had to be
addressed before he could let the man into his confidence.

"Why do you think you were the only person to escape the
German attack on Romek?"

"I was living in the toy factory's basement with Romek and
had no fixed address. I was what Romek called a ghost. I rarely

hung around the factory during the day and didn't get too close to the other fighters." Darek paused. "I can see you're worried, and I understand your scepticism. I still can't wrap my head around being the only survivor. The guilt keeps me awake at night.

"On the morning of the German raid on our base, I was at Chirac's shop delivering Romek's radio transmitter to Marine. From there, I went to Duguay's farm. I was supposed to meet Romek at the Petit Croissant Restaurant on the Champs Élysées at one o'clock, but my meeting with Duguay went on longer than expected. That delay probably saved my life."

Max believed Darek, for now. "I want to meet with Florent Duguay. Will you take me to him?"

Darek's eyes widened in surprise. "No. I don't like the man. I haven't gone anywhere near him since Marine went missing. He doesn't tolerate betrayal, or even a whiff of disloyalty. To be honest, I suspected him of having a hand in Marine's disappearance. I thought he might have killed her because she knew too much, and he didn't trust her to keep her mouth shut about his operation. He's ruthless. I don't want anything to do with him."

Darek's reluctance didn't put Max off. It had been a brilliant stroke of luck meeting him, a coincidence that one might call a miracle in wartime. "Marine is safe. I got her to London."

Darek looked surprised, but he didn't demand details. "Good to hear. Why do you want to meet Duguay?" he asked instead.

"I need you to set up a face to face meeting with him. Tell him that you'll be bringing a British Intelligence agent who wants to offer him and his group British help and collaboration – no names – no specifics. Understand?"

Darek was silent while Max watched the cogs turning.

"If I do this, there's something I want in return," Darek finally said.

"In return for helping to defeat the Germans? What is it?"

"When you leave France, I want you to take me with you..."

"Impossible," Max grunted.

"It's not impossible. You took Marine back, so why can't you take me? I don't know if the Gestapo know about me, but if they do, how long do you think I'll be able to evade capture? I haven't got anywhere to live, and if I stay with Marcel, I will put his group in danger."

He wouldn't say it, but Max was not averse to the idea. SOE could use all the agents they could lay their hands on, and the Poles in London were desperate for dedicated soldiers. "I can't just take foreigners back to England with me at the drop of a hat. We have security procedures and vetting..."

"Major, I know for a fact that Poles are in the British army or have formed their own units," Darek cut in. "I know that Poles were evacuated to Britain during the German invasion either by ship or plane or on foot. You strike me as a man who can find his way around procedures when you want to, so either you give me your word that you will take me to England or you can find someone else to set up a meeting with Duguay. You decide."

******

Max paced the living room floor in the Paris safe house, panicking over his imminent encounter with the communist leader. The meeting was only hours away, and he was very conscious about the promise he had made to Heller. "You know me, Jonathan. I will conduct the meeting in my usual professional manner, and I won't let my personal feelings get in the way of the job."

Promises were easy to make, but sometimes impossible to keep, he thought. The harder he tried to focus on the negotiations concerning collaboration with Duguay, the more he imagined himself sticking a knife in the man's gut.

Irritable, he slumped into a chair. For three days, he had waited alone in the Paris flat for Duguay's answer. Time had dragged, yet the days seemed to have sped by; he had only two more left in which to complete his business before getting on the flight home. Heller's feelings had been clear; he wouldn't take the fall should the mission fail, or if Max didn't make it back to the airstrip near Dieppe in time to meet the plane.

After having a wash, Max wiped the excess shaving soap from his now-hairless chin, then peered at himself in the bathroom mirror to study his blond moustache. He'd already dyed his blond hair black, so the hair on his top lip looked oddly out of place. *Keep it or shave it?* He pondered. He went into the bathroom cabinet and took out another razor blade. The moustache was coming off.

He studied his clean-shaven face and flattened black hair. It was imperative that he change his natural appearance as much as possible, for he wouldn't get ten metres on the Paris streets looking like himself. According to Darek, posters of Paul were still plastered on walls, lampposts and windows throughout the capital. A reward of four thousand Francs, equivalent to two hundred Reichsmarks, was being offered for information regarding Paul's whereabouts. It was a pittance for his brother's life, Max thought, considering what the Reich was charging the French for being in their country.

One of the conditions of the armistice between Germany and France was that the French pay for their own occupation: i.e., the French were required to cover the expenses associated with the upkeep of a 300,000-strong army of occupation. When the British got wind of that information, they'd been genuinely flabbergasted. The burden on the defeated French nation amounted to approximately twenty million German Reichsmarks per day, a sum that would cripple the country for decades to come, regardless of their eventual victory or defeat.

The Germans had also set an artificial exchange rate for the Reichsmark versus the Franc, which established a ratio of one mark to twenty Francs. The Nazi gall was staggering.

Outside, it was an unusually mild early November day with a clear blue sky. Were it any other time, Max would have been savouring the crisp fresh air on the Paris streets or sitting in a café enjoying a café au lait. But he was not enjoying the walk with the aid of a walking stick, he was a bundle of nerves intent on reaching Darek's vehicle without being closely scrutinised by people walking in the opposite direction.

Marcel's food delivery van was already parked on the corner of the street. Max glanced at his image as he passed a shop window and was startled by the mop of black hair that was no longer flat but bouncing with curls. His confidence rose; if he didn't recognise himself as Max Vogel, no one in Paris would see him as Paul. Wearing black trousers, a black jacket, white shirt and braces, he had taken the added precaution of donning dark glasses to hide his turquoise eyes.

Before reaching the van, Max reminded himself that he was one step closer to Duguay and finding out what had happened to Paul. He'd given himself a good talking to before leaving the flat; he *was* a professional, and he *would* hide his murderous impulses.

This was a small victory, for he'd not been confident of getting the communist's permission for a face-to-face meeting. He was angry, yes, and still wanted to kill the man, but he acknowledged that murdering Duguay would be foolish. That, he was not.

When Max arrived, Darek was leaning against the side of the van. He hopped into the driver's seat and turned the key in the ignition.

"If it hadn't been for that expensive-looking walking stick, I might not have recognised you," Darek said.

"Good, then neither will anyone else in Paris," said Max, wincing as he climbed into the passenger seat.

Darek checked the rear-view mirror then pulled away from the kerb. "We're going twenty kilometres south of here. But before I put myself in danger, I have one condition."

"Another one?" Max responded, without looking at the Pole.

"Yes, another one, and it's important."

"Go on then, out with it."

"Duguay's men have enough weapons to repel a German assault, or at least put up a damn good fight. I know you want vengeance, Major, but I can't let you go in there with that gun you're hiding in your sock. Hand it over."

Max had lain awake throughout the previous night, his rage against Duguay bubbling over, and his disbelief that Paul was truly gone still plaguing him. It just didn't feel right. The memory of Klara's testimony was also replaying over and over in his mind as if hearing it again and again would change it. He needed closure, but Darek had been right to warn him against violence, and he was right to ask for the gun now. Still, he wasn't getting it.

"No. I don't think I will."

Darek pulled the van to the pavement, slammed on the brakes and cut the engine. "Look, I did as you asked. I told Duguay's man that you were from British Intelligence. I said you were acting on behalf of your government and wanted to offer your assistance and cooperation. I won't get myself killed because you're hell-bent on vengeance, so you will either leave your pistol in the car before we get out of here, or I will throw you out of this vehicle now."

Max's muscles twitched in his jaw. He could refuse to follow the instruction, but he wasn't quite ready to tell Darek to piss off. To keep the peace, he removed the gun and put it under his seat. "Satisfied? Now drive, or we'll be late."

Chapter Nine

Max got out of Darek's food delivery van minus his gun. He watched Darek drive off, then approached Claude who was standing close to the back doors of his Post Office van. The shock on the Frenchman's face was priceless; the lift of his eyebrows, the widening of his eyes and the step backwards spoke volumes.

"Get in," Claude said.

After he closed the door behind him, Claude banged his fist against the dividing wall between the driver's compartment and the back of the vehicle. "Let's go, Pierre!" Then he asked Max, "Do you have a gun?"

"No," said Max, amused at the Frenchman's blatant security errors, thus far. "And that is your second mistake. You don't know me or if I'm the ally I claim to be. You should have searched me before I got in here. And you shouldn't have let Darek drive off before making sure I was not a danger to you or your driver."

Max got on his knees, trying to keep his balance, as the floor of the van vibrated. He raised his arms. "Search me. You won't find anything but do it anyway."

Claude grunted, but gave no response as he patted Max down. When he finished he pulled a hessian sack over Max's head. "Lie flat on the floor and stay there."

Max did as he was told without protest. It was not the first time he'd gone through this song and dance routine with foreign counterparts. But he was disappointed in the Frenchman called Claude – a name he remembered from Klara's interview. The man had been much too trusting. If he saw to security in Duguay's camp, he should be replaced; sloppiness in the Resistance movement was the main cause of death for its members.

The van was bumping along what was probably a rough gravel road, judging by the amount of stones being thrown up by the wheels. Max heard Claude moving around despite the racket of the old engine and ineffective suspension.

"You know who I am, don't you?" Max said from under the sack.

"Be quiet."

"What did you do with the German doctor's body after you murdered him?"

"Shut up."

Max groaned at the boot to his ribs. Claude didn't have to answer; he'd already showed his hand. He knew exactly who he was dealing with.

Max relaxed his muscles and closed his eyes. His identity wasn't important now that he'd got this far. His mission was straightforward: meet with Duguay, offer him an alliance with British Intelligence, establish Paul's fate, then leave. Simple. Only it wasn't. Heller's orders were not compatible with Max's desire for revenge.

Heller had repeated his instructions at least three times. "Don't raise a hand against Duguay and his men. Don't ask a single question about Paul unless Duguay makes it clear he's willing to give you answers." Well, bollocks to that.

Max rehearsed the words he would use to do his job properly and stay alive, going so very deep into himself he barely noticed that the van had come to a stop and its squeaky back door was opening.

Claude ripped the sack off Max's head. He squinted as a shaft of sunlight hit his face but was given no time to adjust to the brightness before being manhandled out of the van into a cobblestone courtyard.

There, Claude strode towards a two-storey farmhouse, motioning Max to follow him. Max looked around. It was apparent that the property was situated well away from the main road. He spotted a narrow dirt track with trees on either side beyond a perimeter fence. And beyond that, he saw nothing but trees and more trees. The Germans would find this place if they were intent on looking for it, but they wouldn't stumble upon it by chance. It was as perfect a set up as a hideout could be, the sort of place he would have chosen himself as a base of operations.

While keeping pace with Claude, Max noticed a well-kept garden, vegetable patches on his left and a barn on his right, obscuring whatever lay beyond it. Geranium-filled flower pots hung in baskets in front of the stone house while frilly net curtains adorned the windows. The style of building was typical for the area, as were the wooden basement trapdoor and narrow basement window, almost at ground level and close to the front porch.

Inside the house, Max was ushered along a narrow entrance hall. He passed a spacious living room where a rowdy group of men were seated around a circular table playing cards. They stared at him as he passed, and he nodded politely, his sharp eyes falling on the German *Gewehr* Mauser rifles piled against the wall. The group had been busy stealing from the Germans. Good for them, Max thought.

Darek was already in the kitchen sitting at a rectangular table laid with a cream lace cloth, two jugs of wine and four tumblers. A plate of olives and another with hard lumpy cheese floating in olive oil sat next to a breadboard with an uncut loaf and a serrated kitchen knife. Max, relieved to see a friendly face and the welcoming repast, sat down next to the Pole.

"Wait here. Eat. Drink wine," said Claude, before leaving the room.

Darek sipped the rich burgundy wine then leant across the table as if to emphasise his point. "Remember, Major, I will make the introductions, and you will not say a word until Duguay speaks to you directly. He likes to look people over."

Max nodded. "And you will remember our deal, Darek. I'll offer him the British terms, and then I will get answers about my brother."

After a ten-minute wait, Duguay entered from an outside door. His left arm was wrapped in a white cotton sling, his hand hanging limply over the edge. He wiped his feet on the doormat then stood open-mouthed, his disbelieving eyes, wide. "*Mon Dieu*, it's true," he muttered.

Max stood up and returned Duguay's pervasive gaze with one of his own. It took only seconds for him to see the Frenchman as an adversary, to recognise the man Klara had been terrified of, and to get the measure of his cold, unapologetic eyes.

Duguay came to the table. He pulled out a chair opposite Max. Max returned to his seat, his eyes necessarily guarded but his hatred welling inside him like a burst pipe. He pictured the German rifles in the next room and for a split second wondered if he could get to one of them and pull the trigger on Duguay before being shot down.

Duguay shifted his eyes to Darek, and in French said. "Pole, you're a sneaky bastard. You didn't warn me who he was. I'm not happy about this. I don't like surprises."

"I told him not to give you my name," Max responded in perfect French. "Would you have met with me had you known who I was?" Max sipped his wine and set the glass casually on the table. He had imagined this scene many times, but not once had he pictured this stand off so early in the game. He hadn't been asked for his name, rank, or the details of his mission, but it was evident that the Frenchman knew exactly why he was there.

Duguay flicked his eyes again to Darek. "Tell the men in the other room to get out. You go, too. I'll call you when I need you."

Max looked at the bread knife. His pulse thumped wildly in his neck, not only because of his rage but with the grief that was engulfing him. It was real now. Paul was dead, and he was sitting opposite the man who'd killed him. His parents' faces tumbled into his mind. He saw them crying, his father holding his mother in his arms. Hannah, beside herself; it was no secret that Paul had been her favourite brother. And Willie, alone in Russia, would get another letter like the one he'd got from Biermann about their father.

Max's stony gaze followed Duguay's men as they traipsed through the kitchen and out the door into the yard with rifles slung over their shoulders. Duguay was displaying his strength, saying without words that he held all the cards, and should Max want a fight he'd lose and end up as dead as Paul – he clearly wasn't afraid of being in the house alone with his victim's vengeful twin.

"The resemblance is remarkable. Did you really think you could fool me with black hair, Major Max Vogel?" said Duguay, pouring more wine into Max's empty glass.

"The hair wasn't for your benefit. You'll have noticed my brother's face plastered across the city?"

"Ah, *oui*." Duguay sat back. "*Eh bien.* Let us discuss your brother before we talk about the business of war, *d'accord?*"

Max nodded, his mouth a hard line.

Duguay began in a casual manner, as though having a conversation with a friend. "You want to know why Paul was brought here and what happened to him, *hein?* Perfectly understandable."

"I want to know if he is dead, and if so, where you buried him."

Duguay chuckled. "You already think you know the answer to the first question, otherwise you wouldn't be itching to kill me. As for the second ... well ... there really is no need to talk about where..."

"And why is that?"

Duguay smiled. "You're good – calm, patient with a poker face, as you English call it – you think as I do, *n'est-ce pas?* Blind rage is never a good thing, is it? It doesn't defeat an enemy. It is just as destructive as one hanging oneself or blowing one's own foot off – *mais,* perhaps that is an exaggeration."

Duguay went into his trouser waistband, pulled his gun out and placed it on the table. He taunted Max with a humorous smile, inviting him to reach for it. "I don't blame you for coming here. You want to kill me. You want revenge. I understand."

"I doubt that very much." Max eyed the gun, and then dismissed it. Duguay didn't seem like an idiot who'd leave bullets in its barrel.

Duguay poured another glass of wine for himself but then pushed it to the side. "I had a brother, Max ... may I call you Max?"

Max remained silent.

"Very well, Major. My brother was killed in Madrid three years ago during the siege of that city. I loved the boy. He was younger than I and much more idealistic ... he was drowning in his beliefs. I'll never forget the day the Spanish Republican Government begged for help on the radio. Gerard, my brother, left the farm, walked over the Pyrenees and into Spain without a moment's hesitation. He fought with the Russians against that pig, General Franco, and died bravely, or so I was told.

"A communist by the name of Rouge – an apt name, *non?* – fought alongside Gerard and saw him die. Rouge and the other few survivors of that battle were forced to dig the grave for their comrades. He told me that the fascists threw over a hundred dead men into the pit before they sat under trees to eat lunch while watching the remaining communists fill the grave with dirt.

"Rouge was a prisoner for a while, but when the war ended he made it back to France and went straight to my parents' house to inform them – you know what I did, *hein?* – when I got word that Gerard was dead, I went to Spain to search for the place where he'd supposedly been killed. The war was over. Republicans were fleeing the country, half-starved men stumbling into France like downtrodden mules. But I travelled in the opposite direction, because I refused to believe my brother was gone."

Duguay paused to take two long slugs of wine. Max, remaining silent, wondered why the Frenchman was telling the story of his dead brother. He was also surprised to see Duguay blink away tears.

"Rouge had drawn me a map of the burial site, and I was going to dig Gerard up and bring him home. Fascist Spain had taken him, but they weren't going to keep him." Duguay sighed. "*Oui,* it was an overambitious plan, impossible to carry out, but even as I told myself that, I was still determined to search through that pit of corpses to see him with my own eyes. Was my Gerard in that grave? I'll never know for sure – I never found him – I will always wonder."

"It's a touching story," Max said, his voice flat. "So you understand why I need you to tell me what happened to Paul?"

"I do."

"Where did you shoot him? In the woods, inside a grave you made him dig for himself, in a river, in the back of the Post Office van I travelled in to get here?"

"I will answer your questions, Major, but before I do, I need you to answer one of mine."

Max inadvertently eyed the knife, angry at Duguay's procrastinations. It was within reach. Duguay had only one useful hand and was vulnerable without his men…

"Where is Marine?" Duguay asked.

"She's not in France," Max responded, surprised by the question.

"You took her?"

"She was mine to take."

"I see. You were aware of the work she was doing in the photographic shop?"

"Of course. She was my agent."

"I want her back."

"You can't have her."

"Why? There is a notice on her shop door saying the business is closed for family holidays. It's not too late to get her back here to carry on working for me. Bring her or you can leave France without answers and without my cooperation. We don't need the British. You supervised Romek's group and look what happened to him and his people. Marine was giving me valuable information. She was … is indispensable."

"No one is indispensable." Max sat back, the calmer of the two, yet he was still at Duguay's mercy. "Monsieur Duguay, your delaying tactics are not lost on me. You're either bored with your men and enjoy my company, or you're stalling for a reason I can't fathom. Why don't we get down to business, and when we've come to an agreement, you can tell me about Paul and I'll be on my way."

"And you will agree to Marine's return? As I said, she is indispensable."

"Weapons, soldiers, and resources are the *only* indispensable commodities in this war, and I can give you two out of the three. I've been authorised to supply you with whatever small arms and explosives you might need. We will also give you air support when necessary, money, radio transmitters, and an agent to operate them and organise your group into a cohesive force. We will not make demands on you. You will have your autonomy, but we will require your full cooperation on any mission we choose to execute. As for Marine, her talents are needed elsewhere. She is not a bargaining chip on the table."

Duguay seemed to be mulling over Max's offer. His eyes had sparkled as Max unrolled the gifts he was bearing. Evidently, he hadn't realised just how useful the British could be to him.

For a while, the two men continued to talk business. Duguay wanted to know how the system worked regarding the delivery of weapons, where their possible targets would be, how supplies and weapons would be transported, and how committed the British were in France. He also asked for more details about the money he would receive to finance their missions and was pleasantly surprised by the amount mentioned. Max had patiently explained the workings point by point, even forgetting Paul for brief moments until he was reminded why he'd gone there, and his anger bubbled up anew.

"Tell me about Paul now," Max said after a lengthy silence, during which Duguay had started to pace the floor.

"We will carry on with our assassination programme," said Duguay, ignoring Max's request.

Max raised his voice to combat the pounding of Duguay's boots on the stone floor. "General de Gaulle was on the BBC's French language service only a few days ago asking that you, the Communist Partisans, call in your assassins. But you already know that, don't you? As he so rightly said, killing one German will not change the outcome of the war, and my bosses agree. I have been instructed to ask you to rein in that part of your Resistance strategy. You must be aware of the hundreds of French men and women being shot by Germans in reprisals? The General has made it clear…"

"We do not recognise de Gaulle's authority. We don't listen to a man who ran away from his country. We believe in an eye for an eye."

Max refused to get into the game of politics. All he could think about was the cold-blooded way Duguay was talking about the subject of assassination to the brother of one of his victims. He stood and went to the window. He'd done his job, and he'd had more than enough of the demigod-like, over-dramatic Duguay. "Do we have a deal, Duguay. Yes or no?"

"*Oui,* we have a deal."

"My brother?"

Duguay went to the kitchen door leading to the hallway, turned, and sent Max an infuriating smile. "Come with me."

Outside the front entrance, Duguay lifted the basement trapdoor and pointed to the wooden steps. "You want answers, Major, down you go."

Chapter Ten

The Vogel Twins

The basement was lit by a couple of bare light bulbs hanging on a wire across the ceiling. Max stood at the bottom of the steps, his eyes slowly growing accustomed to the dimness and the room's layout. His heart soared then sank, and any fleeting thoughts he'd had about finding Paul alive were dashed in the empty space that looked and smelt like a vegetable storeroom. A door at the back of the room was ajar. Max crossed to it, pushed it open, then stopped in his tracks. An old metal bed frame was pressed up against the far wall, and on it lay what looked like a bundle of rags.

Max gasped, emotion soaring into his throat, tears following in hot pursuit as he ran to the side of the bed where Paul was lying. His wrists were bound above his head with a rope whose ends were tied to the bed post. A gag had been stuffed into his mouth, and that was covered by a strip of cotton bandage wrapped around his face and tied at the back of his head. Tears sprouted from Paul's wide eyes as he tried to move his lower body, but the bindings made it virtually impossible.

Max fell to his knees beside his twin, wracked with sobs as he pulled the gag from Paul's mouth and untied the rope from the bedpost. "Sorry it took me so long to get to you … sorry, Paul …Jesus Christ, Paul!" His mind shut down on him. He was incapable of saying another word, so he buried his head in his brother's lap and sobbed.

"Max … Max, it's okay. You're here now." Paul's newly liberated lips broke into a smile. "Move for God's sake, you're crushing me."

Paul and Max embraced as if it were the last hug they would ever share. When they drew apart, Paul slumped back onto the bed and Max joined him, still overcome by shock and the inability to say anything that would come close to describing how he felt. His brother was alive, pale-faced, but looking well.

"Can you get me out of here?" Paul asked finally. "Tell me before I go mad with not knowing from one day to the next if I'm going to be executed."

"I'll get you out," Max sniffed. "It won't be easy, but I'm not leaving without you." Max picked up the gag and length of rope and waved them at Paul. "Is this how you've been for weeks … tied up like a dog?"

"No. A man called Claude came down here half an hour ago and told me that a British officer was trying to negotiate my release with Duguay. He tied and gagged me, probably because he was afraid that the meeting wouldn't go well, and I'd call out if I heard a British voice – I don't know why these people do what they do."

"Did they treat you well? You don't look hurt or too thin."

"If you mean Duguay, then yes, he hasn't injured anything but my pride. When he realised I had no information about German operations and plans, I thought he might kill me, but a few hours after I was brought here, one of his men was injured and I was asked to patch him up. Since then, I've looked after men who've been sick or wounded, including Duguay, who took a bullet to his shoulder last night. I suppose I've been useful to him."

Paul inhaled a ragged breath. "Max, I thought I'd been abandoned – Jesus, I still can't believe you're here – I never expected to see you again."

Max finally found his normal voice. "I thought you were dead. The woman…"

"Marine? She thought I was you. She called me by your name and kissed me on the lips before she disappeared – you should make better choices in your women – and what the hell have you done to your hair?"

"Your ugly mug is plastered all over Paris."

Paul chuckled. "At least they haven't forgotten me."

"Paul, about the woman. She heard a shot and presumed Duguay had killed you. She's in England now. She told me the whole story, but only after I had left France with her. I would never have got on that plane had I known about this."

"I know. I'm sorry, you must have been frantic. After the woman left, Duguay came back down here. He aimed his pistol right at me and then fired over my head. The sick bastard frightened the life out of me."

"Maybe Duguay wanted to make her think he'd killed you. She said he wanted to teach her a lesson."

Paul said, "Well, whatever his reason for doing that, I'm all right. I probably look better than you do right now."

Max shook his head, "I don't know whether to laugh or cry. It's been hell – thank God I didn't tell the family. By the way, there's something you should know about…"

Footsteps clumped on the basement stairs as Duguay and Claude appeared, halting Max's next words. Duguay studied the brothers sitting side by side on the bed, a mocking smile feathering his lips. "You two really are peas in a pod aren't you

… apart from your dreadful hair dye job, Major. Ah, the sweet reunion, at last."

Paul stayed silent, but Max was furious. "You could have saved me a lot of anguish had you just told me he was alive when I first arrived. No more games, Duguay."

Duguay shrugged. "All right. No more games."

Max got up from the bed, automatically shielding his brother. "What happens now?" he asked.

"Now, I will give you my terms for his release."

Claude remained in the background, his rifle raised although not trained on either Paul or Max.

"Sit, Max … sit. And yes, I'm going to call you Max, whether you like it or not. It's easier for me … Vogel is much too German for my liking." He pulled a chair over to the bed and faced the twins, looking at each of them in turn. "Max – Paul – *vous êtes extraordinaires, vous deux.* The likeness between you … ah … but you must hear that a lot."

"Will you let him come with me when I leave?" Max asked again.

"Oui. I knew he couldn't stay here indefinitely when I decided to spare his life, but he was useful, you see."

"I'm very grateful that you did." Max was surprised at the warmth in his voice.

"*Mais oui,* Max. I don't murder doctors, not even German ones. Marine was very foolish to bring him here, but she did tell me about you. You could say she introduced us in advance, and in so doing, saved your brother's life. Isn't that right, Paul?"

Paul nodded. "As much as I hated her for getting me into this mess, he's right, Max. She did tell him who you were, and that you would come for me."

Max's anger toward Klara softened, but only for the briefest of moments. He had more pressing matters on his mind to deal with than his personal feelings for her. "Duguay, it seems we have a deal. How do you want to do this?" he asked.

"I'll send two of my men with you as far as your departure point. I take it you are going to leave France as soon as possible?"

"Correct."

"*Bien.* He has to leave with you."

"What!" said Paul.

Max shot a warning glance to Paul. Then he turned back to Duguay. "Agreed. Your men can come with us as far as Dieppe. If Paul tries to get back to his Nazi friends en route, I will shoot him myself. I give you my word, he will get on the plane with me."

Max heard Paul's sharp intake of breath but refused to look at him. "Duguay, my brother isn't stupid. He knows he can't go back to the Wehrmacht *and* he knows he will face consequences in England."

Duguay cocked his head, evidently pondering Max's statement. "What consequences?"

"I'll have to hand him over to British Intelligence when we get to London. He'll be detained as a prisoner of war and will probably spend time in a detention centre, undergoing interrogation. That's the only deal he'll get, but it's better than this."

"Max, for God's sake! Is this a bloody joke?" Paul blurted out.

"No, it is not a joke. You're the enemy, Paul. Neither Duguay nor I will let you go back to the Wehrmacht. The Gestapo or SS would squeeze every detail of your capture out of you whether you want to tell them about it or not. Make no mistake about it, if Duguay agrees to my proposal, you will cease to be his prisoner and become mine until I relinquish custody of you to the British authorities."

***

Paul glared at his twin while Max and Duguay discussed his fate as though he were a commodity. He was astounded at his brother, who'd seemed to be agreeing with every demand Duguay made. He hoped Max was merely feeding the Frenchman's ego to get them both out of the farmhouse in one piece. He'd learnt a lot during his weeks of imprisonment, and despite his allegiance to the German army, had been impressed by Duguay's French Communists who, every day, were undertaking dangerous missions to undermine the occupation forces at tremendous risk to themselves. Hardly a day had gone by Paul hadn't treated somebody's wounds.

His freedom was in sight. He was ecstatic to see Max, who was once again bailing him out of a terrible situation, one he never thought he'd survive. But this Max was a different man than the one who had gone to Germany to help him. He was threatening imprisonment and calling his own twin the enemy, and he was being very convincing.

"… I'm taking a huge risk," Duguay was now saying.

"As am I, even by being here," Max retorted. "Look, you need to trust me on this. I never expected to find Paul alive, but now that I have, he cannot be allowed to re-join his unit. It would be lethal for you and other Resistance groups."

Duguay stood and gave Paul a dismissive glance. "Major, you and I will discuss this further upstairs."

When Duguay headed for the stairs, Max got to his feet and looked down at Paul's horrified expression. He held his finger to his lips and whispered, "I know this is not what you wanted to hear, but it's the only way. We're not out of the woods yet and won't be until we board the plane tomorrow night. Don't say anything that might spook Duguay or his men, you hear me?"

Paul was livid. Max was right about most things, but they were alone now, and he needed to clear something up before Duguay and Max continued their discussion. He rose, drawing himself to his full height and standing only inches from Max's face. "I can't let you take me to England. I won't go to prison. Christ, Max I have a wife in Berlin. What were you thinking?"

Paul followed Max to the bottom of the steps. "Max, think ... I can't do it. You have to ... you must find another way," he called out even as Max disappeared, and the trapdoor shut, leaving him alone again

Paul sat in the chair Duguay had occupied. He was elated, not quite believing that soon he'd be free of the constant, terrifying nightmares of dying at the Communists' hands. But he was also distraught. His dreams of seeing Valentina and Berlin were disintegrating and in their place was the vision of him behind prison bars in England. He accepted that Max had acted with good intentions. He recognised the perceived folly of allowing a German officer held hostage by the enemy to return to his barracks with a basket full of intelligence. Max was right; the Gestapo and SS would make him retrace every step he'd taken on the night he'd been captured. They'd force him to join them in a manhunt for Duguay and the location of the Communist base, and they wouldn't stop looking until they found both. Yet the alternatives: England, detention, losing Valentina, were infinitely more terrifying.

He'd been duped by fellow officers. Apart from hearing about a couple of high-profile assassinations, he'd not been privy to German reports of sabotage on their trains and convoys. He'd known nothing about the hijacking of German military trucks and soldiers, nor had he guessed that French Resistance groups operated with disciplined men and women who weren't overawed by the colossal German army. The Third Reich was being challenged, and contrary to the impression given to him by the men he'd dined with in Parisian restaurants, the French were not cowed or accepting defeat.

An hour after leaving him to agonise over Valentina and the thought of incarceration, Duguay returned alone to the basement. Paul stood to attention, desperately trying to show his captor respect and cooperation.

"You're a good doctor, Paul. Thank you for helping my men." He gestured to his arm. "And for this."

Paul nodded, surprised by the compliment.

"Your brother and I have made the arrangements. You will go with him, but if you try to escape, my men will shoot to kill, as will the major. He gave me his word as a British officer."

Paul blinked. "I'll do as I'm told."

"*Bon, c'est fait.*" Duguay stared at Paul; through him, as though not really seeing him at all. "I hate Germans, not just because they are my enemy but for their total disregard for codes of conduct regarding civilians. It is because of your disgusting ethics of killing innocent people that we will fight you to the death. We won't yield to your occupation or your powerful weapons, your soldiers on our streets, or your vengeful slaughters. Your brother was candid with me. He said he'd once warned you not to choose the wrong side because you would … how did he put it? Ah … you would be on the wrong side of history. You should have listened to him, Oberartz Vogel. You should have listened."

Chapter Eleven

Claude's Post Office van was used to take Max, Paul, Claude, and a driver to the Dieppe airfield. It was the only vehicle that could legally break the Germans' night time curfew and have enough space in the back to hide the men. Duguay had taken extra measures to conceal the passengers. The Germans, should they stop and search the van, would see Max and Jean, the driver, wearing postal workers' uniforms and pill box hats and carrying *ausweis* ID cards, albeit forged ones. The hope was the inspectors wouldn't spot the false wall in the back with a hollow space behind it. Erected near the driver's end, the wooden panel had ventilation holes and was partially hidden by the packages and sacks full of letters.

Max had instructed Darek to return the food delivery van to Marcel in Saint Quentin. The men would rendezvous at Marcel's farmhouse that night before travelling on to Dieppe.

The aircraft picking up Max, Darek, and Paul was due to land at 2 am on the same grass airstrip as the one that had dropped Max and the weapons off eight days earlier. Max was buoyant and heady with their success to this point, but he was also nervous about the bureaucracy and questions that would face him when he got back to England. He was the only passenger on the flight manifest, but he was not worried too much about the pilot's reaction to carting two additional men in his plane; Royal Air Force pilots were aware of the secrecy surrounding SOE and MI6 missions and generally trusted the actions taken by agents in the field. Max was, however, more concerned about the slating he'd get once they arrived in England.

Max's superiors in the Intelligence Branch wouldn't appreciate his unilateral decision to bring a German Wehrmacht officer into the country without prior permission. He hadn't followed security protocols relating to the capture and custody of enemy prisoners, nor had he given any advanced notice to the Warrant Officer who'd be meeting the flight in Kent. Given the circumstances, it would be incumbent upon him to handcuff both Paul and Darek before stepping foot on British soil – he wondered how Paul would react to that? It was a hell of thing to have to do to his twin.

His biggest worry now was what would happen to his brother when they got to London. He'd been honest with Paul, stating correctly that he'd be given no special favours, nor would he be regarded as a trustworthy ally just because he was part English and brother to an intelligence officer.

What possibly could affect a positive decision regarding Paul's freedom, or incarceration, was that he'd always been a moderate German who had refused time and again to join the Nazi Party. He'd been forced to enrol in it when he'd signed the SS papers for Hauptmann Leitner, but Max had gathered from his father that Paul had never been in a paramilitary group, at least not officially. Leitner had apparently committed fraud, and when that had been found out, Paul's bogus SS documents and Nazi membership had been torn up and his SS status rescinded, remaining buried under a cloud of secrecy and embarrassment.

Paul could also help his case if he confirmed everything in Max's report about the Brandenburg gas programme and the German plans to expand it, and if he shared intelligence on the Wehrmacht's strategies in France and Germany. It was doubtful that Paul would know anything of importance, but Max was hopeful the authorities would recognise an opportunity to turn Paul's allegiance away from Germany, and in so doing, free him from any military custody and enlist him into the Army Medical Corps. It was a long shot, but an objective well worth pursuing.

After collecting Darek in Saint Quentin and then travelling through country lanes to the outskirts of Dieppe, the Post Office van finally turned into a lane twenty metres from the landing site. Located in a secluded area and hidden by woods on all sides, the airstrip was a devilishly unpredictable spot for pilots to land their planes. There was no room for error. An early or late descent could be catastrophic; the aircraft could hit trees before reaching the grassy strip or overshoot it and crash into the thick coppice at the far end.

A local Resistance report from Marcel had stated that German patrols hadn't discovered the airstrip's location yet, but Max believed it would only be a matter of time before they found it. They would then destroy the ground, making it inoperable or staff it with personnel and use it themselves. He was surprised British aircraft were still landing there, even though they stayed on the ground for no more than a few minutes before taking off again.

Soon, Max predicted, planes would not land in Northern France at all. SOE operatives were now being supported by the Royal Air Force after months of negotiations, but in most cases, the final leg of an agent's journey was by parachute, and always at night. He knew only too well about dangerous landing sites and the damage they could do to one's body.

Max got out of the van and surveyed the area. It was 01:45, a cold night with a soft rain that had been with them since Paris. The weather was in their favour, he thought, for they had not passed a single German military vehicle or foot patrol for the last ten kilometres or so.

He opened the back door and moved the boxes and sacks until he got to the false wall. He tapped on it, then stepped back to watch the panel fall forwards onto the floor.

"The plane should be here in ten. Start digging in the fire torches. We'll light them at the last minute," Max instructed Claude and Jean once the men were outside.

"How long should we wait around here after the plane lands?" Claude asked.

"Don't wait at all. As soon as the aircraft turns around and opens its doors for us, douse the torches and get the hell out of here. It'll be on the ground for no more than a couple of minutes but they'll seem like the longest minutes you've ever lived."

Darek looked around him, his tall, powerful body taut with apprehension. A rifle was slung over his shoulder along with a rucksack carrying his personal belongings. "Max, will I be all right? Your government won't kick me out, will they?" he asked for the second time that night.

"You're going to a friendlier country than the one you're leaving, Darek," said Max with a grin. "Give your rifle to Claude. You won't be needing it where you're going. Keep your eyes on the perimeter. Claude, you too. We should hear the plane any minute."

"I need to pee," Paul said.

Max glanced at his brother. He couldn't see his expression clearly, but he could imagine the emotions playing through his mind. Paul wasn't restrained by handcuffs or rope, but as they strode to a hedge bordering the field, he grumbled under his breath.

"Will you at least let me have a piss in peace?"

"I won't turn my back on you if that's what you're implying," Max answered.

Paul sighed as he fumbled with his trouser buttons. "Jesus, Max, you're taking this prisoner shit a bit far. I'm hardly going to run away when I don't even know where I am or in which direction I'd need to run."

Max's eyes narrowed. "I'll relax once we're in the air, but until then, don't give me any reason to forget you're my brother and that I love you. You have more to worry about than me. If you so much as take a step out of line, the French…"

A soft humming noise and increasing vibration distracted Max as the Westland Lysander came into view only a few feet above the treetops. Max craned his neck at the black sky, leaving his threats unspoken. "Hurry up, Paul."

Paul finished and buttoned his trousers. "What do you think our parents would think of you forcing me to go to England?"

"There's a lot you don't know about our parents, so trust me when I say they'd think I was doing my job and saving your life into the bargain."

The torches guiding the plane in were not as bright as they should have been because of the rain, but despite that difficulty, the Lizzie landed safely, skidding on the wet grass a little on her one hundred and eighty degree turn.

Over the noise of the engine, Max yelled to Claude to begin removing some of the torches. Darek was already running towards the plane's open door, and Jean had returned to the vehicle and was waiting for Claude.

Max's eyes widened like plates, as Paul took off like a gazelle towards the other side of the airstrip. Half way across, he weaved diagonally in front of the plane's nose as it taxied down the runway almost to a stop to allow the passengers to board.

"Merde!" Claude raised his rifle and trained it on Paul's back just before he disappeared.

Max, intending to pound after his brother, first jerked the gun upwards, ruining Claude's aim. "Don't be stupid, man. You might hit the bloody fuselage!"

Stunned by his brother's audacity, Max was further dismayed when the pilot gave the signal to board, then started moving again. Not able to delay take off, he grabbed Claude's jacket and yelled in his ear, "Go after him on foot. Take him alive – alive! If you touch a hair on his head, I'll come back here and kill you myself!"

"Go, go. I don't care about your threats, Englishman. If I find him, I'll kill him. This time he's dead! You hear me? This time we'll kill him!"

Max ran to the plane, his stomach in knots. Darek was at the hatch as the plane was starting its run and he pulled Max on board before closing the door behind them.

Max pulled his knees up to his chest, thumped them with his fists, and growled with rage directed at himself and Paul. "I'll bloody throttle him – damn him – fuck him!"

"What the hell happened?" Darek shouted as the plane lifted off the ground.

Max glared at Darek, then grabbed him by the lapels until they were only inches apart. "You took your eyes off him. You were supposed to watch him, not just think about yourself. It's your fault, you son of a bitch. We lost him. That's what happened!"

******

Paul charged through the wet, black woods without any clue as to where he was, no landmarks to tell him if he was going deeper into the coppice or running around in circles. The noise of the plane taking off over his head was music to his ears, and, within seconds, the rumble faded to a soft purr as it cleared the trees and disappeared into the night sky. He was certain Max and the Pole were on board, therefore no longer a threat. Max would never strand himself in France, not even for his twin brother. Duty would have called him home, despite his blasé to-hell-with-duty – you're-my-twin-brother attitude.

He was getting scratched to hell as he ran, stumbling over boulders, his jacket getting snagged on protruding branches, his skin being stung by nettles. But a bit of discomfort was not going to slow him down or make him think twice about escaping into the murkiest of nights. Max would have sent the two Frenchmen after him, and he was determined to keep the good head-start he'd already gained. Claude wouldn't show him mercy, not this time.

Paul puffed until he had to stop to catch his breath. He groaned and bent over to massage the knife-like pain from the stitch in his side. The wind had picked up, and the rain had intensified, spattering the winter branches, battering what leaves remained, and drowning out any other noise. He couldn't get any wetter. His clothes were already saturated, his hair dripping. Nature's foibles were making his escape even harder.

He stumbled blindly into a thorn bush, the sharp needles penetrating his skin. He clamped his mouth shut and dropped to all fours, cursing as twigs snapped under his knees. Then crawling forward, he held one hand in front of his face and felt around the foliage until he found a gap in the bush's perimeter. It seemed to have a thick trunk in the centre and wide-spread branches like an acacia which afforded enough room for him to wriggle through and conceal his body inside. Ripped to shreds by thorns and sharp branches, he pulled his knees up to his chest and made himself as small as his six-foot body would allow. As well hidden as he could be, but unable to see around himself in the dark, he shut his eyes and considered his next move.

Should he stay where he was, silent as the grave, and in no position to keep an eye out for Claude, should he or Jean appear? Should he make a run for it to the edge of the woods where he'd hopefully find a road and a German patrol? Where *was* the edge of the coppice? Where was the road? As wet as he was, the rain was doing him a favour; it was obliterating his tracks. And if he couldn't see Claude, then in principle, Claude couldn't see him. He would, at some point, give up his search. The Frenchman wasn't stupid; he wouldn't leave his Post Office van parked for hours in its present location.

During his time with the communists, Paul had come to know Claude. Out of all Duguay's Resistance fighters, he was the most committed to killing Germans. He'd made no bones about his feelings towards the Nazi in the basement and had on numerous occasions urged Duguay to get rid of the German scum.

An hour passed. Paul, in pain with bleeding cuts, cramps in his calves and toes, tried to shift into a more comfortable position. Unsuccessful, he remained in his foetal state, squeezed his eyes shut and battled with visions of Max. Guilt, as painful as any physical kick in the guts, desecrated Paul's victory. "Don't tie me up. I won't try to escape," he'd promised. "You know me, Max, I'm not a liar." But he was.

Paul knew Max as well as he did himself, but stark differences in their characters had emerged. Max, though a spy living in a world of subterfuge and deception, would never have given his word to a person, particularly his brother, and then broken it. Without a shadow of doubt, he had left on that aircraft with the bitter taste of treachery in his mouth, a never-ending reminder that his twin had deliberately double-crossed him. He wouldn't understand the motive behind it; how could he when he'd never met Valentina, never been in love? He knew nothing of the power it wielded over men and the loyalty it demanded.

Paul made a greater effort to straighten his cramped legs after deciding to remain where he was instead of taking the risk of being caught on the run in the woods. Max had risked his life to meet with Duguay despite that woman, Marine, insisting that his twin was dead. Max would certainly be reprimanded by his boss when he got back to London, and at some point, he would tell Hannah what had occurred tonight. *I'm very angry and disappointed with Paul, I'll never trust him again.* Hannah would try to comfort him, but she'd also say that she understood why he, Paul, had wanted to get back to his wife, for she'd do just about anything to be with her husband.

Some new noises interrupted Paul's thoughts: the swoosh of leaves being swept aside, heavy footsteps snapping twigs, dog-like panting, and the ground vibrating under his backside. He held his breath as black figures flashed past his hiding place and shook the outer branches of his lair.

Paul remained underneath the bush, stiff, soaking wet, and too scared to move. He was terrified of freezing to death should he spend any more time there. His saturated clothes were useless against the bitter cold which pierced his flesh to the bone. If someone offered him a fortune in gold to stop shivering, he'd not be able to take up the challenge. His biggest worry, apart from the return of Claude and his sidekick, was his body temperature. He was burning up with fever, freezing one minute, then so very hot he was becoming sleepy and hypothermic. He wouldn't last much longer.

Almost at the end of his tether, he heard the snapping of branches and willed himself to concentrate despite waves of nausea making him want to retch. Claude and Jean were whispering just outside his den in what appeared to be an argument. Although he could only understand snippets of what they were saying, he gleaned enough to know they were not happy with their defeat.

"Duguay will kill both of us," said Jean.

"Then we won't tell him...." Claude snapped.

"Okay. If you don't, I won't. We'll think of something."

Chapter Twelve

Paul Vogel

Unsure if Claude and Jean had left the vicinity, Paul erred on the side of caution by not making his move until daybreak. His muscles were stiff, his lips blue with cold, and he couldn't feel his fingers or toes. It had been the most terrifying night of his life, and he still had to make it to a German patrol in an area he presumed was occupied by French rebels.

The woods looked different in the grey light of dawn. Some trees were almost bare, and Paul could now see that the bush he'd hidden under was full of needle-like thorny branches which had ripped his skin, jacket and trousers to shreds. He was a dreadful sight. His uniform was brown with mud and blood, its cuffs frayed, and his shirt filthy. His fingernails were broken and black underneath with dirt and soil. His shoes, without their laces because Claude had made him relinquish them at the farm, were also caked in mud, and his sockless feet were blistered and bleeding. And he stank. Even his foggy breath was rancid.

He peered again at his feet. Apart from removing his trouser belt and socks, Duguay's men had also taken Paul's dark-blue *Waffenfarbe,* doctor's epaulettes and cap. Duguay, like a high-priest about to perform a ritual, had burnt them in the cellar during Paul's first night in captivity. The communist leader had told his men that the fire was a symbol of Paul's defeat; a defeat that would eventually come to all Germans.

Paul tugged at his lapels and straightened his jacket. He may be filthy and barely recognisable as the Wehrmacht officer who had attended a birthday party in the swanky Hotel Lutetia only weeks earlier, but he was still the man his parents were proud of and Valentina had married; when he got the chance, he would conduct himself as such.

A now-visible path snaked through the woods, a well-trodden track that the Resistance probably used to get to the airstrip. Paul began to jog. He did his utmost to ignore the soreness in his feet, the stinging wake-up call to his nerve endings, the use of muscles that had barely been used in weeks, his loose shoes, and the shivers wracking his body. Desperate to get to his unit, to report everything he knew about his abductors and to have them found and punished, he ran even faster, weaving in and out to avoid the branches across his path.

As he ran, he thought about his eventual arrival in the arms of his countrymen, the relief he'd feel, the comfort of knowing he was safe and protected. He had to believe there were convoys and foot patrols in this area. Germany had France by the throat, and the Wehrmacht wasn't only controlling its cities but hundreds of country towns and villages as well.

His most chilling thought was of never seeing Valentina again, or Berlin, the city he loved, or his parents, who'd be frantic with worry. He couldn't quite believe that he'd got away from Max, the Pole, and the two Frenchmen with only moments to spare. Dizzy now with fever, he couldn't recall the instant he'd decided to take off and skirt around the front of the slow-moving plane to get to the trees on the other side. That spur-of-the-moment decision would probably be the biggest act of courage he'd ever achieve in this war.

He glanced behind him, still afraid of being followed even though he'd run a fair distance and had heard nothing. The terror of impending death was imprinted on him like a permanent scar. Every day in Duguay's custody, the communists had made him believe his end could come at any moment. They'd taken him from the cellar, put him against the wall and shot bullets over his head on eleven separate occasions. They had driven him mad with fear, until he'd believed that every footstep, voice, and dark figure appearing in the basement was coming to finish him off. He'd lied to Max about being treated fairly because he didn't want his hot-headed brother to unleash his temper on Duguay. The truth was, he'd endured a more brutal torture than any he could have imagined.

When he reached the main road, his spirits rose. With that came anger and thoughts of revenge. He wanted nothing more than to let the Gestapo and SS know every detail of his captivity: the names of his captors, the group they were affiliated with, the description of the farm and its approximate location. It was not in Dieppe but situated on the southern suburbs of Paris. That was his best guess, for the journey to the airfield had taken almost half a day, and although he'd seen nothing outside the van, he'd heard a mishmash of familiar noises that he'd associated with the capital: some cars, probably German military vehicles, motorbikes, trams, people on foot, trains letting off steam, and the familiar church clock with unique chimes near the River Seine.

He set off along the deserted road, his eyes fixed on the horizon, his ears alert for sounds behind him. But he was also picturing Duguay and his thugs being brought out to a wall, thrown against it and riddled with bullets that wouldn't miss their heads, as the commies had intentionally done with him.

He halted to stretch his sore muscles in a series of calisthenics, and was suddenly struck by a disturbing thought. Yes, he wanted to see Duguay *and* the woman who had abducted him from the Hotel Lutetia dead, but, if he helped the SS or Gestapo to achieve that goal, the rebels might be captured and forced to mention Max during interrogation. He couldn't loosen that Gordian knot, for it would reveal his own somewhat tenuous, but real collusion with an enemy spy.

He began walking again, slower this time. The realisation that he was heading towards a tangled web of lies without a plausible story to satisfy the Gestapo and protect Max's identity seeped into him. His heart punched his chest wall as he became truly cognisant of the trouble he was in and would cause those he loved. Apart from Valentina, his loyalty to his twin stood above all else, all others. Their bond was impervious to war and enemies, politics, religion and ideals. He'd never knowingly damage Max's reputation or put him in harm's way, but that was what he was about to do if he continued down this road. He stood still; he needed to think. *What if...* Before he had a chance to formulate a new plan he heard the loud rumble of a convoy coming towards him.

He squinted as the lead jeep came over a rise. He couldn't tell how many vehicles were behind, but it looked like a large motorcade of trucks. He waved the jeep down, lifting is hands in surrender as it approached. *"Ich bin Oberarzt Paul Vogel!"* he shouted, once it had come to a standstill.

During the brief conversation that followed with a Leutnant from the jeep, Paul confirmed his name and doctor's rank then asked for water. He drank the flask dry, then vomited half of it onto the ground as he crumpled to the side of the road with relief.

"Bring the Assistenzarzt here quickly," the Leutnant ordered.

Paul slouched on the grassy verge and sipped the water slower this time. He was surrounded by soldiers who moved aside when the Assistenzarzt, a junior doctor, appeared.

"Are you injured, Herr Oberarzt?"

"No, just scratches and muscle pain – I might have a fever," Paul added while the young man examined him.

"What happened, sir? What are you doing out here?"

"I was captured some weeks ago, but I escaped my captors last night and hid in the woods a few miles back ... they might still be close by ... I don't know."

Paul struggled to his feet with the help of two soldiers. His legs gave way again, and a stretcher was brought. The men who'd been on the first truck were now lining the road, clapping and cheering as if he were a damned hero. He didn't feel like a brave man. He'd run away; he was good at that.

Soon, news of him reached the soldiers in the second and third trucks, and he could hear them hooting with glee, whistling and clapping wildly.

"The men know your name, Oberartz Vogel," the Leutnant explained. "Everyone thought you were dead. You've given us a victory. You've given Germany a victory."

Paul, barely conscious and wracked with fever, watched in a blur as men patted his shoulders and legs when his stretcher passed the Wehrmacht soldiers lining the road. Shouts of, "Well done, Oberartzt!" rang in his ears, and he closed his eyes in a vain effort to shut out the noise, the faces, the whole palaver.

The Leutnant appeared to be deliberately offering his men a spectacle by marching Paul and his stretcher along a parade-like line of soldiers, as though he were an esteemed general to a file of adoring subordinates. "Look men! Oberartz Vogel is alive!" the man shouted every few paces until the stretcher had reached the ambulance at the back of the convoy.

"We're going to our base just north of Paris. I'll arrange transport for you as soon as you feel ready to continue to the capital."

Paul, woozy with fever, nodded. "All right, but I need to get to Paris as soon as possible… report to the Gestapo and SS in Avenue Foch," he mumbled, before dizziness washed over him and he closed his eyes.

******

Paul had been transferred to the infirmary upon his return to Paris, but shortly afterwards the Gestapo arrived and demanded they be allowed to question him in Avenue Foch. According to the Gestapo officer in charge, Paul, as sick as he was, had a duty to testify about his experience before he forgot the details. Thus, the doctor's orders that he remain in bed until his fever broke were ignored, and Paul was escorted out of the barracks' infirmary and whisked away in a Gestapo jeep.

"Think – think, Oberleutnant Vogel! You must be able to remember a landmark, a church steeple, a road sign – something?"

The Gestapo Kriminalinspektor who had been grilling Paul in Avenue Foch for almost an hour with little success leant across the desk, his eyes boring into Paul's. "You are the only German officer to come back alive. Four high-ranking Wehrmacht officers have been assassinated by the Resistance … four! We are facing a crisis, an enemy capable of not only reaching, but killing our Wehrmacht elite in broad daylight on the streets of Paris. You, Oberleutnant, have a duty to your fallen colleagues. You must help us find this scum before they abduct or assassinate anyone else … think harder."

Paul, a shivering, perspiring wreck, looked helplessly at the Gestapo Inspektor who had given him a very public and effusive welcome at Avenue Foch. Within minutes of beginning the interview, however, his concerned attitude was replaced by annoyance and suspicion.

"I would rather you called me Oberartz, Inspektor. I am a doctor, *not* a soldier." Paul emphasised his point. "I understand your frustration; I do. And if I were in your shoes, I would also be impatient."

Paul's hand shook as he drank the water in his glass, then asked for more. He was parched, shivering yet hot and sweaty. He truly didn't know what to say even though he wanted to maintain his integrity in the eyes of the Gestapo and give them the answers they wanted. His responses, therefore, had been spoken in a weak, sickly tone with no helpful details. He felt as though he were walking through a minefield, skirting probing questions, asking for water, feigning exhaustion and loss of memory. His excuses and repeated requests that he be allowed to rest were not working, and if he went further down this dangerous path, he'd be arrested for treason or held on that suspicion. His choices were clear: protect Max's identity and involvement by shielding Duguay or tell the truth as he knew it and suffer the consequences.

"The reason I've not been forthcoming, Inspektor, is because despite every part of me wanting the scum captured or killed, I don't know where I was being held exactly ... somewhere near Dieppe."

The Inspector nodded. "Good ... good ... go on."

"Yes, near Dieppe, I think," Paul lied again. "I was blindfolded and unconscious on the way there and afterwards I was kept in a dark cellar with no windows. But I do know I was at a farm, a large place with numerous outbuildings. Once, they let me out to wash at a well, and I saw a church steeple in the distance, fields and a tree-lined dirt track that led to … I'm not certain … maybe a highway or village, perhaps? Every now and then I heard the rumble of heavy trucks … and often the sound of a train. Every day, that sound … every day."

The Gestapo's demeanour relaxed, spurring Paul on to invent a not-entirely-false story. "The people who held me were in some sort of Resistance group. I heard a few of them talking in French. They were planning to attack a train…"

Paul let his words hang in the air while he took a sip of water from his refilled glass.

"Yes? Yes?" said the Gestapo officer, who was scribbling on paper while Paul talked.

Paul sat up straight, his tense muscles looser, his mind set on ending the interview. "Yesterday evening, they were taking me somewhere else. I don't know why, or where. But I was thrown into a van … an unmarked van, I think. Then I asked … I pretended I was desperate to relieve myself, and once I was outside the vehicle, I ran and didn't look back."

"You ran? It was as easy as that? I see…"

"No. I don't think you do see." Paul cut him off. "Do you know what it's like being held in a basement with the only breathable air coming through a narrow ventilation shaft on the wall, to live in silence day after day, tortured, put up against a wall blindfolded and being told you're about to die, time and again? You're damn right I ran, even though the bastards were armed and standing behind me watching me piss. Herr Inspektor, on that short journey, I thought they were taking me to an execution site. I *believed* it was all over for me." Paul panted with exertion. He was getting weaker, feeling dazed and nauseous.

"I'm sorry I can't give you any more information. I can barely think straight with this fever … I ran … I ran for my life…"

Paul slumped forwards in his chair, his hot forehead on the cool metal desk. He didn't yet know what these lies would mean to the French people in Dieppe, but for now, he was encouraged by the interrogator's expression. It had visibly softened. The narrowed, suspicious eyes had relaxed, and in its place a sympathetic nod.

"Would you recognise the area if you saw it?" the Inspektor asked.

"If you're asking me if I will search with you and your men for the Communist base, the answer is yes, of course. I will do whatever it takes to see those men hang."

Chapter Thirteen

Klara Gabula

Arisaig, Scotland
November 1941

Klara Gabula was used to Polish winters, but she had never experienced anything like the biting winds or walls of thick grey sea mists that rolled into the Scottish SOE training school at nightfall. Arisaig, located in a remote area of Scotland's rugged west coast, was the perfect site to train secret agents. The inquisitive locals were told it was a training centre for commandos and generally steered clear of the men and woman based there, although Klara had spotted a few children peeking through the perimeter fences.

Arisaig House, as it was known, consisted of several groups of cabins which housed agents destined for the same German occupied country. Klara, billeted with fellow Poles and using her own name for the first time in over a year, had never felt as liberated or as eager to learn. No more hiding secrets or being afraid of the enemy. She had questioned her past actions, confronted her mistakes, and was now looking to the future.

Upon her arrival, she'd been interviewed by Captain Frank Middleton, her principle tutor. During their initial meeting, she was informed that she'd been chosen by her previous handler, Max, as a potential SOE agent because she possessed qualities and traits the section needed. The captain had added that no female SOE agents had, thus far, been sent to her country, but he couldn't see why she shouldn't be the first to pass the Polish course, which differed slightly from the others. She surmised that Max had put her name forward before their disastrous final meeting in which he'd tried to strangle her.

Klara believed she would have made a good candidate even without Max's recommendation. She already had a Polish and French background, spoke those two languages fluently as well as reasonable English, and had already been an MI6 asset in Paris for over a year. When she was asked if she would volunteer to go on a mission with only a fifty percent chance of a safe return, she'd laughed, "Every day might have been my last in Paris. I know danger and death very well, Captain, and I'm not blasé about either."

Klara found the physical training demanding, but also exhilarating. She was sleeping better than she had in years, had shed her guilt over betraying Romek, and had come to terms with losing Max. She loved him still; how could she not when he would forever hold her heart in his hands and be part of her most sacred places forever. For weeks, she'd prayed that he'd appear at the camp on some military pretext, ask to speak to her, and when they were alone, tell her that he'd forgiven her for his brother's death. But as the weeks passed, so too did her hope of ever seeing him again.

She strode up the hill, wrapped in a heavy coat with its collar turned up to protect her face. She was battling a gale that could knock a person off their feet and leave the skin chaffed as if burnt. This morning, she was due to sit an exam on explosives. Theoretical tests were easy for her, as were memory tests, for she was an academic by nature, a sponge for information. She had told Captain Middleton that her greatest asset in Paris had been her photographic memory. When she read texts written in books or documents, she recalled them almost word for word for days thereafter. She'd explained it was like having a camera in her brain without meaning to sound boastful about her gift.

Klara had been surprised to learn that she was going to receive an officer's rank when she'd completed her training. She'd been told that local Resistance groups were more likely to follow an officer. On her first day there, she had also discovered that she would be trained in a brutally physical way. She learnt the rudiments of hand-to-hand combat but did not excel in that department. She had taken part in water landings in dinghies when the Scottish waters had been icy and plagued with dangerous squalls. She was not an aggressive person, nor had she ever hit anyone in her life, therefore, the job of incapacitating someone without the use of a weapon had been beyond her in the beginning. She'd been quick to learn, however, that simple body mechanics, psychological deception, and body control were the most basic and efficient ways to protect and defend oneself in a fight.

As she neared the building, she went over the possible questions she'd face about explosives. In the previous week, she had witnessed their power first hand when a fellow agent had gone fishing, a loose term for what he'd done that day. He'd placed a detonating device into some plastic explosives and dropped the *bomb* into the nearby lake. The explosion killed hundreds of salmon, and she and another couple of agents had scrambled to remove the evidence before the people in the nearby town discovered them. Later, she'd expected the guilty agent to be dismissed from the SOE programme, but instead, his act of violence against the fish population had been applauded in some quarters, because, apparently, he had shown initiative and drive; precisely what the SOE was trying to teach. *The dirtier the tricks you use against your adversary, the better,* Captain Middleton had remarked.

After the test, Klara and her classmates were told to go to the camp's bar. She entered the snug area and luxuriated in the warmth of the fire blazing in a fireplace almost the same length as the wall it was built into. It was one of the most welcoming sights she'd seen all week. It was dark and dreary in her billet and so very cold she'd almost disobeyed the standing order not to get into bed fully clothed. It was a strict rule, one she hadn't understood until Captain Middleton had explained that the worst thing a person could do to their body was to sleep under blankets with garments on and then face the cold air outside with not more, but less bodily protection. She had thought it made sense at the time, so she'd decided to sleep in her underwear ever since, despite the misty breath emanating from her mouth at every exhalation.

"Dick, what's going on?" Klara asked her fellow agent after being handed a glass of whisky. "I don't drink this stuff. Even if I did, it's only eleven o'clock in the morning."

"Beats me, Klara, but I'm not refusing it," Dick winked. "It's just what I need to clear my pipes. Drink up, girl. It'll warm the cockles of your heart."

Klara grimaced, but joined him when he downed the Scotch in one.

"Gather around everyone," said Frank Middleton with a mischievous grin. "Many of you are already in the army and are probably wondering why I'm breaking a rule by trying to get you drunk." He raised his untouched glass of Scotch and studied the perplexed faces around him. "Come on, drink up. There's plenty more where this came from. When you're finished, refill your glasses with whatever tipple you prefer so long as it's alcoholic.

And when you've finished that one, fill up again and again until I tell you to stop."

Klara giggled. The whisky had slid smoothly down her throat but was now burning her chest. As a woman who only occasionally drank alcohol, she worried that the next generous tot would tip her over the edge. She'd been drunk only once in her life with Romek and Max in Poland. The following day she'd gone to work with a terrible headache.

She went to the barman and dutifully asked for a refill, then she caught Frank's eye. "May I have a lemonade instead, Captain? This is very generous of you but I'm afraid whisky will make me feel unwell."

"I don't care how it makes you feel, Gabula. You'll drink what I tell you to drink, or you'll pack your bags."

Klara was shocked but did what she was told while Frank crossed to the centre of the room and held his hands up. "Listen, everyone. Contrary to what you might be thinking, I am not inviting you to drink good Scotch out of the kindness of my heart. This is an informal assessment to test your metal – yes, yes, don't look at me like that. I know it's in direct conflict with the regulations at other armed services' training camps, but here's the thing…" He studied the intrigued faces before him. "I am giving you strong drink to evaluate your level of commitment, and more importantly, to find out if you can handle alcohol. Why? Because agents who can't hold their drink are of no use to SOE. We need you to be able to control any situation with equanimity, and that includes you getting drunk and being up close and personal with German soldiers or enemy agents in the field. We can't have weak-bellied spies falling over or spilling secrets to all and sundry when under the influence, can we?"

"No, sir!" They all shouted in chorus.

"Good, because when you do stop drinking I'll be giving you a test – about what, you don't need to know yet. Drink up!"

Klara was dismayed. She had no idea how many glasses of the disgusting stuff she would have to drink to satisfy the captain, but she was certain that if she failed this test, and the next one, she would not be going to Poland.

"How are you getting on, Gabula," Frank asked her a while later.

Klara, now on her third glass, straightened her back. "Well, thank you, Captain."

"Without turning around, tell me how many plant pots are on the window ledge behind you."

"Four, sir," she answered without hesitation. "The plants in them are Azaleas, Busy Lizzies, and Ivy. The fourth pot is empty." She had remembered looking at the plant pots when she'd first come in and was still sober. She had asked the bartender what the plants were. Memory tests could come anywhere, anytime and she had studied everything in the room including the sign that said, *take off muddy boots* – which no one had.

"Very good. You can finish what's in your glass, then call it a day," Frank said with a nod of approval.

Less than five minutes later, a French woman was unceremoniously carried out of the snug by two of her male colleagues after vomiting on the floor by the ladies' toilet and then falling on her backside. She would be on a train that afternoon; a failure, a reject.

Klara, dejected about losing a female colleague, sat on the bench seat beside the window, no longer trusting her feet to carry her out in a straight line. Men were becoming rowdy, some had started to sing and insult Adolf Hitler, and she found herself giggling at their antics. She swivelled to the window ledge to peer at the plant pots and giggled again as she wondered if they might enjoy a little drink. First, she checked no one was looking, then she poured the remains of her Scotch into the pot with soil but without a plant. Still giggling, she returned her attention to the room and stared straight into the eyes of the man she'd been longing for.

Max – Max Vogel. Klara gaped, blinked, then blinked again. She was not imagining it; he was there. He had come for her. He loved her still and any minute now he would to tell her she was forgiven. Her eyes filled with alcohol-induced tears as she gazed at the man she had been dreaming about for so very long. They shone with love through the cigarette smoke and she made to rise. Until he scowled and turned his back on her.

Chapter Fourteen

Max Vogel

Arisaig, Scotland.

Frank drove at five miles per hour on the winding stretch of road running parallel to the rugged Scottish coast. Rain and mist made it impossible to see more than six feet in front of him, and he'd been forced to stop a few times to get out of the car to look at the condition of the ground ahead before continuing. He had warned Max that the stretch of road between the village and the house was often blocked by rocks and fallen trees, and this evening, rocky landslides were particularly severe.

Max, glad of the bad weather and the delay it was causing, hadn't stopped talking since they'd left the SOE training camp. He was desperate to tell Frank about Paul's abduction and everything that had followed it, before arriving at the house where his mother and Hannah would be waiting.

"So, this Pole, Darek, he definitely wants to fight?" Frank asked when Max finally stopped talking.

"Yes. He's anxious to get involved. He seems hell-bent on going back behind enemy lines. I've told him a bit about what we do and he's all in."

"Where is he now?"

"In detention until the vetting protocols have been completed. When I saw Heller yesterday, he told me he was going to hand Darek over to the Polish headquarters in London, but the sly fox had already reached out to SOE. It will be interesting to see who wins that battle.

"We're desperate for Polish and French agents, Max. See what you can do for us."

Silence ensued until Frank put on the brakes when a large puddle loomed. "Shit, these roads are littered with potholes. It's impossible to know how deep they are, especially when it's dark like this."

Max swore when his head hit the ceiling. "I see what you mean."

Frank manoeuvred the car around the next pothole, then glanced sideways at Max. "You didn't say, so I'll ask, how furious was Heller when you told him about Paul's escape in Dieppe?"

"He was apoplectic." Max chuckled. "Called me every sort of bloody idiot for trusting Paul in the first place then told me to let it go. He's sending another agent over to France to try and calm the waters with Duguay. I cocked up, Frank. We've probably lost the French Partisans' cooperation because of that farce at the airstrip. It'll be a long time before I'll be able to show my face in France again."

"I'm not surprised Heller was furious. He'll get it in the ear from above if the Germans take out that Communist group."

Max sighed. "That's not my biggest concern. After weeks of worrying that Paul might be dead, and then feeling as though a ton of bricks had been lifted off my shoulders when I found him alive, I'm now back to square one worrying myself sick about him. I keep thinking that he got away, that he was smart and didn't panic. But trying to convince myself and knowing it to be true are two very different things – this is not how I want to spend my war, Frank."

"You did your best for him, Max, but you need to come to terms with his choices. It doesn't matter how much you might wish he'd given up Germany to come to our side, the fact of the matter is he chose the Nazis over a year ago."

Frank had a good point, but it still stung like the devil. "Heller said the same thing."

"Talk about a family being split by war. I'm still trying to wrap my head around Paul being married to a Gestapo Major's daughter, Wilmot spending time in a prison camp, and your father being a British spy. What sort of family have I married into?" Frank chuckled, then he stopped the car at the bottom of the lane leading to the cottage. "Joking apart, is there anything you can do to find out if Paul made it back to his unit?"

Max had asked himself that on the train journey from London and had concluded that he couldn't do a damn thing. "If I make another wrong move, I'll be up for treason. Heller's not finished with me yet. You know what he's like when he's been crossed."

"Hmm, not the forgiving type, and he's got the memory of an elephant. Did he think ... did he suspect...?"

"What? Say it, Frank."

"All right. Look, you lost a prisoner, Max, not just a German soldier but your Nazi brother. It might be..."

"Oh, for God's sake, not you as well. You think I helped him get away? Christ, Frank. Do you?"

"No! Don't be daft. I was going to say that it might have looked that way to Heller."

Max recalled Heller's exact words, but he was unwilling to share them with Frank. *You're going down the slippery slope to treason, Max, and you don't even realise it.* "I was desperate to get Paul on that plane and back to England, even if it meant he'd be locked up as soon as he arrived. If Heller thinks otherwise, it's his problem. Not much I can do about the way his mind works, is there?"

Frank's hands gripped the steering wheel as though he'd just thought of something even more disturbing. "Jesus Christ – please tell me you didn't tell Paul about your father's situation – does he know your dad's still alive?"

"No. I didn't have time to talk to Paul about anything other than his release. I was going to spill the beans about our parents being in England after we'd touched down in Kent."

Frank exhaled. "Thank God. I've said this before and I'll say it again, you can't trust Paul anymore. I know that's hard to hear…"

"I agree … and I heard you the first time. He's not the brother I knew a year ago. I saw a Wehrmacht officer in France, desperate to get back to his unit and his wife in Germany, and it cut me to ribbons. Don't get me wrong, he was grateful I'd gone back for him, but not enough to give a damn about the repercussions for me when he ran away. Know what, Frank? I'm lucky Claude and Jean didn't think I'd been complicit in Paul's escape. They'd have shot at me instead."

Once Frank had parked the car outside the house, he changed the subject. "Paul's friend, Judith Weber, is here. Your father sent her to us. You'll like her."

"Interesting," Max said, still thinking about Paul.

******

Laura and Hannah squealed with delight when they spotted Max getting out of Frank's car. It was dark, and the rain was lashing down, soaking the two men as they ran up the garden path.

After a quick hello, they both went straight upstairs to change out of their sodden uniforms. When Max came back down, he noticed another woman setting cutlery on the table, her head bowed to her task and oblivious to his presence. Not wanting to scare her, he called out a soft, "Hello, there," from the doorway. She looked up, promptly dropped the knives and forks and swayed in a faint.

Max rushed forwards and caught her as she staggered backwards. "Are you all right?" he asked, still holding her steady at her elbows.

"Yes … yes, thank you." Her large dark eyes widened further as she held his gaze.

Her exquisite face with flawless pale skin tinged with pink from the Scottish air, was surrounded by shiny black curls to her shoulders. Max stretched out his hand and gently brushed a curly tendril from the edge of her half-parted lips and tucked it behind her ear. Now he understood why Paul had been taken with her. She was stunning.

Embarrassed by his impulsive act, Max took a step back. "I'm sorry if I frightened you," he said.

"No … no need. I thought you were Paul … Doctor Vogel. Are you Max?"

"I am indeed." He pulled out a chair. She sat, her hands shaking as she pushed her hair back from her forehead.

Max sat in a chair opposite her and waited until she had settled herself. "And you must be Judith, Paul's friend from Berlin," he finally said in German.

"Yes. Judith Weber. Hannah told me I wouldn't be able to tell the difference … only your hair…"

"It's not mine … well, of course it's my hair, but just not my normal colour." Christ, he sounded like a prepubescent

143

schoolboy. "I've been looking forward to meeting you, Judith. Frank mentioned that you'd come to live with them for a while. My father talks fondly about you. He said you were very brave when you went across the Swiss border."

"I did what any desperate Jew would do."

"Not true. Many would have stayed in Germany out of fear for the unknown. I've come with a job offer, Judith. Would you like to work in England for the war effort?"

Judith frowned. "A job, for me? I don't speak English very well, only a few words your mother and Hannah have taught me. What could *I* do?"

Max was annoyed with himself for not even giving her five minutes to recover from the shock of seeing him – Paul's mirror image – or giving her a chance to get to know him before mentioning business. He reminded himself that she'd already been pushed from pillar to post since her arrival in Britain and probably wouldn't relish another move.

"Tell you what, Judith, why don't we talk about it after dinner?"

She shook her head. "No, no. I'd like to hear about it now if you don't mind."

"All right. Well, because you're German, we thought you might consider working for our government in the … let's say … the translation section." Max chuckled as her eyes grew round. "Don't worry, Judith. We won't ask you to leave the country or do anything dangerous at all. In a nutshell, we want you to read, speak, and listen to German for us. If you accept, you'll be working in an office with a lot of other people – people from all over Europe – who've escaped the Nazis. I guarantee you'll learn English very quickly and make good friends into the bargain.

Would you be interested in helping Britain defeat Adolf Hitler? Just think about…"

"Yes. Yes, I would like that very much. I'd do just about anything to see that man defeated. I hope they hang him for what he did to my sister and father."

Such sadness in her, Max noted, as her eyes shone. He surmised that the subject of her lost family was still very painful. He recalled Paul saying she didn't know what had become of her father after his arrest, but he knew; Herr Weber was dead.

"We'll talk more about it tomorrow." With a mischievous grin, he tapped his fingers on the table. "Now, let's get this table set before my mother catches us slacking."

"I'd been looking forward to meeting you, Max," she said as Max stood. "Hannah said no one knows Paul like you do, and I wanted very much to talk to you about him. He saved my life, but I was never able to thank him properly."

"Paul is a good man. He is very fond of you."

Judith bent to pick up the cutlery still scattered on the carpet. "I'm being silly, I know, but I'd do just about anything to speak to him. Does he know I'm here? Before leaving Berlin, your father urged me not to tell Paul he was helping me to get out of Germany. He thought Paul would be safer if he didn't get involved."

Max felt his nerves sparking again with yet another conversation about his brother. For days, he'd done nothing but think and talk about Paul, imagining where he was and if he were in trouble. What he needed was time to think about something else, perhaps his own life and where *he* was headed. That was a novel idea. "I don't know what Paul knows. It's possible we won't hear from him again until this terrible business in Europe is over."

"Oh, I see." Judith gave him a sidelong glance then continued laying the table. "I thought I might write to him. I was very happy when your father told me in London that he'd got married. She's a very lucky woman, whoever she is. I'd like to congratulate him, but your mother doesn't think I should send mail to Germany. What do you think?"

"I think my mother is right. Paul is in the Wehrmacht, and is what we would call *behind enemy lines.* We might be able to get a letter through to him via the Red Cross, but because of who we are and what we do for Britain, any personal communication could throw suspicion on him. It's very hard on my family, not being able to get in touch with him, or my other brother, Wilmot. But they are enemy soldiers..."

"Yes, I understand. Your mother explained that to me, and your father also told me that he was supposed to be dead." She shook her head. "That was the first thing he said when I met him again in London. He was worried that I might mention his name to other Germans. I should have known I couldn't reach Paul, but I thought I would ask."

Max studied the graceful curve of Judith's neck as she delicately laid forks and spoons beside the knives. He hoped that was the end of the conversation for the moment. He still had dinner to get through with his mother and sister who would talk incessantly about Paul and Wilmot. Frank had warned him in the car to smile and say he didn't know anything about Willie's whereabouts or Paul's ongoing drama in Paris. Frank had also remarked that, after seeing the devastation left by the Luftwaffe in London, Laura was finding it difficult to accept that her other two sons were enemies of Britain.

Chapter Fifteen

The Vogels

Dinner was eaten at five thirty, much earlier than the Vogels were accustomed to having their evening meal in the south. It was dark in Scotland at three o'clock in the afternoon, and days at the training school began at 6am most mornings, meaning Frank went to bed at around nine thirty or ten o'clock most evenings.

While Laura, Hannah, and Judith were in the kitchen serving up, Max and Frank discussed Judith's situation.

"… it was your father's idea to send Judith up here to Hannah. He wanted us to gauge her character and state of mind," Frank said.

"Where was she before Scotland?" Max asked.

"Billeted as a refugee with an English family in Croydon. Dieter told me that Judith didn't settle in well at all. She didn't speak a word of English, and she was desperately unhappy when your father and Heller went to visit her the day after your dad's arrival in Britain."

A while later, Max and Frank turned their attention to the vote in the United States Senate on whether to allow merchantmen to be armed and permit U.S. ships to enter combat zones.

"Were you surprised when the bill passed?" Frank asked Max.

"Yes, and delighted. The American ships will bolster the supply of food and arms reaching Britain. That, and the failure of Hitler's crazy plan to draw Britain and the United States into a coalition to destroy the Soviet Union, has cheered me up no end."

Laura, who had apparently heard some of the men's conversation, became emotional when she gave Max and Frank their dinners of minced beef, neeps and tatties. "Hannah and I were talking about the Soviets before you two arrived. We were discussing what the Germans did to that Soviet ship. Did you hear about it, Max?"

"Yes, it was in all the newspapers, Mother. I have no love for the Soviets, but the Germans shouldn't get away with that massacre. They must have known the *Armenia* was a hospital ship from the big crosses on her sides and deck."

"Ah, but she also had light anti-aircraft armament, and it's widely reported that she'd previously transported troops and military stores," Frank informed Max.

"What's the latest on how many died? The radio said it was in the thousands," Hannah said.

"It was, darling, and I suspect not just one or two thousand," Frank answered.

"My God!" Hannah rushed to translate for Judith.

"I hate Nazis. They don't care about people's lives unless they're Aryan. They like killing those who can't defend themselves," Judith blurted out in German.

"I hope those responsible for atrocities get strung up when this is all over," Hannah grumbled in English.

"Be careful of what you wish for, dear," said Frank. "All Nations involved in this conflict will have blood on their hands when it's over. One of the biggest curses of war is collateral damage. Ask the civilians in London who have lost entire families and homes, and those in Germany who will lose loved ones when our bombers hit Berlin hard. We will be the ones they call blood-soaked savages."

"I know that, Frank, but I'd like to think that the British would draw a line at sinking ships treating wounded soldiers, and with women on board … nurses for goodness sake. It's appalling."

"Our newspapers will tell a different story to the one Herr Goebbels' propaganda machine put out about the Russian ship," Max said to no one in particular. "They won't tell the German people they sunk a hospital ship. They'll say their bombers acted to protect their ships from an enemy weapons-carrying vessel."

"That's if the story gets out at all in Germany. Goebbels has sunk independent journalism," Frank added.

Max flicked his eyes towards his mother; he could feel her intense gaze on him. "What's wrong, Mother?"

"Darling, I hate to interrupt this conversation, but I'm worried sick about your father. I haven't heard from him in three days. I don't know what to do. I can't believe he would put me through this again after everything that's happened."

"What's he putting you through now?"

"Keeping me in the dark as usual, driving me mad not knowing what he's up to. God forbid he's in trouble again and I don't know about it. I'm still not over what he did in Germany. Thinking he was dead, and then ... oh, Max, I don't think I'll ever be right again ... the grief of burying your father, then discovering he's alive, and now wondering if I'll lose him a second time .... I can't deal with this anymore."

Max wanted to hold his tearful mother in his arms. She looked lost, and it was breaking his heart. He understood what she was feeling more than anyone else in the family. "I was going to leave this news until after dinner, but you might as well know now..."

"Oh, dear God, what's happened, Max? I can't bear it!"

"Nothing. Mother, it's good news." Max laid his knife and fork on his plate and reached for her hand. Jonathan Heller had sent Dieter to Bletchley Park to attend the Government Code and Cypher School, and to remain there afterwards in the German codebreaking section. He couldn't tell his mother that Bletchley was in Milton Keynes in Buckinghamshire, or what went on there, but he had been given permission to escort her back to England and take her to his father.

"Father has been given a government job. It's not in London or Kent, but it is in England. He wants you to join him."

"Oh, Laura, that's very good news, isn't it?" Frank said.

"Yes, but, where will I be going?"

"I'll be able to tell you more en route, Mother. But I know you'll love it. Father's already arranged for a cottage in a village near where he'll be working. And you can stay with him for as long as he's there, which might very well be for the duration of the war." Max, who had tried to tell her without being hit by a barrage of questions, stopped talking as Laura's eyes welled up again. "Come on, Mummy, please don't cry. I know you'll have to leave Aunt Cathy in Kent and Hannah again, but at least you'll be with Papa."

"I'm not upset, dear … goodness, no, I'm happy. I hated the thought of him being stuck at home with nothing to do all day. It would have driven him mad and me along with him. But I disliked the thought of him leaving me even more." Laura, smiling through her tears, shook her head and produced a lacy handkerchief from her sleeve. She dabbed her eyes as she lifted her water glass. "Cheers everyone. This has made my day."

"Max, will your nephew and I be able to visit Mummy and Daddy?" Hannah asked.

"I don't know."

"You might not be allowed to go to near the place," Frank said, without giving a reason. "And to be honest, darling, I'd prefer it if you didn't go back to England at all. You and Jack are both safer up here."

Max agreed. "Frank's right, Hannah. Mother and Father will be using assumed names for their own protection, and we'll all have to be very careful if we're seen with them."

"Oh, for God's sake, Max, you can't think all this cloak and dagger nonsense is necessary?" said Laura, turning on a sixpence. "As far as Freddie Biermann and the Nazis know, your father is lying in his grave in Berlin."

"That's true, but the Abwehr might have spies or sympathisers in Britain who look for information that the Nazis would be happy to pay for. Father's face was often in the German newspapers. He was seen at Nazi functions and was photographed with ministers in the Chancellery. It would only take one German agent to spot him and report back with the scoop. And, it's not only father we have to worry about, it's what the Abwehr would do to Paul and Willie by association if it were to be found that their father was alive and working for the British."

"Honestly, sometimes I think you make this stuff up," said Hannah, scowling at Max. "If they think he's dead in Germany, why would they be *spotting* him anywhere? I'm with Mummy – it's all nonsense if you ask me."

"I'm not asking you!" Max snapped. "I'm sorry, but you don't seem to understand how serious this situation could become."

"I'm not stupid, Max. I lived under Hitler's rule as well as you and Paul and Willie. I know what the Nazis are like, but if Papa's dead to them, he's dead, full stop!"

"Dear, we all know what your father did, but you should listen to your brother. He knows what he's talking about," Laura said, trying to calm the situation.

"Your mother will manage the odd trip up here, darling." Frank tried his best to appease his wife. "Won't you, Laura?"

Hannah was on the verge of tears. Judith, lost in the hurried and heated English conversation, focused on the neeps on her plate.

"Finally, we're in the same country and we can't even spend time together. It's not fair," said Hannah through clenched teeth.

"I know, darling, and it's not fair that we can't see Willie and Paul either. It could be years."

A brief silence ensued with Hannah looking embarrassed, and when she finally spoke it was with a more conciliatory tone. "We'll just have to put up and shut up, I suppose."

"Yes, we will. Just like all the other families who watch their sons and brothers go off to war," Laura said. "I remember the Great War, not knowing if your father and my two brothers would ever come back. No one came home every five minutes on leave, not like our lot."

"To be fair, Mother, the army wouldn't have come home this time if they hadn't been pushed off those beaches in Dunkirk," Max reminded her.

"I'll never forget that day in 1917, when my mother found out that my twin brothers had died," said Laura, completely missing Max's point.

"You never talk about them. Did they die together?" Hannah asked.

"No. They weren't even serving in the same battalions. John was at the Somme, and Paul, after whom your brother is named, was in North Africa. They died three weeks apart, but we got the notifications the same week." Laura sniffed again. "Hannah, darling, we're very lucky to be sitting around this table together, and to have Judith with us. I'll come back to see you whenever I can. War or no war, I won't be kept from you and my grandson."

Laura perked up as the conversation returned to Dieter's secret posting. "My goodness, it must be a very quiet place if no one knows about it. I'll get plenty of reading done, I suppose. Oh, I'm very excited about seeing him. Hannah, I think I'll take him some of that delicious shortbread we found yesterday."

Max was content to listen to the conversation going on around him. Judith, coming out of her shell, showed off what little English she'd learnt and seemed to be quite at home with her hosts. His mother, talking non-stop now she'd absorbed the good news, was convinced she wouldn't be able to sleep.

The longevity of his parents' love for each other never ceased to amaze Max. They were still crazy for each other after more than three decades, and under some trying circumstances. His father wasn't a charmer, nor had he been an overly attentive husband. He'd always put work first, yet after years of hard slog he'd decided to lie to his wife, and up and leave his business in the hands of his somewhat clumsy brother-in-law. His sister's husband, though a loyal foreman in the Berlin factory for years, was a labourer at heart with no diplomatic skills or experience in dealing with Germany's business community, or what was left of it. *What did it matter?* Max thought. The factories and everything in them would probably be sequestered by the Nazis for the good of the Fatherland or blown to smithereens by the Allies. His mother was laughing now, her upset gone. He couldn't help but admire her; she was the strongest and most forgiving woman he'd ever known.

"… no, really, I'm not worried about leaving my homes in Germany unattended when there's so much more to deal with here," Laura was saying to Frank, as though she'd read Max's thoughts. "I was much more upset about having to leave Paul and

Willie behind, and Kurt as well, although I could never seem to get to the bottom of that man."

"But Paul and Wilmot weren't there," Hannah reminded her.

"That's true, dear, but I still felt I was abandoning them. That's why I retained Kurt's services. He'll make sure everything in the Berlin house is just as it should be for when the boys go home for leave."

"Forever the optimist, eh, Laura," said Frank.

As Max listened to Laura, now telling Judith about how she'd met up with Dieter in London and had nearly died of shock, his thoughts drifted to Klara. Months ago, he might have aspired to have something like his parent's long-lasting love with her. He had imagined it often, until traumatic events had smashed his feelings to pulp – a hurdle called Paul had been taller than all the other obstacles he and Klara had faced – he wasn't sure he even wanted to see her again.

"Don't keep Frank up too late, Max. He has to be up early," Hannah called out as she followed Laura and Judith up the stairs to bed.

The two men were drinking tea from floral patterned cups and eating Laura's homemade chocolate cake, a real treat for Max.

"I have to say, Max, I was shocked when your mother told me about what your father had been up to in Germany. It was a courageous thing to do, but I can't imagine me ever letting Hannah think I was dead. If I'm honest, I think it was rather cruel of him." Frank held Max's eyes. "Is he the only reason you're here, or is there a more sinister one?"

Max sighed. "There is something I wanted to run by you." Finally, he could talk to someone who understood him better than anyone, better even than his twin, it seemed.

"Wait, let me pour you a real drink." Frank went to the sideboard and brought out a half bottle of Scotch and two glasses.

Max accepted one but then looked at the clock and saw it was almost midnight. "Sorry, Frank. I'm keeping you up."

"Don't worry about it. I have an easy day tomorrow. My pupils are on the firing range with my sergeant in the morning and then off for an overnight hike in the highlands. I've got a test to mark, but I'll knock off early. Do you want to meet me for a drink around two o'clock?"

"Sounds good." Max cleared his throat. He'd decided to be honest with Frank about Klara, even though her part in Paul's abduction had been concealed. Heller and Blackthorn of SOE had both decided that her reputation should be without blemishes before she went to the commando training school.

"I need a favour, Frank," Max finally said. "I'll understand if you say no, but hear me out first, will you?"

"I'm all ears."

"Christ, this is going to be hard…"

"Max?"

"All right. The thing is I know one of your pupils. Her name is Klara Gabula. I was her handler in France, and I'd like to speak to her in private while I'm here."

"You know you can't do that, not while she's in training."

"You're right, technically, I can't. That's why I'm asking you for the favour."

"I'm sorry, Max, but unless you give me a damn good reason, my answer is no."

Max gulped. "I'm in love with her … was in love … Christ, I don't know anymore. I don't know how I feel. Love, hate, I'm so bloody tired of personal dramas I can't think straight. Look, I wouldn't ask unless it was important. I need to see her, not just because of our personal relationship, but because she thinks she killed Paul." Max downed the whisky, grateful that Frank had suggested the nightcap.

Frank folded his arms. "You didn't tell me about this in the car. Go on."

"Klara abducted Paul thinking he was me…"

Max told Frank about Klara's part in the whole tragic story. "So, there you have it. Now do you see why I have to tell her she didn't kill Paul?"

Frank looked furious. "You lied to me, Max. You said Paul was lifted off the street, not by whom or why. I'm not happy about this. Damn it, I knew there was something off with her, but I couldn't put my finger on it.

"I'm sorry. I wasn't sure if I wanted to mention Klara at all. I didn't want to overload you with information on the drive here. I just thought … well, now that I'm here…"

"I was overloaded the minute you told me Paul had been abducted," Frank snapped, as he refilled his glass. "This explains a lot about Klara's personality. She's a nice kid, but she's a loner, doesn't mix much with her classmates. She looks sad, distant a lot of the time. Her behaviour has been worrying me. I thought she might be too sensitive for the job, or she was having a hard time getting over the loss of her husband." Frank's eyes narrowed. "I hope their separation has nothing to do with you. Has it?"

"Yes." Max closed his eyes. "I think so, yes. Shit, I don't know."

"Bloody irresponsible of you to get involved with a married woman. I'm disappointed in you. You should have known better."

"I take it your answer is still no, then?"

"I'm not sure what to do. She's smart, a damn good agent who's supposed to be going to Poland when we're finished with her. But I can't put a lovesick spy in the field…"

"Trust me, I know. That's why I need to tell her Paul is still alive – please, Frank?"

Max recalled the last time he'd seen Klara. He'd tried to leap over a desk to strangle her. The terror on her face had haunted him ever since, as had his cruel words. He refused to leave Arisaig without telling her that Paul had not been killed on the night she'd taken him to Duguay. He'd go behind Frank's back to get to her, if he had to.

"I don't want to upset her, Frank," Max tried again. "In fact, if you let me talk to her for five minutes, I guarantee she'll cheer up – give me five minutes. I won't ask for more – five, Frank."

"I'm going to bed," Frank grumbled. "I'll inform her in the morning that you're going to meet with her. You can have your five minutes during her lunch break."

"Thank you."

"I'm warning you, Max, if you say or do anything to distract her from her job, I'll come down on you like a ton of bricks."

Chapter Sixteen

Klara Gabula

Captain Middleton's request that she meet with Max at lunchtime had knocked Klara for six. She left the mess hall, her stomach still empty and fluttering like a butterfly's wings, despite her attempt to eat. She washed her face in a sink outside her hut, applied some lip balm to her lips, combed her hair and then rushed to the classroom to meet Max. Surprise, dread, yearning, and nerves were making her legs tremble as she walked, and those were only the tip of her emotional iceberg. Why Max had made the long journey to Scotland to see her was still unclear, but she had already deduced that he must have received confirmation of his brother's death and wanted her to feel even guiltier than she already did. This, she suspected, would be the last time she'd ever see him, and it was going to be a bitter goodbye.

Max stood at the classroom window that looked out over a field of fern and heather. He turned to face her, his stare as intense as the rugged scenery outside. She froze just inside the doorway, struck by the vivid memory of his rough hands reaching for her neck in the interview room at the London SOE Headquarters.

"Hello, Klara," Max said.

"Hello."

Max crossed to her with long strides, and Kara took a step backwards.

"I want to talk to you, Klara, just talk." Max led her to a chair and sat her down. Dressed as the aloof British Major that he was, he stared unemotionally at her, even as her eyes became moist and she folded one trembling hand over the other on the desk.

She squeezed her fingers, and asked, "Why are you here, Max?"

"I need to tell you about my brother, but first, I have to apologise for the way I reacted in London. As a rule, I would never lift a hand in anger. Never, Klara. I scared you, but I was out of my mind with worry..."

"Don't apologise. You have every right to hate me."

"I've never hated you. Disappointed and hurt, yes, but never hate." Max sat at the desk next to her, looking far too big and bulky for the classroom chair. "I was furious. I wanted to throttle you and everyone else involved in Paul's abduction. I was beside myself with grief, and it got the better of me. I'm ashamed of how I reacted. Will you forgive me?"

"Of course, I..." Her words got stuck in her throat when Max touched her arm.

"I went to Paris. I found Paul, and he was alive. He didn't die at Duguay's hands, or at yours," Max uttered.

Klara stopped breathing. Tears sprung from her eyes and she lowered her head before a long, ragged breath tore from her throat. She began to sob as relief washed over her. Embarrassed, she covered her face with her hands, and in a muffled voice uttered, "They lied to me? Claude and Duguay ... they both lied." She finally looked at him and met a kinder face. "Did Paul go back to his unit?"

Max nodded. "Yes, he was heading back to Paris when I last saw him. The point is, you mustn't blame yourself anymore. No more guilt, Klara, do you hear me? I need you to put Paul and Duguay behind you now. You have enough to contend with here."

Max got up to sit on the edge of her desk. He tilted her chin with his fingers and captivated her with that sweet, loving gaze she had come to know.

"It will never be completely behind me. I will always regret what I did." Klara lifted her hand to his cheek, brushing it gently with the tips of her fingers as the first tears spilt from her eyes. "I love you, Max."

Max leant in, his eyes half closed as their lips touched, but then, as though stung, he pulled back.

Dizzy with love, she shivered at his rebuff. "I understand ... no need to say anything."

"I shouldn't have done that," he said regardless, "I promised myself I wouldn't get close to you. We have no future together, Klara. Not anymore."

She shook her head. "You're not thinking..."

"I can't stop thinking. I agonise over how close Paul came to death, how *you* thought I might be working for the Germans without giving me, or him, a chance to explain. But worst of all, I can't accept that you lied to me in the back of the truck. We made love, Klara, but afterwards you could barely look at me or touch me. I spent days trying to understand what I might have done wrong. I can't – I won't forgive that."

She panicked. "I didn't lie to you. I just didn't tell you about it."

"For God's sake, Klara, if you had, I wouldn't have left France. I would have dragged you back to Duguay's base to plead for my brother's life!"

Klara flinched as he got abruptly to his feet and went to the window. She followed him, staring at his back, willing him to turn around. "We can fix this, Max."

When he finally faced her, he folded his arms across his chest, a closed off gesture she had learnt about in class. "Max, I won't try to persuade you to come back to me, but please tell me that you forgive me?"

"I did, five minutes ago. You must understand that this is not some game I'm playing. We're broken, and we can't be fixed. I came here today to tell you that Paul is alive or was the last time I saw him. You deserved that much from me. But our affair, or whatever you want to call it, is over."

She held his eyes, daring him to retract his statement, but when he didn't she shoved her hands in her coat pockets in defiance. "Why did Florent Duguay give Paul his freedom?"

Max raised his eyebrows.

"Oh, come on, Max, it's a perfectly reasonable question. Since being here, I've learnt the importance of secrecy, especially when it involves the locations of safe houses and who is involved with the Resistance. Given that Paul Vogel is now free to report back to his unit with information on how many men Duguay has and possibly the area in which his base is situated, I think it highly unlikely that he would let Paul walk unless something bigger was at play."

The beautiful moment between them had gone with the words, *we're broken.* He and she were like old clocks forever being repaired but never working as well as they had when they were new and undamaged by the passage of time. They'd have no more intimate moments together, she thought. But she'd be damned if she'd let him walk out thinking she didn't have a brain in her head.

"I thought Duguay and Romek were paranoid, but these last few weeks have taught me that one can never lower one's guard in enemy territory, not for a second," she said in a cold, flat voice. "I know now that personal feelings and errors made because of love or fear have no place in the field. They're as likely to bring down an agent as a German bullet, and I will not open my heart again."

"Then you've learnt a valuable lesson," Max said.

"I have, and that's why I can't understand why Duguay released Paul. Had he been in my custody, I would have killed him. God help me for saying that, but as a spy, I would have shot him in the head and buried his body – that should have been Duguay's only safe option – tell me Max, what and who did *you* sacrifice to make your brother safe? What rules did *you* break?"

Max buttoned his greatcoat, then picked up his hat from a desk. Without looking at her, he put it on and made for the door, as though Klara were no longer in the room.

Unafraid of consequences or another berating, Klara rushed to the door, her hands on her hips like a fuming fishwife. "You can't answer that one, can you? You might have put Duguay's entire operation in danger because of your feelings for Paul, but you don't care about that. You used your heart instead of your head, just as I did, and though you may tell yourself that your actions were more professional than mine, you're no better than me, Major Vogel."

Max's eyes became cold as he opened the door. "Move on, Klara. Keep safe. Don't get into any more trouble."

After he left, Klara returned to her hut. She pulled on her socks, hiking boots, and thick quilted jacket. She blew her nose and brushed her hair with such ferocity her scalp stung. Max had said his piece, and she couldn't and wouldn't beg for another chance with him. He was right; they were beyond repair. The damage she had caused would haunt her forever.

She pulled her hood over her head to keep out at least some of the rain lashing down outside, then stared at her pale, forlorn face and the eyes that held no life. She'd had a lover, and now he was gone. He was going back to his war, taking his self-righteousness with him. She had a husband who was hiding somewhere in Spain away from a world at war, at least that's where he'd been heading when she'd last seen him at Duguay's farm. And her, look at her, dressed like a man going into combat with only one thought: killing Germans. That was what mattered now. She was going to show Max Vogel and Florent Duguay just how good an agent she really was. They were no better or wiser than she.

Chapter Seventeen

Freddie Biermann

Berlin, Germany
December 1941

Freddie Biermann clasped his hands behind his back and squinted at the blinding white landscape outside. The recent storm had been relentless, beginning with rain and gales that had lasted throughout the previous night as well as most of the present day. Now the wind had died, but it was so very cold that the rain had frozen mid-air and turned to snow.

Biermann's subordinate, Kriminalinspektor Manfred Krüger, stood in front of the desk, shifting his feet on the thick blue carpet. Having been groomed by the Kriminaldirektor, he knew when to speak and when to keep his mouth shut, and on this occasion, he appeared reluctant to say a word unless spoken to.

Biermann turned from the window and pointed to a pile of documents. "Look at this lot, Manfred. Even with my evidence, they don't believe me. Even with all this!"

"Perhaps they do believe you but don't want to open a can of worms…"

"What can of worms?"

"You know, the SS…"

"Yes, yes, I know them," Biermann grumbled. "My point is, what's the use of having the damn proof if no one will take action? It's preposterous that Herr Himmler won't bring a traitor to justice – no – no! I'm not having it. The sole fact that Vogel hid his artworks before disappearing should have been enough to convince even his biggest supporters that his death was a ruse. I want those paintings. You hear me, Manfred? I want them."

"Shall I pour you a brandy, sir?" Krüger asked.

"Yes." Biermann pushed his frustrations aside and returned to his desk to concentrate on more pressing matters. The news from various fronts and at home was bad, particularly after Germany's winning streak in Western Europe.

"Let's put the Vogel issue aside for the moment," he said, taking a sip of the brandy. "The news from the Eastern Front is not good, and between you and me, the atmosphere here at the Reich Security Office is as frigid as the weather outside."

"I did notice, sir."

"Sit, Manfred, sit." Freddie enjoyed airing his thoughts with like-minded people. It allowed him to offload many mental burdens. He particularly liked the young man now sitting before him, and although he found him a tad sycophantic, he was as trustworthy as a subordinate could be. The Reich was plagued by backstabbers who thought they'd be safe from personal scrutiny if they blamed others of disloyalty. He no longer knew what disloyalty meant, for Hitler seemed to be accusing every man and his dog of betrayal every time Germany made a misstep. It was sad but true that honest and frank conversations seemed to be a thing of the past in the Fatherland.

He picked up a document. "Reports of Adolf Hitler's continuous attacks on members of his High Command have reached the top floor. Everyone is on edge, from Rinehart Heydrich to our most junior SS and Gestapo officers. No one is feeling safe from the Führer's blame game. No one knows how far his rage will reach when he loses his temper…"

"Or who he or his henchmen will target next."

"Precisely." Biermann indicated the files on his desk. "Remember a simpler time? In the old days, I wouldn't have been given access to all this classified material. You and I, we're not military men, and I'm not sure if I'm happy about the Gestapo's current mandate. It's grown to such an extent that we've now got to investigate cases of treason, espionage, sabotage and criminal attacks on the Nazi Party, *including* those instigated in the military. I say, let the Abwehr stick their noses into the army's business. They stick them everywhere else, eh?"

"I absolutely agree, sir. I looked at the Gestapo recruitment files last week and saw that our workload has doubled in the last year, but manpower hasn't. I blame all this disruption on the Jews. We've lost good men to Poland and those ghettos. In a simpler world we'd wipe the Kikes off the face of the earth and be done with them. We don't have nearly enough men to do our proper jobs, never mind babysitting Jews."

Krüger sighed dramatically and shook his head. "Ach, I just don't know … it's no easy task keeping up with the Wehrmacht cases we're being asked to handle and, as you so rightly say, sir, in order to conduct comprehensive investigations into military offences, we need to know what's going on in its ranks. To do that, we need more men on the streets and maybe even in the military barracks."

The Gestapo's growing power was a double-edged sword, Biermann thought. Its basic tenet, which had been passed by the government in 1936, gave the Secret Police Force carte blanche to operate without judicial review; in effect, putting it above the law and exempting it from the authority of the administrative courts where citizens could normally sue the state to conform to the law of the land. The Gestapo's power also included the use of what was called, *Schutzhaft* – protective custody – a euphemism for imprisonment without judicial proceedings.

The police forces seemed omniscient and omnipotent to most people, and the terror they fomented was leading to an overestimation of their reach and strength. It was a faulty assessment, Biermann believed, but it helped to hamper the operational effectiveness of underground resistance organisations who were scared stiff of the German Secret Police in their countries.

"I often wonder if we haven't created a rod for our own backs," Biermann said, still deep in thought. "We adhere to the regime's view that all antipathy to Hitler is not to be tolerated, so we gave ourselves the important, but time-consuming role of monitoring and prosecuting all who oppose Nazi rule, whether openly or covertly."

"I have noticed, sir …. if I might be so bold…?"

"Speak freely, Manfred. What you say here will stay here. You know that."

"Thank you, sir. I was thinking some of the Gestapo systems are rather odd … farcical almost … I mean, we're now asking suspects to sign their own *Schutzhaftbefehl.* To expect any man or woman to request his or her own imprisonment is…"

"Ludicrous, yes, I agree. But as much as it is apparent the detainees do it solely out of fear of personal harm, it does serve a purpose, which is not to have to go to court and waste time in the judicial system."

Biermann scowled at a classified document on his desk. He wondered whether to tell Manfred about its contents – yes, the news would be out in the open soon, slipping through the cracks of secrecy as such skeletons in cupboards always did.

"The last German troops at Halfaya Pass near the Egyptian-Libyan border on the coast at as-Salum have surrendered, meaning General Rommel has now lost thirty-two percent of his forces since Operation Crusader began."

As though reading Biermann's mind, Manfred said, "God help the war effort if the Führer calls for Rommel's head because of this defeat. I'm a great fan of the General's. Experienced leaders like him don't grow on trees."

"My thoughts exactly." Biermann nodded. "We are going to have to monitor the fallout from this. We both know when the Führer dismisses one of his commanders there are often rebellious reverberations further down the chain of command, and when that happens we are called in to deal with disgruntled Wehrmacht officers. And that's a difficult one, Manfred. Having a moan about superiors is not an offence, but openly criticising the Führer is now deemed a crime. It's a very fine line, and we must continue to take care when and if we cross it."

Biermann picked up another classified document. This one, he wouldn't share with Krüger. It was much too disturbing. Generaloberst Erich Hoepner had just been dismissed from the Wehrmacht for ordering his forces to pull back on the Eastern Front without the Führer's approval. Hitler had also deprived Hoepner of his pension and the right to wear his uniform and medals. It seemed their *stickler for details* leader didn't care that by doing so he was contravening the law and Wehrmacht regulations.

Freddie put the classified document back into its file and then picked up another while still thinking about the General. It was distasteful to him, for he knew General Hoepner personally. He and Dieter had served with the man in the First World War, and the three of them had met regularly during the post-war years. He was a good, honourable man, a hell of a leader, and undeserving of such a disastrous end to his career.

Although Freddie had never met Adolf Hitler nor been in meetings with his top generals, he'd been hearing rumours from reliable sources that the Führer was regularly overruling the Generals who were commanding the Russian Campaigns' Northern, Central, and Southern Armies. It was said he was disregarding the opinions and advice from the men on the battlefields, believing he knew better than veterans of the Great War and long-serving military officers with vast experience. It had not been noted in the document, but it was also rumoured that before Hoepner was fired, he'd insisted he either be relieved of command or given the freedom to direct his forces as he wanted. Hitler had apparently chosen the former.

Apart from the outrageous slur against Hoepner, the Führer's unilateral act of malice set a dangerous precedent. In the military and police forces, commanders, officers and foot soldiers lived by a code: an unbreakable set of rules and regulations. Without them, there would be anarchy and chaos. What message was Hitler sending when his actions were outside the boundaries of all known protocols? How could any general lead with confidence when his strategies were being overruled by a man who knew little or nothing of tactical warfare? It didn't bode well for future campaigns. It was like taking dough out of a baker's hands and giving it to a coal miner to bake.

Biermann looked at the clock on the wall and then at Krüger, whom he'd ignored for the last few minutes. "That will be all, Manfred. I'm having dinner at the Einstein, and I'll be late if I don't get a move on. Tell my driver to have the car ready. See you tomorrow."

The first thing Biermann noticed when he entered the Einstein Club was that it was extremely busy despite the freezing temperatures and harsh driving conditions outside. He went to the club most Thursdays to enjoy its relaxed and unguarded atmosphere and to glean information from patrons who had asterisks next to their names on his list of possible troublemakers. He had never arrested or reported anyone as a direct result of anything they'd said or done in the club; that would be counterproductive. Instead, he stored information to be used against the person, or not, at a future date.

Extramarital affairs at the club blossomed in full view as men got drunk and tittle-tattled. Arguments occurred, but people generally let off steam, contradicting their disciplined facades. Should the Gestapo, or SS for that matter, be stupid enough to detain a person in the Einstein for airing their views or making a fool of themselves, the clientele would completely dry up. So too would the gossip and all the useful rumours about the state of the war and the men who were leading the country.

Claus and Dietrich, Biermann's dinner companions, were already seated at a table. He waved as he crossed the room to join them. Both men were aides, glorified secretaries to Martin Bormann, the head of the Nazi Party Chancellery. They had shared interesting tit-bits about their boss with Freddie in the past, in return for slap-up meals and champagne, which the Gestapo paid for. It was a win-win situation for Biermann.

Bormann had gained immense power after succeeding Rudolph Hess, who had flown to Britain, never to be seen again. Answerable only to Hitler, Borman was also responsible for all NSDAP appointments. The foreign organization branch of the National Socialist German Workers Party, NSDAP accepted members outside the country only if they were actual citizens of the German Reich with a German passport. Being Hitler's private secretary made Bormann a powerful ally for those he could manipulate, and a dangerous adversary for overly ambitious men who threatened his position, which he used to control the flow of information and access to the Führer.

After a few drinks, Claus and Dietrich often referred to their boss as the *Brown Eminence* but they emphasised that they'd never dare call him that to his face or let anyone other than themselves say the name. Freddie acknowledged that while Claus and Dietrich's inadvertent slips of information involving Bormann were never top secret or illegal, they did give him insights into the powerful man's psyche, thoughts and moods, and thus, the Führer's frame of mind as well.

Freddie ordered a large Scotch from a passing busty waitress who was known to take advantage of drunken men with deep pockets. He couldn't blame the girl for trying to make a little extra money on the side by having sex with gullible patrons. Times were hard for Berliners.

For a while, the men talked about their families. Biermann was excited about Valentina's recent announcement that she was pregnant; however, when he gave the men that news it was somewhat eclipsed by the update on his son-in-law's recent brush with death.

"... and apart from Valentina being overjoyed about the baby, she got the news that Paul, her husband, had been found safe and well."

"That's wonderful news, Freddie. I know how worried you were about him the last time we spoke," Claus said.

"Did they capture the people responsible?" Dietrich asked.

"Yes. Paul gave the Gestapo what he could on his abductors, but he'd been kept blindfolded and wasn't exactly sure where he'd been held. My colleagues searched from Dieppe to Saint Quentin and captured or executed dozens of rebels."

"Good. Well done to your son-in-law," Claus said. "What now for him?"

"He's coming home. He has a week's leave, but he doesn't know if he'll go back to Paris or if he'll be posted elsewhere after that."

"I hope for his sake it's not the Eastern Front. Those poor devils are freezing over there," Dietrich grumbled.

"I'm disappointed in the way the High Command is handling that problem," said Claus, jabbing the ice in his whisky with a cocktail stick. "They're supposed to excel in predicting and combatting the harsh Russian winter. It's just a matter of using simple statistical analysis, yet they were totally unprepared."

"The problem is the hubristic attitude of the German commissariat," Freddie responded. "They didn't send anything like enough woollen hats, gloves, long johns or greatcoats to Russia." He was reminded of Wilmot Vogel's latest letter. Part of him didn't want to read about the terrible winter conditions in Leningrad. It was common knowledge that there was a desperate need for millions of such clothing items, over and above what could be looted from the Russians and the Poles. On the radio, Joseph Goebbels had even broadcast an appeal for warm clothing to send to the troops, saying: *Those at home will not deserve a single peaceful hour if even one soldier is exposed to the rigours of winter without adequate clothing.*

Freddie thought it ridiculous to blame the civilian population for the lack of warm garments. Two years of clothes rationing meant there was little to give the soldiers at the front, but he suspected Goebbels already knew that and was following Hitler's habit of blaming everyone but the Third Reich when things went wrong.

Claus said, "I have a son serving with the Northern Army at Leningrad."

Freddie was surprised he didn't already know that. "You didn't tell me that, Claus."

"Ach, I don't like to talk about him. I'm worried sick, Freddie. It makes me angry when I think about the military's lacklustre behaviour towards those poor souls living in trenches … and I know what I'm talking about. I was with Herr Bormann at Berchtesgaden in October. The Führer held a dinner. I wasn't at the table, of course, but I *was* in the room and heard the conversation about the Russian weather. Herr Hitler said one couldn't put any trust in meteorological forecasts. I suppose he thinks he's as much an expert in meteorology as in everything else."

"Claus, you shouldn't be talking about private conversations between the Führer and Herr Bormann," the other Bormann aide warned.

"I'm only saying what I think, Dietrich. Adolf Hitler is a world-class know-it-all." Claus threw more wine down his throat. "He said weather prediction is not a science that can be learnt mechanically. What we need, according to him, are men gifted with a sixth sense, who live in nature and with nature; whether they know anything about isotherms and isobars doesn't matter apparently."

"A damn stupid thing to say if you ask me," Freddie chuckled. "What else did he have to say about it?"

"He said that as a rule, these men with a sixth sense were not particularly suited to the wearing of uniforms. One of them would have a humped back, another would be bandy-legged, a third paralytic. Then he added that simily … sorry … similarly, one shouldn't expect them to live like bureaucrats."

Claus sounded like a madman blubbering nonsense, but he was, he assured Freddie, relating the conversation between the Führer and Bormann word for word.

"You'll have to excuse me, Claus, I might have had too much wine, but I don't really understand why you're talking about bandy-legged men and the like," Freddie said, trying to keep the amusing story going.

"Human barometers, Freddie – that's what Hitler dubbed these elusive people – said such men should have telephones installed in their homes free of charge, so they could predict the weather for the Reich. You see, these woodland folk – the Führer's words, not mine – would be people who understood the flights of midges and swallows, who could read the signs, who felt the wind, and understood the movements of the sky. Hitler told Herr Bormann that elements are more reliable than mathematics, but I don't think Herr Bormann was impressed." He shrugged. "Ach, I suppose there are things beyond our understanding that only the Führer's genius perceives. That's why he's the leader of the Fatherland, and I'm a nobody."

Freddie had asked no more, but upon separating Hitler's ludicrous musings from the harsh reality of the situation, he couldn't help but feel worried about the Russian campaigns. For the Germans to be defeated in the field of battle was one thing, but for them to have been improperly provided for by their own leadership and the General Staff was quite another. It was appalling and should have been avoided with level-headed forward planning.

Chapter Eighteen

Biermann slept on his office couch until 07:00 the next morning. He was groggy, and his head was pounding with the after effects of too many glasses of red wine at the Einstein Club.

He got up, stretched, and then went to the window. It was still snowing, but the ground was covered in dirty grey slush. Vehicles were moving, albeit slowly, and people were arriving for work as usual. He had a quick wash in the bathroom but left his overnight stubble alone. Then, he changed out of his civilian clothes and put on his Gestapo uniform.

An hour later, Biermann's driver dropped him off at Spandau Prison on Berlin's Wilhelmstraße. Most of the political dissidents and traitors who had plotted against the Nazi Party had already been transferred from Spandau to the concentration camps at Dachau and the marshland prison camp at Esterwegen. A few remained, however, including one who was of great personal interest to Biermann.

The prisoner was handcuffed and slouched over a table in the interview room. His cheeks were swollen to twice their normal size, and his right eyelid resembling a piece of raw flesh was forcing the eye shut. Sores had become infected on his lips after they'd been repeatedly punched, and a ring of fingerprint bruises was wrapped around his neck. But for all the physical evidence of suffering, the most telling was the way his filthy clothes hung on his emaciated body.

After dismissing the Gestapo guard, Biermann sat at the table opposite the prisoner. The man had been an impossible nut to crack, and this, the fifth interrogation, was going to be the last chance to get answers to a long list of questions. Biermann planned to lie through his teeth today and use every dirty trick he knew. Failure wasn't an option, not when Dieter's artworks were at stake. He was counting on those to boost his measly retirement pension further down the line.

Biermann didn't bother to hide his frustration as he glared across the table. He was determined to break Dieter Vogel's driver, Kurt Sommer, the man he had arrested the night Laura Vogel left Germany. He lit a cigarette and offered one to Kurt.

******

Kurt eyed Biermann with suspicion but accepted the cigarette, which he jammed between his scabbed lips. Something was different about the Kriminaldirektor today, he thought, letting Biermann light the cigarette with a match. Apart from arriving earlier than usual at 07:30, he was in Gestapo uniform and had an air of victory about him, something that had been missing during previous interrogations.

"Thank you, Herr Kriminaldirektor. What can I do for you today?" Kurt mumbled.

"At about ten o'clock last night, something came to me. I know it was ten because my wife was just clearing the table and mentioning that she didn't like to eat that late in the evening. I asked her what time it was, and she told me – sorry, I'm digressing. Anyway, it came to me that I've never asked you if you knew Captain Leitner – August Leitner?"

Kurt shook his head, his expression deadpan.

"Come now, Kurt, you must recall the visits he made to Herr Vogel's houses in Berlin and Dresden ... such a lovely villa, that one in Dresden. Shame it's abandoned now ... so, Kurt, Captain Leitner? He worked with Paul Vogel in the hospital at Brandenburg?"

"No. I've never heard of him. A lot of people visited Herr Vogel over the years, and to be honest, one man's Nazi uniform is the same as the next to me."

Biermann's lips twitched, then spread into a broad smile. "We'll come back to Leitner another time, shall we?"

Kurt shrugged.

Biermann shuffled some papers. "I'll miss our chats together, even though they've been largely one-sided," he smiled again. "What about you, Kurt? Will you miss me? Berlin? Your freedom? I hear the Sachsenhausen camp is a rough place full of Soviet prisoners and traitors. I know one of the camp commanders. His name is Gustav Sorge. Have you heard of him?"

Kurt shook his head, his gaze steady. Was this another Gestapo trick or was he finally going to be moved from Spandau? If it were the latter, he might as well kill himself now. He'd hidden his cyanide pill inside a fake tooth at the back of his mouth on the day Laura Vogel left. He'd suspected that Freddie Biermann was closing in, a sixth sense, professional instinct.

"...he's quite the talk of the place, this Gustav," Biermann was still talking about the concentration camp. "People call him *Der eiserne* Gustav – Iron Gustav, an apt name. He doesn't like Soviets or dissidents. He won't like you, Kurt."

"Why are you telling me this?"

Biermann spread his arms as though the answer were evident. "I wanted to let you know that I have everything I need now to send you to the death ... maybe that's too harsh a threat ... your long incarceration." He sat back in his chair, looking as satisfied as a man who had just enjoyed a T-bone steak and a fine bottle of wine. "I can stop the transfer or get you sent to another camp that will be more hospitable. Would you like that, Kurt?"

Kurt sniggered. "And in return you'll want me to give you a false confession, craft the story you want to hear, make you look good in front of your superiors when you run to them waving my testimony in their faces? Blah, blah, blah. Herr Direktor, you can write a love story to your bosses and cover the pages with kisses, but as I've said many times before, I won't be signing my name on any piece of paper." Kurt took another drag of his cigarette and then leant in. "For the fifth time, I have nothing more to add. Dieter Vogel died, just the way I told you, just as the SS recorded in their report, and I have committed no crimes against the Fatherland." Sitting back in his chair, he added, "We both know I've been wrongly detained, and you don't have a shred of evidence that will stick. Why don't you stop this pathetic game of yours and let me go home?"

Biermann opened his briefcase and pulled out another file. He set it on the table, closed the case and leant it against the table leg. "This has been a long time coming, but the proof that you lied to me, to Laura Vogel, and to the SS, is inside this file. The question is, what should I do with it?"

Kurt eyed the name on the cover. *Dieter Vogel, case 176392.* "I haven't lied to anyone."

Biermann scowled. "The only reason it has taken me this long to prove what I've always suspected is because Laura Vogel refused to allow the pathologist to conduct an autopsy on her husband's body. Had he done one, he would have discovered straight away that Dieter Vogel was not a victim of the factory explosion."

Freddie tapped the matchbox on the table, shaking the matches inside.

"This is crazy," Kurt snapped, incensed at the suggestion, and irritated by the noise the matches were making. "I saw and felt the explosion ... you saw my injuries ... you were a pall bearer at Herr Vogel's funeral. You watched the coffin go into the grave."

"The coffin I dug up. When Laura Vogel crossed into Switzerland, I no longer needed her permission to exhume Dieter's remains, as she no longer had the right to object."

Biermann lit another cigarette. "For weeks, you've kept to your story about Dieter going into the chemical plant with two guards just minutes before the explosion, and for weeks I wanted to shove your lies down your throat. Today, I feel justified, no, satisfied with my evidence."

Kurt swallowed, but kept his eyes turned away from the file. He had not been brought up in a family environment that encouraged emotions, whether they be sad or happy. He'd never displayed fear or hatred, for his father had frowned upon those feelings; hysterical outbursts, he had called them. Now, for the first time in his life, he was unravelling inside. It was all about Dieter's teeth – the bloody missing teeth – it had to be.

Biermann flicked through the documents in the file while Kurt tried to relax in his chair. The Kriminaldirektor had bided his time, probably to try and find out who else might be involved in the conspiracy against the SS gas plant. He wondered if the Gestapo knew about Herr Brandt or Dieter's connection to MI6, or *him* also being a spy?

"Don't you want to ask me why I feel vindicated?" Biermann eventually asked.

"Why? I'm sure you're going to tell me."

Freddie opened the file, pulled out a piece of paper and slid it across the table to Kurt. "Read it."

Kurt looked at the heading, then scrolled down, much of which was medical jargon, like a foreign language he didn't understand. Impatient to learn the laboratory results, his eyes jumped from one line of mumbo jumbo to another until he got to the last sentence: *The remains, therefore, cannot be those of Dieter Vogel.*

"That's right," Biermann said. "It was the missing teeth that gave you and Dieter away. Any good dental surgeon who'd been given the chance to examine the skull's mouth straight after the explosion would have concluded that two teeth had been recently pulled. The gums, although badly burnt were..." Freddie turned the document to face him. "Ah, yes, here it is. *Gum and bone tissue had recently been cut away using a non-surgical instrument – ends were ragged, and gum bone was chipped.* What did Dieter use to pull out the dead guard's teeth, hmm? Pliers? A knife? No, never mind, don't bother answering that question. I'd much rather know where Dieter is now. I suspect England with Laura. How nice for them both – and where is his art collection? You remember all those marvellous paintings he hung on his walls – the Goya, the Rembrandt among others? They seem to have disappeared? Why don't you tell me where they are, Kurt?"

Kurt smiled through his cracked lips. This was contemptable. Biermann was more interested in Dieter's artworks than finding justice for the Third Reich. *Good luck with retrieving the paintings and lining your pockets with money for your retirement,* Kurt wanted to say, but instead, he uttered, "I have nothing more to say to you. You've concocted this whole story to rattle me. If Dieter isn't dead, I say, bravo, but here's the thing, I had nothing to do with any of this. I have no idea what happened to Herr Vogel after he went into the gas plant, and I certainly wasn't privy to any plans he might have had for his paintings." Pleased with his lies, he added, "Ask the factory's night-watchman about me. He saw me running towards the exit just before the place exploded. How many times do I have to tell you that?"

"Kurt. *Kurt,* you're missing my point. Dieter's body was not *in* the building."

Without another word, Freddie shuffled the papers, slid them into the file, and then left the room.

Minutes later, Kurt was dragged back to his cell where he reflected upon his failure. Laura had been told at the time that the corpses were unrecognisable. Yet even after weeks in the ground, the medical authorities had still managed to determine that the remains with the missing teeth were not Dieter's. The skull's bones and gums had revealed enough to convict, apparently, but what precisely was *his* crime? At best it was conspiracy to arson and vandalism. "Fuck Biermann," Kurt mumbled. He wasn't signing the already-written confession. He'd rather kill himself than hand the bastard a victory.

Kurt recalled that before setting the timer for the explosives, Dieter had stripped an SS corpse naked and had redressed it in his own civilian clothes. Then, he'd dressed himself in the dead man's ill-fitting SS uniform. Kurt also remembered that Dieter had planted his wedding ring on the young guard's body and had then ripped the corpse's two bottom teeth out using pliers, just as Biermann had suspected. Not wanting to leave evidence, Dieter had taken the precaution of putting the teeth in his jacket pocket. The plan had succeeded to the letter.

Dieter's *body* had been buried after a high-profile funeral in Berlin's cathedral with Nazi Party members in attendance giving tear-jerking eulogies about Dieter's loyalty to the Führer. Later, Laura had left the country, just as Dieter had wanted.

The Gestapo had arrested Kurt on the night of Laura's departure for England. That day, he'd driven her to the train station and afterwards he'd returned home to close the house and store the Vogel's expensive ornaments. The paintings from both houses had been removed during the days before the explosion. Dieter had told Laura that he was putting them into storage because of allied air-raid threats. He'd also advised her to feign ignorance about the artworks' removal. Money was tight for most people, and thieves were breaking into houses to steal expensive items to later sell them on the black market. Laura Vogel was not a stupid woman. She must have known that the paintings had been stolen from Jews in the first place, yet she had agreed not to say a word, specifically telling Dieter she didn't want to know where he'd taken the canvases.

Laura had never been his friend, Kurt knew, not like the other members of the family. Their conversations had always been polite, rather formal, and she'd never mentioned the paintings to him in the days after Dieter's supposed death, nor had she to Biermann. The Gestapo was pissing against the wind with that line of enquiry.

On that last evening, Kurt had sent a transmission to Heller from the cabin in the forest, telling him that Laura had left Germany. Then he'd returned home to Dieter's house to fill the car with his belongings. Laura had instructed him to live in the Berlin house to make sure it wasn't looted or damaged from neglect, but Dieter had ordered him to leave Berlin as soon as Laura got away safely. Unfortunately, Kurt had made his departure too late to escape Biermann's Gestapo.

Terrified of what might come next, Kurt stared at the cell door and thought again about his kill-pill, and whether he had the balls to crack it open in his mouth. Was Biermann really going to send him to a concentration camp or try a more robust form of interrogation to get the information he needed to find Dieter? Would he arrest Wilmot? Had he the gumption to incarcerate Paul, now a member of the Biermann family? Was he going to try and find whoever he and Dieter had been working with? Just how far would the Gestapo go to hunt down Dieter, the man who had foiled Himmler and Heydrich's plans for their precious gas programme?

Chapter Nineteen

Kurt Sommer

Kurt had spent weeks in solitary confinement. He'd been left naked, freezing, and starved of food and drink apart from one lump of bread a day and a tin cup of water every eight hours. The chamber pot, never emptied since his incarceration, had overflowed numerous times, forcing him to sit in his own piss and choke on the stench of his excrement. He had pleaded, to no avail, for a scrap of paper, water, or soap, and had sacrificed one cup of water a day to cleanse the filthiest parts of his body. He was skeletal and losing muscle strength from lack of exercise and nutrients. And though he had the means, he still couldn't bring himself to end his own life.

Every three hours or so, a guard came to Kurt's three metre by two and a half metre holding cell. He slid open the small window half way up the iron door and blew a horn for ten minutes, and when the noise ended, he told Kurt a series of lies: guards were coming to take him to the interview room, he might be going home a free man or taken to a camp, or this was to be his last day in the cell. Kurt had long since figured out that it was all a ruse to deny him sleep and continually jar his nerves.

During his confinement, he'd braced himself for what was to come by envisaging every possible Gestapo torture known to him. Biermann wanted solid confirmation to incriminate Dieter, but that wasn't Kurt's biggest worry. For years, he had been one step ahead of the Secret Police. He was a Jew by birth, and in possession of forged papers and a carefully devised false background story that had, up until now, fooled everyone. That backstory had been concocted by the British Secret Service in 1935 after he had approached them in London to offer his services as a spy.

His biggest regret in life was that he'd never contacted his family to let them know he was alive and still living in Germany. He'd hidden from them to keep them safe from the *Einsatzgruppen Schutzstaffel,* the SS paramilitary death squads who had been after him for months during that period in 1935. But despite his bid to protect his Jewish parents and sister, they had died in an unrelated event on November 10th, 1938.

On that day, the Reich had conducted a pogrom against Jews throughout Nazi Germany, using the SA paramilitary forces and German civilians. It had been said at the time that the German authorities had watched the whole thing without intervening, but the Reich had later denied those reports. They had also stated that they did not condone violence against Jews, which Kurt had seen as a blatant lie, like all the other untruths coming out of Nazi mouths at that time.

The day after the riots, he had driven Dieter into Berlin where they'd seen the damage first hand. Jewish homes, hospitals, and schools had been ransacked. The attackers had demolished buildings using sledgehammers. A week later, Dieter had got hold of *The Times* of London, in which a journalist had eloquently written: *'No foreign propagandist bent upon blackening Germany to the world could outdo the tale of burnings and beatings, of blackguardly assaults on defenceless innocent people, which disgraced that country yesterday.'* And for weeks, dribbles of information leaked from authorities into the public domain until the full extent of the destruction became shockingly clear: over one thousand-four-hundred synagogues had been burnt to the ground, seven thousand Jewish businesses were either destroyed or damaged. At least ninety Jews had been killed, and over thirty thousand Jewish men had been arrested throughout the Reich and incarcerated in concentration camps. No one at the time had been able to verify if the number of casualties was entirely accurate, but they'd been close.

Germans, when they talked about those two nights of brutality, referred to the Pogrom as the *Reichskristallnacht* – the night of the broken glass – for all the shards of window panes that had littered the streets. Who cared what they called it, Kurt had remarked to Dieter. The event would live on in infamy, a stain on Germany for a thousand years.

In the aftermath of Kristallnacht, Kurt had found it difficult to separate fact from fiction. Every time Goebbels got on his soapbox, he spewed lies about the reasons behind the violence: the Jews, according to him, had attempted to bring down the Führer's Nazi Party in a violent coup, and had it not been for the intervention of real Germans, they might have succeeded. Another: a Nazi German diplomat, Ernst vom Rath had been shot multiple times by Herschel Grynszpan, a seventeen-year-old German-born Polish Jew living in Paris. And Goebbels' final statement: that the assassination had been organised by the Jewish councils. The last part was utter fabrication.

Kurt rested his head against the wall and recalled his and Dieter's trip to Munich three days after the riots. Worried about being recognised in his home city, but desperate to find out what had happened to his parents, Kurt had asked Dieter to make discrete enquires in his parent's Jewish neighbourhood. The news had been devastating: neighbours had told Dieter that Kurt's parents, sister and brother-in-law had either been killed or transported to a camp.

The consensus among the stunned Jewish communities was that predominately well-to-do families had been specifically targeted. That rumour had been confirmed when, sometime later, Biermann had remarked to Dieter that the Reich had seen Kristallnacht as an opportunity to beef up Nazi revenue streams from the deported Jews' holdings and possessions. Kurt believed that scheme was still being used in the many Jewish deportations taking place in every corner of the Third Reich.

In retrospect, he had never accepted Goebbels' pathetic justification for the attacks that had wiped out the people he'd loved. Even now, he struggled to grasp that almost one hundred innocent people had been battered to death in retaliation for the assassination of *one man* in Paris. He also found it hard to stomach that the average German man and woman had condoned or stayed silent about the Nazis' slaughter against Jewish citizens in their own cities.

The cell door opened for the first time in six days, letting in a slanting shaft of sunlight from the hallway. Kurt, blinded by the brightness, shielded his bloodshot eyes with his hands and kept them there while he was dragged out of the cell; his faeces-stained backside skidding across the concrete floor.

After a long walk through a maze of hallways, Kurt was taken to an empty room with a wet floor and bare brick walls. He breathed in the pungent, mouldy stench mingled with his sweat and sewage-covered body, and choked as the guards bound his wrists and ankles with rope.

"I presume this is the physical torture part of your interrogation," he chuckled through cracked lips. For weeks, he had endured mental abuse and physical beatings in his cell, and now they were going to officially brutalise him. Maybe they'd do him a favour and finish him off.

The guards used a pulley to raise Kurt's arms up until only his toes were touching the ground and his arms were stretched above him. Beyond terror or embarrassment at his nakedness, he squeezed his eyes shut and bit his lip. Fuck them, he wouldn't give the bastards the satisfaction of seeing him squirm or beg.

The men were chatting together, ignoring Kurt as though they had done this job a hundred times and were immune to their victim's suffering. He wondered when the questions would come and who would ask them? It didn't matter. They could send in Hitler himself and he wouldn't say a bloody word to the insane dictator or his equally demented minions.

His collarbone cracked as the head of his humerus slipped out of joint causing his shoulder to dislocate. He screamed in agony but was rewarded with a punch to his ribs.

"He stinks," one of the guards said to the other.

"We better get to it before the Kriminaldirektor comes in here," said the other, tying off the pulley rope.

One of the men dragged a hose across the floor. Kurt, gasping with pain looked down the length of his body to the floor and saw the drainage holes. Dazed and losing consciousness, he murmured, "A shower ... how nice of you to think of it."

When the freezing water hit Kurt like needles pricking every inch of his skin, he screamed again. The force of the spray combined with the water's icy temperature turned his body purple, and finally, unable to breathe, he squirmed in silence, lips set in a tight line and turning blue, his eyes squeezed shut, and pain wracking his whole body until he slipped in and out of oblivion.

After they'd turned off the water, the guards cut Kurt down and made him lie on his stomach over a chair while they beat him with clubs on his back and behind. Then, they threw him on the floor and kicked him in the stomach and genitals.

Kurt curled himself into a ball, his body shivering with shock and the agony of his bleeding backside and dislocated shoulder. His teeth began to chatter as the cold air hit his wet, naked body and seemed to frost the hair on his head. He focused on the concrete floor and a circular patch of blood staining it, and prayed for unconscious bliss…

"… I know, but we can't leave him like that. The Direktor won't be happy," one of the guards was saying.

Kurt screamed again, as the guards rolled him onto his back. One lifted his arm in the air while the other held him down. Then without warning, the guard manipulated Kurt's arm and clicked the joint back into its socket.

After the men had left the room, Kurt rolled back onto his side and let the cold air soothe the cuts to his backside. He didn't know what was worse, the physical torture or not knowing what was coming next. He ran his tongue over his fake tooth. It was time. He knew better than to hope he'd get out of there a free man. Worse was coming, more pain, death by firing squad, or a short, miserable life in a camp. *Yes, it was time to end it.*

Kurt's fingers went to his mouth, but they instantly retreated as Biermann strolled in. Kurt stared up at the Gestapo Kriminaldirektor, Dieter Vogel's friend, and Paul's father-in-law. It was hard to imagine now that he and Biermann had shared a toast at Paul and Valentina's wedding. He'd been in Frau Biermann's kitchen numerous times drinking tea, eating her sponge cake while waiting for Dieter to finish some meeting or other. It was difficult to reconcile Freddie Biermann, the good man, to this torturer with the sadistic eyes of a monster and a razor-thin smile.

Biermann pulled Kurt to his feet and then pushed him into the chair he'd been doubled over earlier. Kurt flinched again with pain. "I'd rather stand if you don't mind – sore arse."

Biermann, ignoring the request, took two cigarettes from his pack, put them to his lips, and lit them both. He gave one to Kurt before pulling over another chair and sitting opposite his prisoner.

"What's just been done to you is only the start of our new relationship, Kurt." Biermann smiled. "I call this round one, as in a boxing match that might or might not have ten or twelve or even more rounds to go." He waved his hand. "Ach, you know what I mean. I've also decided to leave you in solitary confinement a while longer, and on days of my choosing, you'll be brought here for your shower." He sighed. "Call me selfish for not sending you to the camp I mentioned, but I'm not ready to let you go until you tell me the truth."

"I told you I don't know anything about anything. You're wasting your time."

"Maybe I am, but I'm betting you will eventually tell me where the traitor, Dieter Vogel, is. *Precisely* where he is."

Biermann leant in and the stench of stale wine and tobacco hit Kurt's nostrils.

"Can you imagine, Kurt, how it must feel to find out that your closest friend in the world is a man you never really knew at all, a lying, deceitful stranger with no empathy or conscience?" Biermann asked. "I know he's alive and laughing at me and the country he claimed to love. I am suffering a torrent of misery…"

"Is it like the torrent of nonsense you're talking now?"

Biermann sat back, eyes blazing. "You-will-tell-me!"

"Fuck off," Kurt croaked.

Biermann wagged his finger in Kurt's face and sniggered. "I expected that answer today. It's your first time under the whip, shall we say, and you still feel you can beat me at my own game. But I wonder if you'll feel the same way when it's your third or fourth time, when your arse is so sore you can't sit down, and every limb is out of joint. By the second go around, your sores will be infected by your excrement and piss. You'll be starving because we'll only feed you enough to keep you alive. You'll not know if it's day or night, or for how long you've been here, and a part of you will want your life to end. I admit, Kurt, the predictability of this job gets tedious after a while. I've never met anyone who didn't tell me what I wanted to know at some point or another."

"Does your wife know you're a cruel sadistic predator?" Kurt asked. "Or does she only see the loving husband and father who cried at his daughter's wedding?"

"Mention my family again and I'll kill you where you sit!"

Kurt enjoyed his small victory then spat a lump of blood from his mouth onto the wet floor. "You have nothing on me, Biermann."

"I have enough evidence on you to shoot you here and now…"

"… why don't you do it, then?"

Biermann slapped Kurt's face. "I have enough proof to write a report stating that Dieter is a traitor, and as such, so are his children by association. Do you really think I want to go to Russia or Paris to arrest Willie and Paul? Boys I've known from the day they were born?"

"No, not unless you want to break your daughter's heart." Kurt held Biermann's eyes. "Leave the Vogel boys out of this sham. Whatever this is, it's between you and me." He tried to sit up straight but couldn't breathe without feeling a stab in his side; cracked ribs. "Come on, Herr Direktor, do you … do you really want to drag this ludicrous investigation into the open? You'll be laughed at from here to the Russian Front ... hypothetically, even if Dieter is alive, which I know he's not, what are you going to do about it?" Kurt steadied his gaze and despite the pain pushed his shoulders back and his chest out. "Do you really want to risk your career on an absurd accusation?"

Biermann charged to his feet, knocking his chair over, then went to the door and yelled for the guards. Before he left, he said. "Kurt, I'm a patient man. I can wait a day, a month, a year for the information I need. Can you?"

Five minutes later, Kurt was taken back to his cell. It had been cleaned, and a dish of cold, congealed stew and a lump of bread were sitting on a tray. He choked as he ate, his hunger more urgent than swallowing the meat carefully. Afterwards, he curled up on the floor and closed his eyes. Ten minutes later, the guard with the horn arrived.

Chapter Twenty

Romek Gabula

Madrid, Spain.
December 1941

Romek was living in the Legazpi neighbourhood of Madrid, a vast complex of ornate stone and brick buildings standing near the banks of the Manzanares River. The sparsely furnished and somewhat dilapidated lodgings didn't bother him in the slightest, he'd told his handler upon his arrival. He wasn't a snob who needed to be surrounded by fancy ornaments or furniture; in fact, he much preferred staying in a working-class area with people he could relate to.

One wet mid-morning, he left his tiny one-bedroom flat, said *buenos dias* to a crinkly old man in the hallway, and then ambled down three flights of stairs. At the exit, he kept the door open for a young woman struggling to get her baby's pram inside. She thanked him with a broad smile and then rummaged in her shopping bag, her eyes lighting up with excitement as she unwrapped three pork chops from newspaper.

"I bought them…"

Romek listened to her rambling in Spanish, not understanding most of what she was saying apart from she'd bought them and *tu y yo, esta noche,* which meant you and me tonight. She was inviting him to dinner.

"Si, gracias … comida," he responded when she'd stopped talking.

Romek, who had chosen the name Juan to avoid awkward questions about his Polish heritage, smiled at the woman he'd been having sex with for the last two weeks. He'd met her on the day he'd arrived in the neighbourhood. She, like many of the women living in the complex, was a widow of the recent civil war and had gone to great pains to show him her husband's death certificate issued by the defeated Republican government almost two years earlier.

He couldn't speak more than a few words of Spanish, but sign language came in handy. She'd been left with a fatherless baby and he'd chuckled inwardly at the lie. The baby, no more than a year old, was evidently not the child of the woman's dead husband who had died two and a half years earlier, according to the death certificate. Or he, Romek Gabula, was terrible at arithmetic. It was more likely that the baby had been fathered by a conquering Nationalist soldier, who had probably disappeared as soon as he'd found out she was pregnant.

Romek freely admitted that he'd taken advantage of the woman's desperate situation. She saw him as her last hope for a respectable future, going to extraordinary lengths to please him in every conceivable way, despite his often rough and verbally abusive behaviour towards her – he negated the verbal abuse because she couldn't understand a word of Polish – and he had recently deduced that he wasn't over Klara's betrayal with Max after all, and needed to punish someone of the fairer sex to make himself feel better. He wasn't proud of this side of his character but lashing out from time to time tamed the beast inside.

After he left the woman and her baby, he covered his mouth with his handkerchief and strode at a brisk pace along the street. The downside to staying in this area and having as much sex as his body could physically take, was his flat's proximity to the city's main slaughterhouse. The robust stench lingered far beyond its high stone walls and deep into the neighbourhood. The widow had probably fucked the abattoir's butcher for the fatty chops, but the thought of that didn't bother him in the slightest.

Romek was not enamoured with Madrid, or with the Spanish people. In the ruined streets of a war not long ended, he witnessed the Republican defeated being intimidated by General Franco's victorious soldiers. The bullying tactics reminded him of the German power-crazed officers in France who'd picked random hostages to be shot without laying charges of any misdoing at their doors. That he was now working for the German demigods who destroyed people's lives never ceased to amaze him, but then neither did the fact that he had made it out of France a free man but his Resistance fighters in Fresnes Prison had not.

After he had passed the Hotel Tryp Gran Vía, Romek zigzagged through the streets around Puerta del Sol. He sidestepped a mule and cart as he crossed the narrow Calle Victoria, and after another couple of twists and turns reached Calle de Echegaray, its cobblestones sparkling from that morning's rain.

La Venencia, an old bar where men in flat caps and tweed jackets sipped sherry from tall, narrow glasses, and bartenders wrote their tabs in chalk on the bar top, was the regular meeting place between Romek and the head of the Abwehr in Madrid. Karsten Portner – probably not his real name – was already seated at a table near the back of the room, and he waved at Romek as he wound his way through the crowded tables and chairs.

Portner pushed a glass of crisp *Mistela* towards Romek who nodded his thanks. He sipped it while the Abwehr officer lit a cigarette from a gold-plated lighter. He'd never trusted the slim, good-looking German whose movements were like those of a big cat. He was amiable enough, but Romek never forgot that he was a hostage of sorts, and he was constantly aware of not making false statements, lest they come back to haunt him in the future.

"I was ordered to handle you with love and care, Romek, to do my utmost to help you. I hope you'll agree I've done just that?"

"You've been very kind, Karsten," Romek said, raising his short-stemmed glass.

"Did you know that La Venencia was, and in some ways still is, a haunt for Republican and Communist sympathizers?"

Romek looked around him. "No, I didn't know that. Seems strange you should like it here."

"Yes, strange indeed. On paper, I'd have no reason to mix with the likes of these Marxist scum, but we have a saying in the Abwehr: the best way to destroy a group is to become part of it."

"I suppose that makes sense," said Romek, his bile rising as he thought back to Oscar's betrayal in Paris. Not wanting to commit himself further to that conversation, Romek said, "Tell me more about this place."

"Ah, I have many stories. During the civil war, it is said that Ernest Hemingway came here to get news from the front. You know Hemmingway's work?"

"I can't say I do – never heard of him."

Portner pointed to a sign on the wall and translated it. *In the interest of hygiene, don't spit on the floor.* "The Venencia has a few old rules from its recent past. The second is no taking of photographs. I suppose because it prevented visitors from being incriminated by possible Fascist spies during the war. The third rule: absolutely no tipping, because the Republican loyalists considered all workers to be equal. They think they're all the same, you see, and the barman deserves no more than the men who pay him for their drinks – they're a strange lot."

Romek, now bored by the uninspiring conversation from a man who clearly loved the sound of his own voice, mumbled, "Fascinating."

Portner stood up abruptly, gesturing for Romek to follow, then zigzagged to the exit. For a while the two men strolled along the streets in silence. Romek, used to following blindly without asking questions, was surprised, however, when he was ushered into the German Consulate, a place he had not visited since first meeting Portner there shortly after his arrival in Spain.

"In you go, Romek," Portman said opening his office door. "Take a seat at the desk."

Romek felt a flutter of excitement as Portman took a cardboard box from his desk drawer and pulled a forged passport from it. He had learnt a great deal about what the Germans would want from him when he eventually got to Britain. The Abwehr had trained him in spy work, how to recognise, write, and decipher their codes, and their techniques in constructing and dismantling their radio transmitters.

Portner smiled, the white teeth and thick lips that charmed the most pious of Spanish women aimed now at Romek. "I will miss you, Romek, but as with all good things, our direct association must come to an end."

Romek eyed the passport. "I'm leaving?"

Portner smiled again; then, like a magician pulling rabbits from a hat, he went into his box, pulling out items one by one. First, he held two crystals in his palm. "You will use these to begin the construction of your radio transmitter." He set them down on the desktop next to Romek's false passport. "This is your invisible ink," he said, shaking a small bottle. "This document is your questionnaire. In England, you will study the list of targets and answer each question before sending it back to us. This is the address where you will stay in England, and the name of your landlady, a loyal Nazi supporter."

Romek's eyes widened at the pile of British pound notes and coins Portner deposited in front of him.

"There is plenty more where that came from, Romek," said Portner, going back into the box. "And finally, this is your cyanide capsule."

When he'd calmed himself after seeing the pill that would kill him should he be captured, Romek began to gather the items and put them back into the box. "When do I leave?"

"This evening."

"That soon?" *No pork chops for me tonight,* he thought.

Portner took a document out of a file and lay a pen on it. "Read this and sign. I know you were informed in France that should you betray us we would have the right to execute your family members in Warsaw. This takes that agreement a step further, Romek. It confirms your consent for such executions to take place."

"And here I thought we were getting along so famously," Romek said.

Portner walked around to the front of his desk and went to the door. "My code name is Matador, yours is Cicero. Don't forget that. From now on, Matador and Cicero will be the only names that matter to us." Portner extended his hand. "I wish you all the best. We *will* meet again, perhaps when you least expect it."

Chapter Twenty-One

Max Vogel

London, England.
December 22ⁿᵈ, 1941

Max sipped a cup of tea in a café near Oxford Circus, his head buzzing with apprehension. He smiled at the waitress then nodded to two soldiers who entered and saluted him. "At ease, gentlemen. Enjoy the scones. You won't find the likes of these anywhere else in London."

A sense of elation had surged through him when he'd cleared the cobwebs from the gloomy basement he'd called home for more than a month. Stuck behind a desk compiling and filing personnel records was a mind-numbing job, one a trained monkey could do blindfolded. He'd been like a rat in a crypt, nibbling scraps of information that filtered down through the floorboards from upstairs. In his kingdom of one, he'd been ignored, deliberately left out of the intelligence loop, and forbidden to go anywhere near Blackthorn's office, or to communicate with him by letter. But, as humiliated as a major in the king's army could be under such circumstances, he had swallowed his pride and completed his sentence in resolute silence. He'd deserved the punishment; Blackthorn had called it a lesson in humility.

His administrative job had been his penance for the debacle in France with Paul. News of his secret November mission to Duguay's base had reached Blackthorn only one day after Max's return to London from Scotland. A series of communications from Pasqual, Max's ex-SOE sergeant in Saint Quentin, had informed

Blackthorn that the Gestapo and SS had purged the Dieppe area to the south of Saint Quentin looking for Paul's captors. They'd gone door to door in every village and town, had snatched people from the streets and from their homes and used them as hostages for information, but they had not gone anywhere near the Parisian outskirts where Duguay's base of operations was located.

Max had learnt that Blackthorn and Heller had made a deal after they'd read Klara's initial report. In it, Blackthorn had offered to supply an asset from SOE to track down Duguay and his Communists, and once again, offer them British collaboration if Heller would lend SOE the Westland Lysander aircraft for the mission. Blackthorn had been livid when he'd discovered that Heller had used Max in the covert operation they'd agreed upon. But despite his vitriolic threats to put Max on a charge and report Heller to the Foreign Office, Blackthorn had relented at the last minute, giving Max a mundane job in SOE's basement along with a verbal warning to Heller, which had gone no further than the two men.

Max, though he'd hidden his feelings well at the time, had been ecstatic to hear that Paul had made it back to his unit unscathed. He was, however, saddened and remorseful about the deaths of innocent French men and women, which had been caused by his and Paul's actions.

The news of Paul's escape and return to the Wehrmacht had been confirmed by Heller's agent. He'd been sent to France in the aftermath of Max's failed mission to develop relations with Duguay, who had threatened to kill Max if he ever showed his face in France again.

Max paid the waitress and left the café to face the bitter cold outside. It was only three days before Christmas and in the best British tradition, decorations were strung between lampposts and above shop doors. Selfridges had also gone all out this year, he noted, looking down the street. The English had stuck two fingers up at Göring and his Luftwaffe who had failed in their ambition to reduce London to ashes. Just about every building still standing in Central London was making a statement, and it was a simple one: "We're still here, you Nazi bastards!"

Max jumped at the sound of a car horn at the corner of Broadway near St James's Park Underground Station. The driver waved him over and he walked hesitantly towards Blackthorn's vehicle. He'd not seen his boss for five weeks.

"Get in," Bernie Blackthorn snapped. "It's bloody freezing."

Max opened the passenger door nearest the kerb and slid into the back seat next to Blackthorn.

"I take it you're on your way to the airport, Vogel?" Blackthorn asked.

"Yes, sir. Thanks for letting me in on this meeting. I'm feeling more like my old self again."

"Old, new, I don't care how you feel. If I'd had my way, I'd have locked you up in that basement and thrown away the key." Blackthorn shot daggers at Max, leaving him in no doubt that he'd still not been forgiven.

"I'm sorry. I…" Max muttered.

"A Polish Government official will be at the meeting," Blackthorn interrupted Max's apology. "The Poles want this Romek Gabula for themselves, but I'm betting Jonathan Heller will have him. He usually gets what he wants."

Blackthorn paused and instructed his driver to go straight to the airport.

Max, glad he didn't have to take the train, trod lightly with his next words, "I haven't spoken to Heller, but he probably thinks he has first dibs. He recruited Romek before the war began, and I suppose he's loath to let him go anywhere else."

"Hmm, you may be right. Even so, I'll put my case forward for SOE."

Blackthorn offered Max a cigarette. The air inside the car was blue already with smoke, but he accepted nonetheless.

"You know the Pole better than anyone else, Max. Were you surprised to hear he was coming to London?" Blackthorn asked.

"Surprised and sceptical."

"You're not the only one. His arrival in Britain has sent the intelligence services into a tail spin. What's he like, as a person?"

Max chuckled. "He has a flair for the dramatic. He's conceited, flamboyant, and loves nothing better than to hold an audience spellbound with his exaggerated stories of heroism. He enjoys being the centre of attention. He's a showman, a bit of a smug bugger when he wants to be. I don't know why he's here, but he'll relish telling us."

"You don't trust him?" Blackthorn looked surprised.

"I didn't say that. He's always proved loyal in the past, but this … I can't put my finger on it. If you don't mind, I'll reserve judgement until after I've spoken to him."

Blackthorn puffed repeatedly on his cigarette until the ash fell on his coat. He brushed it off and said, "We've had our ups and downs, Max, but you're wasted in that basement. We need you back." Blackthorn sighed as he looked out of the window. "I've received more intelligence on the aftermath of your cocked-up mission."

Max tensed. "As I said, I am very sorry about it all…"

"Oh, shut up with the apologies, Vogel, and listen. The consensus among the Saint Quentin Resistance group, which lost two of its members to the Gestapo, by the way, is that Paul must have passed on false information to the Germans. Why, Pascual didn't say or doesn't know, but your brother's information led to the deaths of at least thirty people in the Dieppe area, most of them civilians with no ties to the Resistance at all – scapegoats, that's all they were."

Max, unwilling to give his opinion or views on why Paul had guided the Germans to Dieppe when he must have known he'd been held nowhere near the northern town, asked, "Does this mean Duguay is back in business?"

"Yes, and he has requested Marine as his liaison officer."

Max shook his head. "The man's got gumption, I'll say that for him. But he can whistle for her. She's going to Poland."

"No, she's not. She's dropped out of the Polish course."

Max swallowed. "She failed?"

"Yes – no – it was her choice. Said she wasn't cut out for the Polish Home Army. She requested a transfer to F Section."

"Will you take her back?"

"Damn right, I will. She's a good asset despite her shaky past. She's familiar with the Paris area and knows Duguay better than anyone else we might send. Anyway, Colonel Baranoski of the Polish section was always against the idea of having female agents on his front lines. He wants to wait until they've got a tighter grip on things in Warsaw."

"She wants to go back to France?" Max mumbled, still coming to terms with the news. He'd been an ass to her in Scotland and hadn't been in touch with her since that final cold goodbye in the classroom. He had struggled to understand his feelings that day. Beautiful as always, still herself with the brightest of smiles and shining, love-lit eyes, she had been for him no more than a mishmash of sweet memories soured by lies and betrayal. It had been a wonderful, heady affair at the time, but it had lost its allure; tarnished by the ugliness of war and events that had brought out the worst in him. His decision stood, and though he still felt the void in his heart, he also felt strangely liberated from the tangled mess they'd once got themselves into.

"She's already on her way to him, Max, so don't even think about contacting her again – you hear me?"

"Yes, I understand, sir. No contact."

Chapter Twenty-Two

Romek Gabula

London, December 1941

Romek had arrived from Madrid openly carrying one small leather valise but hiding an array of secret treasures on his person and clothes. Secret documents containing the Abwehr questionnaire were concealed inside the sole of his left shoe. Another two pieces of paper giving targets and their locations were in a knotted condom up his backside. Two crystals to make the radio transmitter nestled in the heels of his shoes. A small bottle of special ink was concealed inside a jar of cold cream. His combustible notebook, which contained film that would ignite when triggered by his pencil, was in his jacket breast pocket looking perfectly innocent to the untrained eye. He was also in possession of a cyanide pill, which was dug deep inside a fake tooth; it was a necessary evil, he'd been told, but vital if things went badly.

Before reaching customs, Romek had been picked up by British officers who'd recognised him from the MI6 records that Heller had sent over. Romek, assuming he'd been expected, had volunteered his name before being asked a single question and was immediately escorted to a military style detention complex.

Left alone in an interview room furnished with a table and two chairs but no windows, Romek rehearsed his story for the forthcoming interview with British Intelligence. His handler, Matador, had said it was all about strategic deception before going into his homily about how to be a good spy. "You're a performer now. You must play your role even when you think you are alone, or with a person you believe you can trust. Never be Romek Gabula – always be Cicero. Cicero is your name and your mission in life is to serve the Abwehr."

Romek had been relieved but not surprised that his arrival had been anticipated. He'd agreed with his handler in Madrid that he should use his French connections to inform the English of his impending arrival. By doing that, he might avoid invasive body searches and a barrage of unwanted questions. Matador had, after the brief discussion, deployed one of his Abwehr agents, in the guise of a French Resistance fighter, to inform the French rebels on the Spanish-French border about Romek's travel details. The Rebels had been told that Romek was afraid to leave Madrid for fear of being captured by German agents.

Once detained in London, the customs officer had told Romek that he wasn't going to be arrested, searched or questioned until the appropriate authorities arrived. The officer had not articulated to which authorities he was referring, and Romek hadn't asked. He surmised they would include MI6, which meant he might see Max; that backstabbing, wife-stealing bastard who'd get his comeuppance at the appropriate time.

Romek's nerves were tingling with apprehension, and compounding his fear was the struggle with his conscience. That he was working for the enemy was evident. But he'd accepted his Abwehr role because he was, in his mind, as much a prisoner of Germany now as he had been in Fresnes Prison in France. The only difference was that these new German chains would, in theory, allow him to make a life for himself and save his Polish family from harm.

During his training with the Abwehr, Romek had been given the task of memorising a list of questions to which the Germans wanted answers. He was also subjected to fake interrogations to make sure his false story would hold up. Matador had told him to stick as close to the truth as possible, which Romek found difficult to achieve when under pressure. He had also been coached in speaking slowly to cover any hesitations, and that had also been hard for him as he tended to have a high, accelerated voice whenever he was nervous or under stress, and especially when he lied.

Romek had decided on the plane that the less he said the better. If he gave the British too much information about his time on the run in France and his stay in Spain, he might get questions he would rather avoid. If he were honest, he'd spent as much time picturing himself with a gun in his hand shooting Max's handsome, double-crossing face than he had thinking about how his *friend* would react to seeing him in Britain. Within five minutes of his arrival, that *gówienko* – piece of shit, Max, would confirm that Romek Gabula was a good, loyal Resistance fighter and give him a glowing report. Romek in his new role, would be equally complimentary about the treacherous pig.

While thinking about all the terrible things he'd like to do to Max, Romek's mind wandered to the British Intelligence Service and how they might react should he reveal his true mission. They might see him as the enemy, even execute him as a spy, or lock him up, throw away the key, and let him rot for the duration of the war. Or maybe they'd give him a decent welcome, a house, money, and a career as a double agent. He knew from his disastrous experience with Oscar that such two-faced people existed. He'd like to betray the Abwehr while coining in the money they were going to send him for living expenses, but if they were to discover his duplicity, they'd kill him and his family in Warsaw. This was the hardest dilemma he had ever faced.

Two hours and half a cup of disgusting British tea later, Romek was taken to another room where Max and three other men were waiting. Romek's heart pounded, his pulse raced, and he was dry and could hardly swallow. He should have drunk the tea. His time in the detention room had unhinged his resolve and his courage with it.

Romek's first instinct was to behave in a formal and polite way when seeing Max, but that plan was taken out of his hands when Max rushed forwards and gave him a bear hug. Matador's words about him being an actor came to Romek's mind and he began his portrayal without knowing his lines or how the scene would play out. This was no longer a rehearsal, but the performance of his life.

"Max, my old friend. I've never been happier to see a familiar face. I feel safe for the first time in over two years." He gave Max a hefty pat on the back then drew away. "My God, it's good to see you again."

Max gestured to the other men present. "First things first, Romek. Let me introduce you to my colleagues. They've been looking forward to meeting you."

Romek searched the faces of the other men seated at the conference table. His eyes settled first on the Polish army captain. The soldier, so very tall that his head towered above the man next to him, had a long, clean-shaven face, and had what Romek would describe as a mean-spirited gaze – not the friendliest-looking fellow.

"Welcome to Britain on behalf of the Republic of Poland's government in exile. I am Captain Bazyli Kaczka of the Polish 1st Grenadier Division."

"Thank you, Captain. It's a relief to be here," Romek responded in Polish.

"This is Jonathan Heller." Max indicated the second man in the room. "He is Section Chief of the British Secret Service, MI6 division."

Romek felt a twinge of guilt as he stared at the man wearing a grey pinstriped suit. He was number two on the Abwehr's list of targets; the man to whom Romek was to get as close as possible. This was easy, he thought. Not three hours in the country and they were all in the same room.

Romek then turned to the third stranger. Dressed as a British major, he eyed Romek from his chair. No hand-shaking, no welcoming smile.

"You don't need to know my name just yet," said Bernie Blackthorn.

Kaczka began the interview in Polish with a series of questions about Warsaw: what was Romek's job before the war, his home address, his marital status, and the names of family members? He also tested Romek's authenticity by asking him to give Warsaw street locations, the names of restaurants he might have frequented, and the floor plan of the German Embassy where he had worked for years.

Next, Romek was invited to talk about his time in France, and he gave a flawless recital, a glowing account of his work with the Resistance. Only when he described in detail the group's downfall, his incarceration in Fresnes Prison and his eventual escape into Spain, did he falter. The last part, which had been carefully rehearsed after hours of Abwehr coaching, sounded false and weak even to his own ears, but he pushed on nevertheless until a middle-aged woman wheeled a tea trolley into the room. Romek pulled a face, the only honest gesture he'd accomplished all day. He'd already decided he didn't like the typical English beverage.

"Before we continue, tell me, Max. Where is my wife?" Romek asked with a straight face.

Max's discomfort was laughable, but Romek was too damn angry with his old friend to find his hesitation amusing.

"You do know where she is?" Romek repeated his question.

"In France where you left her." Max casually crossed his legs. "She's all right. That's all I can tell you. You understand … security and all that?"

Romek nodded. "But you've seen her? You can tell me if you think she's safe in Paris or in danger from the Gestapo and SS, can't you? After all, she is my wife, the woman I love. You know that better than anyone, Max."

"We can't say any more about one of our agents until you've been fully vetted," Heller said, coming to Max's rescue.

During the short pause that followed, Romek managed to glance at one of the pages in the open file sitting across from him and in front of Kaczka. Though the writing was upside down, familiar names jumped from the paper: Darek Lukaszewicz, Florent Duguay and Marine, the code name for Klara, followed by dates and places. He opened his mouth to speak but then snapped it shut as Max and the two Englishmen rose and abruptly left the room, leaving their tea behind. Kaczka, however, lingered in his chair and lit a cigarette, signalling that he wasn't finished with Romek yet.

"Our Polish Headquarters could do with an experienced man like you, Romek," Kaczka said after sipping his tea from the green government-issue teacup. "I'm sure we'll find something useful for you to do."

Romek was wary. The Pole's friendliness was forced and unnatural, like the Germans' attempt at being nice to the French in Paris. While speaking, his eyes had flicked to Romek's hands as if he were watching for signs of nervousness; a tremor, a clenching of fists. The young captain also reminded him of one of the mock interrogators in Madrid who'd oozed charm one minute and was antagonistic the next. He knew the game more than Kaczka could possibly imagine, and – more disturbing – the others, including Max, had upped and left the room without a word or explanation, as if their exit had been rehearsed beforehand and the tea had been the signal. Had they left him with the Captain for some sinister reason yet to unfold? Or was this about him being asked to join the Polish campaigns?

"Is there anything you would like to ask me?" Kaczka asked, surprising Romek.

Romek pointed to the file left by the British officer. "Yes, this. If you already knew everything about me from that report, why were you testing my loyalty to the Allies and trying to confirm I was from Warsaw? I've already proven myself."

"If we, and by that I am referring to the Polish Security Service, didn't test the loyalty of every Pole who came into this country, we wouldn't be doing our job properly. We're satisfied that your escape was genuine, but you will still have to earn our trust … *my* trust."

He picked up the file. "There's a story about you in there, Romek, and I'm duty bound to find out if it's fact or fiction. That might seem straightforward to you, but it really isn't that hard for a person to fabricate events or places or to feign loyalty to one's enemy. More than once, I've heard men proclaim their devotion to the Allies only to find out that they're being paid in German Reichsmarks to spy on us."

Romek exuded confidence. He wasn't just a man who'd walked in off the street. He knew what he was doing. "Max and his associates will collaborate everything that's in that file. It was

MI6 that probably gave you the information about me in the first place, and it's safe to assume you read everything in it before I even got here." He turned to look at the door. "I don't know where they've gone, but if you're waiting for me to deny my heroic acts in France, you'll be getting pins and needles in your arse. I'm everything those pages say about me: loyal, trustworthy, diligent, and the Germans' worst enemy."

The Captain sniggered. "Well said, but it's not your level of loyalty to the French Resistance in Paris that concerns me. It's what you did after you escaped from Fresnes prison. That part of your story isn't in the file, is it?"

"I'm not following..."

"Then let me explain. According to you, every member of your Resistance group was apprehended and later transported to Germany, yet you escaped from a German military transport and managed to evade further capture. You then made your way back to the French Resistance who helped get you into Spain. You spent almost eight weeks in Madrid with no money, but despite that obstacle you managed to arrange for another French Resistance fighter to travel back to the Spanish-French border to inform yet another Resistance cell that you were coming to Britain – Romek, you're either a very lucky man, or you've been turned by the Germans – which is it?"

Romek choked. "You think I'm an enemy spy?"

"My job is to presume that everyone I meet is a spy until proven otherwise. As I said, you will have to earn my trust, and thus far, you haven't done that, not by a long shot."

Romek had been convinced that his record in France would be more than enough to endear him to both the British and Polish authorities. Kaczka's well-founded suspicions, however, threw his Abwehr interrogation training out the window. "You, a pen-pusher, are lecturing me on trust?" he blustered as his burning skin turned crimson. "You were probably sitting behind a desk wearing your fancy military uniform that's probably never seen a battlefield while I was fighting the Boche in enemy territory. I've been tortured, hunted, and shot at. I've lost good men and women to concentration camps. I lost my wife because of my commitment to the Resistance. I lived alone in Madrid, starving and sleeping under bridges ... I risked everything to get here because I want to carry on the fight. And you, a bureaucrat, suggest I might be working for the Nazis ... fuck off, Captain!"

Romek, shaking with fury, got to his feet and looked down at the Pole. "Why don't you get off your backside and try a spot of fighting instead of questioning those of us who have done their fair share of it?"

With a stony face, Kaczka got to his feet, picked up a drab brown walking stick, and headed for the door.

Romek gaped when he noticed the limp, the false foot, and, on closer inspection, the ridge of a prosthetic leg connected at the thigh.

"I lost it at Dunkirk," said Kaczka, his hand on the door knob. "I'll be back with the others in a minute or two. Enjoy your tea, Romek."

Chapter Twenty-Three

Max Vogel

"Well, what do you think, Max?" Heller asked.

"I think he's not himself. He looked staged," Max answered, then he asked Captain Kaczka, "How did Romek know his Resistance fighters had been sent to concentration camps?"

"I don't know. He said it without being prompted."

Max frowned. "He couldn't have known that unless the Germans told him. I got the news from the Saint Quentin Resistance, and he was nowhere near that group's location. No, this is not right. We were friends, but he could hardly look me in the eye. Something's up."

"He's on the defensive, and as I said, he was aggressive. I agree with Major Vogel, he's hiding something," Kaczka said.

Max, Heller, Kaczka, and Blackthorn huddled together in a small office down the corridor from the conference room to discuss their initial meeting with Romek. The French Resistance in Spain had reported by radio transmission to Heller that Romek was arriving in Britain. But in a coded footnote they had added that a French Resistance member from Madrid had delivered the travel details, not Romek.

Heller said, "I wanted your personal thoughts before we got into any more discussions with Romek. I have reason to think he's tainted."

After Heller had shown the others a copy of the French Resistance's message, he continued, "This code at the bottom is used when an agent is suspected of colluding with the enemy. But this and my gut feeling are all I have to back up my theory."

Kaczka said, "He's just told me in there that he survived alone in Madrid, never spoke to another soul or had any help. So how did he employ another Resistance fighter to deliver the message at the Spanish border? He gave me no explanation when I questioned him about that."

"Let's not jump to conclusions," Max jumped in.

"I'm not happy, Max. He's either slipped up, or he's deliberately being sloppy. I want to have another go at him," Heller said, looking at Kaczka. "Captain, you and I will play our game. Max, you will stay quiet unless Romek speaks to you directly." Heller then said to Blackthorn, "Bernie, we'll take it from here. I'll keep you updated."

Bernie nodded his agreement. "Okay, but if he is clean, I want him."

"Get in the queue," Kaczka said.

The second part of the interview proceeded with Kazcka's aggressive questioning and Heller's fierce defence of Romek. It was common practice in the intelligence game to play two interrogators off against each other; the friendly chap going soft on the suspect versus the antagonistic cynic coming down like an iron rod. The strategy was used to make suspects feel as though they had someone in their corner, a defender, a shield against the rougher, tougher cross-examiner. Max had often remarked that this age-old playacting tactic was overused and predictable; a cliché, but it almost always got the required results.

Max was concerned about two things: Romek was unlike other refugees whose backgrounds were unknown. He already had ties with Britain, and on paper, should have been congratulated upon his arrival, not suspected of batting for the other side. But he *was* a suspect, and the more Heller stepped back to allow the more hostile Kaczka to rattle Romek, the more Romek appeared guilty of something. He was unnerved; his skin was beaded with sweat despite the unlit gas fire and freezing cold room. And he was being curt, to the point of rudeness when Kaczka asked him to answer questions he didn't seem to like.

"… Major Vogel, do you agree with me?" Heller was asking.

Max, so deep in thought he hadn't heard the most recent exchange, had no idea what to agree or disagree with. He looked at each man in turn, a little embarrassed. "I'm not quite sure what to think, yet," he said.

"Oh, come on, Max. You know I'm right. He should stick to what he's good at," Heller said. "You're a spy at heart, and a damn good one, aren't you, Romek?"

"Yes, I am good. I was born for this job. Sending me to Poland or putting me in a uniform as Captain Kaczka has suggested would be a waste of my talents."

Romek's eyes narrowed as he stared defiantly at his fellow Pole. "I will serve MI6, or I will do nothing at all. I've lost everything and everyone I ever cared about, the least you can do is settle me in Britain with Mr Heller, who is the only man here not to have abandoned me."

"You've been given a free rein for too long, Gabula," Kaczka snapped "You're deluded about your own self-importance, so let me remind you that contrary to what Mr Heller says about you having a choice, you will do as you're told or be deported back to where you came from. As a Pole, you are expected to help liberate *our* country before France or Holland, or any other occupied territory. And the only way you can do that is by following your government's orders, not Mr Churchill's."

"Get off your high horse, Captain," Romek sneered at Kaczka. "I'm not in the Polish army, or what's left of that rag-tag useless bunch of refugees. I'm a free man and *I'll* choose where to put my talents to good use, not you or your pretend government sitting in their fancy offices in London."

At first, Max had assumed that Romek's brusque personality change had everything to do with his recent traumatic experiences and nothing to do with his present situation. But he'd now concluded that the honest man he'd known in France was not the one sitting opposite him. He *was* on the defensive, distracted, and at times jumpy, as though waiting for someone to walk in the door to arrest him. But Romek was more than this unrecognisable nervous wreck; he was a clever man, not the petty, blustering fool he was portraying. Max could only conclude, therefore, that Romek was deliberately opening himself up to suspicion and *wanted* to be caught.

"… he'll be sent back to Poland to fight with the Underground. His experience will be invaluable." Kaczka stood now as though to leave.

Romek shot to his feet, fists tight in anger. "I want to stay in Britain. I *want* to be a spy."

Max's eyes bored into Romek's, and in them, he saw a plea for help. "Captain Kaczka, Mr Heller, might I have a word with you in private?"

******

Romek choked on the water, gasping for air when it went down the wrong way. His pulse was racing and all he could manage were short, sharp breaths. *Was he having a heart attack?* The Germans had warned him of British intelligence tactics, how they charmed and snaked their way under their victims' skins until they peeled away the deceit and secrets. This wasn't an interview; it was an interrogation being expertly conducted by Heller's flattery and Kaczka's appeals for patriotism. All their talk of how wonderful and sought-after he was had probably been a prearranged act to lower his guard.

He'd handled hard, probing questions with ease under the Abwehr's watchful eyes in Madrid, but this was a different beast. Heller and the Pole were working in tandem, toying with him, at times goading, concerned, attentive, manipulative. German spies in Britain would have to be absolutely dedicated to their cause to succeed – lying, cheating, killing, and stealing information could only be done well when it was achieved with great commitment, without conscience or regret. He'd reached that state of mind in Paris, but only because his heart had been in what he was doing. His cause had been just and pure. He couldn't say the same about this smutty game of subterfuge against the British. His guilt was killing him, and his hatred for the Abwehr was far stronger than his fear of telling the truth and facing the consequences. Traitor be damned – the Germans could piss off!

He heard footsteps and stared at the door. They'd be back any minute; Heller, desperate to have him on his team, the brave Captain Kaczka, a man he admired for his devotion to duty despite losing a leg at Dunkirk, and Max, who had already noticed that something wasn't quite right with his old friend.

Romek fidgeted in his chair as the men traipsed back in and took their seats. He glanced at Max, who was staring back at him with eyes black with suspicion – the hypocrite, the liar, the man who had betrayed their friendship by having sex with his wife in *his* bed. He'd get to Max another time.

He sniggered, knowing the game was up. "Look at you three, sitting there, caught up in this little charade of yours, waiting for me to confirm what Max already suspects."

Heller's eyes shot to Max, and Romek chuckled again. Sweet liberation. The truth would set him free or have him locked up before 13:00; either scenario would be better than being a Nazi whore. "Here's the thing. I really don't want to play this game with you. My heart's not in it. I feel dirty, and somewhere between our first and second interview, I decided not to pursue other people's goals when mine are completely different." Romek paused to meet Max's eyes again. "You remember my cousin and his pregnant wife, Max? You met them in Warsaw on the night of the German invasion."

"Yes?" said Max, eyebrows raised.

"Well, it seems I've got my family in a spot of bother with the Germans. They have me up against a wall."

"Who are you working for?" Max asked.

"Ah, so I was right. You already suspected," said Romek, surprised by Max's calm restraint.

"Of course, I did."

Like a man about to entertain friends with a good story, Romek sat back in his chair and finally relaxed. "I was approached by the Abwehr while I was in Fresnes Prison. They offered me a deal, which they said would save my thirty fighters from execution and my family from death. And I, being a loyal man to those I care about, agreed to become an Abwehr agent even though my stomach heaved, and I wanted to reach over the table to choke the life out of the smug Nazi bastard sitting across from me."

Heller's shoulders heaved as he removed his glasses and placed them gently on the table. Max appeared unruffled. Kaczka looked furious.

Romek swallowed. He was about to throw all his cards on the table at once, knowing he had a bad hand and no aces up his sleeve. "I have come to Britain with the Abwehr's expectation that I will spy for them. Let me show you?"

Romek stunned the men by taking off his shoes and producing two radio transmitter crystals from his heels. He then tore away the soles and retrieved the questionnaire on specific English targets. "I have other documents, but I'd have to go up my arse to get them…"

Three bemused faces stared back at him. "My principal mission for the Germans was to report on aircraft production in this country. I also agreed to use the contacts I would develop among Polish and British leaders." He waved a hand around the room. "You three perhaps? I was then to report any high-level political information I might come across."

He took a measured sip of water. "I also had a more farsighted assignment, which was to foment discontent among the Polish armed forces, and if possible, organise a new Polish column that would be sympathetic to Germany. Why they thought I would have the power or know-how to manage that, I really don't know, but I can tell you they were very insistent that I would soon be joined by many more German agents on this island."

Romek stared at Kaczka, holding the captain's eyes, as he said, "The Abwehr went as far as to hint that their agents were already embedded in the Republic of Poland's government in exile. Right here in London, Captain."

Kaczka shot Romek a contemptuous glare, but behind his anger was a flash of surprise. "Go on."

"My Abwehr handler in Madrid, the man who trained me, was very clear that if I didn't fulfil my obligations to Germany, the Gestapo would execute my family in Warsaw, whom they said were already in their hands … shoot them between their eyes one by one with the children dying first so the adults could watch, they specifically said." Romek looked at his ripped-apart shoes. "I love my family, and I despise the German pigs who think they own me now. I don't … never did want to work for them … and I would have told you all this, if not now, then tomorrow or the day after. I could *not* have gone through with it."

With all the cockiness drained out of him, he added, "My goal, my *only* goal, is to persuade you three to accept me as a double agent, and to let me do all I can to destroy the Nazis' plans for me and my family. And I will do whatever you ask of me. Without any qualms. I will murder, lie, and cheat my German handler with false information. If you'll have me, I will give you my loyalty and my life – here, on this piece of paper – see that? It's the address of my safe house. It's run by a German woman who works for the Abwehr. My first job will be to get her for you."

Romek paused, then flicked his eyes to Heller. "I want Max to handle this…"

"You're not in a position to make demands!" Kaczka shouted. "I could shoot you today, and no one would bat an eyelid!"

"Hear him out, Bazyli. He hasn't spied on anyone yet," Heller said.

"Thank you, Mr Heller." Romek gave Max a sideways glance. "I will be the best double agent you've ever recruited, but if you want the best from me you have to give me the best to work with. Not a Pole, not another British spy, but Max. He's the only man I trust."

For the next half hour, Romek took the men through his training regime, holding nothing back and even going as far as to talk about his fling with a Spanish woman who had made his life a bit easier in Madrid. Finally, he put his fingers in his mouth and took out the false tooth with the cyanide capsule inside. When he stopped talking, he stared long and hard at Max. "Now you see the real Romek, don't you?"

******

Max, Heller, and Kaczka left Romek in the conference room under guard and retreated to Heller's office. Romek's bombshell had hit Max hard, but he was not as shocked as Kaczka, who had earlier planned to go out on a limb for Romek by recommending that he receive a commendation for his work in France.

The three men, scrambling to make decisions, found themselves at odds with each other. Max maintained that Romek hated the Germans with every ounce of his being and that he'd make a highly effective double agent. Romek had asked that he be given the chance to prove himself in that role, which demonstrated that he had thought long and hard about committing himself to the most dangerous section of the spy business; that of playing for both sides. He had also given the address of a German safe house, a treasure for British Intelligence. Heller, however, seemed sceptical of the whole matter and wanted time to think about the best way to move forward.

"Romek vowed in there that his aim is to help us, but he must have sworn the same oath to the Germans," Heller said. "And if the Abwehr trust him enough to get him to Britain, what's to stop him from forming some sort of triple-cross? He's certainly a more sinister individual than you or I ever thought, Max."

"True. But convincing the Nazis of his loyalty doesn't mean he planned to hold up his end of the bargain. I believe him,

Jonathan," said Max. "I don't think he ever intended to go through with this. His feeble attempt to hide his guilt was more like him giving me a sign that he was in trouble. Romek is no fool, trust me, he wanted us to know. He probably just didn't know how to tell us."

"Well, what are we going to do with him today?" Kaczka asked.

"You can take him into custody," Heller suggested.

"No. I don't want him near the Polish headquarters. If what he said is true about there being Abwehr spies in our offices, I will need to clean house. Romek was your man in France, Jonathan. You fix this."

Max had another alternative. "Bazyli, Jonathan, your choice is simple. You can imprison him as an enemy agent or you can use him to cause havoc for the Germans. Might I suggest that we agree to take him on but keep him under close watch? We can tap his telephone, monitor his correspondence, and have an MI6 handler with him in the Abwehr's own safe house."

Heller stood up. "No. We're finished here, at least for today. If Bazyli doesn't want him, we'll take him to our holding cells at MI6 and pick this up again tomorrow morning."

"Very well," Kaczka agreed. "Does eight o'clock suit you?"

Max had trouble keeping up with Heller as he strode along the corridor to where two subordinates had been waiting for orders. "What the hell was that all about? Why did you leave in the middle of it?" Max asked before they'd reached Heller's men.

Heller slowed down. "If we take Romek on, MI5 and MI6 will be forced to share an unacceptable amount of classified information with the Polish authorities. More than we have in the past." He stopped walking. "Having British or German nationals as double agents is one thing, but Romek is still answerable to his

Polish exiled government who will want to know what we and the Germans are doing with him. I need to go higher with this one, and if we *are* given the green light to take him, and he still insists on working with you, you will have to leave SOE and come back to MI6. Have you considered that?"

"No. But if you think he's important, and Blackthorn agrees, then yes, I'll return," Max said, surprised by his own eagerness.

"You should never have left in the first place," Heller grumbled, walking ahead. "Go home, Max. Think about what you'll be getting into. Think about what it'll be like being a twenty-four-hour babysitter to a man who's been trained by our enemies. I'll see you in my office in the morning – and before you ask, I will clear your return to MI6 with the Foreign Office and Blackthorn – Christ, he's going to love this."

"What about the German woman?"

"I'll put surveillance on her immediately. Let's see if she leads us to other enemy agents before we arrest her."

"We could put Romek in there with her?"

"We could, but I'd rather get rid of her and replace her with one of my people."

Heller got to his office door. "Get some rest, Max," he repeated. "This has been a good day."

***** *

After spending four hours in the flats' garden bunker during a ferocious air raid, Max had gone back to his room blue with cold. The silly gits who managed the building had forgotten to take gas for the bunker's heater and lamps, and he'd sat in his pyjamas and dressing gown in a black, wood-panelled shelter with neighbours, including an elderly widow from next door who'd peed herself and farted for England. God bless her old gums.

Life twisted and turned on a sixpence, he thought, still shivering in bed and unable to get warm. The previous morning, he'd pictured a clear path forward with SOE, a new beginning and perhaps another overseas posting coming up for him. But as much as he loved his job, he now found the prospect of working with Romek more appealing than spy work on foreign shores. Handling a double agent was tricky, challenging in the extreme but highly rewarding when handled right. He'd be mad to turn it down, despite Romek's thinly veiled digs at him when he'd enquired about Klara during the initial interview. Was it possible that he'd found out about the affair? No, Romek would have punched him in the face.

Max lay on his back and stretched out his hand for his cigarettes on the bedside table, felt the lamp stand and then heard it crash to the floor. It was so dark, he couldn't even see the damned black-out curtains.

He rolled over again, the cigarettes forgotten, and felt a quiver of excitement and the warning that went with it. No point planning anything in wartime, his inner voice told him. One minute he was going somewhere and the next he was on a path travelling in a different direction. No use projecting what his future might look like, or what people might do, or who was in his life and who would leave it.

Paul came to mind, leaving Max with mixed emotions. He was over the moon that his twin was safe, but he couldn't seem to get rid of his disappointment. They would get over this bad patch between them, eventually, but in the meantime, he wasn't going to contact Paul again.

Klara replaced Paul in Max's thoughts, making him groan. His body was tired, but his mind was still active. What was Klara to him now? he wondered. A beautiful memory? The woman he would always love, the one who'd got away in the chaos and cruelty of war, or someone who would forever leave a bitter taste in his mouth?

He punched the pillow, frustrated at not being able to sleep, then he slipped his hand under it and retrieved his torch. To hell with this carry on, he'd have a cup of tea.

Chapter Twenty-Four

Max was looking forward to spending Christmas Eve and Christmas day with his mother and father. Heller's orders that he deliver classified correspondence to Dieter by hand, had come as a complete surprise. The letter was urgent, Heller had said, and he didn't want to send it by military post, nor with anyone else.

Max spent most of the train journey to Bletchley Park in Buckinghamshire, thinking about Romek. He was still in MI6 custody in London and would remain their prisoner until the British reached an agreement with the head of Polish Intelligence about what to do with him.

Max's prediction that he'd be re-joining MI6 as Romek's handler had almost immediately come to pass, leading Max to believe that a deal for Romek had already been struck. Max's transfer had not been smooth, however, for it had caused a full-blown argument between Blackthorn and Heller behind closed doors. Blackthorn had argued that Max was not a toy to be passed back and forth between sections. SOE had invested money in him, and it was not willing to let him go at a time when experienced agents were needed in occupied Europe. Heller had reminded Blackthorn that Max was an MI6 agent on loan to SOE, and therefore, not Blackthorn's property to begin with.

When he'd been given the chance to speak, Max had been honest with both men. He would miss SOE and the hands-on approach behind enemy lines, but he would return to that section as soon as Romek no longer posed a security threat. With this, he'd placated Blackthorn.

Heller had already agreed to make the transfer temporary but had later reneged, somewhat, when he'd pointed out that Max was going to work with Romek and his challenging situation for however long it might take to defeat Germany. He'd added that the Pole was a wild card and not completely trustworthy because of his earlier promises to the Abwehr and his concern for his family in Poland.

Another troublesome question for Heller had been whether the Germans would fully trust Romek because of his previous association with the British in France, again putting forward the idea that Max was probably the only man who'd be able to see signs of deceit and subterfuge. If Max had to spend the rest of the war by Romek's side, then so be it, he'd repeated numerous times.

Max walked the short distance from the train station to the row of terraced house in the village near Bletchley Park. He was carrying three bags, two of which were full of family Christmas presents that he'd hastily purchased the day before, including one for Judith Weber. Laura was going to Scotland to spend New Year with Hannah and Frank and would take their presents with her. The third bag contained a change of clothes and toilet bag, as he planned to stay two nights with his parents.

"Darling, this is the best Christmas present ever," Laura told Max, after kissing him in the hallway.

He looked past his mother to Judith Weber. Before Max had left London, Heller had informed him that the German girl had recently joined Laura and Dieter after accepting a job in Bletchley's decoding and translation section. She was a welcome surprise, and Max found himself unable to peel his eyes away from her. Beautiful, in a festive red dress with a white frilly apron and a sparkling tinsel bow in her black hair, she looked like a shining angel in the dimly lit passageway; a cliché, perhaps, but precisely how he saw her. "Hello, Judith. How are you?"

She gave him a demure smile as she walked towards him, and he wondered if his face were as flushed as hers. He cleared his throat and asked Laura, "Where's Papa?"

"Your father will be home shortly," Laura replied, looking first at Judith and then at Max. "I'm very busy in the kitchen, darling. Why don't you be a love and take Judith for a walk. The poor girl never gets any exercise except when she walks up to Bletchley Park in the morning and comes home at … whatever time that is. Honestly, Max, she'll make herself ill working all the hours God sends."

"Do you feel all right, Judith?" Max asked.

"Yes, I like my job. It hardly feels like work at all."

"Don't listen to her. She's working six days a week," Laura grumbled. "The other day she left here at three thirty in the afternoon and didn't return until after midnight. And sometimes she doesn't even start until midnight."

Max, his feet barely in the door and still holding the bags, smiled at his mother's concern. She was clearly very fond of Judith, who was now clasping and unclasping her hands at her waist in a sweet, innocent gesture that melted his heart.

"Tell you what, Mother, let me put these bags down before I go out," he suggested.

"Oh, yes, of course, darling. I didn't mean to rush you."

Max put the presents in the living room, looked longingly at the blazing fire, and wished he didn't have to go out in the cold again.

"Right, off you go, you two," said Laura, waiting for him at the front door with Judith's coat already in her hand. "You can have a nice chat on your walk while I finish peeling the potatoes."

Max shot a warning glance to his mother not to embarrass him. She had apparently seen his admiration for Judith and was trying her hand at matchmaking. She was out of her depth with him, he thought. The last thing he needed was another romantic entanglement.

He set Heller's envelope on the hall table and said, "Make sure Papa sees that when he gets home, will you, Mother? Jonathan said it's important." He then helped Judith with her coat while wondering whether his mother had tried to partner up Judith and Paul when he'd taken Judith to the Berlin house. He thought not. His mother was a romantic at heart, but she wouldn't have wanted her son to get involved with a Jewish woman in Germany no matter how much she liked the girl.

Five minutes after his arrival, Max and Judith were clumping across a field getting mud and cow dung on their shoes. He'd just had what was commonly known as the *bum's rush*. His mother hadn't even offered him a cup of tea.

"How is your English coming along, Judith?" he asked in German after a rather long silence.

"Better than last month. To be honest, I spend most of my time listening to and speaking German. Your mother is helping me. We speak English together at home."

Judith stopped at a stream, lifting her coat and skirt to jump to the other side. Max, when he'd joined her asked, "Are you happy?"

Her expression changed. She grew serious as though thinking about how to answer. "Yes. I suppose I am. This Christmas Eve has been hard for me. I couldn't stop … I was thinking…"

"I can't imagine how much you must miss your father and sister," said Max, instinctively knowing what was on her mind.

"Paul told me what happened to them. Do you want to talk about it?"

"No, thank you. I try not to think too often about my papa and Hilde. It hurts too much. I just say to myself every day, well, Judith, you're doing your bit to defeat the people who killed your sister and took your father, so put everything you have into it. That makes me feel better."

Max knew not to ask what she was doing at Bletchley Park. He surmised that she was listening to radio transmissions and reading correspondence, as were the other vetted exiles employed there. It was also possible that she was involved in detainee interviews in London. Since finding out that two German translators had lied during interviews with German defectors to deliberately mislead the MI6 agent, the section had ordered that a *silent* German speaker be present to report the translator's discrepancies, should there be any. People like Judith, who now spoke just enough English to get by, travelled from Bletchley to MI6, posing as secretaries. In the interviews, they took notes of questions being asked by the intelligence officer, and the German detainee's answers being repeated by the official German translator in English. Judith would be a good candidate for this sort of subterfuge; she was a young, pretty woman whose presence wouldn't threaten the official translator.

Judith slipped on a patch of grass, white with frost, and squealed as she fell backwards. Max pulled her up and then to him, but instead of letting her go when she'd righted herself, he continued to hold her. He stared at her face: her pink cheeks, the reddened tip of her nose, wide, watery brown eyes, and lips slightly parted in fright; her beauty captivated him.

Their heavy, misty breaths merged in the frigid air. Max, still mesmerised, drew her closer to him and in a moment of impulse, kissed her lips.

"Was I … I'm sorry … I was wrong to do that?" Max finally let her go and watched her run her hands down her coat fumbling with its buttons, which were already in their buttonholes. He'd had no intention of kissing her before the walk or while he'd been thinking about her job. This wasn't like him. He barely knew her and was stunned by his lack of control. He looked at her fawn-like eyes and blurted out, "I know I'm not Paul." *Damn it!* He could kick himself for saying that.

She smiled and touched his icy cheek with her gloved hand. "No, you're not Paul. I never thought you were. I never saw him the way I see you. The first time we met, I didn't think about your brother at all except for the few moments when we spoke about him … to ask how he was … you remember?"

"Yes, I remember."

She blinked. "Max, your brother saved my life and tried to help Hilde. He will always be in my heart. But you're … well, you might look like him and talk like him, but you are as different from each other as any two people could be." She lowered her head. "You must think I'm terribly forward, but I told myself that if I ever met you again I wouldn't be like one of those women who never say what they feel because they're afraid of being brazen or rejected." She touched his cheek again. "Life is precious to me, and so are moments like these."

They walked in silence, their gloved hands touching, until they had almost reached the wooden gate at the edge of the field, where Judith halted, put her hand on Max's arm and said, "I felt something between us in Scotland. Did you, Max? Did I imagine it?"

Max hesitated to answer both questions. He'd admired her looks, but he hadn't felt an immediate attraction to her. At that time, he'd been too busy planning his meeting with Klara the following day and trying to sort out his feelings for her. He still wasn't used to the strange sensation of thinking about her without the familiar ache in his stomach, the desire coursing through him, the want, the need, the frustration. She seemed a million miles away, like an object shrinking to nothing on the horizon. She was no longer cluttering his mind; it felt tidy, as clean as a mopped floor. He didn't know how else to describe his feelings. Was he fickle or just ready to move on? Was Judith so very special that he was forgetting Klara, or had his obsession for her finally run its course?

Coming back to the woman standing before him, he said, "You're beautiful, Judith, and you're strong and courageous. I was drawn to you, but in the spirit of honesty, I had a lot on my mind that night and..."

"No, please ... it's all right. Don't say anything else. I opened my mouth and that popped out. I won't mention our kiss or this conversation again. But I would like us to be good friends, Max. We can start there, can't we?"

He could stop this in its tracks, say yes, we can be friends, before it went any further, he thought, but he didn't want to. She was refreshing, like this brisk walk in the countryside without the London smog or deadly air raids. With her, he could breathe.

Damning the consequences, he leant in and kissed her again with a passion he'd thought lost for good. She felt wonderful; he was exactly where he was meant to be. "We can be friends, but we could also be more. Maybe, if you come to London, we could have dinner or go dancing. Would you like that...?"

"Yes, very much," she said, before he'd even finished the question

This time he kissed her forehead. "We should go back. My mother will be getting worried about us."

"Get in here, Max, now," Dieter grunted as soon as Judith and Max entered the house.

In Dieter's study, Max stood like a schoolboy in the headmaster's office without a clue as to what his crime had been. His father, scowling as he read aloud from the letter in his hand, finally looked up and threw the pages at Max.

"How could you keep this a secret from me?" Dieter demanded.

Max's face reddened, but he was in no mood for an argument. "Keep what a secret? What are you on about?"

"You've been deceitful, Max, that's what I'm on about. Why did you not tell your mother and I about Paul? About you running off to France without Blackthorn's permission to negotiate with the criminals who abducted your brother? He almost got himself killed and you didn't say a word to us. I had to find out like … this … then you lose your brother in a French forest!"

Max was furious, not because his father was yelling at him but because Heller had gone behind his back and spilled the beans before he'd had the chance to do it in his own way in his own time. "I was going to tell you…"

"Don't lie. You've known about this for weeks."

"What did Heller say?"

"You tell me." Dieter picked up the pages and went on to read another excerpt aloud.

Max gulped. Jonathan had been thorough. "What good would it have done to tell you about Paul when I didn't know at the time if he was alive or dead? Hmm, what would you have done?"

Laura opened the door and then slammed it shut behind her as she entered. "I can hear every word you two are saying from the kitchen, and so can Judith." She stood, hands on her hips as was her way when she was angry. "Your father showed me Jonathan's letter, but I want to hear it from your lips, Max, and you had better not leave anything out if you know what's good for you."

"Does it have to be right now? You know Paul's all right…"

"Max…"

"He's back at his base…"

"Max! *Halt die Klappe und hör' zu!* – shut up and listen!" Dieter stood up and clung to the desk as the veins in his neck bulged. "Did you tell Paul that I'm alive?"

"No. Absolutely not."

"Are you sure? Did you let it slip? Think!"

"Of course, I didn't let it *slip.* Why don't you believe me?"

"Kurt has been arrested."

Max slumped into a chair. "Oh, no. How did you…?"

"The point is, he's been taken by the Gestapo, and if they torture him he might give me away. He won't want to, but you know what they do to Jews like him … to anyone who opposes the Führer. If he talks, I'm finished, and so are your brothers – remember Leitner?"

Max raised an eyebrow. "Kurt is a Jew? Since when?"

"What do you mean since when? Since always, apparently," Laura snapped.

Max, as worried but slightly more confused than his father, asked, "Who arrested him? On what charge?"

"The Gestapo. Who do you think arrested him? The transmission from our mutual friend in Berlin was short on details, but it had to be Freddie Biermann."

Max presumed their *mutual friend* was Herr Brandt. "Papa, I'm sorry about Kurt, and I understand why you're worried, but I can only assert that I never said a word to Paul about you being alive. I presumed he got the notification of your death at the same time Willie did, but he and I didn't talk about family when I was in France. We hardly had time to talk at all. Mother, you said Biermann was writing to them both about father's death?"

"Yes, and I'm sure he kept his word. I just don't understand why he would arrest poor Kurt when he had nothing to do with anything."

Max got up and offered his mother the chair, then threw his father a scathing glance. "Father tell Mother the truth, the whole truth, including why I was in Berlin two summers ago. Tell her about Kurt's involvement in everything you did. If you don't I will."

Laura's eyes shot to her husband. "If my sons are in danger, I want to know *everything,*" she demanded.

Max went to the door.

"Get back here, Max!" Laura shouted, now turning her anger on her son. "If Kurt is tortured – oh, what a dreadful thought – but if he is, and he knows your father is alive, Wilmot will be targeted." Laura glared at Dieter, back to Max and then to Dieter again. "How could you leave Kurt in Berlin to deal with Freddie when you knew he was a Jew?"

"I ordered him to leave as soon as you did," Dieter mumbled.

Laura's eyes widened further. "Would Freddie torture Paul for information? Tell me the truth."

"No, of course not. Paul is his son-in-law."

"Max, do you think Paul will be all right?" Laura asked.

"Yes," Max said with less conviction. "To be honest, Mother, I've put up with enough drama surrounding Paul in the last couple of years to last a lifetime. I wanted to bring him back here to save the lives of men and women who are fighting Germans in France. But Paul wasn't having it. Oh, no, not him. He ran back to the Gestapo and pointed them in the direction of French Resistance fighters. Dozens of people were executed because of his betrayal, and God knows how many other innocents were imprisoned. Don't you worry about him, Mother, he's probably playing the hero now with his Nazi comrades and sticking his middle finger up at me."

"That's enough of that talk, young man!" Dieter shouted.

Max stormed out and bumped into Judith in the hallway. "I'm sorry … I'm sorry you had to hear that, Judith."

Laura appeared behind him with tears glinting in her eyes. "Let's not fall out over this. Your father wants to speak to you. I want to speak to you. Please, Son, let's not spoil Christmas."

Max looked at the two women and realised he must be scaring them to death. He turned to the half-open study door and nodded. There was more at stake than him keeping secrets from his parents, and his father who, it seemed, was still being dishonest with his wife. Max looked at Dieter who had come to the study door. Kurt, complicit in his father's escape from Germany and in the death of Captain Leitner of the Abwehr, now posed a serious threat to the Vogel family. Perhaps it was time to have a heart to heart with dear Papa.

"Okay, we'll talk, Mother, but only if Father promises to tell you the whole story."

Laura sniffed. "Yes, Dieter, you must. I'm tired of the lies in this family. I'd rather we ate burnt turkey than have any more secrets between us. I'm sick of it. I'm sick of everything. I miss my boys."

Chapter Twenty-Five

Paul Vogel

Berlin, Germany
January 1942

Freddie Biermann handed Paul a brandy then dropped with a sigh into an armchair. "I'm sorry you had to find out about your father and mother the minute you got back to Paris. I imagine you had enough on your plate to deal with after your terrible ordeal. It's my fault. I should have let Valentina tell you in a telephone call instead of writing to you, as I did with Wilmot. Her voice would have given you more comfort than my cold words on paper."

Paul, sitting on the couch with Valentina facing his in-laws, said, "It's all right, sir. It was good of you to let Wilmot and I know."

"I do wish you had telephoned me the minute you escaped from those terrible people who abducted you. I was frantic with worry," said Valentina, clinging to Paul's arm.

"I couldn't, darling. My privileges were revoked. I wasn't allowed to write to anyone or telephone Germany, although the Gestapo assured me at the time that they'd contact you on my behalf."

"Valentina, dear. Paul is a hero," Biermann said. "Because of him, some very bad people in France were punished. Don't tell him off for something he had no control over."

Paul, appreciating the warmth and affection from his wife and her parents, welled up. Never had he valued the love of family more than he did now. He wondered what his father-in-law would say if he knew about Max's part in his release? He trusted his wife's father and hated having to keep secrets from him.

After kissing Valentina on the cheek, Paul addressed Biermann. "To be honest, I don't see myself as a hero. Your people, the Gestapo in Avenue Foch, certainly didn't think I was one. They were sceptical of how I successfully got away from my captors. My interview with the Kriminalinspektor in Paris felt more like an interrogation."

"How dreadful for you," Olga Biermann grumbled. "How could they possibly have thought you wanted to be held prisoner by those murderers? Of course, you ran away from them. It was your duty to escape."

"The Gestapo were doing their job, Olga. They had to be thorough," Biermann reminded her.

"That's true, Frau Biermann. Apparently, I was the first abductee to make it back alive, and they had a hard time believing me," Paul continued. "I can understand their vigorous questioning now, but at the time I was reeling about the news of my father's death. I wasn't reacting well or thinking straight, and I hadn't slept in two days."

"Oh, poor darling. I can't imagine what you must have gone through. They should have let you come straight home," said Valentina, patting his arm. "It was unfair of them to treat you like a criminal, and not allowing you to speak to me in person was … well … quite barbaric. They should be ashamed of themselves, if you ask me." She sniffed as she flicked her eyes to her father. "Papa, you should complain about those Gestapo officers in Paris. Have them reprimanded."

"They followed protocol, dear," Biermann responded indulgently. "They had to be sure that Paul hadn't been coerced, or God forbid, brainwashed. Keeping him incommunicado for security reasons was the correct procedure under the circumstances."

Paul let out a tired sigh and stretched his legs. "I suppose that's what happens when one's mother is English, a twin is fighting for the enemy, and a younger brother has been locked up in Dachau for attempted murder." He squeezed Valentina's hand. "Forgive me, darling. I would have done just about anything to hear your voice on the other end of the telephone line."

Paul looked at Biermann who was staring at his brandy glass as if it had all the answers. He suspected his father-in-law also wanted to know what had happened during his captivity and escape, but he was desperate for a few minutes alone to gather his thoughts before being grilled again, as he probably would be after the ladies went to their beds. The ambiguities in Paul's story had stood up to Gestapo scrutiny in Paris, but Freddie Biermann was extraordinarily diligent in his job, hence his rank.

"Why don't you let me run a hot bath for you, darling? Your hands are freezing cold," Valentina said to Paul.

Paul took a large slug of brandy and grimaced as it burnt the back of his throat – his father was dead, his mother had fled to England, and his wife was pregnant – how sweet that last piece of news had sounded to his ears amidst the shock and sorrow that had hit him like a cast-iron mallet.

"I'd like that." Paul nodded, leaning his head towards her. The bathroom would give him the privacy he desperately needed. It was hard trying to hold himself together when all he wanted to do was curl up in a corner and weep.

"As I mentioned, I wrote to Wilmot. I told him about your father's death and that your mother had emigrated," said Biermann, delaying Paul's escape. "He's a prolific writer, your

Wilmot. He's sent several long letters to me since November – you're welcome to read them."

"Thank you. I'd like that. And thank you again for informing Willie about our father. It was very kind of you." Paul took one long swallow, finishing the brandy and feeling the familiar heat running through him. Valentina returned, having run his bath, her eyes reflecting his sadness. Olga was dabbing her eyes with a handkerchief while sniffing loudly for more effect. Biermann was looking on with sympathetic eyes, but he was clearly uncomfortable with Paul's visible emotion.

Paul cleared his throat. "Kriminaldirektor … ladies … I'll have that bath now if that's all right with you."

"Take your time, darling," Valentina kissed him. "I'll come up in a minute…"

"No. I can manage." Much as he adored Valentina, he wanted to be alone.

"We'll eat whenever you're ready," Olga said, as Paul left the room.

In the bathroom, Paul eased into the bathtub, flinching as he immersed his cold body into the steaming water. After ducking under, he re-surfaced and let out a ragged breath. His father, the indomitable Dieter Vogel, was dead – dead – it had hardly seemed possible when he was in France, but now that he was back in Berlin it seemed all too real.

While he soaked in the tub, Paul mulled over the reasons why Max hadn't said a word about their father being blown up and killed. He'd just left Kent and would have already spoken with their mother about how Papa had died. God help her, she was probably lost without father. He'd been her world. How would she cope without him?

Paul scrubbed his skin until it was red and tingling, then he angrily pushed the loofah under the water. Trying to make Max the villain of the piece was covering up the truth. *He* had betrayed Max, the person least deserving of disloyalty. He'd spat in Max's face after he'd risked his life at the communist base, and that, Paul knew, made him an ungrateful swine.

As he got out of the bath, Paul recognised that he didn't regret scuttling Max's plans. He hadn't seen himself as a German prisoner of war in England. No. He was a German soldier, sworn to protect the German people and the Third Reich, and although Max would be spitting mad, he should also understand the part loyalty had played in the deception at the airfield.

As he shaved, it struck Paul that the Vogels, the upstanding Aryan family headed by an important Nazi industrialist father, were no longer united geographically or ideologically. According to Valentina, his mother, Laura, was being called a traitor by her circle of friends, unlike his papa who was being heralded as a hero of the Fatherland. Wilmot, apparently, was also persona non grata in Berlin after his incarceration in Dachau for attempted murder, and as for Max, Hannah, and Frank? It had been a long time since anyone had even mentioned their names.

Kurt remained the bastion of the Vogel estates, Paul thought, clinging to something positive. In the morning, he'd pay his respects at his father's grave and afterwards he'd go to the Vogel's house to speak to Kurt about the night of the factory explosion. He'd know more about what happened than anyone. He was the man to help him through this. He was dependable, loyal and trustworthy. He was family.

Paul dressed, combed his hair, and stared at his reflection. The last time he'd studied himself like this had been in his Dresden bedroom just before his graduation party. He hardly recognised himself. The outer edges of his eyes had deep crow's feet spreading toward his hairline, and the lines between his outer nostrils to the sides of his mouth had deepened. His face was gaunt with prominent cheekbones, and his eyes had a bewildered look; a reflection of how he was feeling.

Olga and Valentina refused coffee and went straight to bed after they'd cleared the dining table. Dinner had been served much later than usual, and the clock had struck midnight while they were eating dessert. Biermann and Paul took their brandies into the living room where Biermann became sentimental with florid admiration for Dieter.

Paul privately disagreed with his father-in-law's view of the man who had loved the Nazis as much if not more than his wife and children, but he stifled his feelings and tried to move the conversation along. "Berlin will feel strange with my parents gone. I thought I might take Valentina to their house in Dresden for a few days? I'm hoping she can take some time off work."

"She can leave now. She's pregnant, and I don't know about you, but I don't like to see her working in that delicate condition. It's not right."

"I agree. I'll suggest she leave the job straight away." Paul stretched out his legs and sighed. "I'm going to be a father. I still can't believe it; it makes me never want to leave her again."

"At last, some good news, eh?" Biermann agreed. "That's a good idea about going to Dresden, Paul. It will give you some well-deserved time together. When you left for Paris straight after your wedding, my Valentina couldn't quite believe she was a married woman. She seemed bereft without you. I don't think I've ever seen her that sad."

"I can imagine. I know I hated every minute I was away from her." Paul sipped his brandy, calmer and more content than he'd been an hour earlier. "It'll do us good to have some time away from everything … not that I'm ungrateful for your hospitality. It's been … you've been marvellous to me."

"Will you go to the cemetery? I can come with you if you like."

"I was thinking I might speak to Kurt. I'll let him know he can stay in the Berlin house for as long as he wants…"

Silence.

"There's something you should know about Kurt Sommer." Biermann rose to refill his glass. "He's not the good man you think he is. He might even have had a hand in your father's death."

Paul flinched then gulped as the pulse in his neck jumped. What the hell was the man talking about? "Is this a joke, sir?"

"No, and it's not something I take lightly. I didn't want to talk to you about this tonight. It's bad enough you having to deal with your father's death and your mother's abandonment, but you would have found out tomorrow that Kurt is not at your parents' house. He's in custody at Spandau Prison and has all but admitted being a British spy. Paul, as hard as this is for you to hear, I believe he killed your father because he got found out."

Outrage and denial stuck in Paul's throat. He was haunted by the image of Captain Leitner's car on fire with his dead body at the steering wheel staring sightlessly through the windscreen. Kurt had been there that day. He'd seen everything. He'd helped carry Leitner's dead body. He'd been loyal, especially to Dieter, and hadn't uttered a word to anyone about the murder, or Max's profession. It didn't make sense. He didn't believe Biermann, and that in itself was shocking.

Paul took a deep breath, then let it out with a tepid response. "I would never question an esteemed Kriminaldirektor such as yourself, but are you certain? Kurt loved my father. He joined the Nazi Party because of him. He's almost one of the family, like an older brother..."

"My dear boy. Oh, Paul. Spies are very often the people closest to you," Biermann asserted. "Were that not so they wouldn't be able to winkle out their victims' secrets. It was *because* he was an enemy agent that he feigned loyalty and affection for your father, and to you and Wilmot, and that other brother of yours. I will break him, and when I do he will be severely punished for taking your father away from you – from us."

Paul still didn't believe Biermann, but he held his tongue. He was not talking to his wife's father now, he reminded himself, but a Gestapo Kriminaldirektor who seemed to have damning evidence. "May I see Kurt? I know him, and spy or no spy, he won't lie to my face."

"No. No, I'm sorry, Paul, it's against our policy."

Paul, undeterred, tried again. "Please, can't you make an exception for me, for the sake of my father's memory? Kurt will tell me the truth."

"Ach, this is a terrible state of affairs," said Freddie, slumping back in his chair with an overdramatic shake of his head. "You're putting me in an awkward position, Son, but for your father's sake, I'll give you five minutes with Sommer. That's all."

"I appreciate it. How long will you hold him?"

"He's been at Spandau for months. I'm supposed to hand him over in the next three days to one of our prison camps where the Gestapo use more advanced interrogation techniques. If only he would stop lying to me. I won't be able to help him once he leaves Berlin."

Paul was dizzy with tiredness, shock, and too many brandies. This was not what he'd expected to find on his leave after the terrible ordeal he'd been through in Duguay's custody. He had steeled himself to visit his father's grave, but not to see Kurt in an infamous Berlin prison. He was drained. His head hurt, and he could no longer think straight about anything, let alone this latest blow. His beautiful wife was in bed upstairs waiting for him. He desired her more than ever, but he'd be capable of no more than a kiss, a cuddle, and words of love. He hoped that would be enough for her tonight.

"I think I'll go to bed. I'm exhausted. What time do you want to leave for Spandau in the morning?" Paul asked.

Biermann stood and placed his hand on Paul's shoulder. "Seven, no later. Get some rest, Paul. You've been through hell, but I have other news for you." Paul's face fell, and Biermann tittered, "Now, don't think the worst. I think it will please you, or at least give you a fresh start. Ach, it can wait until tomorrow. Goodnight, Paul."

Chapter Twenty-Six

As Paul approached Spandau Prison in Wilhelmstraße, he was struck by the building's austere and dated façade. Built with red brick in the 19th century, it was enclosed by high walls of differing heights and topped with electrified wire accompanied by a wall of rolled barbed wire. Its entrance was castle-like, with two towering turrets on either side of the avocado-green entrance doors beneath a row of medieval battlement blocks that gave it an air of foreboding, even if one didn't know it was a prison.

He looked up and spotted a soldier on duty manning a machinegun in a guard tower. It was raining and the man was covered from head to toe in a rain sheet with a wide hood covering most of his face. Paul was reminded of one of Wilmot's childhood games of ghostly hauntings, except that the soldier was infinitely more terrifying than Willie had ever been.

As a young boy, Willie had made it his mission to scare his older brothers using their mother's bed sheets. He was frequently punished for cutting holes in the expensive Egyptian cotton to make peep holes for his eyes, dragging it through the house and garden, fraying the ends and staining them so badly it was impossible to get the dirt out. Wilmot had thought himself unrecognisable and incredibly menacing in his spectral outfit, as he glided into Max's and Paul's bedroom at night bellowing, "Wooooo! I'm coming to get you!"

"Impressive, eh, Paul?" said Biermann, staring up at the same machinegun post. "Spandau used to serve as a military detention centre, but it has housed civilian prisoners for over twenty years now. I was surprised when you told me you'd never been here before."

Paul took his eyes off the ghostlike figure. "It's not a place I would ever want to visit unless it was to plead for the life of someone I love, and I do love Kurt, sir. I hope you'll listen to what I have to say about the man before you condemn him to a concentration camp."

Inside the building, Biermann ushered Paul to an office. He closed the door behind them and invited Paul to sit. "I want to show you something before you tell me all the reasons you think I should release Sommer," Biermann said, taking a brown leather-bound folder out of the desk drawer. "You think highly of Kurt because you know him as your father's driver, a loyal friend, whatever. But he's much more than that." He pointed to the file. "When you see what's in there you'll change your mind about him and understand why I arrested him."

"I'll always think highly of him, Kriminaldirektor," said Paul, using Biermann's official title as he eyed the folder.

Biermann uncurled the string wrapped around a disk glued to the leather binder. Then he took out a newspaper clipping with a faded photograph on it. "Do you recognise anyone?"

Paul stared at the group of men in the picture and pointed to one of them. "That's Kurt."

"No. You think that's Kurt, but he's Karl Ellerich, and when this was taken he was a twenty-nine-year old Jewish activist and journalist of a subversive newspaper that was banned in 1935. Ellerich, your Kurt, was a member of a dissident group that lobbied for Jewish rights in Germany. Now, I don't have a problem with anyone demonstrating for their rights if they do it peacefully..."

"I thought the Gestapo had zero tolerance for demonstrations of any kind," Paul interrupted, sounding bolder than he felt. "I know it's a fine line you have to tread."

Biermann's eyes narrowed. "Not with these sub-humans. They tried to destabilise the government *and* the law by circulating anti-Nazi propaganda and inciting violence against the Third Reich and the Führer. As I said, Paul, you'll see that his arrest is justified when you read what's in these pages."

Paul looked again at the faces of the five men in the picture, noting that all of them, including Kurt, were wearing the *kippah,* a brimless cap made of cloth. It was worn by Jews to fulfil the customary requirement held by Orthodox halachic authorities that the head be covered.

Biermann smirked and for the first time, Paul saw him as something other than the benevolent father-in-law. His hubris was nauseating; he was enjoying himself.

"I see." Paul could think of nothing else to say. Biermann, however, was flicking through the papers and just getting started.

"If only he were here for a simple case of fraudulent identity." Biermann pushed a document across the desk to Paul.

Paul read the damning evidence of violence and sedition, and his gut twisted with dismay. "What will you do to him?"

"Ah, that is the question. Kurt … Karl Ellerich, caused civil unrest on too many occasions to count, but for some reason only a few of his rebellious acts in the name of Judaism were properly documented. On one occasion, an SS squad tracked him to one of his illegal meetings in Munich. At the time, the SS believed the Jews were planning violence against high-ranking members of the Nazi Party, and under orders from Herr Himmler, they bombed the building where the illicit gathering was taking place. After the smoke had cleared, it was reported that Ellerich had died with fourteen of his Jewish activist colleagues. In reality, however, he was already on his way to Switzerland by train."

Paul poked the documents. "Has Kurt confessed to any of this?"

"Kurt doesn't know I've uncovered this information, or that I found out he's a Jew. He was arrested on quite a different charge … one he has confessed to … a crime he'll be severely punished for."

Biermann placed another Gestapo-headed loose page in front of Paul, then closed the folder and put it back in the drawer. "I'll have Ellerich taken to an interview room. Read that Paul. We'll talk again when I return."

Paul stared unseeingly at the paper. Kurt was a Jew. Kurt, with fierce Germanic looks, blue eyes, perfect blond hair, a member of the Nazi Party, a man who had always spoken his mind to Dieter Vogel and his sons, a loyal man with no family of his own who had claimed to love the Vogels. Paul groaned. He knew exactly what was going to happen to Kurt. He'd never see the light of day again.

The numbered paragraphs on the page held enough accusations to warrant a firing squad. Kurt was a foreign agent. He'd been a Gestapo suspect for months. Suspicious radio frequencies had been detected in the Vogel's neighbourhood, and on the day that Laura Vogel left for England, Kurt had apparently made the mistake of transmitting a radio message to persons unknown.

Paul read on. *After an extensive search, a radio transmitter was found in a hunter's hut in the Grunewald Forest, which is only a couple of kilometres from the Vogel's house. A scrap of paper had lain next to the radio with a few indecipherable words. The Gestapo, under the command of Kriminaldirektor Freidrich Biermann, had checked Sommer's handwriting against the numbers and letters on the piece of paper, and had determined that it was written by the same hand.*

As he waited for Biermann to return, Paul's mind reeled with questions, and a sadness almost as intense as the grief he felt for his father. Biermann was lying about there being a radio transmitter. The Gestapo twisted facts and made up stories to suit themselves the way *he* had in France with the Gestapo. They wanted Kurt to burn, not because they believed him to be a spy, which was ridiculous, but for being a Jew – it was always about being a bloody Jew!

Paul wondered whether his father might have known that Kurt was Jewish. It was unlikely, he decided. Had Biermann shared his suspicions with anyone about Kurt being a foreign agent? Was he fabricating the story about a radio transmitter? It was possible. Trumped up charges seemed to be the order of the day in Germany. Did Dieter Vogel die at Kurt's hand because he'd found out about the latter's espionage activities? No, it was preposterous to even consider those possibilities.

What was his father-in-law playing at? His evidence, though abundant, was as scrappy as the bit of paper they'd apparently found. He saw no mention in the document about who Kurt had sent the radio messages to, or who he was supposedly working for. Had Kurt confessed, as Biermann suggested, he would have come clean about the country he was loyal to – and where was Kurt's signature? It wasn't in the file – it was all a lie. This was about Judaism. The rest was garbage.

Chapter Twenty-Seven

When Biermann returned, Paul was taken to a room one floor below in a completely different part of the complex. The atmosphere changed as soon as they left the stairwell and entered the main hallway beyond the double iron-barred doors. The rancid stink of urine, shit, and sweat assaulted Paul's nostrils. He shot a sideways glance at Biermann who'd covered his nose with a handkerchief. If he was aware of the appalling stench, why had he not done something constructive to clear it up? Paul was fuming. He was finding it hard to speak to or even look at his father-in-law; the man had become a stranger.

The corridors were dimly lit by an occasional gas light hanging from thin wire on the bare brick walls. Every door they passed was reinforced with steel and had peep holes and hatches big enough for food trays to slide through. Paul halted mid-step to look out of a window onto a garden area beyond. It was barren through lack of care but was nonetheless a strange sight in the middle of a city prison.

Biermann also stopped walking and pointed to the door closest to them. It was guarded by two soldiers leaning against the wall with rifles slung over their shoulders. They came to attention, their boredom eliminated by their respect for the Gestapo Kriminaldirektor.

"He's in there, Paul," Biermann said, gripping Paul's arm. "Remember what I said on the way here. I'm doing you a favour by allowing you to see him, so I expect you to respect my instructions. Say goodbye to him, but do not mention his Jewish heritage, or anything else you've read about or heard in my office. Do I have your word?"

Twice, Biermann had reiterated those orders. Was he worried that Kurt might contradict the carefully laid-out accusations and embarrass the Gestapo? Paul wondered, giving a curt nod. "Yes. You have my word."

Biermann gestured to the guard, who opened the door to let Paul enter. Disappointed, Paul felt his father-in-law follow him in. Damn Biermann for not giving them the courtesy of saying their goodbyes in private.

Kurt was handcuffed against a wall. He wore a dirty grey shirt and striped trousers that looked like pyjama bottoms, like those Paul had seen men wearing at the Brandenburg Prison.

The man Paul had always admired was an emaciated shadow of his former self, a pitiful, beaten man with blackened eyelids and cheekbones, his lips white and crusty with scabs. His puffy eyes brightened as he gave Paul a weak smile and raised himself to his full height.

Paul turned sharply to Biermann, dismissing forever the respect and appreciation he'd once had for the grim sadistic torturer leaning nonchalantly against the closed door with his arms folded. A bigger and more courageous man would beat the life out of the piece of Gestapo shit! "I'd like five minutes alone with him?" Paul spat.

"No. Say your goodbyes. That was the deal," Biermann replied.

Paul swallowed his fury as he walked to Kurt. He couldn't think of a single thing to say with Biermann breathing down his neck in this abhorrent place of suffering.

"It's good to see you, Paul. Thank you for coming," Kurt muttered.

"I came as soon as I could. I have my father-in-law to thank for this visit."

Paul, noticing the vicious curl of Kurt's lip as he looked past him to Biermann, tried to ease the tension. "I won't lie to you, Kurt. I was shocked to hear about you being in here. I'm not allowed to know what you did or ask you any questions about your alleged crimes, but I can ask you about the night my father died. You were with him just before the explosion. Will you tell me what happened? It will help me to understand."

Again, Kurt looked past Paul to glare at Biermann who gave a brisk nod of approval.

"Your father was desperate to see the gas plant shut down. He planned to use the basement as an extra factory floor, to meet the high demand for medical equipment." Kurt began, his eyes now fixed on Paul. "He went inside to check the gauges with the view to having the gas holders removed the following day if they were empty. He was taking your mother for a break to Dresden and wanted to leave his instructions with his brother-in-law."

"What caused the explosion?" Paul asked.

Kurt sighed and shrugged, "I've asked myself that question a thousand times, Paul. Berlin suffered an air raid just after your father went into the gas plant and locked the reinforced door from the inside. I watched him and two of the guards check the gauges as planned … and … then I felt a violent tremor beneath my feet, like an earthquake. Inside the plant, sparks were flying, and your father rushed back towards the door and gestured to me through the glass panel to leave. At that point, I ran up the stairs and back to the entrance, thinking that your father would be safer inside the contained space than I'd be in the main building should we be bombed by the British. But I was wrong. When the explosion occurred, it took down the entire gas plant, the basement area outside it and the floors above it. And I … well … as you can see, I'm still in one piece."

"That's enough, Paul," Biermann said from the doorway.

Kurt and Paul locked eyes, the former's silently pleading with Paul to stay a bit longer.

"Paul, that's enough," Biermann snapped.

"I'm sorry, Kurt, I won't be able to visit again. Stay strong," Paul said, tears prickling his eyes.

"I don't think I'll be here much longer." Kurt tried to smile. "You take care of yourself, and always remember that your father loved you. He was a very proud man at your wedding, and right up to the moment he died. Goodbye, Paul."

Back in Biermann's office, Paul accepted a cup of tea. Biermann, once again his charming, caring self, seemed pleased with the visit.

"That went rather well. You got a better picture of what happened to your father, and you found out what a lying traitor Sommer really is," Biermann said, after slurping his tea.

"I didn't expect to see him in such a dreadful state," Paul dared to say.

Biermann waved the comment away. "Ach, don't worry about that. Scuffles happen when prisoners refuse to cooperate, that's all."

Biermann returned his cup to its saucer then rubbed his hands together like an eager storyteller. "I'm glad we got that nasty business out of the way first. Now we can both go home with the news I'm about to tell you. I wanted to speak to you about it before I told Olga and Valentina, so you could have time to take it all in."

Paul, feigning interest but still horrified at Kurt's inhumane treatment, smiled. "I'm all ears."

Biermann took a satisfied pull on his cigarette, making Paul cough as the smoke drifted towards him.

"The thing is, Paul, I'm not a young man, and being of a certain age I always thought I would spend the war in Berlin." Biermann began with a chuckle. "It appears that the powers-that-be have other ideas for me. Can you imagine how taken aback I was when my superior told me I was to be posted outside Germany?" He took another puff of his cigarette, exhaling slowly, then stubbing it out in the ashtray. "What do you know about Łódź, in Poland?"

"Not much. Why?"

"I'm being sent there for an extended period to help run the Litzmannstadt Ghetto with the *Schupo – Schutzpolizei.* I started my police career in that force. It'll be like going back to the good old days of policing and keeping the peace – a completely different pace to what I've become used to in Berlin."

Paul digested the news. He shouldn't be surprised. Germany was at war, so why should his father-in-law be immune to the upheaval it brought? He was no different than the million other servicemen who'd been sent beyond Germany's borders.

Biermann continued to talk about his new job with boyish enthusiasm. "Of course, I was adamant that my Olga should accompany me. Other officers have been allowed to take their wives to permanent postings that are not close to our front lines. I couldn't even imagine leaving her behind."

Paul, unsure if Biermann was genuinely happy about the move or playacting, said, "I don't know what to say." He lifted his cup to give his still-shaky hands something to do. The man was like a tap that ran hot one minute and cold the next, and Paul was quickly learning to measure his words before speaking. "I'm pleased for you, sir, but you … have I displeased you in some way … the way you're looking at me…?"

"No. No, you have the wrong end of the stick, Paul. I was studying your reaction. You see, I've used what little power I've got to secure you a posting to one of the Reich hospitals in Łódź. You're coming with us."

Paul gaped like a fool. "I'm going to Poland?"

"Yes. But that's not the best part. You also have permission to take Valentina with you. Although, had the worst come to the worst and you hadn't been allowed to take her, I would have arranged for her to accompany her mother and me, what with her being pregnant and having no other family in Berlin. She'll be sorry to leave her job at the main security office, I suppose. You know how much she loves it. But when she finds out that you and she can set up home together in married quarters in Poland *and* have her mother and me just around the corner, she'll be delighted." He stared hard at Paul. "Aren't you happy?"

Paul was astonished. He was still open-mouthed and uncertain of his father-in-law's motives. "I really don't know what to say apart from what about Paris? Will they agree to my new posting?"

"Yes, yes. You were never going back to France, Paul, not after your ordeal."

Paul squirmed under his father-in-law's scrutiny. Living in Poland was not what he'd envisaged for himself. He knew damn well who was in the Łódź Ghetto, and he wanted no part of it.

"Don't take this the wrong way, Paul, but your superiors see you as an embarrassment, a reminder that the Resistance can take German officers off the Paris streets at will. You *are* a hero, no doubt about it. You might even get a medal…"

"Why?" Paul blurted out.

Biermann spread his arms wide and let out a contented grunt. "Why? Because you made it possible for the Gestapo to execute thirty or so rebels in Dieppe. It was a great coup for us. They won't be abducting anyone else in a hurry, will they?"

Paul blushed crimson, as he recalled the Wehrmacht's celebrations in Paris. He didn't want to be reminded about the people he'd helped to kill...

"Paul ... Paul?"

"Sorry, sir. I was thinking about Łódź," Paul lied.

"Look, I know this must be a shock after all the other shocks you've received recently, but I feel Poland is the right place for you ... for our family. I had to call in a lot of favours to make these two postings work in tandem. Tell me you're pleased ... say something."

"For God's sake, give me longer than a heartbeat to take this in!" Paul snapped, still thinking of the French men and women who'd died because of him.

Biermann gasped, his indignation evident. But Paul's cup of wretched news was overflowing. Hans Rudolph came to mind. The homosexual murderer of children, who had wheedled him into making a hasty decision about Brandenburg, had done precisely what Biermann was doing now; cornering him, badgering him for a decision he didn't want to make even though he suspected it was already out of his hands. "I apologise, Herr Direktor. I had no right to speak to you like that," Paul finally repented. "I was thrown when you said Łódź was a ghetto ... what did you call it?"

"Litzmannstadt."

"Oh, yes. Who lives there? I assume it's guarded?"

Biermann tapped his fingers impatiently on the desk and scowled. "Jews live there. But you already knew that, didn't you?"

"Yes."

"Paul, don't make me regret sticking my neck out for you. There are ghettos all over Poland. The biggest one is in Warsaw. It's becoming overcrowded and sickness among the Jews is rife. Thank your lucky stars you're not being sent there, or to the Russian Front without Valentina or me at your back."

Jews again. Max's patronising words over a year earlier came back with a vengeance to haunt Paul. *The Jewish situation will only get worst. Do you really think the Reich will feed and clothe those people in camps and ghettos? You can run from Brandenburg, Paul, but not from the Jews or the politics and death surrounding them.* To please Biermann and give himself a break from the man's coercive stare, Paul grinned. "Forgive me, sir. I was surprised for a moment, that's all. I can't wait to tell Valentina. She'll be as thrilled as I am."

"I'm sure she will be." Biermann's eyes widened, as though he'd been struck by a thought. "Ah, Kurt Sommer. Yes, Sommer."

"What about Kurt, sir?"

"It's something you said earlier about him going to a concentration camp. I might have an idea that could help him avoid that fate. I should have thought about it before now, but until I saw how fond of him you are, I admit I didn't care where he went. I'm not a monster, Paul, although at times I'm forced to do monstrous things."

"What are you thinking?"

"I'm thinking of recommending a gentler sentence for Kurt, one where he can live an almost normal life in the Litzmannstadt ghetto. He'll work, live in a house with other Jews, and be able to wander around the place – within its walls, of course – what do you think about that?"

Paul's eyes brightened. It was certainly a better option than torture in a prison camp. "Failing his release, it would be a vast improvement. Thank you."

Biermann brought out a half bottle of brandy from his desk drawer, then two tubular snifters. "Then it's yes to Łódź for all of us. We're going to make the Fatherland proud, Paul. Shall we toast to our bright futures?"

The Vogels

Chapter Twenty-Eight

Klara Gabula

Klara, along with two crates of weapons, was parachuted into France an hour before dawn. After walking two hundred metres or so, she came to a stream. There, she stowed her chute in a crevice between rocks and took her map and compass out of her rucksack. She was panting with exertion. The chute had not seemed that heavy when she'd first gathered it up in her arms, but after walking with it over her shoulder and dragging at least half of it on the ground behind her, it had become unbearably cumbersome.

She switched on her torch to check her map, noting the markings of water and woods to the right confirmed that she was very close to the rendezvous point south-west of Paris.

Worried that the parachutes carrying the crates might be tangled in the trees, she headed towards the forest. While she'd been floating down, she'd followed the paths of the crates and their parachutes and believed that their landing sites were just inside the treeline.

According to the coordinates, Duguay's men were going to pick her up at a point where the stream widened, and as she walked towards the trees, she spotted the place only a hundred metres ahead of her. It was quite beautiful; not only did the stream widen into a river, but the moon's light reflected off a two-metre high waterfall that splashed deafeningly into the foaming water below. As she approached, she was reminded of similar cascades in Scotland's rugged countryside.

She was in high spirits. She had dreaded the parachute jump almost as much as the thought of being shot down as she hung in the air, yet she'd made it unscathed and felt proud of herself for getting over what had been an enormous hurdle for her. The Frenchmen hadn't arrived yet, which gave her time to look for the weapons crates.

After ten minutes' search, she found the parachutes where she thought they would be, stuck on branches with the crates dangling about three metres off the ground. She left them there, went back to the river, and settled down near the waterfall to wait for Duguay's men.

The sky was clear with countless stars and a three-quarter moon, but it was cold. She shivered, pulled up her collar, and huddled closer to a rock that acted as a windbreak. What would Duguay say to her when he saw she had returned to work with him? She knew precisely what she'd say to him; she'd rehearsed her speech many times.

Her thoughts drifted to her last meeting with Max. She was still undecided whether to mention the state of their relationship, or lack thereof, to Duguay. Max had made it clear he didn't want to see her again. He hadn't replied to any of her letters, written feverishly in a last-ditch attempt to mend fences. It was over; she'd accepted his decision. Max had mentioned in Scotland that he wasn't going back to Paris in the foreseeable future, and because of that, she had left the Polish SOE Section in favour of France, following Duguay's request that she work with his group. That was proof enough that her relationship with Max was well and truly finished, wasn't it?

She was hurting, but in time, the ache in her heart and the sadness she felt would ease then fade away completely. She didn't live and breathe for anyone but herself now; she was her own person. She hadn't lost her name upon marriage; she'd been born Klara Gabula, a common surname that had matched Romek's.

During her years in Poland, she had studied, taught others, lived, laughed, cried, and experienced many things before either Max or Romek had come into her world. Neither man had made her or saved her. They had not come to her rescue; she had rescued herself, surviving with stoic determination on her own. She was now free of the guilt of being an adulteress, and of almost killing her lover's brother. She had turned a page and would never go back again, not for Romek, and certainly not for Max Vogel.

At 06:15, three of Duguay's men made their way towards her along the rocky embankment. She remained hidden, however, until she recognised Claude's tall, gangly figure and heard him call her French name, *Marine*. It felt strange hearing it again.

Duguay was waiting for Klara at the farm. He'd cooked a breakfast of pork sausages and scrambled eggs and had brewed a strong pot of coffee, along with hot fresh bread from the oven. She found him much changed since their previous encounter when he'd insulted her for her stupidity and had ordered her into a van while he shot over Paul Vogel's head. She was now an SOE agent, and although he didn't know that section even existed, he was aware she held an officer's rank in the British Army. He was pleasant, respectful, and grateful for British help, or so it seemed.

After breakfast, when she was drinking the last of the coffee, she set about outlining the British government's long-term goals.

"When and where are the two other agents arriving?" he asked.

Klara pushed her plate aside and pulled a map from her rucksack. "Two days from now – here." She pointed to the map, marked by a series of numbers. "A British vessel – I don't know the exact type of boat – will put the men in an inflatable dinghy off the coast, here."

"Yes, I know the place."

"Good. They'll row into this cove – you see? From what we can gather, the Germans have a series of concrete bunkers along the entire coastline as well as sentry points on roads into harbours and jetties, so you'll have to make your approach to the cove on foot."

"I also know that. The German military are monitoring everything from fishing boats to enemy planes and shipping. They're also checking the boats as they unload and are grabbing the best of the catches for themselves before allowing the rest of the fish to be sent to local markets. I'm surprised the British are even attempting this. Why didn't they parachute in with you?"

"I don't know. Perhaps they're carrying sensitive materials. They must have their reasons. Don't worry about it, Duguay. The curfew means there is no fishing at night, so there shouldn't be any German military trucks on the road. All we need to be concerned about is that the dinghy isn't spotted before the agents sink it out of tidal sight and come ashore."

For an hour, Klara and Duguay discussed the way ahead. She had brought four radio transmitter crystals and explained how they were used to construct two radios. She also handed over money to Duguay and a list of British objectives and targets including railway lines and canals.

Klara was gaining confidence as Duguay kept eye contact, listening and agreeing to all she said; until she brought up the Vogels. "Do we need to talk about the Vogel twins?" she asked.

"No. That episode is closed, but what happened will haunt us forever." Duguay rose and carried the cups to the kitchen sink.

Klara spoke to his back. "I know what happened to the Resistance in Dieppe. But as much as I'm sorry for the loss of those French lives, you and your operation are still afloat and now you have vast resources at your disposal. I learnt through your communications that for whatever reason, Paul Vogel didn't give you up, never mentioned his brother, you, or me by name, or where he'd been held. Why do you think that was?"

"Do you still see the brother, Max?"

Thrown by his question, Klara scratched her cheek. "I thought you said that episode was closed."

"I'd like to know where I stand with you. Have you spoken to him?"

"Yes, but he and I won't be speaking to each other again – that relationship is over."

"I see. Do you understand the damage you caused? Have you any idea what we had to do when Paul Vogel escaped?"

Klara's face reddened. "No. But I imagine you took precautions..."

"We did more than that. We moved out of here, lock, stock, and barrel. We ceased operations and scattered like leaves. We lost targets and twenty men who never came back – even now, I'm not sure if we should remain here..."

"Florent, I apologised to the British for my bad judgement with Paul Vogel, and I will apologise to you, but only once more," she interrupted. "What's important now is that this is a new operation. I have my orders from England, the equipment we need to destroy bigger targets, and the means to keep in contact with the British. Again, I'm sorry your operations were disrupted, but you must move on with me now. We have a job to do."

An uncomfortable silence ensued while Duguay returned with fresh coffee. "Why don't you get some sleep? I've set up a place for you in the barn. It's discrete and will give you some privacy."

"You want me to sleep in a barn?"

"I've made it habitable. Would you rather share a room with Claude?"

Klara picked up her rucksack and followed Duguay across the courtyard behind the house until they came to the barn where she had last seen Romek. She followed Duguay's lead then nearly bumped into him when he paused mid-step and turned to face her with an inscrutable smile on his lips.

"You wanted to know why Paul Vogel didn't mention this place?" he asked her.

"Yes … yes, I suppose I do."

"It's quite simple. He didn't want to get his British spy of a brother involved. But apparently, he had no qualms about sentencing men and women in the Dieppe area to death, who, by the way, had nothing to do with Vogel's abduction at your amateurish hands."

Klara flinched. "As I said, we must move on…"

He sniggered, "You want me to move on with you? No. You're mistaken. You're not equipped for this job, or for any other job in France. You didn't cause the temporary ruin of my operations or the death of dozens of innocent people – that was Paul Vogel's doing. But you are ruled by your female heart, not your head or your training, and I could never … *never* trust you again or allow anyone else to rely on you."

"Now, wait a minute. Why did you request me if you don't trust me? You told the British you wanted me to work with you…"

"The only reason I asked them to send you back was to do this." Duguay put his hand into his waist belt and pulled out a gun.

"What are you doing?" She took a step backwards and bumped into Claude, who gave her a sharp push forward. Her hand shot to her throat. She couldn't breathe. Then her fingers began to tremble as she stretched out her hand to Duguay, her eyes pleading with him to stop what he was doing.

Duguay released the safety catch. "I won't let you put any more Frenchmen or women in jeopardy. You're a liability, Marine. You can't be allowed to leave this farm to meddle in our affairs ... ever again."

Klara's throat was pulsating as though her heart had shot up to her mouth. Her eyes, wide with terror as they tried to make sense of what was happening, filled with tears and overflowed onto her cheeks. She tried to imagine death; the pain beforehand, oblivion, darkness, but she couldn't even begin to comprehend what it would feel like.

"Claude, move away from her," Duguay ordered. "Marine, get your knees."

"No, Florent, don't do this ... I'm begging you ... don't kill me because of one mistake..."

"One mistake? You mean one unforgivable mistake that can *never* be repeated? All the lives that were lost because of *your* actions?"

Claude pushed her to her knees, then walked to Duguay's side.

Klara, caught off balance, looked up at the two men, tears streaming down her cheeks. "You won't get away with this ... you won't ... the British will punish you. They'll never help you again," she croaked. "Duguay, they will smash you and your communists to pieces for killing one of their own – think – think!"

The tip of the gun barrel touched Klara's head then moved back a couple of centimetres. Blinded by terror, she screamed, losing all control. "No. Stop it! I'm more use to you alive than dead – Florent, don't – please don't..."

Duguay pulled the trigger, the deafening ping of the bullet echoing against the wall of the barn.

Klara's body crumpled sideways onto the ground, her legs bent at the knees, one arm tucked beneath her and the other with its hand clenched in a tight fist.

"Bury her in the woods but leave a grave marker. I want to show it to the British agents when they get here," Duguay said.

Claude nodded, his face ashen in the moonlight. "What will you tell the agents when they arrive?"

"She had an unfortunate accident when she landed – broke her neck. We found the details of their arrival in her rucksack along with a map with their landing point – we put two and two together. Don't worry about it."

"What if they want to see the body?"

Duguay sighed with impatience. "Why are you asking stupid questions? The British have no reason to doubt my word."

"What will you say to our men about this?"

"My men are loyal to me. They'll understand why I did it. Do *you* understand, Claude?"

"I suppose … yes…"

"Say it. Do you understand why she had to die?"

"Yes. She was a liability."

"Good. Now get this done. We've got work to do and crates to unpack."

Duguay took one last look at Klara, the tidy hole in her temple seeping black blood, her eyes clouded over in death. He sighed with neither regret nor relief, but instead set off at a brisk pace towards the house.

Chapter Twenty-Nine

Wilmot Vogel

Russia, January 1942

Wilmot and his fellow German prisoners of war stood in silence on the cramped boat that had taken them across a narrow river. Talking was not a good idea, nor was complaining about feeling sick, a lack of food or warm clothing. Wilmot had learnt that keeping quiet, head bowed, and staying on one's feet was a Russian prisoner's best chance of surviving the Soviet guards who liked to take pot shots at uncooperative Germans.

After the boat docked, a painstakingly slow debarkation process began. For days at a time, the prisoners had been marched through snow and ice-bound wastelands, travelling further north away from the German Forces and any chance of rescue. Physically and mentally, they were no longer the same men who had been captured at Leningrad. Wilmot, although trying desperately to hide his feelings, was irritable, hyperactive, and impetuous. Twice, he'd gone back to his old ways of lashing out with his fists, provoking fights with other prisoners just to get the prickliness out of his system.

He had a good idea where they were being taken, but he still couldn't understand why the Russians were moving towards the Karelian Isthmus, an area mostly held by Finnish troops. He and the other prisoners had concluded that the Russians were planning another assault on the Mannerheim Line, at present also held by the Finns. Perhaps the Russkies needed labourers to dig ditches, or maybe, as a German officer had suggested, they were going to fortify territory as close to the Line as possible, to hold it against a Finnish attack? The officer had then calmly deduced that regardless of what those two armies were planning, they, the prisoners, would probably be executed when they were of no further use.

Two hours after the vessel had docked, Wilmot marched in formation through a town where every sign had been painted over with either graffiti or the name *Stalin*. He felt the urge to chuckle as he imagined Russians running around deliberately hiding the names of streets and inconsequential towns. Maybe they had scrubbed out the names because they were previously inside Finnish territory? Who cared, he thought, as he pushed his body on. All he wanted to do was find was a sheltered corner, a roof, and a blanket to shield himself from the wind and snow. But he'd be lucky to come across any one of those.

As though his prayers had been answered, Jürgen, Wilmot's constant companion since their capture together at Leningrad, pointed out a train station up ahead of them. "Do you think we're going on a train?" the youngster asked.

"I don't know, but imagine that we are – imagine it, Jürgen – a roof, a dry space, straw floor maybe, and at the end of the journey a warmer place to stay."

"Now you're dreaming, Vogel." Another man poked Wilmot in the back.

Suddenly, the men in front of Jürgen and Wilmot halted. Wilmot's heart punched against his chest as he peered at a large hut and a goat pen in a field with wooden fencing separating the animals from the railway tracks. Behind the fencing, three Russian soldiers with rifles slung over their shoulders, were throwing a large ball to each other. Wilmot was struck by the relaxed way those men were handling sub-zero temperatures; the weather had already killed half the German prisoners.

"How many of us are left, Jürgen?" said Wilmot with a macabre giggle. Every day, the two men took a guess at how many German prisoners had disappeared or died during the night. At first, the game had been a silly, ghoulish joke, a way for them to concentrate on something other than their miserable situation and the fear of death every time the column halted. In Leningrad, there had been far too many prisoners to even contemplate counting, but since leaving that city many of their number had died, weakened by disease, malnutrition, mistreatment or murder at the hands of over-zealous Russian guards.

The men had stayed in various camps on their journey. Most had been damp and bitterly cold. Wilmot recalled one such place they'd been in for over three weeks. The cells, which had glassless windows set high in the walls, had no heating, but there were two wood-burning stoves in the long corridor outside. The cell doors had been kept open day and night, so that the prisoners didn't freeze to death. Thick layers of ice had formed on the walls of Wilmot's cell, which had been on the corner of the building, and at night, the undersides of the straw mattresses got covered with hoarfrost.

He recalled being allowed to congregate in the corridor where the stoves gave off a welcome warmth. Wilmot's cell was farthest from the heater and deemed uninhabitable, so he and the other eight cell mates had carried their mattresses into the passageway at night. That didn't stop two of the men in his cell from dying of pneumonia. They'd whimpered and cried right up until they'd breathed their last without having found a sympathetic ear, medicine, or an extra blanket. He still wondered why he'd been spared, why their lungs had filled with fluid and his hadn't.

Food had been scarce, sometimes non-existent. On one of the coldest days he'd ever experienced, the Russians had thrown food into the corridor. Forty men had tried to share three kilograms of bread, a half a can of *Schokakola* – the bitter-sweet, caffeine and kola nut dark chocolate – and four grams of fat. He, at the edge of the emaciated horde had got nothing but a brief lick of the empty can.

"Start counting, Jürgen," Wilmot whispered again.

"I don't want to play, Willie. Just let me stand here. I'm too hungry and knackered to speak to you," Jürgen muttered as he picked lice from his hair and cracked them open with his thumbnail and finger.

Wilmot stamped his feet to stop them from going numb. He took off one of his gloves and then studied his damaged hand. It had been stitched up by a Russian doctor during the first night in captivity. That man had done more for him than the German Medical Corps who claimed to serve the Wehrmacht and the soldiers in it. He wondered if Paul was waving away injured men because he couldn't be bothered tending to them the way that doctor had done for him at the Leningrad Line? He had to force thoughts of that day to the back of his mind. Had he been sent back to the German line for treatment, he wouldn't be in Russian hands now, dying a slow excruciating death. Germany had sentenced him to die, not Russia.

He cast aside his thoughts of death while a German officer was being led across the narrow dirt track to the hut. Then another was pulled out of the line, and another after that. Ten minutes later an infantry Schütze was frogmarched away, followed by another.

The two Russians weaved in and out of the lines, stopping every now and again to study the prisoners' faces. That usually spelt disaster for the unfortunate Germans, for when the guards did that it typically meant they were being chosen to die. There was no system to the selections, no special type of man, rank or age, height or weight; they were singled out on the whims of low-ranking Russian soldiers who delivered them to their bored, sadistic officers.

When the two guards reached Wilmot's line, he lowered his head, froze, held his breath and prayed. His terror was absolute, but only the beaded sweat trickling down his forehead into his eyes displayed it. Eight men had left his column so far, but he had seen up to ten being taken away at one time, and no one ever returned.

The guard came to Jürgen and halted. The lad's loud panting breached Wilmot's woollen hat even though he'd pulled its flaps over his ears. *Please, God, not Jürgen,* he thought. *And not me, either.*

A whistle blew and the inspecting Russians by-passed Wilmot, moving away from the column towards the hut where the German prisoners had been taken.

Wilmot turned to the boy behind him, a seventeen-year-old from Hamburg who'd let out a guttural sob after the Russians had left.

"It's over, Hans. Hans, it's over. Get a grip on yourself."

The boy's eyes widened like saucers as he stared at the field. Wilmot followed the lad's gaze and gasped. The Russian soldiers were carrying or dragging German bodies from the hut across the stony ground, and they weren't hiding the blood around the dead men's throats.

Wilmot looked down at his feet, hunched his shoulders, and exhaled a mighty breath. He was already aware that for most Russian soldiers, any instinct for pity or mercy had died somewhere on a hundred battlefields between Moscow and

Warsaw. The veneration of Adolf Hitler, the magnificent Führer, had not reached Russia or their Soviet territories. On the contrary, many of his fellow prisoners, including himself, were beginning to agree with the hatred Russians felt for the German leader. *Hitler Kaput!* the Russian guards shouted every five minutes.

After years of not being able to voice an opinion, or even think one that might insult the Führer or his supporters, Wilmot and many of the other prisoners were, for the first time, beginning to discuss all that they didn't like about the Nazis. Wilmot saw no need to hide his ugly experience in Dachau from the other men since he was in a situation he was unlikely to survive. His main gripe was the murder of Jews in the back of Polish steel-covered trucks, he'd told a group of men one night, and he'd then divulged his crime of attempted murder.

Wilmot noted that some, especially the officers, were still indoctrinated, refusing to listen to any seditious talk against Hitler. They disagreed with Wilmot's assessment about the killing of Jews, saying that Kikes deserved to die after all they'd done to impoverish real Germans. He'd always thought the term *real Germans,* was a subject of debate. He was born in Germany, making him a *real German,* but hundreds of thousands of Jews were also born in Germany, yet they were defined by religion and not nationality.

Most of his comrades were past caring about what their officers thought, and a lot of them deliberately threw their opinions in their superiors' faces for the fun of it. Adolf Hitler, the saviour, the man who was to make Germany great again, was a liar and a conman who didn't care about the tens of thousands of men who were dying in Russia.

Wilmot sucked in his already caved-in belly as a Russian guard approached the area where he was standing. Traumatised by the recent selection of prisoners who'd just been murdered, he closed his eyes and prayed again.

"Move, all of you!"

As the Russian barked this command, Wilmot exhaled with relief and, to take his mind off things, he played his and Jürgen's game, counting the men in his line of sight. The day before, he'd calculated that there were around five hundred prisoners left. That number had altered in the last hour with the death of eight men.

At the sound of an approaching train, he stopped counting and nudged Jürgen. "They're putting us on an animal transport, Jürgen. It'll be dry, and there might even be straw on the floor. We'll have a lie down, eh?"

"Do you really think we'll be able to sit down?" Jürgen said, his voice croaky.

"Probably. If we can, I hope it's a long journey. We'll feel better after a decent sleep."

"Do you think we'll get food?"

"We'll get the usual daily allowance, I imagine."

Jürgen stumbled. His face was as white as the fresh snow, his eyes sunken and unfocused. "It's not enough to survive on, Willie … only for dying slowly."

Although he agreed with Jürgen, Wilmot refused to verbalise his fear of death as the youngster often did. After almost three months in Russian custody, the short, skinny Jürgen was showing signs of starvation, as were they all.

Like his brothers, Wilmot was about 1.9 metres tall, and his weight, although he couldn't confirm it, was probably hovering around fifty-six kilos. He was anaemic, had diarrhoea, his body was covered in a rash, and his heart fluttered in a strange way, especially when he lay down. He was scared, and his morale had sunk lower than a snake's belly.

Wilmot stared at the dead Germans piled outside the hut's door. He felt sorry for them, but he also wanted their boots and gloves. He'd take everything off them if he could; his soles were flapping at the toes, his pullover was full of snags and rips, and his hands could do with another pair of gloves to pad out his own torn and holey ones.

Two soldiers came out of the hut. They were laughing, and one of them was talking while cleaning blood from his hands with a sheet of old newspaper. Wilmot imagined getting out of line. If he had a knife handy, he'd cut the man's throat and have the pleasure of seeing a Russkie choke on his own blood.

"These men collaborated with Fascists! They deserved to die. Do any of you object to what we did to them?" the blood-stained Russian officer shouted at the prisoners.

Wilmot noted the silence. Where was the Geneva Convention? he wanted to scream.

Chapter Thirty

The wagon doors slid open and ramps were attached. Wilmot glanced behind him and grunted. The Russians were stripping the dead Germans, then throwing them in a pile and dousing them with gasoline. His comrades, men he'd walked with, talked to, and struggled alongside had had their throats slit for sport. He guessed what would come next. He had witnessed Russian disposal methods in other places; the smell of gasoline, a couple of matches, the whoosh as the liquid ignited and the eventual bonfire of Germans to keep the Russkies warm.

"I don't think we'll be going north," Wilmot heard the man behind him say.

"Why not?" Wilmot grunted without turning around. "I don't think they know where the hell to take us."

"They're not stupid, Willie – stands to reason if they go much further north they'll eventually bump into the Finns – they're going to get us on that train and head south, probably west to avoid Leningrad."

"You're full of shit," Willie said, shuffling forwards.

Minutes later, Wilmot pulled Jürgen up the ramp behind him and into the wooden wagon where about eighty men were already packed in, hardly able to turn around, never mind lie down. Over the heads of the others, Wilmot spotted a latrine bucket on the floor in the corner. He struck out towards it, barging his way through the tightly knit men. He was desperate to relieve himself and get as close to the bucket as possible before it became impossible to reach it. Despite daily indignities, no one wanted to shit or piss their trousers and then live in them afterwards.

Jürgen looked crushed as the train pulled away from the platform. "I don't see any food or drink ... not even a water bucket ... oh, Jesus Christ, Willie, I'm sick with hunger!"

Wilmot ignored the moaning lad who was trying to follow him to the bucket. For some reason, Jürgen clung to him like a limpet, constantly sapping his energy. How the hell did such an infantile mama's boy even get in the army with all his weeping and wailing?

"Willie, I asked if you saw any food being loaded?"

"No. Shut up, Jürgen. I'm thinking."

It was dreary outside with slate-grey skies shedding a light snowfall that had started the previous day and hadn't stopped for a single minute. Only a pale gleam was coming in through the wagon's window. Wilmot noted the wide spaces between the bars, of which there were only three. If pushed aside, a man his size just might be able to squirm through with a helpful push from someone inside.

The first few times he'd seen his comrades and officers being murdered, he'd felt ripples of shock that had made him feel sick and shed tears of panic. Now, he accepted that soon his own luck would run out, and he'd be the one being dragged into some hut and mutilated. He couldn't live with his pathetic acceptance of inevitable death any longer. He'd go mad. He'd rather die jumping out the train's window.

The wagon held about ninety men. Twice, men's boots trod on Wilmot's feet, but despite the discomfort of being jostled and cursed at, he eventually managed to reach the window for a closer look. The bars were red and coarse with rust but almost two handspans apart.

Spurred on by the miniscule chance of escape and the fear of not lasting another week with the Russians, he said in a loud voice, "Has no one else noticed this window? It might be big enough to get through, even for a man of my size."

"You'll never get the bars off, Willie," a voice said from somewhere in the crowded space. "Shut up. Keep your stupid ideas to yourself," another grumpy voice shouted.

"We don't need to get them off, just prise them apart," Wilmot insisted. "This is the best chance we've had in months. We can do this. Come on, who wants to get out of here?"

"We'll be dead as soon as we jump from the train. Did you not see the machineguns and searchlights on the roofs?" someone asked.

"I spotted the guards manning machineguns up there," said a man standing next to Wilmot.

"We all saw them, Gunther, but I'd rather break my neck and get shot at than waste this chance of getting away," Wilmot maintained.

A short scuffle ensued while an officer barged through the men to get to Wilmot. "Move away from there, Vogel. Don't let me hear you talk of running away again. You'll get us all shot," the skeletal Hauptmann said.

Wilmot noticed the man's badge and stopped what he was doing. No one argued with a captain of the *Einsatzgruppen,* the Nazi death squads. One showed such people respect, even if one didn't care for their ambiguous yet telling mandate. Wilmot recalled the Einsatzgruppen when Army Group North had crossed into Russia from the Baltics. They'd given him the rifle and told him to shoot the people at the mass grave. They were cold-blooded bastards.

A man pulled at the bars and said, "The Hauptmann is right. You'll never move them, Vogel." Then, finally, an enlightened soul took Wilmot's side. "Hmm, I don't know. I'm with Willie. If we all take turns at pulling the bars we just might do it. They're rusty and old. They might even snap."

"Look at the state of us, discussing whether we go or not," Willie said, gaining confidence. "Where are your balls? You saw what they did to our men at the station. Do you think they won't kill the rest of us? They don't have enough food to feed their own people never mind us. I don't understand why you won't even try to make a run for it."

The man who'd agreed with Wilmot said, "Listen to him. Don't you want to die knowing you at least tried to escape?"

"He's right," Wilmot said. "We're all going to die as soon as they run out of grub, so we might as well lose our lives on our own terms. I say we should go for it."

The Einsatzgruppen Hauptmann, the only officer present, remained silent as Wilmot pushed his way to the latrine bucket. It had only a couple of pee's worth in it, the men having not been on the train for more than ten minutes, and with little or no food or drink in them, few had any urine to dispose of. He looked at those who were nodding, and without a word removed his coat, jacket and pullover. Then, he shoved the pullover in the bucket, unbuttoned his trousers and pissed.

"Willie, you're off your bloody head," a man said, his mouth agape.

"No, he's not," another disagreed, "If the pullover is wet it'll be stronger, and it'll strengthen his grip on the bars. We could spend hours trying to prise them apart with our bare hands, and we'll probably reach our destination before we make them wide enough. Make room. I feel a pee coming on."

In the next five minutes, several men donated their urine to the pullover until it was saturated. While fighting to overcome the stench, Wilmot wrung it out, made it into a rope and then wrapped it around one of the window bars. It was humiliating, having other men's pee soaking his hands and wrists, but he was spurred on by the anticipation of freedom, even if it were to last only minutes before he was shot down.

The Hauptmann who'd ordered Wilmot not to try anything, appeared to have changed his mind. No one would give him their pullovers, so he took his off and dipped it in the latrine bucket. Then, he followed Wilmot's lead and wrapped it around the second bar.

"We'll all take turns, right, men? Every one of you will have a pull whether you're coming with us or not. It is our duty to escape and to get back to our forces to continue the fight."

Up yours, Herr Hauptmann, Wilmot thought. *My fighting days for the Fatherland are over.*

The men moved back as far as they could to give Wilmot and the Hauptmann room to pull. They were standing on either side of the window, poised as though they were about to start a tug of war.

Wilmot grinned at the expectant faces and pointed to the ceiling. "Keep your voices down, and don't get too excited, you lot. Them up top might hear us and think we're up to something."

Chapter Thirty-One

As daylight waned, Wilmot stuck his head through the newly bent bars, which had been prised back sufficiently for most of the skinny prisoners to get through. On his left the dense forest lay about two hundred metres from the train which was chugging at a snail's pace on snow-laden tracks. He slid his eyes right to the same landscape: flat snow-covered land with white-topped pine trees stretching as far as he could see.

Inside the wagon, most of the men avoided his gaze. So far, only seven, including the Hauptmann, were committed to his plan. Others thought the whole idea was suicidal, as did Wilmot, to be truthful. Still, he didn't care who came and who stayed. Every man was free to live or die as he pleased. The rank system had all but disintegrated and camaraderie hung by a thread as every man fought for food, usually thrown at them as though they were animals in a zoo. He was becoming immune to the feelings of others. Death had taken too many friends, and he was losing his sense of self, not only because of starvation and cold and having the shits and shakes, but with the loss of his fighting spirit and dreams of a future outside Russia. He'd be damned if he'd end up like Jürgen, a suppurating mess who had to be led everywhere by the hand pleading for the bullet that would end it all.

"Look at the lot of you. I've seen harder spines on caterpillars. You're all waiting for death as though it's your only option. I pity you…"

"We're going now or not at all," the Hauptmann interrupted. "It's none of your business what the rest of them decide to do."

Wilmot nodded. "Fine. We might break our necks from the fall, or catch a few bullets in the back, courtesy of the snipers on the roofs, but if we make it to the trees we'll have a fighting chance of getting away. It's more than I can say for them."

"What do you call a fighting chance?" Jürgen asked.

"I'd say about twenty percent. I don't think you should come with us. You're too weak and you won't make the hike if we survive the first part."

Jürgen's eyes smarted. "Don't leave me. I want to go. I won't hold you back, I promise, Willie – I don't want this life – I don't want it."

"No."

"Let him come, Vogel. He has the right to try like every other man here," the Hauptmann said.

"It won't work with him. I had to drag him up the bloody train ramp because he was too weak to walk up it himself."

"I'm going. The Hauptmann said I could," Jürgen huffed.

Wilmot looked at the boy and felt his own chances of survival lessen. The lad was going to be like a rope around his neck. "All right, but if I make it, Jürgen, I'm not hanging around for you to catch up with me."

Jürgen pulled himself up as though to solidify his courage. "I understand, Willie. But twenty percent odds are better than no odds at all, and I'd like to take them."

Wilmot pulled his jacket and coat on and began buttoning them up. The others glared petulantly at him but made no move to follow. He found their reluctance incomprehensible but was secretly glad that only a handful were going. He didn't want a mad rush of men falling out of the moving train. The smaller the group the more chance they had of getting away unnoticed. Looking out the window, he also deduced that the first and second man to jump would have a better chance of escape than those who came afterwards. Eventually, the guards on the roof manning the machineguns would notice and start mowing people down as they tried to run in the deep snow.

Wilmot inhaled a long breath and then let it out slowly. "This is it. After you, Herr Hauptmann."

"No. The honour is yours, Schütze."

Wilmot supposed the Hauptmann wanted to see how far someone could get before committing himself, clever git. "If I die in a hail of bullets, don't follow me, okay, boys." Wilmot chuckled yet his knees were knocking with fear.

The Hauptmann boosted Wilmot to the window. Once there, he knelt on the ledge while two of his comrades held the back of his coat so he could manoeuvre one leg after another out of the narrow window like a contortionist. Once sitting sideways on the ledge, he reached out and slotted his fingers between the wagon's wooden slats, then pulled himself outside, his nose almost touching the wood as his feet searched for another foothold.

Perched on the edge of the wagon, he nearly lost his balance as the ferocious wind hit him in the face. The chugging noise of the train, although travelling slowly, was deafening. His left ear was stinging as the freezing air hit it, but he continued to cling on until he saw the Hauptmann's head appear out the window. Then the silly git nose-dived as though he'd been shot from a cannon. Gone in a flash, Wilmot didn't even see the captain hit the ground.

Wilmot and the others had agreed to meet up in the forest if they made it that far – he was going now, not waiting for the other men to jump. Every second that passed took him further away from the Hauptmann, and closer to being detected. Now was not the time to play hero, to make sure men like Jürgen got away safely. This was his idea, his chance to survive. "Jump – jump," he howled into the wind. "What are you waiting for? Now – now!"

Wilmot leapt, using the concave shadow, as the train went around a corner. When he landed, he tumbled down a small slope and rolled like a ball until his body came to a halt. Then, with no other thought than to escape, he charged, zigzagging for the trees, a hail of bullets chasing him as he ran.

A few metres into the treeline, he halted and fell to his knees. The train was still chugging down the track, but even as the high-pitched squeal of its wheels faded, the intensity of machinegun fire from its roof reverberated through the forest.

Every part of Wilmot shook. His teeth chattered with shock and his throat was burning. If he died right now, he'd go to his maker a happy man. He was free. He'd got away from the Wehrmacht and the Russian pigs who laughed at dying men and spat on their corpses. If he only lasted five minutes, he'd be grateful for every one of them.

He started to weep, then howled with full-blown laughter. He didn't give a damn about being in the Russian wilderness. He'd just jumped off a moving train and survived! Aware he was becoming hysterical, he finally shut himself up by grabbing a handful of snow and shoving it in his mouth.

When Wilmot's euphoria faded, exhaustion and numbness hit him. He lay down, a shivering mess on a bed of snow. He was afraid of falling asleep but too drowsy to care about the warnings of hypothermia when one dozed off.

A few seconds later, the lower branches of a tree made a whooshing sound as piles of snow plopped to the ground. Wilmot sat up, dizzy with the sudden movement. "Who's there?" he whispered.

"Is that you, Vogel?" a small voice called back.

"You made it, sir," Wilmot nodded, noticing his Hauptmann's figure picked out by the light of a sliver of an early moon reflected off the snow.

The Hauptmann staggered forward, panting for breath, his face ghostly, his expression dazed. "Did you see the others … anyone else?"

"No. They hadn't come out the window by the time I jumped. I don't know if the krauts' attention was on me or those who came after. I heard the machinegun fire from the train, but it faded a few minutes ago."

The Hauptmann ran his trembling fingers through his snow-wet hair and collapsed beside Wilmot on the ground. "The train didn't stop. I'm going to wait for the others."

Wilmot shook his head in defiance. "You do what you want, but I'm not staying here. We need to head north to the Soviet-Finnish battlefront…"

"The Mannerheim Line?"

"That's the one. If we can get within striking distance, we'll stand a chance of hooking up with the Finns."

"You're off your head, Vogel. You'll run into Russian divisions if you go in that direction."

"That's the second time today that someone's told me I'm off my head, yet here I am, a free man. Look, Hauptmann, I'm not trying to tell you what you should do, but to the south there's only Russians and more Russians between us and the German armies…"

The Hauptmann staggered to his feet, leaving Wilmot's words hanging. "Shh…"

Wilmot heard the snow crunching and clambered to his feet as Jürgen appeared.

"I'm alright, Willie. I hurt my knee when I landed. I knew I'd find you if I backtracked … we're free… we did it."

"Did anyone else get away?" the Hauptmann asked.

"Two men jumped before me, but I didn't hang around to see what happened to them. I thought someone was running behind me, but there was a lot of machinegun fire and I didn't turn to look. It was a miracle I dodged the bullets. I think they all might be dead. Do you think they'll stop the train and come after us?"

"The train's gone." Willie grinned at the youngster. "Now we go home."

The Hauptmann dithered. "I'm not sure about going home, Vogel, but we do need to move – all right, we'll go north – we might pick up our men on the way."

The image of over four hundred German prisoners getting on the train popped into Wilmot's mind. He felt guilty for leaving them behind and wondered if they'd be punished because of the escapees. He glanced at the Hauptmann and wondered if he also felt guilty.

"Hauptmann, we might not get far today. It'll be pitch black soon in the forest. Maybe we should make some sort of shelter." He could feel snowflakes tickling his cheeks. "If we don't, we'll freeze to death before morning."

"On the upside, Willie, we shouldn't bump into any Russians in this Godforsaken forest," Jurgen said, his voice unusually calm.

An hour later, and only a short distance from where they'd started their trek, Wilmot felt bile rise in his throat. His stomach heaved as he slumped against the nearest tree trunk. His head was spinning, unrelated objects swimming towards him then back and forth. A sudden heat suffused his body and he rolled onto his knees to push his face into the snow.

Beside Wilmot, the Hauptmann's chest rose and fell like a panting dog. Jürgen was lying flat on his back with his eyes shut. The snow was still coming down and the trees were dropping great lumps of the stuff onto the ground.

"Your name's Willie?" the Hauptmann finally asked.

"Wilmot ... but, yes, Willie to my friends and family, sir." His tongue was swollen in his mouth, and he couldn't swallow. He grabbed some snow and sucked it into his burning cheeks. "May I ask your name?" he croaked.

"Max – Max Albrecht– and you can drop the sir, Willie."

"Max, eh," Willie mumbled through chattering teeth. "That's a name I like."

"Max is Willie's older brother," Jürgen said, taking a peculiar furtive look around. "He's in the British army."

Lifting an eyebrow, Max Albrecht said, "I'd like to hear how that happened." Then he took on a serious look. "We left our own behind on that train…"

"Or they left us," Wilmot interrupted, rubbing his face again with snow.

"Maybe. My point is, whichever way you two look at it, we three should make a pact not to desert each other – we can do this – we can make it home but only if we stick together."

Wilmot sighed. He'd sat down for five minutes and his extremities were already numb. It was a nice thought, but he didn't believe a word of it. They weren't going to reach home; they were dying men in their final throes.

Chapter Thirty-Two

Paul Vogel

Łódź, Poland
February 1942

Paul left Berlin alone for Łódź, Poland's second largest city. Valentina, Biermann, and Olga were to join him four days later because his father-in-law had loose ends to tie up from an ongoing investigation in Berlin. Paul had suggested that Valentina travel with her mother and himself, but Biermann had made other arrangements for the ladies.

"They will travel in comfort, Paul. I have arranged a private compartment for us. You don't want your pregnant wife to sit for hours on the crowded Wehrmacht trains that you have to use, do you?" Biermann always seemed to finish his questions with a *do you* or a *don't you think?* Like a challenge to contradict. Paul, though desperate for Valentina to join him, was secretly pleased to have four days to himself in which to settle in and track down Kurt, who'd been deported to the Litzmannstadt-Łódź Ghetto at the end of January.

Fewer than half the train carriages carried Wehrmacht soldiers, SS, and Gestapo on this, the last leg of his journey. The windows in the last four ancient third-class carriages were blacked out, and inside they were crammed with deported Jews. Paul had many outstanding questions regarding the fates of the Jews going to Łódź, but the failure to learn about the ghetto was entirely his. He'd been too busy enjoying himself with Valentina in Dresden, and he hadn't wanted to spoil his leave by thinking about what was to come. Paul now wished that his father-in-law had given a bit more background into the place. He'd been cagey about the whole thing, especially when Paul had specifically asked about Kurt's fate.

"I told you, he's got off lucky." Biermann had deemed that was all his son-in-law needed to know.

Only one other man was sharing Paul's section of the carriage, an SS officer eating a ham sandwich. He must be from an affluent family, Paul deduced. It was not a common sight nowadays to see a thick cut of meat wedged between slices of bread, nor was the sterling silver tea flask the man was using.

"Have you been to Łódź before?" Paul asked, noticing snowflakes slicing into the windows.

The young, fair-haired Untersturmführer finished chewing his ham and peered at Paul.

"Before? Hah, I was born there. I'm Polish on my mother's side. My Father was German, but I didn't know him. He died just after the Great War. I was in Berlin visiting my German cousins. One of them got married yesterday to an Oberstleutnant. She's done very well for herself."

"Do you have anything to do with the Łódź ghetto?"

"I've been there for over two years. In fact, I was there right at the beginning."

"The beginning of the ghetto?"

"The beginning of everything." The man smiled displaying white teeth and thick lips spotted with breadcrumbs. He seemed friendly enough, but then, so had Hauptmann Leitner when Paul had first met him.

"How many Jews were in the city before the ghetto walls went up?" Paul asked.

"Over 230,000 when our forces occupied the city in '39. But we don't call it Łódź anymore. It was renamed Litzmannstadt just after we got there. You heard of a German general called Karl Litzmann?"

"No, sorry. I can't say I have."

"He led the army in 1914. You don't know your military history very well, do you?"

"I'm afraid not." Paul was beginning to feel uncomfortable in the SS officer's company. His spell in the SS, albeit for a short and devastating period of his life, had taught him to expect an almost fanatical attitude from its ranks, who were not above reporting members of other branches of the military to the security authorities for myriad misdemeanours that, in their eyes, were disloyal to the Führer. Still, he was desperate to learn all he could about the ghetto, and who better to ask about Łódź – Litzmannstadt – than an SS Untersturmführer who'd been there since its inception.

"Hmm, I must read up on the general. You see, this posting was very last minute," Paul said.

"Ach, don't worry about it. It's not like you're a real soldier. I don't suppose the Medical Corps have to learn all that military history stuff. You have enough on your plate learning about the anatomy, eh."

"Yes, how right you are." Paul smiled, warming to this Untersturmfürer. "I'm Paul Vogel," he said extending his hand.

"Gert Wolff. Call me Gert, please."

"Gert, will you tell me a bit about the ghetto?"

"What do you want to know? It's big. It still holds one of the largest Jewish communities in Europe, second only to Warsaw. Having said that, the Reich intends to purify the city by expelling every single Polish Jew to the *Generalgouvernement*. The ghetto is only a transitional centre. The Reich's aim is to burn out entirely this pestilent abscess from Poland."

"Does that mean the Jews will be looked after by the German authorities and not the Poles?"

"Exactly. It's getting that way now. When our authorities took the city, they ordered the Jewish residence to be limited to specific streets in the old City and the adjacent Bałuty Quarter – you'll get to know these places in the ghetto when you have a good walk around it – anyway, the big push into the ghetto happened in May of '40 when they had the pogrom. The SS weren't supposed to be directly involved. We were just standing by in case the Orpo Police got into trouble when they launched the relocation of the Jews across the city. The Kikes were given fifteen minutes to leave their apartments. After that, those who were found inside them were shot."

"When you say launched, do you mean with guns?"

Gert laughed. "Ach, Doctor, you've got a lot to learn about the Jews and how uncooperative some of them can be. They hide from us and cheat with false identity cards. They try to run – many of them did – and there are those, the worst of all, who refuse to move out of their houses. Have you never been to a Jewish detention camp before?"

"No. I was in Paris…"

"Lucky sod." Gert was still chuckling and wiggling his tongue around his teeth as though trying to dislodge a wedged piece of ham. "Look, Paul, the only way to get the Jews into line is to use deadly force from time to time as an example to others. On that day, two years ago, the Kikes didn't want to see reason, and the Orpo shot about three hundred and fifty of them in their houses. Some might say it was a bit heavy-handed, but it taught the other Kikes a lesson they wouldn't forget in a hurry. After that, they were like little yellow-starred sheep with their battered leather suitcases and little Jew children hanging onto their arms as they filed into the ghetto without a chirp – they still call that day, Bloody Thursday. Umm … where was I? Ah, yes, during the next two months we erected wire and wooden fences around the area to cut it off from the rest of the city. Electricity and water were cut off, and we kept non-Jews out by issuing a warning that the area planned for the ghetto was rampant with infectious diseases."

Paul's mind went back to the fences and warnings around the area where Judith's family had lived. He recalled his disapproval at the time, thinking that their confinement was the worst thing that could happen to them.

"The Ghetto is run by the *Erweitertes Polizeigefängnis, Radegast* – you know, the German Order Police and Gestapo – our authorities also established a Jewish Council inside the ghetto's walls. The Kikes call it the *Judenrat*. A Jew called Chaim Rumkowski runs it. He thinks he's a king, but we just let him get on with it. Our officials thought it better to give him the power he needs to properly maintain order and organisation in the Ghetto. The other Jews seem to respect him. They listen to him. I suppose without him, there would be a lot more work for us to do, and chaos for our administrators."

Gert stopped speaking and took a long, bold look at Paul. "So where are you going to be based?"

"I've got to report to Radogoszcz Prison with my orders first. After that, I'll be working at Hospital No.4."

"Ah, on Mickiewicza Street."

"That's right. My father-in-law is a high-ranking Gestapo officer. He'll be arriving later this week with our wives."

"Is that right? Your wife is being allowed to join you?"

Paul chuckled as Gert Wolff's expression changed from *I know it all* to *I'd better be respectful.* He hoped to capitalise on the man's new-found deference by requesting that he show him the way to the prison when they got off the train.

"I take it we're going to the only train station in Łódź? I'm not sure where the ghetto is, but I was told that the station is right on its boundary," Paul said.

"That's right. We in the SS have a saying about Radegast train station because it links the ghetto to the outside world. All roads lead to Litzmannstadt, but if you leave as a Jew your only destination is a long sleep – get it? They don't want to go into it, but they never want to leave the place when we deport them because there might be something worse outside the ghetto's walls."

Paul didn't have a clue what Gert was on about but kept up his friendly façade and smiled regardless. "It seems I do have a lot to learn. I must sound like an idiot, so forgive me for asking why the Jews don't want to leave the Ghetto?"

Gert hesitated. "Would you like a sandwich? My aunt made far too many. I've only got cheese left though. Is that all right?" He avoided answering Paul's question by removing the lid of his stainless-steel goody box and offering the sandwich inside to Paul, who gratefully accepted.

In return, Paul took out a sponge cake, baked by his mother-in-law for his journey, and cut a slice for Gert. "My mother-in-law's. She'll be upset if it doesn't get eaten." Paul handed the young, enthusiastic Nazi a piece, then bit into the sandwich. Gert could be a great source of information. Shame he was a Jew-hating bigit.

"Hmm. Delicious, Paul, thank you," Gert mumbled with a piece of cake in his mouth. "Getting back to your question about the Jews leaving the ghetto. You see, Paul, I don't think our lot expected as many Jews as they got. The ghetto was originally intended as a preliminary step on a more extensive plan of creating the Judenfrei province of Warthegaut. Instead, about forty thousand Polish Jews were forced out of Warthegaut and its surrounding areas and shoved into Litzmannstadt. Then, to make matters worse, they started transporting foreign Jews from Vienna, Berlin, Cologne, Hamburg, Luxembourg, the Protectorate of Bohemia and Moravia, *and* the citywide Theresienstadt concentration camp.

"When word got back to Germany about the ghetto bulging at the seams, Heinrich Himmler came to see for himself. No doubt about it, he helped calm the situation. Shortly after that visit, most of the patients in the ghetto's psychiatric hospital were taken away, and thank God, they've not returned – that must have been a bloody awful place to work – Jews are bad enough, but mad Jews?"

Paul replaced the top of his tea flask as he listened to the knowledgeable Gert. The patients from the psychiatric hospital were probably dead by now, and while he was reminded again of Brandenburg and Herr Rudolph, Kurt also came to mind.

"Did the over-occupancy problem inside the ghetto get solved?" Paul asked.

"Ach, if you ask me, it won't be solved until every Jew is expelled from Europe." Gert sniggered. "But, having said that, the authorities seemed to be getting to grips with the overcrowding. Just last month, ten thousand Jews were deported to Kulmhof – the Poles call it Chełmno – and things are looking up. I know for a fact that more deportations are on the cards for later this year. I can't say any more on that subject. You understand, Paul?"

"Of course. Thank you, Gert. Your information has been invaluable. I now know what to expect. I imagine I'll be kept very busy at the hospital."

"Oh, you'll be kept busy, alright." He cocked his head as though he were looking for a hint of dissension. "You seem scared, but it's not all bad, Paul. We've got trams on the ghetto's streets now. They transport food, fuel, and raw materials from Radegast station to various departments, and the goods produced in the ghetto go on the return journeys back to the station."

Gert got a map of the ghetto out of his rucksack and ran his finger across it. "Look, here. Tram lines have been built along Brzezinska, Marysinska, and Jagiellonska streets. And see these side tracks? They were built to serve the most important departments."

"Departments?" Paul hadn't a clue what he was supposed to be looking at. He couldn't even pronounce the street names, never mind know what the important departments were.

"This one," Gert was still pointing to the map, "is the tailoring department at Jakuba Street, where clothes are made, repaired or dished out. And this line here stops at the vegetable market on Lagiewnicka Street. There's talk of the trams being made available to the public, to transport people to work, but no news on when that's supposed to happen."

Paul smiled. "I'm very glad I met you, Gert. You've been a big help."

Chapter Thirty-Three

Before getting off the train, Gert handed Paul a note with the directions to his barracks and the name of a bar-restaurant situated outside the ghetto walls. The German military used it, although only officers were entitled to membership. Paul and Gert promised to keep in touch then parted ways, leaving Paul to lug his suitcase in one hand and his papers and a map of the ghetto in the other.

His priority was to look for Kurt, but he decided to postpone his search until after he'd registered with the Gestapo and deposited his heavy suitcase in his billet. He was staying in the city's military barracks until the Biermanns arrived. His father-in-law's detached house with a garden would be much grander than the one-bedroom apartment he'd been promised, but Valentina would make it look like a palace.

Paul would probably never know how the Kriminaldirektor had managed to obtain married quarters for a junior officer in the Medical Corps, but he supposed it was entirely possible that his father-in-law's Gestapo rank was more powerful than he'd led his wife and daughter to believe. One never knew what to think when it came to the Gestapo, apart from it being prudent to guard one's political opinions when in their company.

At the ghetto gates, Paul set his suitcase on the ground and handed over his papers to the German Schupo officer for inspection. Afterwards, a Jewish ghetto policeman offered to escort Paul to the prison. He even insisted on carrying the suitcase, much to Paul's embarrassment.

Radogoszcz prison, a German Police and Gestapo establishment, had originally been a four-storey factory with an adjoining floor. Biermann had talked at length about the prison in which he was going to work, although he'd been reticent about the ghetto itself.

Paul lingered outside the building, somewhat loath to enter. His father-in-law had made a point of telling Valentina and Olga that the first thing the Nazi authorities did when they took over Łódź was to arrest members of the city's intelligentsia. It had been an excellent plan, he'd agreed. "We always knew that to truly occupy a city, we would first have to get rid of its leaders." That strategy had been highly successful in Łódź because they'd not only incarcerated local and state bureaucrats, social and political activists, but also teachers and artists.

"What on earth did the Gestapo want with artists, dear?" Olga had asked innocently.

"As I said, Olga, strip a city of its leaders, journalists, and cultural examples and you will control an ignorant and vulnerable population. Do you understand now?"

"I suppose so," she'd answered with an unconvinced frown.

Paul had not been as easy on his father-in-law as his wife and daughter had been. Both women tended to listen and nod a lot when Biermann spoke about the war. He wished that Valentina would question her father, ask about how the war was going, give her opinions on political matters. Hannah always had, and he was all for women having their say and airing their thoughts. He hoped that by being married to him, Valentina would come to disagree with some of the Reich's policies, such as the one that dealt with Jews. It would be nice if she responded to her father one day, saying, "Jews are people, Papa, not animals, as you and Herr Hitler call them." She, like many Germans, had been brainwashed by Herr Geobbels' anti-Jewish propaganda machine, and evidently by her father whose nightly lectures concentrated on the merits of exiling Jews and dealing with them in the *toughest way possible.* Paul suspected that Biermann was preparing the ladies for what they would witness in Poland; if only he were as prepared and excited as the women seemed to be. He was not looking forward to working in the ghetto hospital at all.

That evening in Berlin, after the ladies had gone to bed, Paul had pressed Biermann for more information. The women had not asked what had happened to the city's leaders after their arrests and incarcerations, but that question had been on the tip of Paul's tongue. Reluctantly, his father-in-law had responded with a wishy-washy answer in which he'd explained that arrests had been made based on proscribed lists, and after a trial by a summary court, the people had been sentenced to death. "Why? For being respected leaders of the community?" Paul had questioned, keeping his temper in check.

Biermann had cut him off without an answer. "I'm going to bed, Paul. I shouldn't even be talking to you about this." That memory was still fresh in Paul's mind as he went through the registration procedures.

After he'd signed the necessary papers, Paul was escorted to his temporary barracks, situated four streets away from the ghetto's outer walls and barbed wire fences. Alone at last, he emptied his suitcase, and hung his clothes in a wardrobe big enough for only three hangers and with no shelving for underwear or socks. Then he put the food items he had brought from Berlin into his rucksack.

As he slung his rucksack over his shoulder, he imagined the poor buggers who had to live in the barracks' dingy, musty rooms with peeling wallpaper, black, damp patches on bare brick and putrid odours that caught in his throat. Duguay's basement in France had been more comfortable than the officers' quarters in Łódź.

Paul took more notice of the entrance upon his return to the ghetto from his barracks. Signs with large black letters saying JUDEN, were hung on sturdy branches. Long, white planks of wood were also nailed into trunks and stretched from one tree to another like pretty, white picket fencing. A young Gestapo Kriminalassistent and a policeman wearing a yellow star stood outside the security booth at the gate while two other Jewish policemen searched the bags of those going into the ghetto.

Gert had mentioned that the ghetto measured about one and a half square miles and housed around one hundred sixty thousand people, but on first impression, Paul thought the area was even smaller than he'd pictured. Gert had also mentioned that the German authorities had insisted that the ghetto be scaled down so that the factories could be situated outside its perimeter.

As he trudged through the slushy snow, Paul cast his eyes around him, storing the images of people and streets. The ghetto, isolated from the outside world, seemed to be divided in two, but wooden bridges had been built so Jews could cross between the two sections. Wire fencing also separated different sectors, and children stood up against one such partition with their noses peeking through the diamond-shaped holes.

Paul looked at a street sign: Zigurska Street, and then checked it on the map given to him by a policeman in the prison. It was an Aryan street apparently, and like many of the locations on the map, had a notice attached, this one specifying that Jews couldn't go there.

He observed a wooden bridge that was accessed by about sixty steps at either end. It was overloaded with people bumping into each other as they crossed in opposite directions. Why it hadn't already collapsed under their weight was beyond him.

Further along, two men, harnessed like mules, were pulling a cart carrying hundreds of loaves of bread lined up on end. The wheels were having difficulty turning because of the slush and ice on the ground and a few men loitering on the street corner joined the effort by pushing the sides of the cart.

At the corner of this street, the first signs of human suffering hit Paul. A row of men sat against a wall eating watery soup from battered tin bowls, every one of them with gaunt, grey faces, sunken cheeks and eyes, bony fingers, and emaciated hands. They lowered their heads as he neared, wary of looking him in the eye.

In the next street, Jews were going about their business. Some of them seemed to be bartering with each other for goods that were piled up on ground sheets, despite probably standing in the frigid air for hours.

Children were throwing slushy snowballs at each other. Paul smiled at them and they ran away. Further along, a man trudged through a minefield of concrete blocks and steel from the remains of a destroyed synagogue. He took off his cap and bowed his head as Paul passed, then replaced it and walked on. A pillar with the Star of David carved into the stone leaned at an angle jutting out of the snow like a memorial. It painted a stark contrast to the perfectly intact church with two tall spires that Paul spotted in the distance.

At a main road, he bumped into two Polish policemen who were running after a young man gripping a long loaf of bread in his hand. Biermann had told him that to ensure there was no contact between the Jewish and non-Jewish populations of the city, two German Order Police formations had been assigned to patrol the perimeter of the ghetto. Within its walls, however, a Jewish police force ensured that no prisoners tried to escape or committed crimes. So far on his walk, he had seen sixteen Jews carrying batons, dressed in police uniforms sporting the Star of David. A strange sensation swept over him. He saw them as Jews, yet also as traitors to their own race; keeping other Jews in order by force if necessary. It was a personal observation and not one he would share.

As a work-related question, Paul had asked Gert about the area specific to German Jews. He'd suspected that Jews with the same ethnicity would live together as would other minority groups such as Roma and clergy who had spoken out against Hitler's policies. If he were lucky enough to find Kurt, it would be in the designated German section.

Paul had wondered whether Biermann's motives had been benevolent or sinister when he'd deported Kurt to Łódź – Litzmannstadt – to hell with it, he'd call it Łódź. He was going to work with Polish doctors, and they were going to hate him for being German. The least he could do was get the name of their city right.

As he walked on, Paul thought again about Kurt and the reasons behind Biermann's sudden change of heart. This ghetto wasn't an unusual resettlement. Thousands of German Jews had already been deported to the city, but Biermann's unexpected decision was troubling, as were his strict orders.

"You mustn't go near Kurt Sommer, Paul. It's very important that you respect me in this," Biermann had insisted when Paul was leaving Germany. It was an unreasonable order and not one Paul would obey. He suspected that Biermann was using it as a loyalty test, but he also believed that his father-in-law wanted to interrogate Kurt further, and knew the only way he could do that would be to have Kurt close at hand. Paul didn't know how Biermann operated or what was in his mind, but he was convinced it wasn't kindness that had brought Kurt to this miserable place.

He stopped walking when he came to a junction. On the other side of the wide road, a building stuck out because of its three-metre half-open iron doors, each divided in the middle like stable doors but with a large square peephole in the upper section. He crossed the road, entered and then walked into a series of courtyards surrounded by the tenement buildings and a patch of snow-spattered greenery. This was the place Gert had eloquently described as the German district.

Paul checked the time and calculated that he had about three hours to spare before he was due at the hospital for his first meeting. He studied the buildings in front of him. They were four floors tall with innumerable windows, some with balconies. Outside the downstairs entrances, children were sitting in the slush. They all had runny noses, malnourished bodies and faces with huge dark-ringed eyes; not how children should look. Few had coats, gloves or scarves, and they looked half-starved, like the men he'd seen earlier with the watery soup. He was overwhelmed with pity while he gently shooed them indoors.

Paul entered a building and stopped short at the stairwell. The wall was pitted with bullet holes, the concrete steps sank in the middle and three were stained reddish-brown with what he could only presume was blood. He shuddered, recalling Gert's story about the police assault on the Łódź Jews.

He knocked on the first ground floor door he came to. A scrawny child answered then ran away as soon as she saw him. A man and women appeared, followed by four more adults, two of them carrying babies. Fear in otherwise dull eyes, stared back at him, but no one spoke.

"I'm looking for a man with the name of Kurt Sommer – Kurt Sommer," said Paul, then a thought struck him. "I'm sorry, I meant to say Karl Ellerich."

A man in his twenties came forward. He bowed his head before speaking, a wholly Jewish gesture borne of fear and defeat, that irritated Paul.

"Well, do you know him?" Paul asked.

"Yes, sir. I know Karl Ellerich. He lives on the third floor … he works … I think he's not at home."

"What time does he finish work?"

The man shrugged. "Forgive me … perhaps … maybe five o'clock, sir."

Paul thanked the man, then told the people with him to keep warm. A look of surprise crossed their faces as they closed the door.

On the third floor, Paul met a woman going into a flat. He asked her for Karl and she pointed to another door. An old man answered it and told Paul that Karl did live there but wasn't home yet from the factory.

Downstairs, Paul looked again at his watch and decided to wait for a while. After everything he'd seen, thus far, he wasn't leaving until he'd spoken with Kurt.

Chapter Thirty-Four

Kurt Sommer

Kurt's hands and feet were frozen. His flat grey cap was threadbare and sopping wet, and melting snow dripped onto his nose from its peak. His thin-soled boots trudged the last couple of blocks, the strength he'd had that morning long since spent on the heavy machinery he operated in the factory. A bath, hot stew with plenty of potatoes, and a coffee to finish off with in bed; what a fantasy that was. Such bliss he felt when dreaming about luxuries.

He pushed open the entrance door to his tenement building and did a double take when he spotted Paul sitting on the staircase. Kurt's mind flashed back to his last interrogation at Biermann's hands when he'd been branded with a hot poker on one of his buttocks. "You'll be seeing a lot of me, Kurt. I am following you to Poland. We'll have many chats in the future." At the time, Kurt had perceived the news as a threat, a way for Biermann to carry on his investigation into Dieter's death. But not once did he mention that Paul was also going to be based in Poland. Seeing Paul sitting there, his friendly face and eyes shining with affection, heartened Kurt no end; it was the best thing he'd seen in weeks.

The two men hugged. Kurt basked in the embrace, the first display of affection he'd received or given since his and Dieter's final farewell in the Vogel factory. Physical contact with another human being was priceless. He'd almost forgotten what intimacy felt like. He saw it every day; the Jews hugging each other for comfort. Loving and being loved kept every dream alive, every flame of hope lit, made every day a little more bearable in the ghetto.

Kurt drew away to hold Paul at arm's length. "You look good, Paul."

Paul shook his head. "I'm sorry, Kurt, but you don't look good at all. You're soaked. Do you want to dry off? We could go to your flat?"

"No, let's not," Kurt chuckled. "I live with eight other people in two rooms. We should talk here. It'll be quieter, and I won't have to answer a hundred questions after you leave."

"You look terrible," Paul repeated.

Kurt felt ill. Twelve-hour days on his feet in a factory making bullet and shell casings with hardly any calories or protein to sustain him, then sleeping on a hard, cold floor with children crying all night had weakened him to the point of giving up on life entirely. And he'd been there for less than a month.

"I'm all right," he lied, staring at the packages Paul was taking out of his rucksack.

"You're not all right at all. Any fool can see you're starving. Christ, Kurt, I've seen nothing but walking skeletons like you all day. Here, take these." Paul handed over the parcels wrapped in old newspapers and grinned as Kurt ripped them open one by one, his eyes gleaming with joyous tears like a child opening presents.

"Eat as much as you want but slowly," Paul urged. "Are they treating you well? Do you get enough rations?"

Kurt sniggered as he tore off a lump of bread with his teeth. He chewed, his eyes closed in ecstasy. "We're not given enough of anything to survive," he eventually said. "The hardest thing to see here is the children's gaunt faces and bloated stomachs. Some of them don't even have an appetite anymore, and the smell of food makes them nauseous. I've only been here three weeks and I've seen six dead children and two infants being thrown onto a hand cart outside and taken away."

"They're starving you?"

Kurt nodded slowly. "Yes. I think that's their plan; that, or they have no organisational skills. Coal and wood are in short supply. There's not enough of either to keep the cold at bay, let alone cook food. We don't have fires, so we're forced to eat black, rotten potatoes and other vegetables that would normally be cooked. A week ago, a crowd of people went to the wooden fences and outhouses and tried to tear them apart – they were punished, of course – kicked, beaten with sticks, stoned, shot in the head."

Kurt sighed, the sound more like a sob. "We get 20 grams of coffee for the week, and a loaf of bread every eight days, but it lasts me about two days if I stretch it out. Look at me. How can a man my size get by on that? I'm sick of seeing people with haggard skin, bones, and eyes collapsing and dying every day on the streets. You can't work a body like a mule without the fuel to keep it going…" Embarrassed Kurt cleared his throat and chuckled. "I'm a thief now, Paul. I've taken to running behind potato carts and using a stick with nails on the end to drag the potatoes off."

Paul's sorrow was palpable. He took a furtive look around. "I'm going to help you, Kurt. I didn't think the Nazis' madness could get any more outrageous but after what I've seen … well … I don't know what to say …"

"I'm all right, just so damn hungry and tired all the time," Kurt said before devouring another lump of bread.

When he'd eaten as much as he thought he needed to keep him going, Kurt jammed the packages of cheese, lard, more bread and an apple into his coat pockets. He'd give the lard to one of the women in the flat and slices of apple to the children. If they could stomach it and their tiny bellies got fuller, they might let him get some sleep.

"What's this job you've got?" Paul asked.

"It's in a factory. New businesses have been opening every week since I got here. They work us hard, and those that can't be useful are dealt with."

"What do you mean?"

Kurt bit his lip, his fingers opening and closing as he recalled January's terrible events. "Apparently, the problem with overcrowding started before I got here. The authorities took in five thousand Roma in December, and the council elder, Mordechai Chaim Rumkowski, told the German officials that Jews couldn't or wouldn't live with them. He said they'd rob people and set fires everywhere, including the factories and materials in them."

"I've heard that man's name mentioned before. What's he like? Is he a fair man?"

Kurt wanted to say, *He's a Nazi loving traitor, an arrogant bastard with an iron rod stuck up his arse. He hasn't a care for anyone but himself, is lining his pockets with blood money, and systematically getting rid of his political opponents,* but instead he replied, "He's sixty odd and full of self-importance. He was brought in to organise and implement Nazi policy within the ghetto. I don't know why he was chosen. Rumours are that he was nobody of importance before the war. He'd had an unremarkable life, selling insurance, managing a velvet factory, and running an orphanage."

Feeling calmer and warmer and more like his old self, Kurt continued, "You'd think he was the bloody Chancellor. He's replaced German currency with ghetto money that bears his signature – can you believe that? People call the new money *Rumkies.* He's also created a post office with a stamp in his image. The only decent thing he's done is build a sewage clean-up department since the ghetto has no sewage system."

"Maybe he's doing some good?" Paul suggested.

"Doing good would be feeding the children and keeping the elderly warm, and that takes me back to why I mentioned the man in the first place. When the Roma arrived in December, they were housed in a separate area of the ghetto because of Rumkowski's protest. But shortly after, and I can only tell you what I heard from a man who's fond of licking Rumkowski's backside – you know, does his bidding, runs errands for him, finds out what Jews are saying about their situation and what they truly think of their Jewish leader – anyway, this man told me that the Nazis had wanted to deport twenty thousand Jews out of the ghetto. Apparently, Rumkowski talked them down to ten thousand. The lists of deportees were put together by ghetto officials and the Sinti and Roma were at the top of it. Next were people who didn't work, had a criminal background, or were related to someone in those two categories. When I got here in January, the deportations had already started. I saw children and the elderly being put on trucks and driven away with their families running, screaming and weeping after them."

"It's like Brandenburg all over again." Paul shook his head.

Kurt's mouth settled into a tight line. "Why are you looking so glum? You had your chance, Paul."

"What do you mean?"

"You know damn well what I mean. You could have gone to England with Max over a year ago. You of all people know what your kind is doing to Jews, so don't sit there looking shocked."

Paul flinched. "My kind?"

"Yes. You're working for the Nazis, the Jew killers. Once you put that uniform on, you became the executioner you were in Brandenburg." Bitterness coloured Kurt's words. "We're starving to death, Paul, slow, horrible deaths. Women, children, men who used to be strong, wealthy, and law abiding are falling in the streets like sacks of bones. It makes no difference to the Gestapo or SS who dies, and you being here won't change a bloody thing."

"You're being unfair…"

"Am I? Tell me, are you the doctor you aspired to be?"

Paul looked sheepish. He had no response to Kurt's words.

"Well, are you a good German doctor?" Kurt goaded.

The two men held each other's eyes until Paul finally broke the silence. "We'll talk about my failings another time. Go back to your story. Where did they send the deported people?"

"I don't know, but I was working in a factory near the train station and saw at least a thousand people being put on trains every day during the last two weeks of January. We were told they'd gone to Polish farms to work – liars – babies, children and the old who had to be lifted into the train carriages, and we're supposed to believe they were going to work in the fields, in January? Ridiculous."

Another uncomfortable silence followed. Kurt stared at his sodden shoes, turning his fury inwards. Paul's face was ashen, his jaw muscles jumping under his skin.

"I'm sorry, Paul. It's good to see you, but it's hard to keep a cheery face in this God-forsaken place. Sorry for my foul mood, and for not telling your father I was a Jew. I hope you understand." Kurt lied, aware now that he couldn't share any secret with Paul because of his association with Biermann. Dieter had known from day one that he was a Jew, and he had not told a soul, not even Laura.

322

"It wouldn't have made any difference to us," Paul asserted. "My father, for all his Nazi-loving ways, wouldn't have thrown you out or had your name put on a register. This is me you're talking to, Kurt. I am *not* a Nazi. I'm your friend. I always will be your friend no matter what my uniform says or forces me to do. And if my father was still alive, he'd have had something to say to Freddie Biermann about your predicament."

Kurt took out another lump of bread and began to chew slowly, savouring every morsel. He wondered what Paul might say if he saw the letter *J* for Jew branded on his left buttock? He hadn't been able to sit down for days. Paul didn't know his father-in-law, not the real Biermann. He hadn't the slightest notion of what the cruel bugger was capable of or what he was investigating, and that was a good thing.

It was clear that Paul believed Dieter to be dead. Had he thought otherwise, he'd have asked outright if it were true or false, regardless of Biermann's presence. The Kriminaldirektor, even now, was deliberately keeping that gem to himself, which meant he had neither the solid evidence he'd claimed to have nor Dieter's artworks. Kurt was desperate to tell the lad that Dieter was alive, but to do so would make him a target for Gestapo interrogations.

"I presume your father-in-law will be arriving soon?" Kurt sighed. "Don't tell him you've seen me."

"He'll ask me," Paul responded with a bitter smirk. "When I came to Spandau prison to see you, he made me read the charges against you. He accused you of being a British spy. Is he right?"

"No. It's fabricated nonsense. I was imprisoned and deported because I'm a Jew ... me ... me, a spy? Absurd." Kurt cocked his head to one side as a thought struck him. "Don't you find it odd that you were given the same posting as your father-in-law?"

"Yes." Paul nodded. "I also think it strange that he forbade me to see you, when he must have known you'd be my first port of call. I might be wrong, but I think he wants me to get information from you. He claims that my father's artwork in the Berlin and Dresden houses was either stolen or taken somewhere before the factory explosion. Apparently, my mother didn't know where the paintings went either. Do you know anything about that?"

"No." Kurt exhaled another lie. "You should go, Paul. The ghetto police patrol this area when people are coming back from the factories. Sometimes they come in to do head counts in the buildings."

Paul's misery was etched on his face as he pushed his cap down his forehead.

Kurt, regretting his earlier outburst, said, "Paul, I'm very grateful to you. I know you want to help."

"I do, and I will."

"Could you find out where the Roma and Jews were sent? I'd like to be prepared for whatever might be planned for me."

Paul nodded. "I'll tell you whatever I find out, but you mustn't tell anyone else."

"Of course. No one trusts anyone around here. Everyone's scared of spies, and Jews telling tales on other Jews to the Nazis, hoping for more food or special treatment in return. And don't you trust Biermann for one second. Don't tell him anything."

Paul grimaced and slung his rucksack over his shoulder. "That bastard's getting nothing from me." And as reached the door, he added, "This is a bloody awful situation. I'll be working in one of the hospitals, and I don't know how often I'll be able to see you, but I'll bring food and medicine whenever I can. I'm going to get you out of this place, Kurt. I don't know how, but I swear to God I will."

The two men shook hands, then Kurt watched Paul disappear into the falling snow. Life had just become a little more bearable. He had a friend.

Chapter Thirty-Five

Paul and Biermann

Litzmannstadt Ghetto, Łódź, Poland
February 1942

After they made love, Paul purred like a contented cat as he ran his hand over Valentina's developing tummy. "It's good to be home, darling. I wish we didn't have to go out. I could stay like this until tomorrow morning. To hell with dinner," he whispered playfully in her ear. "To hell with the world."

"To hell with you, Paul Vogel," Valentina responded by removing his hand. "I'm starving, and I promised my mother and father we'd be there by seven o'clock. They're looking forward to spending time with you. You don't want to let Papa down, do you?"

Paul yawned and looked at his wrist watch. It was five-thirty in the afternoon and he was just beginning to relax. He'd give anything to let *Papa* down. He'd got home at 15:00 after a particularly trying morning. Heart disease, tuberculosis, and malnutrition were rife in the ghetto. Two cases of typhus had been confirmed, and in both cases the patients were elderly Jews who had died shortly after being brought in. He stroked Valentina's hair. He wouldn't tell her about the horrors he saw at work. His job upset her.

His place of work, the medical centre called Hospital No.4, was located on Mickiewicza Street inside the ghetto. It was an aesthetically drab, four-storey building with a dirty cream façade and an ugly entrance and interior. Since his arrival, he'd learnt a lot about the place. The nurses and orderlies were all Jews, supported by five doctors, two of whom were Christian Poles. The centre's chief administrator was also a Jewish physician, but Paul had never seen him treat or even speak to patients, most of whom were ghetto residents.

Patient care was shockingly bad. Ambulance orderlies were sent to retrieve patients in horse-drawn wagons or large wooden handcarts looking more like wheelbarrows. They didn't seem to care if their patients got to hospital alive or dead, probably because those who ended up in the Centre were so seriously ill they usually died shortly after admission. If Paul could see patients beforehand, he'd tell them to refuse to go to the hospital. They had a better chance of recovery, or a nicer death, at least, in their own squalid rooms being looked after by family. Love was a powerful medicine.

The hospital was fortunate enough to have salvaged a pre-war X-ray machine, but broken bones were splinted with rough wood and torn fabric. There was a dire shortage of medicine and, of course, food. It was a pitiful excuse for a health facility in which many nurses, orderlies, and doctors were afraid to get too close to their patients. Diseases such as typhoid and tuberculosis put the staff's lives at risk; all they had in the way of protection were pieces of cloth to tie around their noses and mouths.

Paul was unpopular with the hospital staff. Doctors were reluctant to talk to him about anything other than medical matters, and nurses skirted around him as though afraid of coming to his attention. The reasons for their animosity were easily explained: he was a German, a Wehrmacht doctor in a supervisory position, and a member of the enemy's occupying forces. They loathed him, but not enough to refuse to answer his questions about the hospital's history since the beginning of the occupation.

The staff had sent a representative to speak to Paul in private about the incident that had changed the make-up of hospital number 4 in a single day. The young Jewish doctor had looked terrified while clumsily explaining that the elderly patients who had once filled the hospital had disappeared in the space of a morning and were never seen again. Paul had asked him what he thought had happened to the people who been removed, but he'd received an ambiguous and muted response. "Perhaps they went somewhere else."

"You are looking forward to this evening, aren't you, Paul?" Valentina interrupted Paul's thoughts.

"Yes. I'm looking forward to seeing your parents," Paul said, pulling Valentina to him and pushing thoughts of work away. "I'm being selfish. We've had so very little time together lately." He kissed her softly and again ran his hand over her swollen stomach. "Hmm … I adore you like this."

"No. Stop it," she said, removing his hand from between her thighs. "We won't be able to do this for much longer. You *were* naughty – Paul, please, don't – think about the baby."

Paul chuckled as he raised his offending hand in the air. "I'm sure we'll find a way to make love that won't harm the baby. Don't worry, dearest, you can trust me. I'm a doctor."

She giggled, and he silenced her with another gentle kiss on her lips. She was his refuge, his escape from the ugliness of the world outside. He loved her excited chatter about the baby clothes she and her mother were knitting, the names she'd considered for their unborn child, and the colourful stories she told about the excursions she and Olga had taken around the city in a chauffeur-driven Gestapo car. She was vivacious, in good health, and not missing her job at the Reich Security Office in Berlin at all. If only he were half as happy as she was.

Valentina had a selective view of life in Łódź, which was vastly different to the one held by the Poles and Jews. She didn't seem to notice the destroyed buildings, German soldiers, and ghetto walls. From her perspective, days in the city thus far had been entertaining and stimulating. She'd taken tea with high-ranking military wives, where they'd apparently discussed everything and anything one could imagine … except for the war and the vast number of people starving in the cut-off northern part of the city. He assumed she and the other women either didn't know what was going on in the ghetto or didn't like to discuss it, for neither Valentina nor her mother had asked a single question about it.

******

"I can't find a good selection of maternity clothes anywhere, Papa. I wish I had bought dresses in Berlin before we left. I'm going to look stupid in mother's home-made frocks. Her patterns are ancient. Don't Polish women get pregnant?"

"Darling, a lot of the shops in Litzmannstadt were bombed," said Biermann using Łódź's German name with a patience he reserved only for his wife and daughter.

Paul intervened, "There's a shortage of everything in the city, not just clothes. Keep in mind, dear, that most of the clothing shops and factories were owned or run by Jews. It's not their fault that they can't continue to trade."

Biermann scowled at Paul. He wasn't happy with his son-in-law's sharp tone or his attitude towards his Valentina who was in a delicate state. "Valentina, why don't you tell Paul about your visit to Frau Schmidt's house the other day?"

"Oh, yes. She's wonderful, darling," Valentina gushed. "She's the wife of *Generalleutnant* Braun, a lovely man by all accounts. It's such a pity she went back to Munich."

"Where did you meet her?" Paul asked.

"She and her husband were staying at the Hotel Bristol. Generalleutnant Braun was touring some place or other, and she invited five of us permanent Litzmannstadt wives to tea. After eating *delicious* cakes that she'd brought with her especially from Germany, she entertained us all at the piano – Bach, I think, wasn't it, Mama?"

"Yes. She played very well, but you haven't told Paul the best part, dear," Olga said.

"And what was that?" Paul smiled.

"Well, she said if any of us would like to have a holiday, we could join her at her second home in Bavaria. And you'll never guess – it's very near to the Berghof where the Führer sometimes goes. She told us that she'd once seen him in a café eating cakes, and the people with him said hello to her. Isn't that marvellous?"

Biermann smiled indulgently at his daughter. Unbeknownst to her and Olga, he had already spoken about a holiday in Bavaria with Frau Schmidt's husband. Fritz Braun was a friend of his from the Einstein Club and had been delighted with the suggestion that the ladies get together while the menfolk were away. Biermann suspected that Fritz was equally pleased that he'd have more time to spend with his Berlin mistress.

"… Papa, did Mama tell you about our walk along the embankment yesterday? The River Jasień is *full* of ducks."

"Is that so?" Biermann replied.

"We sat on a bench for almost an hour making the most of the milder weather, and I remarked to Mother that I don't know how those poor ducks are surviving. Not once did I see anyone throw bread to them."

"If there's not enough bread to feed the people, they're hardly likely to give what they have to the ducks," Paul said, irritated. "I hate to tell you this, but I'm betting those ducks will live only until they're big enough or fat enough to net and cook. Hopefully, they'll feed a lot of hungry families."

"Oh, don't upset us, Paul. I won't sleep now for thinking about those poor creatures," Valentina moaned.

For a while, the men listened to the ladies describing in detail how they passed their days when left to their own devices. Then, when he'd had enough, Biermann lit a fat cigar, giving Olga her cue to leave the room with Valentina. He'd hardly seen his son-in-law, and there was much he wanted to discuss with him in private.

"I thought we'd see a lot more of each other, Paul, but it seems our paths rarely cross," Biermann said pleasantly enough, after the ladies had left.

"I kept meaning to visit you at the prison, but my shifts at the hospital keep running over. To be honest, I'm pleased Valentina has her mother for company. It was a splendid idea of yours to have them living near one another."

"You won't catch me at the prison," Freddie mumbled, puffing on his cigar. "We've left the local police to run it. We're still in charge, of course, but I've been travelling a bit more than I thought I would. Our new offices are in Alexanderhoffstrasse. Stop by and say hello."

Paul looked surprised, but Biermann didn't want to give his nosey son-in-law any more information, for now.

"How is your job at the hospital?" Biermann asked after another couple of long, drawn-out puffs.

"It's hard, sir. We have far too many patients and not nearly enough medicines, food, or equipment. It's not easy to cure a person of malnutrition when we can't give them the nutrients they need. I haven't said anything to Valentina, but we're also seeing typhus cases."

Freddie was appalled. "In the hospital? Did *you* treat them?"

"No, they were in a quarantine room on the top floor. They died soon after being admitted." Paul sipped his coffee. "Don't worry, the illness is not transmitted from person to person, like influenza…"

"But it can spread?"

"Yes, it can."

Biermann frowned. "I worry about my Valentina being exposed to that and other diseases going around."

"As do I. The ghetto is the perfect breeding ground for arthropods which can jump from person to person. If there are six people sharing the same room and only one bed, or a head of hair is infested with fleas, mites, lice, or ticks, you can bet your life that the disease will spread like wildfire within days. And if those infected continue to come to the hospital, we're all in trouble. I suggested we keep the sick inside the ghetto and take preventative measures. It can be curtailed by controlling the rodent population and disinfecting the contaminated areas. Unfortunately, no one seems to agree with me that doing something is better than doing nothing." Paul dropped his coffee spoon onto the table. "To be honest, sir, had I known the conditions in the ghetto were this abysmal and inhumane…"

"Now, now, I'll have none of that nonsense," Biermann snapped. "What did you expect? Do you think we should have given the Jews rooms in fancy hotels, eh? You don't understand the mechanics of it all. They had to go into an environment they're used to, like the tenement blocks. The only difference now is that they're forced to share their rooms with other families. That's not so very bad, is it? A lot of those Jews were living in houses far too big for them, anyway. And what more can they need? They're pigs. They don't require more gravy in their troughs, do they? No, no. In my opinion, they're being treated better than some of our soldiers on the Russian Front." Biermann started counting with his fingers. "We have allowed for outpatient clinics, first aid stations, dental clinics, a disinfection facility, and several pharmacies."

Biermann grimaced. He'd seen a truckload of Roma leaving the train station. Their stink had been on him the entire day. "Those filthy Roma are no better than animals. They're more used to sleeping under bridges and such-like. I hope you're not treating *them* for typhus? Any doctor who does will be severely punished. You know that, don't you, Paul?"

"Yes, sir. Weren't they deported in January?"

"Yes, but like the bugs you mentioned, they keep coming back."

Biermann was disappointed in Paul. He'd genuinely liked his daughter's new husband, but all too often now he was seeing a side of the man he didn't approve of. A few months earlier, he'd spoken with Hans Rudolph, who'd worked at Brandenburg. He was now at another hospital in Berlin, but he continued to criticise Paul's abilities as a doctor and his troublesome attitude towards his superiors. He'd also had a lot to say about Captain August Leitner, the dead Abwehr agent; it had been an enlightening conversation and one Biermann hoped to raise with his son-in-law in the future.

Biermann accepted that Paul wasn't a Nazi at heart. He'd said as much to Hans Rudolph, but Vogel's openly sympathetic views of the Jewish situation were disturbing, and frankly, with him now as a son-in-law, an embarrassment.

Days earlier, Valentina had let slip to her father that she suspected Paul of smuggling contraband into the ghetto. She didn't know who he was delivering the food and medicine to, but she worried he might get into trouble for pilfering rations from the hospital and then giving them to Jews. She knew for a fact he was doing it, she'd emphasised. She'd searched his rucksack whilst he was taking a shower and had discovered all manner of goodies.

As Biermann was recalling the conversation, Paul excused himself to go to the bathroom. Biermann puffed on his cigar, giving the room a smoky haze that took its time to waft out of the slightly open window. He'd already known about Paul's trips to the ghetto's German section; he'd had a man following his son-in-law since the day he arrived in Poland. Nonetheless, he had questioned Valentina further, squeezing answers out of her like a dripping sponge without her even recognising his motives. She didn't know much about Paul's job or what went on inside the ghetto, she'd said. Paul didn't talk about those things to her and she never brought up the subject; such things upset her.

When Paul returned, he poured more coffee from the pot into his cup. "That was a lovely dinner. Thank you, sir," he said.

"Have you been to the ghetto?" asked Freddie, holding Paul's eyes.

"No, the Polish doctors do the inspections. I've never been inside the place."

"So, you don't go into the ghetto at all?"

"No. Never."

Freddie stared at Paul through the cigar smoke and forced a smile. "Thank God. At least you won't get infected by this typhus disease you mentioned."

"Yes, true. And if the hospital administrator does as I ask, we won't be inundated with cases at the hospital."

Paul continued to talk about his job, but Biermann was becoming bored with the subject of hospitals and diseases. Paul was in Litzmannstadt for only one reason: to get to the truth about Dieter from Kurt Sommer and find the location of the art collection.

Biermann sighed, also frustrated with his own work. Dieter's deception was eating away at him, and he didn't know if his fixation on the matter stemmed from diligent police work or from the gut-punching hurt he felt every damn morning when he woke up. He drew heavily on his cigar again until his face was flushed and obscured by smoke. The Gestapo, SS, and Abwehr; they'd all laughed when he'd shared his suspicions and the autopsy results he'd fought so very hard to get. They'd thought him mad, and, outraged by his accusations, had banished him to Poland.

Heydrich's aide had spoken to Biermann on the sly, giving him some insight into why his superiors had reacted so violently to the accusations. The Reich didn't want a scandal, especially one which involved any suggestion of disunity within the Nazi Party. They had balked at the very idea of an important industrialist and Party financial contributor colluding with the British and faking his own death. Even if it were true, which was ridiculous, such news could never reach public ears. The Fatherland was at war, and the people needed to see harmony in the leadership and its ranks.

Thus, the Vogels' good name was intact. Dieter's factories were still open for business and being run by men who had worked in them for years. That situation was going to change, however, and change soon, Biermann consoled himself. The Reich would requisition the factories as soon as Hitler's demand for more armaments grew, and those demands were ramping up now.

Biermann's wandering mind came back to Paul, sitting in silence as though afraid to speak. He was weak, a trait Biermann had recently noticed in his son-in-law. "Did you hear about Fritz Todt's death?" he asked.

"No?" Paul eyebrows shot up. "Wasn't he the Minister of Armaments and War Production?"

"Yes. He died a few days ago in a plane crash shortly after taking off from the Führer's eastern headquarters at Rastenburg. You know, the speed with which Herr Hitler makes tough decisions is quite remarkable, and they're usually correct. I've just heard today that he's already appointed Albert Speer as Todt's successor to all his posts." Biermann puffed hard. "It's well known that Speer is Hitler's favourite pet. He's a wonderful architect – even Stalin wanted his services – did you know that?"

"No, I'm afraid I'm a bit slow to catch up on news."

"Speer will probably revolutionise the weapons production sectors," Biermann continued. "Those idiots, the five *supreme authorities,* as they like to call themselves, claim they don't have the money for major armament production, but I'm betting Speer will sort them out."

Biermann, tiring of Paul's blank expression when it came to politics, stubbed his cigar butt in the ashtray and got up. He'd get his revenge on Dieter once he had cracked Sommer with Paul's help. Then he'd have the art collection and a more than decent retirement payoff. It would take time, but he had that in spades.

"I miss your father, Paul. You do, too. I can see you're still grieving," Biermann muttered with a sigh.

Paul also rose. "I am grieving. I just wish I had been able to say a proper goodbye to him. There's a lot of things I would have liked to have said, but you know, the hardest thing of all is not being able to speak to my mother. I understand why she decided to leave Germany, but it's hard."

Unsure if he'd heard correctly, Biermann asked, "You do understand her, or you don't?"

"I understand why she left Germany. Her family is in England, along with Hannah and Max. I would have urged her to go had I been in Berlin when my father died. Willie probably won't get leave from Russia, and I was bound to be off somewhere or other. I feel we, her children, let her down when she needed us most. Thank you for looking after her. My father would have been grateful to you."

"You're welcome. Your papa would have done the same for my wife." Biermann patted his son-in-law's broad shoulder. "It's time you got your wife home. Goodnight, Paul."

Chapter Thirty-Six

Wilmot Vogel

Somewhere in Northern Russia
March 1942

Unbeknownst to Wilmot, Jürgen, and the Hauptmann, they had escaped the train on the last day of February and were now into the first week of March. Only four days and three nights had passed since they'd escaped out of the wagon's window, but it felt like weeks. Everything seemed to be moving in slow motion: their pace, thoughts, self-control, and conversation. They now ambled rather than strode, had difficulty with their coordination and memory, at times returning to the same spot without realising they'd been there before. They were lost and had no idea how far they had come, or if they were still going north.

They had been determined to walk each day until they dropped. The act moved them closer to their goal and the exertion kept their bodies warm. They were no longer worried about Russian soldiers or their captors on the train; their principle concern now was the time and effort it would take to reach friendly forces at the Finnish defensive positions.

Neither Wilmot nor the Hauptmann talked about how they were planning to cross the Russian lines to get to the Finns, but Jürgen had enough pessimism for all three of them. He claimed that they were going on a suicide mission and that Wilmot's boasting about being able to read the North Star and shadows in the clouds wasn't going to save them from the thousands of Russian troops they'd find at the Mannerheim Line. Wilmot had smacked the boy over the head, telling him not to speak again until he had something useful to say.

The men were starving, but they had managed, thus far, to survive on handfuls of berries and pine nuts found under the snow. The berries had a pleasant, sweet taste, and they also seemed to calm Wilmot's diarrhoea. Jürgen, with his wild brown hair and the beginnings of a stubbly beard, had yelled like a delighted child when he'd found a wild winter mushroom patch. But, being an impulsive lad, he'd shoved them in his mouth, one after the other, without first nibbling on one and then waiting to check if it was poisonous. Afterwards, he'd vomited for the Fatherland, delaying the men's progress.

At first, they'd had no knives, matches, guns, or any other type of tool that could help them hunt, kill, or cook prey. Wilmot had snapped off one of the lower branches from a pine tree, and using a sharp stone, he had whittled it down at the end to made himself a rough spear. He hadn't been able to try it out yet, as the lemmings he'd seen had kept their distance, and he wasn't strong enough to chase after them.

It was late in the afternoon when the men gave up on their journey for the day. Jürgen was too weak to walk another step. His muscles were failing. He was staggering like a drunk with a blood-stained scarf around his head, having injured himself that morning. Bemused as to where he was and what he was doing there, he'd started rambling on about his mother and how she'd smack him for being late home for dinner.

Wilmot crouched at the base of a tree trunk and studied his companions resting a couple of metres away. Not comfortable calling the Hauptmann by his Christian name, Max, he'd met the captain half way and now addressed him as Haupt. He was sitting against another tree, holding a semi-conscious Jürgen as a man would cradle a child. Overcome by exhaustion and incipient hypothermia, the boy was curled up with his head on Haupt's lap.

Wilmot plopped down next to Haupt and shouted in his ear, "This wind is going to get a lot worse. There's a blizzard on the way. Jürgen won't make it unless we find shelter."

"Do you see any houses? Let me know if you do … we'll … I know, we'll pop in for a cup of coffee."

Wilmot observed his travel companions in silence. He was worried about having to take care of them both. Haupt seemed to be drifting off a lot and couldn't remember Jürgen's name half the time. All three of them were irritable, but Jürgen had gone a step too far by trying to kill himself. The silly bugger had bashed his addled skull against a tree trunk until Wilmot had dragged him away and pinned him down. The boy wanted death, craved it. "Kill me, Willie. Use my scarf to strangle me. I just want to go now," Jürgen had begged. Wilmot, thinking of the German prisoners the Russians had murdered, and the soldiers blown up or shot in battle, had reacted badly by punching Jürgen and telling him he was a selfish bastard.

The wind was whipping Wilmot's face. Desperate to get out of it, he tried to make Haupt see reason. "Haupt, listen to me. The forest is thinning out. There's a clearing ahead. I can see the path to it. If I'm right, the snow will be thicker, the ground won't have as many tree roots in it, and it'll be softer to dig out."

Wilmot's eyes focused on the brightness beyond the trees. It was like a light at the end of a clichéd tunnel. "When we were at the Leningrad Line, I came across a Russian manhole with a Russkie in residence. After I'd killed him, I examined his dugout. It was about one and a half metres deep and wide enough for him to sit down with his knees at his chest. It had a roof of pine and spruce tree branches like the ones breaking off with the wind here, and it was almost warm inside." His mouth snapped shut. It seemed like a lifetime ago, so he wouldn't tell Haupt about the hole he'd helped Geert and Claus dig before the assault on the Russians. It had not saved his friends' lives as intended, it had killed them. "We can outlast this blizzard, Haupt, but you've got to help me. We need to dig a hole and get in it before the storm hits … do you hear me? For God's sake, wake up, Haupt … it's coming!"

Haupt's eyes were glazed. His mouth lifted and twitched at the corners, as though he were about to have a fit of the giggles. "Branches don't fall off pine trees or spruces or larches willy-nilly … I know about trees. I know every tree in Germany … look at him. Look at Jürgen. He can't dig. And we've got no spades. Have you got a spade?"

"Of course, I bloody don't. Look, if you don't want to help, I'll dig a hole just big enough for me."

"You wouldn't fucking dare, traitor…" Haupt snarled like a dog.

Wilmot lurched away. His captain had gone mad.

"Right, that's it. I've had enough of you two. You can both stay here and freeze your balls off."

Wilmot disentangled Jürgen from Haupt's arms and dragged him closer to the tree trunk where his back was to the wind.

"I'm not taking Jürgen to the clearing. He's got a bit of shelter from the wind here. I'll come back for him when the dugout is ready," Wilmot told Haupt. "Will you come with me or not?"

Haupt got to his feet and staggered towards Wilmot. "Of course, I'll come. Can't have you wandering off by yourself, can we?"

Less than a hundred metres from Jürgen's tree, Haupt and Wilmot found a bright, white world of snow and sky. They peered into the swirling wall of snowflakes, their eyes unable to penetrate it, yet Haupt's brain seemed to be rallying with the exertion.

"We'll dig here," he said, already on his knees.

"We can't see a damn thing." Willie pulled a face. "We might be facing a Russian defensive line."

"Or we might be alone in this wilderness. We've not had a single sign that their forces are anywhere near here. No army is going to move in this."

At last, Haupt was thinking straight and talking sense. Both men, intent on making some semblance of a shelter, got to work without any more complaints. Haupt was right; they didn't have the luxury of feeling scared of what if or what might be. If they couldn't see more than a few metres in front of their faces, neither could the Russians, even if they were in the area.

With Willie's optimism somewhat heightened, he shouted, "This is our only hope of surviving, Haupt! Branches *are* falling off, which means that we're in for a hell of a storm."

The men began to dig like dogs, on their knees scooping out the snow with their gloved hands and arms until they hit ice-encrusted ground beneath it. They paused, looked at the ground, and then at each other.

Wilmot, undeterred, began jabbing the snow with his tree-branch spear, but to no avail. "Bugger it! Nothing short of a pickaxe will penetrate this frozen earth."

"We'll build up, then – a three-sided wall of snow against the direction of the wind?" Haupt suggested.

Willie panted, his breath catching in his throat. He inhaled, exhaled then inhaled again, each time deeper and stronger until he managed to hold a slow but steady breathing pattern. Although the walls were still only a couple of hundred centimetres and not high enough to shelter them from the elements, the act of constructing it gave him hope. His hands moved slower with each pile of snow he lifted, but the good news was that ice was forming almost immediately, making the structure stronger and igloo-like. Death was coming, he felt it knocking at his door, but he wouldn't give into it until it hauled him kicking and screaming all the way to hell. He wasn't Jürgen or Haupt. He was a Vogel.

A wolf, howling somewhere in the semi-darkness, had been following the three men since the previous night. They'd first heard it at nightfall and were convinced that it was a lone predator. It had howled for half an hour, but afterwards it had quietened, not making a sound again until two or three hours later when it repeated the pattern. Haupt had suggested that the wolf's erratic behaviour: advance, howl, and then retreat, was a sign that it was going to give up on the idea of attacking the men. Wilmot, however, suspected that there was nothing erratic about its actions and that the animal was cleverly exploring and investigating the vulnerabilities of its victims. He did agree, however, that wolves were not prone to attacking humans when they were outnumbered.

Both men peered through the thick treeline to where they'd left Jürgen. The violent gale had grown louder, obscuring all other sounds including that of the wolf's yowls. Haupt stopped gouging the snow and staggered to his feet. "We should go back for the boy."

Willie wasn't happy. "You go. I'll keep building this up."

"No. I can't manage Jürgen on my own. Sod the walls. C'mon, Willie, we shouldn't have left him alone."

Haupt was making sense, forcing Wilmot to agree with his captain's suggestion. Jürgen was dead weight when he passed out every five minutes. Haupt, even with stoic determination, was almost as physically weak as the lad and wouldn't even be able to get the emaciated boy to his feet. Wilmot gestured to the fallen branches that had broken off the pine trees behind them. "Take one, just in case the wolf attacks," he shouted to Haupt over the din.

The two men battled the elements to get back to young Jürgen. Wilmot still didn't hear as much as a wolf's whimper above the squealing storm, but that didn't mean it wasn't close by and stalking the half-dead boy sitting against a tree. Wilmot gripped his sturdy tree branch with its sword-like tip in his hand and pushed hard against the wind. He wouldn't be beaten by a wolf, not after everything they'd been through.

Both men gasped for breath, but when they got close to the tree, they held it. A brown, scrawny wolf was gnawing at Jürgen's leg, ripping off pieces of flesh and swallowing them whole. Startled, it looked up from its meal, first with irritation, then with outright hostility. Its yellow eyes gleamed in the dusk and held Wilmot's stare. Blood dripped from the beast's mouth, a stringy piece of Jürgen's flesh hanging from its large canine teeth.

Wilmot glared back in a silent game of wills. Jürgen, his face and torso partially obscured by the animal, wasn't making a sound or movement, not a twitch or a snivel. Wilmot, more angry than afraid, scanned his memory for everything his father had ever told him about hunting in the Grunewald Forest. *Don't stare at a wolf. Don't make eye contact. Don't look scared. Don't run away. Build a fire ... build a bloody fire?* Of course, why didn't he think of that? The wolf would sit around and wait until the flames were burning brightly then join the men for marshmallows! Where did people get these bloody stupid ideas?

"Back away, Wilmot," said Haupt, already taking a step backwards.

"Sod that, Haupt. I don't know about you, but I'm not letting this overgrown puppy take another fucking bite out of Jürgen." Wilmot sprang into action, screaming at the top of his lungs and brandishing his tree-branch javelin in the air.

"Bastarrrrrd!" Haupt yelled, charging at the wolf.

The wolf blinked but held its ground, determined not to give up its dinner. Wilmot, taking advantage of the animal's uncertainty, swung his weapon as one would a baseball bat and smashed the beast under its chin, snapping its neck upwards. It yelped, but then Haupt struck it across the head, leaving it bloodied and befuddled, too dazed to run off.

Wilmot released his pent-up fury as adrenaline flooded his system. "Die! Die! Die! He smashed the wolf's head to a pulp then dropped shaking to the blood-spattered snow, stunned at the ferocity of his attack.

Haupt and Wilmot knelt on each side of Jürgen. The boy was dead. His eyes, wide as saucers, were surrounded by icy, white lashes and snow-encrusted eyebrows. Wilmot closed Jürgen's green eyes, groaning as an eyelid dropped off like a piece of withered skin and stuck to one of his fingers.

"Jesus Christ … aw, God Almighty ... is this what's coming for all of us," Haupt moaned. "I should have stayed on the bloody train…ach, Jürgen."

Wilmot, examining Jürgen's body, had regained his calm and was focusing on what to do next. He looked at the dead skin with icy lashes stuck to his index finger and flicked it off with another soft groan.

Jürgen's legs had been mauled from thigh to ankle. Large chunks of the left thigh were missing and probably still being digested inside the dead animal. Wilmot shivered. "The wolf went straight for Jürgen's legs. Look at the bloody state of them."

"Did those bites kill him? I didn't hear him scream, did you?" Haupt said wiping his blood-splattered face with his coat sleeve.

Wilmot stood. He looked down at Jürgen's white face, stress-free and unwrinkled like that of a child. "I don't know, Haupt. He might have died before the wolf attacked." He sighed with sadness. "God, I hope so, for his sake. I don't see any signs of a struggle. He's just sitting there where we left him with his hands on his crotch."

Haupt was now examining the wolf, his eyes flashing with lust. "I'm going to eat it raw. It'll save us, Willie – do you hear me? We'll be saved."

Wilmot, still trembling with the shock of the boy's death, looked skywards and felt the snowflakes and wind stinging his face. Soon, the adrenaline would fade, and he'd be ravaged again by weakness and cold. He was starving and would also eat the wolf raw even if its blood ran down his chin and tasted of iron, but if they didn't get their shelter finished, they'd die before being able to rip off the animal's fur to get to the meat.

Wilmot began stripping Jürgen's body. Unable to put the boy's coat on over his own, he laid it to one side and went for the lad's pullover under his jacket. He also removed the blood-soaked woollen scarf, hat, long john's covered in shit stains, mittens and shoes. Unfortunately, his socks had been shredded by the wolf, and his trousers were almost destroyed and of no use to man nor beast.

As quickly as he could, Wilmot removed his own coat and jacket then pulled on Jürgen's woollen pullover. He'd refused to put his own back on after soaking it in the latrine bucket on the train. He was all for brothers in arms and all that camaraderie stuff, but he'd drawn the line at dressing in his comrades' collective piss.

He put his jacket back on, immediately feeling the added protection the new jumper provided underneath it. Then he covered his head with Jürgen's scarf and knotted it under his chin as he'd seen other men do, and finally, he wrapped his own scarf around his neck.

Wilmot struggled to pull Jürgen's mittens over his own five-finger gloves. The lad had scavenged the white mitts from a dead prisoner. The man, dressed from head to foot in white camouflage gear, had collapsed and died on one of their long hikes. His body was stripped naked within minutes, with a determined Jürgen managing to get to both mittens first. Quite a feat.

As a memory of his mother surfaced, Wilmot pulled his woollen hat down as far as it would go. She'd given her children the same instructions, and reasons for them, every winter, and he'd never forgotten them. "People catch colds and flu when they don't cover their heads and feet properly. You see, body heat comes out of a person's head, so it stands to reason it should be covered whenever you're outdoors. Like the roof does for a house, it holds the heat in. And when you die, your soul will also come out of your head." He'd always wondered why she'd added that, but he'd believed her. Having a scarf and two hats covering his head was bliss.

Wilmot turned his attention to Haupt. "What are you doing?" Aghast, he watched his captain biting into the wolf, his bared teeth and hands ripping its fur away. Wilmot staggered sideways as the wind almost blew him off his feet. He dropped to his knees, gripped Haupt's shoulder, and shouted, "For God's sake, man. Leave it! We need to finish the shelter."

"Bugger off, Willie!" Haupt shrugged off the hand before licking the blood on his bottom lip. His eyes, like grey ice, glared at Wilmot with the same crazed look he'd worn earlier. "You dig and shovel and build walls to your heart's content. I'm bloody famished and if you try to drag me away from my dinner, I'll rip your throat out!"

"Haupt, we'll prepare the shelter, get the animal in there with us, and we'll be safe from the blizzard, then we can fill our stomachs," Wilmot shouted again. "You know I'm right. Haupt, please see sense!"

"Get lost – go on, get away from my fucking wolf!"

Defeated, Wilmot put his head down and battled his way to the clearing, praying he'd reach the half-built shelter in time.

Chapter Thirty-Seven

Armed with Jürgen's coat, Wilmot reached the clearing. There, he set about scooping, placing and patting the snow on top of the previous layers, concentrating on building a back and side wall. He planned to huddle in the joint of both walls, which should be the most sheltered spot unless the wind changed direction and hit him on all sides. The blizzard was moving in fast and the trees were providing no discernible shelter. The snow walls were his only hope of survival, but that outcome was, at best, a long shot. Truth was, he was a nudge away from death.

He lodged a long, sturdy branch into the ground and packed snow around it. When it stood erect, only a couple of centimetres from the wall, he hung Jürgen's coat on it. The top of the coat rested a few centimetres above his head and was jammed between the wall and the thick branch, and in his scrunched-up position, its bulk shrouded him completely.

Despite the gales, Jürgen's headscarf and hats were still in place. He removed his neck scarf, however, to wear it like a mask, tying it in a knot at the back of his head. He then pulled the edge of the coat a couple of centimetres away from the wall, lest he not be able to breathe later because of the weight of snow on it. The scarf protected his face, but able to respire through it, he instantly felt the air hitting him through the tiny gap he'd made. Finally, he pulled one of the woollen hat rims over his eyes. He wasn't going to end up like Jürgen without an eyelid.

He couldn't feel his toes. They no longer seemed to belong to him; it was strange losing sensation in parts of one's body. He couldn't feel his genitals either. He was probably going to lose his prick. He'd seen some unforgettable sights; a man screaming when he lost one of his bollocks, another giggling hysterically when he scratched his ear and the blackened lobe fell off. His name had been Kurt, like the Vogels' driver, Kurt – he missed *his* Kurt. He'd always been a good listener, better than Max or Paul – and as for poor earless Kurt; a Russian guard had shot him in the head to shut him up.

Wilmot had given in to the idea of having to piss himself where he lay; not that he was pissing much lately. He'd not had one all day, despite his damned bladder being full of icy water. Before long, he'd feel uncomfortable, but it wasn't the first time he'd sheltered like this, and he was used to cramped muscles. On the upside, he felt warmer, and he was beginning to believe he might survive this after all.

The noise was deafening: violent winds and creaking, snapping tree branches. He supposed that as the snow piled up on top of him, the noises would fade, but that comfort forced him to think again about being in danger of suffocation. Determined to maintain the flow of air, he ran his finger down the length of the narrow gap between the wall and edge of the coat and flicked the snow away. "You'll breathe Willie … you will … as long as you keep your air tunnel clear, you'll be all right."

He was desperate for sleep but terrified that if he dozed off, he might never wake up. What of Haupt, was he all right? Guilt struck Wilmot, but only for a moment. The last time he'd seen his captain, he'd been more like a rabid dog than a soldier – not a sight he'd get out of his head in a hurry. He'd tried – begged Haupt to bring the animal to the clearing with them, but Haupt wasn't having any of it, couldn't seem to grasp that another hour without food wouldn't kill them, but the blizzard would.

He muttered under the coat, "You're a stupid bugger, Haupt." He'd behaved like a bloody savage, ripping the wolf's flesh from its bones through the hole in the fur he'd made with his teeth, and filling his mouth with fur and blood and flesh without so much as a grimace. He was probably dead now, his mouth stuffed with paws.

Wilmot was heartened; he felt warmer, he really did. Again, he cleared the snow away from the narrow gap directly in front of his mouth and nose. Then he removed one of his mittens and fully extended his middle finger into the frigid air. He sneered then screamed, "Fuck you, Mother Russia!"

******

The thought of suffocating had kept Wilmot from falling asleep. Every time he'd closed his eyes and begun to drift off, he'd caught himself and repeatedly shifted snow away from his tiny window. He was in excruciating pain. Unable to move for fear of dislodging the snow and blocking his life-giving air tunnel, he remained in his cramped position, moving only his mouth to curse God and the Third Reich. He had no idea how long he'd been there, but he thought that the worst of the storm might have passed.

After drifting off for the umpteenth time, he felt a sudden rumbling on the surface. He panicked as the full weight of the coat collapsed on him and snow bled into his shelter. He tried to scream, a pointless act, but an instinctual one from a man who thought he was dying. He opened his mouth and inhaled, sucking in powdery snow that blocked his throat. He pissed himself, something he hadn't done since first getting into his shelter. The hot urine warming his thighs was almost pleasant. Then without warning, a glimmer of white sky appeared along with Haupt's face peering down at him.

"Good God, Willie, you're alive. Jesus ... I thought I'd lost you." Haupt gripped Wilmot's hands and pulled him out of his snowy grave.

Wilmot spat the snow from his mouth and gasped for air, wheezing loudly as he inhaled. He stretched his back, bent at the middle, then flexed his arms and legs. He couldn't believe they were still attached and working. It took a while, but eventually he pulled the scarf off his nose and mouth and croaked, "How are you alive? How are we alive?"

"I'm alive because I'm a clever sod. You, I don't know. I thought you were a goner. I saw the mound of snow and got ready to uncover a dead body. You're a lucky man, Willie Vogel."

"I might say the same about you. I left you in a blizzard gnawing at *wolfy* like a bloody caveman. I thought you'd lost your mind."

"I think I did for a while. It was disgusting, but that wolf probably saved my life. I felt heat running through my body, the likes of which I haven't felt for weeks. I threw up most of what I'd eaten, mind you, but it brought me to my senses."

Haupt glared again at Wilmot. "I was furious when I saw you'd stripped Jürgen of his clothes. You could have shared something with me before you ran off."

"I would have, but I was scared you were going to take a bite out of me," Willie retorted, but then smiled. "How did you shelter from the gale?"

"When I finished eating, I pulled poor Jürgen over my legs, then I lay on my side against the tree and covered the rest of me with the wolf's body. I managed to get my hands and arms inside the wolf's belly through the hole in its coat – I broke a tooth eating that thing, but nuzzling my face into its fur was marvellous, despite the stench."

Wilmot grimaced at the thought of Haupt's nose being that close to the wolf's innards. "You survived. That's all that matters."

"No thanks to you," Haupt spat back.

Wilmot looked at the piles of snow surrounding him and then sheepishly at Haupt. "We can debate who was right and who was wrong another time, but I do want to say thank you for pulling me out of there. You're one tough bastard. I suppose you had to be in the Einsatzgruppen … you know, killing all those dangerous Jews and what-not."

Haupt was sitting on the snow beside Wilmot, studying him with red-rimmed eyes. But at the mention of his former job, they narrowed to angry slits. "Get up, Vogel. We need to make a move. You won't have noticed our surroundings yet, but we're no longer in the forest. We're going to be out in the open from now on."

Wilmot vowed to himself never to mention the SS death squads again, as he stood to take in the landscape before him. The air was clear, and the sky boasted some blue patches. The snow had stopped falling for the moment, allowing him to see hundreds of metres of plains before him.

"Not a tree or house in sight," he muttered.

"That could be good news or bad news," Haupt said. "The bad news is that we don't know where we are, but the good news is I've left you half a wolf. What do you say we gather some kindling? You were in the Hitler Youth, Willie. You can light a fire with stones and whatever, can't you? Let's cook us a wolf stew."

Willie's morbid thoughts of what lay ahead dissolved with the thought of eating cooked meat. They'd not even attempted to light a fire before for fear of being spotted by enemy soldiers, bears, or wolf packs. "I can try. I suppose I could use dry fur and pine cones for kindling and sticks for friction – whether I'll have the strength to make it is another matter – I'm knackered, Haupt." Then he thought about their dead friend and dismissed his self-pity. "We should bury Jürgen first."

"We'll cover him in snow. That's all we can do."

Wilmot stood, stretched his muscles again, and looked around him. "I agree. We need to eat and move forward. I'm more determined than ever. Not many people survive these forests, but we did. We beat them, Haupt. And we're going to make it to the Finns, even if our cocks fall off on the way."

Chapter Thirty-Eight.

During the next few days, Wilmot and Haupt managed to maintain a decent pace. Each night, they constructed a crude snow cave and used each other's body heat for warmth when the temperatures were at their lowest. Helped by the flat terrain and plentiful snow, the shelters had become sturdier, and for the first time in months, they managed to sleep more than an hour at a time.

Along the way, they'd eaten most of the wolf's flesh and disposed of its bones. The meat had remained fresh because of the freezing conditions, although the cuts were not as good as they'd been when there was more flesh to dig into. Wilmot had also speared a couple of lemmings that he'd found when he dug into the snow in what must have been a rest burrow. Both Wilmot and the lemmings were surprised, but Wilmot's speedy reactions had caught two, and he'd eventually managed to light a fire to cook them.

The bad news for the men, however, was that they only had enough wolf meat left for one final meal, and in this flat, almost treeless expanse, they'd not found any berries or mushrooms to bolster their diet. Still, as Haupt had reminded Wilmot that morning, the beast had taken Jürgen's life, but it had given them theirs. The boy was a hero in his mind, and they wouldn't let him down by dying.

They had eaten every piece of skin, flesh and organs apart from the bitter gall bladder, and had even gnawed on paws and ears, leaving nothing of the wolf but dry bones. Their attempt at skinning the animal had been easier than they'd imagined, but because of Haupt's initial ravaging, no piece had been whole enough to make a decent shawl or head covering. Nonetheless, the men had not discarded even the smallest fragment of fur, instead, they'd used them to cover their most delicate parts and had instantly felt the benefit, especially on and around their backsides and genitalia.

Wilmot was in higher spirits than he had been before the wolf attack. It was depressing to consider what might happen in the days to come so he and Haupt had made a pact to only discuss the present and past. Straight after the blizzard, they'd experienced an eerie stillness, but they were now moving into lighter snowfalls and a friendlier landscape. Two nights earlier, they'd also made a breakthrough regarding their route when they'd spotted the North Star in a clear night sky. They were getting closer every day, a little nearer to salvation, or equally, to a Russian bullet.

Five days after losing Jürgen to the wolf or the cold – they'd never determined which had killed him – the men came across a dilapidated wooden house close to a coppice of trees. It was the first house they'd seen since the day they'd got on the prisoner train. Wilmot was excited, desperate to get under any semblance of a roof, but Haupt elected to err on the side of caution before approaching the structure.

"We'll watch it for a while, just in case it's still being used," Haupt insisted.

"Does it look lived-in to you?" Willie asked, his voice laced with sarcasm.

"It's still standing, isn't it?" Haupt grumbled, as he lay on his stomach. "Get down here, Willie. That's an order."

Willie flinched but did as he was told. Since the day of their escape, Haupt had never once pulled rank or given an order; on the contrary, he'd seemed happy to follow rather than lead.

"Can we get up now?" Willie asked after a few minutes. "I'm freezing like a bloody statue here – come on, Haupt, no one is in there."

Haupt nodded, got cautiously to his feet, and did a one-hundred-and-eighty-degree scan of the area. Then the two men ploughed through the snow towards the house.

Inside, they saw that the single-storey building wasn't as derelict as they'd first thought. Two rooms at the back of it were intact, as was the kitchen with a door leading to the back garden. In the bedroom, one window still had half of its glass intact. Against the back wall was an iron-framed bedstead with a torn straw-filled mattress on it.

"I feel as though I'm in heaven!" Willie shouted to Haupt, who was in another room.

"Come and see this!" Haupt yelled back.

Willie stood beside Haupt and gazed in awe at a Russian bomber lying on its side only thirty or so metres from the house. But an even more glorious sight was the barbed wire entanglements strewn across the fields behind the downed aircraft.

"If this plane was shot down by the Finns, we must be getting close to the Mannerheim Line," Wilmot said. "Those entanglements are purely defensive. I think we should try to cut our way through them. That's the border with Finland, Haupt."

"Wait a minute, Willie. Before you do summersaults, we've got to assume that if it were that easy to cut through the barbed wire, the Russians would have already done it. The whole area's probably one big minefield, and we're more likely to bump into a

Russian unit than a Finnish one. Back in Leningrad, there was talk of us eventually coming at the Russians from both sides. The idea was simple, on paper. The Finns would hold their position north of the line and we'd sweep through Leningrad and hem the Russkies in at the southern edge – what if we actually did it?"

Willie, still staring at the aeroplane, sniggered. "Don't make me laugh. We couldn't even *take* Leningrad, never mind surge north to the Russian-Finnish front lines. Come to think of it, you and I have got further than the German army ever did."

Haupt rubbed his chin, his eyes peeled on the vista outside. "The questions now are, how far are we from Leningrad and where are the two armies positioned today?"

"They're easy. Should we take our chances with this potential minefield or find another route?"

Wilmot frowned. It was a miracle that they'd not once come across Russian units on their journey, nor seen many dead bodies, destroyed and discarded heavy weaponry, or tanks. "I don't think the Russians have advanced this far up the Isthmus. We took the perfect route without even trying."

Haupt ran his fingers through his scraggly black beard. He and Wilmot looked like brothers with the same dark, curly hair reaching their collars and half their faces concealed with beards that were well past their chins. Only their eyes differed in colour and shape, Wilmot's being the darker of the two.

As though he hadn't heard Wilmot, Haupt continued, "A Finnish officer was present at a staff meeting I attended with General von Leeb…"

"You met the general?"

"Yes, many times, but I'll tell you about him another day. The Finnish officer had a map of their defensive lines, and they were discussed at length. The Karelian Isthmus is about a hundred and twenty kilometres wide. The Mannerheim line runs from the coast of the Gulf of Finland in the west, through Summa to the Vuoksi River and ends at Taipale in the east, and that's supposed to be … I should say, reportedly, hundreds of kilometres long…"

"Is that why the Finns weren't participating in the Leningrad siege?" Willie scowled. "I thought they were useless buggers, and to be honest, I didn't see the point in having them on our side…"

"You see, that's the problem with the lower ranks, Willie. You lot never see the point of anything because you're not privy to classified information or the bigger picture, which in this case involves the Finns. You've no idea how much planning goes into every single advance, have you?"

Haupt shoved his hands in his pockets and continued to stare outside. "What you don't know is that the Finnish Army halted its offensive thirty kilometres from the centre of Leningrad and then besieged the city by cutting its northern supply routes. They had no hope of advancing on Russian forces ten times their size. Their goal was to hold out long enough for *us* to help them, not the other way around."

Willie, yearning for the bed in the other room, asked, "So, what now?"

Haupt looked around the empty room. "Search the house for a map, plans, anything you see with writing on it."

After a thorough search that yielded nothing but dirt and a couple of tin cups and plates, Willie went outside to fill the cups with snow. At first, the noises from within the coppice were faint and muffled: a twig snapped, shuffling feet, a horse snorted, and skis scraped icy patches. Wilmot tensed, dropped to the ground and scanned the trees – nothing – until the noises, unlike any he'd heard in weeks, grew louder.

He eyed the door, willing himself to get off his knees and make a run for it. His breath rasped the back of his throat, but as he started to rise his legs gave way.

He held his breath, still on the ground, unable to get to his feet. The sounds, now directly behind him, were clearer: skis swooshing across the snow, rifles clicking, horses' hooves crunching the icy ground, and footsteps approaching left him in no doubt that he'd been spotted. He scrambled to his knees, raised his arms in the air and stared at the door of the cabin, praying that Haupt wouldn't suddenly appear and get shot.

Any second, a bullet is going to hit me in the back of the head. Strange, Wilmot thought, he'd rather get a bullet than be captured again by the Russians.

Willie stared at the front door. It opened, and instead of Haupt a man wearing white bed linen as camouflage snow gear appeared. A rifle was slung over his shoulder, and most of his face was concealed by a balaclava. He stepped outside, then Haupt, grinning from ear to ear, appeared beside him in the doorway.

Wilmot, his mind still frozen in fear, remained on his knees.

"Get up, Willie. They're Finns, our allies," Haupt shouted.

Wilmot rose on shaky legs, struck dumb like a wide-eyed idiot as he stared at two horse-drawn sledges carrying artillery. He counted ten men dressed in white garb with ski poles, skis, and rifles. They reminded him of explorers until he noticed the dead reindeer on a wooden wagon on skis instead of wheels. He let out a long, relief-filled breath, still coming to terms with this rescue. He was finally liberated from the Russian yoke that could have so very easily carried him to his death, but he couldn't quite believe it.

Haupt was speaking to one of the Finns. Wilmot was largely ignored until a man approached him and handed him a loaf of bread – a full loaf – stale but perfectly edible baked food. He nodded his thanks and shoved as much of it as he could into his mouth, ripping into the crusty dough with his teeth. He had just been given more bread than he'd had in a week while he was a prisoner of war.

"Thank you … thank you," Wilmot finally mumbled tearfully to the men. Words couldn't adequately describe his feelings of joy and relief, but his wet eyes spoke louder than gratitude.

When he came to his senses, Wilmot walked through the centre of the group of men to Haupt and the man he was talking to. Unlike Wilmot's emotional state, Haupt was behaving like the perfect officer; calm, focused, authoritative, but with all the visible signs that he had gone through hell and was struggling to stay on his feet. Wilmot, wanting to follow his friend's example, drew himself up and listened.

"… and get you to our line … Germans there," the Finn was saying in broken German.

Haupt finally addressed Wilmot. "We're going with them, Willie. From what I can gather, we're only three kilometres from their lines. This is a reconnaissance party."

"They've been hunting as well, I see," Willie responded by pointing to the reindeer on the ski wagon. Then he asked the Finn, "Where are the Russians?"

The man took off his mittens, put up eight fingers, and pointed south. Then without a word, he gestured Haupt and Willie to follow him to the wagon.

The Finn pointed to the back of the wagon, which boasted a bed of furs. He and two of his men helped Haupt to get in. Willie followed suit with another two men hoisting his emaciated body onto the wagon. Willie was handed a flask while still clutching his partially eaten loaf of bread. He took a long slug, and then coughed when the alcohol burnt his throat. "Haupt … try this stuff," he croaked. "It'll blow your head off."

The Finn in charge, said, "Sleep," then the group moved off towards the Russian bomber.

Haupt curled up under the furs and said to a worried looking Wilmot, "Don't worry about a thing, Willie. They know what they're doing and where they're going. Get some sleep. We made it."

"We did, didn't we?" Willie choked, his bottom lip trembling. *We bloody did it, but all our men on that prison train are probably dead by now.*

Chapter Thirty-Nine

Max Vogel and Romek Gabula

London, England
30 March 1942

Max and Romek sat down to breakfast in their shared house in Camden, North London, paid for by the Abwehr. Romek's two guards and Max's driver had already eaten, and Mrs Mullins, the housekeeper tasked with looking after the men, was supposedly going to visit her sister then call in at the grocer's shop to pick up the weekly rations. The busty woman in her early fifties, who seemed to permanently have rollers in her hair, was an MI5 agent on loan to Heller. The headscarf covering the rollers, the lack of makeup and dowdy clothes were all part of her disguise, she'd explained to Max, who'd first met her at MI6 headquarters looking and talking like a well-to-do, smartly coiffed lady.

She had the acting skills of a female Laurence Olivier, mothering the occupants, gossiping about and with the neighbours in her soft cockney accent, which came naturally to her, being a Londoner. She feigned ignorance of what was going on under her nose and managed to hover around Romek while being unobtrusive. Yes, Mrs Mullins played her part well, Max thought, watching her flipping a fried egg in the pan.

The previous housekeeper, the woman employed by German intelligence to look after the house and see to Romek's needs, had been arrested after Max, in the guise of Romek, had gone to meet her. It had taken only five minutes for her to mention the Abwehr and give the Nazi salute of Heil Hitler, giving Max the go-ahead to arrest her and put Mrs Mullins in her place without the Abwehr or Romek getting a sniff of the change-over.

Max had commented to Heller that Mrs Mullins was a remarkable woman whose reality was very different from the one she was portraying. She was the eyes and ears in the house when Max was absent. She reported directly to Jonathan Heller, was married to a retired Colonel who was still very much alive and commanding his local Home Guard troop, and she lived in a large six-bedroom house with a permanent housekeeper of her own. Romek, although he never said, was probably aware of her British Intelligence background and the true purpose of her job, but she was not there to fool him; she was to fool the neighbours by projecting an air of normality around the Polish occupant and his housemates.

"What time do you think you'll be back, Mrs Mullins?" Max asked her when she'd served Romek and Max a plate of one egg, a sliver of bacon and a slice of dry bread.

"I don't know. I've got a lot to do. It's 'ard trying to fit everything in, what with only 'aving one day off a week. I just don't know 'ow we're supposed to manage with these new decreases on rationing. As if things weren't bad enough already, we're now getting less electricity, coal, and gas, not to mention clothing coupons. I lost my George in the Great War. The poor man will be turning in his grave to see us going through all this 'ardship again. And for what? I'll tell you for what, that little upstart in Berlin with his silly moustache and arm going up and down like a bleedin' fiddler's elbow! Hah, you mark my words, my George would've gone over there and put a stop to 'im before this terrible war even broke out."

"Don't worry, Mrs Mullins, I'll make sure you don't go short of anything." said Romek wagging his finger.

"Aww, Son, you and your lot are good people, you Polish are. I can't think of a bad word to say about any of you, 'cept I wish you 'adn't 'ad to get out of yer own country for those Nazis. It breaks me 'eart, so it does."

This morning, Max planned to conduct business at the house. A transmission had come in from the Abwehr with their latest list of questions, to which Max had already written brief answers. It was a tricky business. He and an assembly of other devious minds had to devise solid ripostes that met the Abwehr's demands while not giving away information that could be detrimental to Britain, or her allies.

When the house was quiet, and they'd cleared the table, Max got out the file and typewriter, and as always, advised Romek about how he should sound in the messages to Matador, his handler in Madrid. "Your answers must be written in a personal way, as you would speak them to a friend. But don't overplay your hand or be too informative. It's vitally important in deception work that you forget what *you* know and what *you* would do. This is all an act to make the Germans think they've got to work hard to reach their conclusions. If the intelligence is too easily given, they'll suspect it…"

"You've told me that a dozen times, Max," Romek interrupted.

"And I'll tell you a dozen more," Max snapped. "I don't think you grasp just how vulnerable this programme is. One stupid error, one blown agent and the whole thing could come tumbling down around our ears."

After MI6 and the Twenty Committee had decided to try Romek out as a double agent, his first task had been to request new codes from the Abwehr and to confirm that he was in place in the house without encountering any issues. By changing the codes, MI6 and their counterpart, MI5, who would at some stage take over Romek's case since he was a domestic agent, were able to halt the exiled Polish government's interference in Romek's operations, and at the same time, block any security leaks that might come from the Poles' London headquarters.

The Poles had swiftly retaliated, telling Heller that Romek was their man by right and insisting that they owned him body and soul. They'd capitulated, however, after Heller had reminded the crippled Captain Kazcka that all Poles living in Britain were enjoying the hospitality of the British government, and as such, they were guests and had no right to demand anything.

Thus far, Romek had been kept on a tight leash. He could communicate only the routine information given to him by the British and was not permitted to take part in any operational deception. He was rebellious, sullen, disappointed, and extremely angry with Max who had not demanded that his agent be shown more respect for past loyalty. Their relationship had reached an all-time low with both men avoiding conversations of a more personal nature. Indeed, Klara's name was rarely mentioned.

Max worked diligently with Heller to come up with a suitable backstory for Romek, but their responsibilities didn't stop there. Romek also had to be fed, clothed and sheltered, which was no longer an easy job because of the growing number of double agents in Britain and increasingly scarce supplies.

As part of his long list of duties, Max was responsible for managing and organising Romek's day to day life, and for providing him with an identity card, ration cards, and clothes coupons. But breaking through Romek's wall of surly and unpredictable mood swings was proving difficult, for it went much deeper than their professional differences. The atmosphere between them had become increasingly tense and was alleviated only when other members of the household were present; those being the two guards, using the covers of civilian dockyard workers, and an officer with a car who brought and collected Romek's information and occasionally drove Max into the West End for meetings.

Max had also been charged with coming up with a notional job to give the impression that Romek was self-supporting. Romek had been quite happy when handed the employment card stating he was a librarian at the Islington North Library. Books had always interested him. He was an avid reader, and looked forward to reading in English, he'd told Max who'd recalled the full bookcase in Romek and Klara's Warsaw flat. *Thank God something made him happy,* Max had thought at the time.

Angry at Romek's continuing belligerence, Max tapped his fork on his plate then threw it carelessly on the table. "You don't have to like me, but if you don't take this seriously and show me you're enthusiastic, you'll be disposed of."

Romek's lips twitched with his own barely concealed anger. "Charming. You've changed, Max, and I'm not sure I like who you've become. We used to be friends, have a laugh and a beer, talk as equals, but look at you now, all stiff and uppity like most of the English I've come across in this country. I think you left your sense of humour behind in France along with your faith in me."

Max agreed, for much of what Romek said was true; he wasn't the same man at all. He was tired of keeping secrets and still furious with Paul. He was scarred with family dramas and a barely-healed broken heart.

Looking across the table at Romek, who was scraping the last bit of yolk from his plate with a crust of bread, Max came to a decision. "We've both changed, me with my secret and you with yours. Why don't we get this over with, then perhaps we can move on with a clean slate?" he asked.

Romek tossed the thumb-size crust of bread onto the plate, then sat back in his chair and crossed his arms. "Go on then, get it out. I'm not going to help you," he said.

Max exhaled and sat forward. "All right – I want to come clean…"

"About you and Klara? Yes, go on."

Chilled by Romek's monotone voice, Max focused on the Pole's fingers, now tapping the table very close to the bread knife. He had just confirmed that he knew about the affair, yet for months he'd borne that knowledge in silence. Why? The more important question was, now that it was out in the open, what would he do about it?

Max, keeping his own tone steady, asked, "How long have you known about Klara and me?"

"I suspected your affair a long time ago, but I *knew* it was true when I met her at Duguay's farm. She defended you when I called you a bastard for abandoning us, which you were by the way, and don't try to deny that you hung us out to dry."

"There was a good reason I couldn't…"

"I don't want to talk about your reasons. What's important is the way my wife talked about you. Her eyes betrayed her feelings. I never saw that look of love when she was married to me. It was then that my mind went back to our time together in Warsaw and Paris. I'm stupid. I should have seen the signs, the smiles, the hours you and she spent together while I was working, the way you looked at her when you said goodbye, and the day of the first German air raid on Paris when both of you arrived back at the flat only minutes apart – yes, Max, I *knew* on that day."

Max shook his head. "If you knew, why didn't you tell my bosses about it as soon as you arrived in Britain? You could have torn into me and no one would have blamed you. I took your wife to bed. I made love to her under your own roof and betrayed our friendship.

Max was deliberately goading Romek to illicit a more emotional response from him and, in doing so, finally diffuse the tense atmosphere between them. Thus far, his approach wasn't working. "What I did was unforgivable, yet you said nothing and aren't saying anything now, either; in fact, you look as though you're gloating. What do you want me to do? Should I stand still and let you punch me or stay silent while you tell me what you think of me? I'll do it, whatever you want, just get on with it."

Romek's expression was neutral, no trembling lips, or angry frown. "You're asking me what you should do? Hmm, I don't know, Max. You had sex with my wife with not a thought for your good, old friend, Romek. You accepted my hospitality in Warsaw, ate at my table, and had my meagre possessions at your disposal. I watched your back and risked everything in Poland *and* France to please you, to make you proud of me, and you repaid my kindness and diligence by thumbing your nose at me with whom I thought was my darling, faithful wife. You tell me, Max, what can you do for me when you've already done it all?" Romek swallowed the last of his coffee.

No point in denying the accusations when they were all true. Max pondered the Pole's strange quiescence. The only question now was what was Romek planning to do about it? So far, he hadn't moved, pulled a knife, yelled or threatened; instead, he continued to drink his coffee as though Max wasn't even in the room.

"I apologise, Romek. I am deeply sorry for the pain I've caused you and for being an arsehole. I'll put my hands up. I was a selfish bastard, and you're right, I did betray you. If I could go…"

"Aw, shut up, Max. Shut up! Don't insult me with your *if I could take it back I would,* shit. You prised Klara and I apart like a wishbone. You witnessed our marriage breaking, but you still encouraged her to be with you."

"I never wanted to hurt you or lose your friendship."

"Friends, you and me? You're not worthy of that word," Romek sneered. "You're the man I work with, that's all. You and Klara are in the same filthy box of infidelity. You're both dead to me … dead."

Max cringed at Romek's mention of Klara being dead. Weeks earlier, the two SOE agents on the ground with Duguay had confirmed her death, and a fiery debate between Max and Heller had ensued about whether they should they give Romek the news or allow him to continue believing she was alive.

Max had been devastated when he'd heard about the accident, and although he was not a man given to tears, he had sobbed like a baby in the privacy of his bedroom. Klara had meant the world to him for a long time, and that his love for her had recently begun to fade and then turn in another's direction only hardened the blow and accentuated his guilt.

She had died alone, a twenty-four-year-old woman with a difficult past behind her and her future full of hope, albeit she'd known the risks of war. She'd had a quick death; a kindness, Heller had stated matter-of-factly. Death, quick or not, was never kind to the young, Max had retorted, finding no comfort in the agents' reports that her neck had probably snapped in an instant. He recalled his own final, terrifying seconds before hitting the rocks on French soil. She would have felt the same terror just before whichever part of her body hit the ground. Heller had never jumped out of an aeroplane in his life. What did he know about it?

"… I won't give Klara a divorce, so don't make plans to marry her," Romek was now saying. "*Jezus Chrystus,* I can just imagine the two of you laughing when I was captured. You were probably hoping I'd be executed and out of your hair for good. Well, sorry to disappoint you both…"

"That's enough! You're wrong. Klara was beside herself with worry. Come on, Romek, you know that's not true."

"I *know* she loved you. She admitted it to my face."

Max had rehearsed his denial a hundred times for just this occasion, but now, when it mattered, he had no idea what to say.

"The great Max Vogel is stuck for words, eh?" Romek taunted.

"She and I are not together now … it's over," Max stuttered, his head bowed.

"Aw, poor Max and Klara, boo-hoo. Shall I send you flowers, shed tears for you?"

Defeated, Max sighed, "Can we move on from this? We have to live together…"

"Yes, we do. And we will do our jobs well and hope this war ends sooner rather than later."

Romek pushed his chair back and got to his feet, poking his finger in Max's face. "Make no mistake, Max Vogel. I will knock you into next week and tell your superior officers all about your betrayal. I will stamp on your head until the handsome face my Klara loves is crushed to pulp. I will ruin you, but when I do those things it won't be because you're sitting at this table, giving me your *permission.* And this," he said, pointing to his own face, "this is the new Romek ... this face full of disgust ... it's all you're going to get from now on."

With no worthwhile reply, Max watched Romek go to the stove. Romek's eyes had teared up during those last ominous vows. The fiery Pole was finally airing his feelings.

"What are you doing now?" Max asked.

Romek turned to Max and scoffed. "We have work to do. I'm making a fresh pot of coffee."

He returned to the table and poured coffee into his cup, deliberately leaving Max without a refill. "Work – work, you lot call it. It feels like a stupid game to me. I used to fight the Germans, but now all I do is correspond with them using your lies – say it this way, say it that way, think like this, don't think, just write. I'm not doing anything of use. I'm bored, and I feel like a bloody prisoner with Mrs Mullins pretending she's a civilian and those two guards in the other room monitoring my every move. I'm surprised they don't follow me to the bathroom when I take a shit."

Max stayed silent. He had told the truth and felt better for it. One day, Romek would take his revenge, but until that day came, he'd continue to serve Britain as a double agent or in some other capacity. Like most of the Poles in Britain, Romek was dedicated to the task of defeating the Nazis. It was a sure bet he would put aside his personal feelings, as he evidently had until today, for as long as the Germans occupied Poland.

Max nodded and turned to the job at hand. "Do you know what our objectives are?"

"Some. But go on, enlighten me, as you love to do."

Max lit a cigarette without taking his eyes off Romek and said, "For a start, this work is far from boring. We're controlling the German spy system, you and me, and others like us. We're learning about Germany's spymasters, their personalities, methods, and what's acceptable or not to them. We're making money off the generous allowances they send to their so-called *agents* for living expenses. We're learning about the Abwehr's cypher work and their plans through the questions they ask *you*. And we're influencing enemy plans with your answers and deceiving them about our goals and operations. You don't have to be a visible enemy to beat the Nazis, and you don't have to be in uniform. Always remember that, Romek."

"Yes, yes, all right. Enough, now, Max. You're giving me a headache," Romek said, swallowing his coffee, then rising from the table again to check the typewriter ribbon. "I'm ready. Let's start with the questions."

Max ran through the long list of questions pertaining to aircraft and aerodromes located in Scotland and the current situation of a company called Vickers-Armstrongs, Limited, who owned factories at Brooklands. "… and this last question is more of a request. The Abwehr want sketches showing Vickers' shipbuilding sites at Weybridge."

Based on Max's pre-written answers, Romek fashioned his responses to those questions, along with many others. He was a talented storyteller with a natural tone in his writing, Max admitted.

Hours later, Romek sat back and twisted his neck from side to side. "Ach, I remember this muscle pain, sitting at a desk all day, my wrists and fingers sore from typing. Brings back memories of my embassy job in Warsaw … seems like a lifetime ago I was a bureaucrat working for the Germans and living in my own country. I miss Poland." He looked at Max, slouched in his chair, casually smoking a cigarette. "Seeing as how you're sitting there like a languid lesbian, why don't you make *me* a cup of coffee for a change?"

Max rose from his chair and then responded with a mock bow. "Your wish is my command."

Ignoring the sarcasm, Romek continued, "I'm not happy about this last answer. It seems too succinct."

"Read it aloud," Max said, spooning coffee into the pot.

Romek began reading his answer, ending it with this final paragraph. '*... the ninth air support group is concentrated in the Kent area, which is to be its theatre of operations, on aerodromes between Ashford and Tunbridge.*' I want to finish it by saying I am looking forward to going to *Unsere Lieblings-bar für eine Mistela.* We went to a bar in Madrid. It was full of communists, but Matador liked the Mistela – that's a type of sherry. He'll know it's really me writing this if I put that personal stuff in."

"That sounds fine," Max said, bringing the coffee to the table.

"I don't know, though … should we not? I was thinking I should tell him how many soldiers and airmen I saw, and maybe give him a date for a fictitious mission. You know, give them something meatier?"

"No, this is exactly why you have Charlie monitoring your transmissions. You're not telling the whole truth to begin with, so don't try to embellish your answers with unnecessary lies."

Max put the papers into a folder then looked at his watch. "I have to go out. I won't be back until tonight, so amuse yourself after you finish your shift at the library."

"You're too kind."

Romek followed Max into the hall. A minute later, the two guards came out of the living room. "Fancy getting your arse kicked at poker before you start work, Romek?" one of the men asked.

"Might as well. Nothing else to do around here except the bloody dishes."

Chapter Forty

After leaving Romek and his two security guards to their daily game of poker, Max rode in the back of the MI6 car to their headquarters in Central London. It was a mild March day with a blue sky and a scattering of white clouds, so he asked to be dropped off in Piccadilly, where he'd walk the rest of the way and take advantage of the dry weather.

As he strolled passed the Ritz, Max noted that the air was cleaner than it had been since he'd last set foot in the capital. The city had been suffering terribly with smog and dust from the Luftwaffe air raids that coated buildings with thick grey powder. The fire brigade periodically dampened them down, but with a wind and only a day without rain, the dust was hovering once again in the air. According to Max's driver, the Germans had not bombed the heart of the West End for three days. It was palpable; the difference when one inhaled was profound.

When Max arrived at Jonathan Heller's office, Marjory, Heller's secretary beamed at him, remarked that he looked well, then added that Mr Heller was waiting, and he was to go straight in.

Heller was on the telephone. He looked up and gestured to the visitor's chair. When he finished the call, he asked Max, "What did you tell Romek about the upcoming mission?"

"Nothing, yet," Max answered.

Heller placed a copy of a transmission in front of Max. "Orders have come through from the top. It's been brought forward to Thursday's full moon. You and Romek will leave for Grimsby on

Wednesday morning." He handed Max two train tickets. "You'll have three Royal Navy crew members with you. They're originally from Belfast and will be disguised as fishermen. They'll be on board a trawler in Grimsby harbour with the coordinates of the meeting place. You'll find the trawler's details in the briefing pack."

"And will Matador be coming in person or is he sending another Abwehr agent?"

Jonathan handed Max copies of three transmissions; two having been received the previous day. "Charlie has already decoded them. Read them and ask your questions when you've finished."

The first radio transmission was from Matador, Romek's spymaster. In it, he requested that he and Romek meet in person. *I want to introduce you to a new technology that will greatly increase the amount of information you supply us.*

Max presumed Matador was talking about microphotography and microfilm, which could reduce data on a full-size sheet of paper to the size of an easily concealed postage stamp. His eyes widened, however, when he read the next paragraph: *Here is the name and location of a British man who can handle this technology for you. He is willing to work for us. His code name is Horace. Important you bring him to the meeting. More details to follow.*

"I take it we're going to bring this Horace chap in?"

"I'll get to him in a minute. Read on – questions when you finish," Heller reminded Max.

Max moved on to the second transmission, this one was Romek's reply to the first. It was short and to the point and confirmed that Romek had understood Matador's orders. Romek would contact Horace immediately, and they'd both attend the meeting. Charlie, the radio operator writing in the guise of Romek, had added that he hoped they'd have time for *ein glas Mistella.* And he had used the German, not the Spanish spelling, as Matador did.

The third transmission from the Abwehr was just as succinct as Romek's, with the day, time and coordinates of the meeting. Matador was arriving on a German U-Boat in the North Sea at 03.00 on Thursday morning, and the Germans requested confirmation of the rendezvous.

Max lay the transmissions face up on the desk and frowned. "The Krauts are taking a hell of a risk just to give Romek technology and explosives. There's got to be more to this. He must be bringing something else or needs to ask Romek something in person? Foolish, if you ask me."

Heller fidgeted with his lapel. He was prone to do that when he was about to tell Max something he might not want to hear. "There is one more transmission, Max. Charlie sent it an hour ago. We told Matador that Romek had found the Abwehr agent, Horace, but the truth is, *we* found him and have him in custody."

"What have you learnt from him?" Max asked, fishing his cigarettes out of his pocket.

"Quite a lot. His family is originally from Belfast, Irish discontents who migrated to London when he was a baby. He married a woman from Dublin four years ago, a year before they set up home in Tottenham. According to him, they're both Irish Republicans and members of the IRA. He hates the British and wanted to blow up the Houses of Parliament. He went as far as telling us he contacted the Germans in Portugal and asked them to use him for sabotage operations. He's also quite an expert in technology, which I presume is why the Abwehr want him to work with Romek."

"His speech?"

"He has a predominantly London accent, with the occasional Irish lilt thrown in."

Max stared at Horace's mug shot, taken by MI5. "Damn traitor," he mumbled. "Don't tell me you're going to try to turn him?"

Heller grumbled. "No, he made his feelings quite clear. He wants Hitler to invade Britain and win the war, thinks the Irish Republicans will get Northern Ireland out of Herr Führer."

"What does his future look like?" Max asked, disgusted.

"Bleak. I've decided to keep him locked up for a couple of weeks, or until I'm satisfied we've elicited every bit of information he has on his Abwehr contacts. Then we'll hang the bastard in the Tower. The ravens will be excited about the prospect; they love a bit of carrion."

Max, having no sympathy for the man whatsoever, asked, "Is this why we're using Northern Irish sailors?"

"Yes. English fisherman wouldn't be believable, not even if they're supposedly chartering their trawler for money. Should Matador speak to them, they will tell him that they need Herr Hitler's help to oust the British from Northern Ireland … we'll go along the same lines that Horace used ... you know what they say, the enemy of my enemy is my friend, and all that."

Heller paused to pick up the telephone. "Marjory – yes, bring tea for Major Vogel and myself – and, Marjory, afterwards, I don't want to be disturbed."

With a nagging suspicion that Heller was delaying his next question, Max decided to pre-empt his boss with one of his own. He had a good idea what Heller wanted from him. "I presume you need a Horace to replace the treasonous bastard you have in a cell downstairs?"

Heller smiled and passed over a thick file. "You know me too well. Yes, you'll take his place."

Marjory arrived with a tray which she set down. She looked at the men's earnest expressions and left without pouring. She always seemed to know when a meeting fell into the top-secret category and immediately retreated, closing the door softly behind her.

Heller handed Max a file. "This is what we have on Horace. Study it and remember even the smallest details. If we have this, you can bet the Abwehr do as well." Heller poured the tea and added, "His recruitment wasn't done through the normal Abwehr channels, so they don't have a picture of him."

"Hmm, lucky for me."

Heller handed Max the cup of tea, but without milk or sugar. "Sorry, old chap, I know how you love your sugar, but we ran out this morning."

Max responded with a wry smile, "I see there's no biscuits either. Civilisation is going to the dogs."

Heller sipped his tea then continued, "Back to it. As I said, you'll accompany Romek as Horace, but say as little as possible, stick to your London accent but use the odd Irish lilt if you can … one word here and there, and don't talk German. Horace doesn't speak a word of it. Romek can handle Matador on that front."

Max was already dreading this mission. "Got it. I don't speak German," he mumbled.

For a while the two men went over the planning and objectives of the operation, but a question about an entirely different aspect of the operation was running through Max's mind, one he presumed would have nothing to do with Romek or himself.

"A German U-Boat would be a good catch, don't you think?" Max remarked as he slipped the file into his briefcase.

"I do. That's why we're going to blow it out of the water once it has left the rendezvous site. Not only will the Germans think twice about having tête-à-têtes with our double agents, they'll be extremely worried about the future of their U-Boats in the North Sea."

Heller laid out a map. "Look here. We're giving you the Royal Navy's latest coordinates of their minefields. These are a series of mines that were laid to protect friendly vessels and create a safe zone. The naval lieutenant accompanying you has already been briefed on the mission and will keep the trawler within the safe lanes. We're also sending a minesweeper to the area beforehand to guide you, but it will be long gone before the meet. It means you'll be hanging around for a couple of hours at the coordinates."

Another question struck Max, "Have the Royal Navy and Air Force been briefed?"

"Yes. They'll not bother you or the sub during the meeting. Two Motor Torpedo Boats will be standing by to deal with the U-boat. As soon as it moves or dives, we'll strike."

"What's the chances of the MTBs being spotted by the U-boat's periscope?"

"Less chance than if we used frigates. We'll position the MTBs in close harbours, north and south of the meeting's coordinates. This is still being put together. I'll have more information for you on the day."

Heller sipped his tea then completely changed the subject. "How are you, Max? How's the family?"

"They're well. I spoke to my mother last week. She's settled in nicely at Bletchley. My father is happy enough, she said. They're both worried about Paul and Willie, of course, but my father's genuinely enjoying his job." Max chuckled. "C'mon, Jonathan, you know more about them than I do."

Heller picked up the phone. "Marjory, I want you to locate Judith Weber. She's somewhere in the building." He covered the mouthpiece. "You don't have lunch plans, do you Max?"

Max shook his head, and Heller went back to the call. "Ask Miss Weber to wait in the lobby. Major Vogel will be down shortly to escort her to lunch."

Max was hit with a pleasant fluttering in his stomach. "This is a nice surprise," he said.

"I thought you'd like it. She's a charming girl. Your mother asked me to look after her, but I don't have the time today."

Max got up without asking Heller what Judith was doing in London. She'd tell him herself, he presumed.

"Wait, Max. There's one more thing before you go," Heller said pulling an envelope from his top drawer and handing it to Max. "Open this when you get back from the mission."

Max turned the envelope over in his hand.

"*After* the mission. That's an order," Heller warned again. "Good luck, Max."

Chapter Forty-One

Judith Weber

"Hello – hello, Judith!"

When Judith saw Max in the entrance hall she halted mid-step and grinned. Her tummy lurched in a soft feathery way that left her stuttering in English to the two women with her. "My friend … he's here … thank you."

"What a delight, Judith. I had no idea I'd see you today," Max said with a broad smile.

"I am in luck … yes … and how are you, Max?" Judith responded haltingly, since she'd been ordered to speak in English whenever she was not at her workplace.

"All the better for seeing you. I was just going for a bite to eat. Will you join me?"

She stared at him, mouth agape. German words wanted out, but English ones were stuck in her throat. She seemed to have forgotten everything she'd learnt in the last year.

"I'm going to a restaurant not far from here." Max slowed down. "You might know it, Lyon's Corner House near Oxford Circus?"

"No … I don't think … no, sorry."

Max gave the two women escorting Judith a boyish grin. "Ladies, you don't mind if I take Judith to lunch, do you? I'll have her back here within a couple of hours. You have my word."

One of the women giggled, "Yes, you can take her to lunch, Major. We were already informed of her date."

The other woman said, "She was all of a tizz, Major."

Once the two women had left, Judith said, "Thank you, Max. Lunch is a nice idea."

The Lyon's Corner House was busy as always, full of men in military uniforms and women who had evidently paid a lot of attention to their appearances. Waiters carried trays at shoulder height, and the hustle and bustle went on under the watchful eye of the maître de.

"It's very nice to see you again, Judith," said Max, once they were seated at their table. "I had no idea you were going to work with Mr Heller for a few days. How do you like your job? Are you enjoying our capital?"

"I'm happy. I love London," she replied, although she'd only experienced a few busy long streets whose names she couldn't recall. She cast her eyes around the packed restaurant. She'd seen Max slip a handsome tip to the maître de, and subsequently they'd been given a table in the corner. It was partially hidden from the main dining area by two pillars and was quite a way from the tables in the main room. She was hopeful that if she got stuck for something to say in English, she'd be able to revert to German without being overheard. Perhaps that was why Max had paid the man at the door for privacy.

She peered at the menu, a grubby mustard coloured brochure outlining a vast array of dishes. She wondered how much on the menu was available. She didn't understand much of it, but after many months in Britain she'd become accustomed to being told by waiters that a dish was off the menu that day because the restaurateurs hadn't enough meat or whatever to make it. She was particularly fond of cottage pie.

She glanced at Max who was also studying the menu. The British people she'd met thus far seemed to understand and accept the difficulties war entailed. She'd noticed that they complained less about food shortages and rationing than Berliners had, and they didn't blame religious groups for their hardships, or Adolf Hitler. At Bletchley, a German dissident – in the eyes of the Reich – called the Führer *the midget corporal.* He loved to wallow in his hatred and the freedom he had to express it.

The English seemed calm and optimistic, despite the danger lurking off their shores and the blockades creating endless food shortages. Berliners had kicked up much more of a stink when they couldn't get sugar and the like, and although she'd not been allowed into grocers' shops towards the end of her time in Germany, she'd seen plenty of women traipse out of them mumbling under their breaths with faces set to burst. Berliners were like parrots. 'The Jews are to blame for not having enough to eat, for having no work and no money. It's the Jews, the dangerous Jews who have destroyed the Fatherland!' Yet she missed Germany and all the people she'd known in her tenement block, even nasty old Frau Rosenthal.

She peered at the writing inside a box on the top left corner of the menu. It read: *Notice is hereby given that margarine of the finest quality will be served with all goods except bread and butter.* Pity … she liked margarine on her bread. Another larger box at the bottom in the centre crease read: *Save for victory, buy National Savings Certificates.*

"What would you like to eat, Judith?"

Her thoughts of Germany and margarine interrupted, she smiled and replied, "I like English pie."

Max gave her a tender smile and pointed to a dish on the menu. "I enjoy the meat pudding here. Do you want to try that and a farmhouse pie? We can share both. I think you'll enjoy them?"

"Yes, please." Judith's forehead creased; she'd been told pudding was a dessert.

"Are you staying with someone while you're in London?" Max asked, after he had ordered one meat pudding, a farmhouse pie, and two slices of bread from the waiter.

"I go tonight to the Isle of Man for five days." Again, she looked around, saw that no one seemed to be within earshot, and rushed out in German. "I am going to take notes for the official translator at the detention centres. He says there are thousands of Jews in a camp on the island, and the British want to make sure there are no spies amongst them. All those poor people are locked up, but they've done nothing wrong. It's not fair. They've risked their lives to get out of occupied Europe, yet they're still being treated like criminals."

She paused, then as an afterthought said, "Had it not been for your brother and father, I might be in a detention camp somewhere."

"Nothing will ever happen to you," Max said slowly in English. "You got security clearance only after vigorous vetting. Mr Heller and my father vouched for you, and they wouldn't trust you with a job if they didn't think you were completely reliable. You have nothing to worry about, Judith."

"I'm very fortunate, Max. I know I'm not qualified to be a translator, and I struggle with English. Look at me, I'm just a Berliner from a tenement block. What do I know about politics and spies?"

"What does any person know about the workings of war until they're asked to get involved?" he whispered, reverting to German. "Most civilians at Bletchley are new to this, too, but they've all been chosen for a reason. They saw something in you, Judith. What you did in Berlin, actively spreading the truth about what was going on in Brandenburg. That took tremendous courage…"

"It got my father arrested." Judith's eyes smarted. The postcard ploy had been her crime, but she had let him take the blame whilst watching his arrest from the corner of her street. The guilt was killing her. How she missed her papa – who could be alive or dead – and Hilde, who'd be so very proud of her had she lived. Their loss was as great now as it had been all those months ago when they were taken from her. She still cried, was shrouded in darkness at times, and felt utterly alone in the world. She blinked then wiped her eyes with her handkerchief. "I'm sorry. I don't know what came over me."

Max patted her hand and her heartbeat accelerated.

"Max, may I talk to you in German about the people detained on the Isle of Man?"

"Yes, of course, but stop when the waiter brings our food, all right?"

"I will. I've been warned not to talk in our language. I understand, I do. I sometimes wish I didn't know a word of it. I'm ashamed…"

"Don't ever be ashamed of being German, Judith, or Jewish," Max interrupted, taking her hand in his. "Those who want to follow Hitler's vision have betrayed our country, not you, and not the common soldier or citizen who has been swept along by the madness of the men in power. It has taken Hitler's sycophants, the Nazi law makers, and fanatical paramilitary groups like the Brownshirts and SS to create the disastrous policies that have ruined Germany for everyone else."

"And what about the millions of people who voted for the Nazi Party and burnt Jewish businesses, calling for us to be thrown out of our own country? Everyone seems to believe in the Führer and Herr Himmler, and that liar, Goebbels. I believe the ordinary German man and woman would die for Hitler or kill a hundred

Jews if he asked them to … and apart from your brother and your parents, I never met a single German willing to help me. I think … I might have been killed were it not for Paul."

"Oh, my dear girl. You must know by now that there are many good Germans helping…"

The conversation halted when the waiter approached with their food. Max spoke to the man while Judith recalled the meeting she'd had with the official translator of the Isle of Man Jewish camps, he'd called the situation there, *the Jewish problem*. He'd also explained British policies for refugees and how they'd come about.

Following Kristallnacht in November 1938, Jewish and Quaker community leaders had met with the British government to explore ways in which children could be saved from the actions of the Nazi regime. Judith wished she'd known about the programme at the time. She'd have got Hilde on the list and had her shipped to England before the war began. The British government had allowed ten thousand Jewish children without visas into Britain through the Children's Transport program called *Kindertransport*. It had ended in August 1939, too soon to save her Hilde and tens of thousands of other children with Jewish ancestry.

When the waiter left, Judith aired her thoughts with a bitter, grisly tone that sounded foreign even to her own ears. "Tell me, why are the Jewish refugees being caged?"

Max raised an eyebrow, surprised by the question.

She persisted, "Your government call the Jewish refugees *enemy aliens*. But we're not the enemy; we're Nazi victims. Why lock us up?"

Max cast his eyes around the restaurant and then leant in closer. "I have to stop you. If you must speak in German, Judith, speak softly and stop as soon as anyone comes near us. I know it's uncomfortable for you, but you've got to try. Emotions are running high, and not all English people will see you as a victim. Do you understand?"

"I'm sorry ... I do my best, I do."

He tucked an errant tendril behind her ear as he had the first time he'd met her, and then spoke softly in German. "There is a fear in Britain that anyone with a German accent could be a spy. We know through experience that there are a few Nazi sympathisers pretending to be refugees. We can't let them wander around Britain unsupervised, can we? Who knows what they might do with information they come across. You'll find that people in the camp have been put into groups by tribunals depending upon how dangerous they might be."

"Yes, I know, and that determines how long that they might be held and where they are located. Still, it's sad and wrong. It's like the ghettos in Berlin."

"War is sad, Judith, and those that suffer the most are usually the people without any say in the matter. I'm afraid it's the way of the world. The men in power make the decisions and people like us suffer the consequences of their actions, which in most cases are purely self-serving to begin with. But what we're doing to the Jews in this country is nothing like what's happening to them in occupied Europe. No country at war is without its atrocities. No one is all bad, and no one is all good."

"That sounds very noncommittal to me. It's what everyone says, but the depth of evil I encountered in my country makes me believe that the Nazis are *all bad* with not a smidgen of good in them." She tilted her chin. "I'm sorry if you disagree, but that's how I feel."

After what had been a serious and sombre conversation, Judith shifted the language to English and began to talk about his parents. She wanted Max to be proud of her accomplishments and the speed with which she had adapted to the language. Laura Vogel was the most patient teacher, she told Max, but his father was often too tired or too irritable to talk to her in English.

After a meal of meat pies and one vegetable – on this day cabbage was in – Max suggested they take a stroll in Green Park before returning to MI6.

Judith was pleased with herself. She'd held her own, had talked about a variety of things, and, like his mother, Max had been a very good listener. All right, she wasn't fluent, but he had understood her and hadn't laughed at her mispronunciations, not once.

The park's verdant landscape was beautiful, like an oasis in a jungle of old buildings and ruins. But lovely as it was, it was now mid-afternoon and growing colder and duller than it had been earlier in the day. She was shivering and hoping Max might put his arm around her as he had the last time they'd taken a walk together.

The cold had kept people away, she surmised. She'd only seen five other people walking near them, and now she saw no one at all.

"I've had a lovely time, Max. I'm very happy that we met again today," Judith said in German. Then she looked over her shoulder before placing her hand on Max's arm. "Your father asked me to tell you something. I didn't say anything at lunch because we were in a public place and your father told me not to speak of it unless we were completely alone and couldn't be overheard."

"What is it, Judith?"

"It's about Frank. He's been posted overseas."

"What? Frank? I spoke to my mother only last week and she said nothing. What happened to Scotland? How long is his posting?"

"I don't know the answers to those questions. Your father didn't tell me where he'd gone or for how long."

"Good God. I knew nothing about this," Max repeated, looking deep in thought. "And where is Hannah and the baby?"

"They're living with your Aunt Cathy in Kent. Your mother has gone to see them. She's hoping Hannah can come to stay with us in Bletchley, but your father says there are security issues. Really, Max, you should talk to your father in person about this. I know your parents would love to see you."

Judith's lush, black curly hair fell across her face with the wind. She pushed it away and boldly slipped her arm through his. "It's my birthday the week after next. Your mother wants to make a special lunch. Will you come?"

Max replied absently, "Yes … yes, if I can, of course I will."

Max fell silent. Judith, happy to be close to him, didn't want to ask what he was thinking. She imagined he was still pondering Frank's whereabouts.

"Thank you for telling me about Frank," Max said eventually.

"Your mother and father will be pleased when I tell them I spoke to you about him, especially your mother. She cries a lot, Max. She's very worried about you and your brothers. She and your father had a blazing row the other day because she asked him to use his job to find out if Willie was still in Russia. She often bursts into tears and calls herself a bad mother for leaving him."

"What does she say about Paul?"

"She doesn't understand why he didn't come back with you, and she also appreciates why you were angry with him. To be honest, Willie concerns her the most. She fears he might be dead.

She has nightmares about him lying in an unmarked grave. Can anything be done for her? I can't bear to see her weeping?"

Max pressed his lips together. He was suffering too, Judith knew, and she thought it a shame that, unlike women, men tried so very hard to hide their feelings. "Could you ask someone you know for news of Willie?" she urged.

"I don't know what any of us can do," he finally said. "I think about my brothers every day. I'm desperate to give my mother news of them, but both she and my father must know how difficult it is to get information out of Germany."

"Maybe your father can't do anything because he's supposed to be dead."

"Hmm … true." The sky had darkened, and it was starting to spit icy rain. Max stopped walking, pulled Judith's coat collar up and then hugged her. "Don't say anything to my mother, sweetheart, but I might be able to find a way to track my brothers down. We might get lucky."

Judith clung to him for a short while. Then strolling again in the light drizzle, she talked about how much she missed the Berlin she'd known as a child. For the first time, she spoke about the day her father was taken away by the Gestapo and the day she'd met Paul when he had removed Hilde from her home. Her voice, broken with the memory of that day, finally quietened, and they walked in companionable silence, each in their own thoughts in the peaceful, but wet London afternoon.

Their time together was nearing an end. It had sped by, and Judith didn't want to say goodbye. The feeling of being cherished and protected by a man was still alien to her. She had never experienced this wonderful sense of belonging before; it filled her even when Max wasn't there. Just knowing that he shared her affections gave her dark, grief-filled world a dash of colour. Every day seemed less daunting; every night, less lonely.

"Max, I think about you every day," she blurted.

Max wrapped his arms around her and crushed her to him. "Thank you, Judith. I think about you, too. I'd like to take you on a real date, show you parts of London you don't know dance with you, or watch a movie whilst holding hands in the dark. I enjoy your company very much. You've brightened my life."

Her tummy did another somersault, as they continued to lock eyes. "I'm glad. I hope we can do all those wonderful things together."

"May I kiss you?" he asked.

She coiled her arms around his neck and gazed into his turquoise eyes. She gasped softly as his lips met hers and pulled her even closer. Joy, sweet joy; she was in love with Max Vogel.

Chapter Forty-Two

Paul Vogel

The Łódź-Litzmannstadt Ghetto, Poland
March 1942

Paul walked along the corridor after doing his last ward round of the night. The hospital had been relatively quiet since midnight with only three deaths and five new admissions, four of which had been people with typhus-like symptoms. He usually worked the day shifts during what people called *office hours*, but as supervising officer, he'd decided to stocktake while the hospital was at its quietest. He had only two hours left until the end of his eight-hour shift and was looking forward to spending the following day with Valentina whose tummy was expanding rapidly. She hated being alone in the apartment at night.

He reached the door to the doctor's staff room and put his hand on the doorknob. "Damn it," he mumbled. He'd left his stethoscope on the ward he'd just inspected on the first floor. Not wanting to go back down there but suspecting that someone else might pick it up, he made his way to the staff's private stairwell. The medical instrument was a gift from his parents, a constant reminder of his family, and the only thing he had left of them.

As he reached the second-floor landing, he halted mid-step to listen to the soft footsteps and heavy breathing on the stairs below him.

"We must hurry," a voice said.

"I can't go any faster," another man snapped.

"Are you certain we'll get past the guards this way?" a third man asked.

"Yes. It'll be all right, Abraham, we have a way out. We've done this before," the first man asserted.

Paul stuck his head over the railing and looked down. Anatol and Hubert, the two Polish Christian doctors he worked with, were giving piggy-backs to two fully-dressed men. Paul couldn't see their faces in the semi-darkness, but one had been called Abraham, and both were struggling to breathe even though they were being carried.

Intrigued, Paul took off his shoes and tiptoed down the stairs after them. The men below were going at a snail's pace and talking in whispers, but eventually they reached the stairwell door on the basement leading to the mortuary where bodies were wrapped in sheets and then hauled to the Jewish cemetery in hand-carts.

Paul sat on a step, slipped his shoes back on and tied the laces. His heart galloped in his chest, an excitement permeating his being. He was not fluent in Polish, but he now had an ear for the language. What he'd witnessed was not a normal patient's discharge procedure, and what he'd heard led him to believe that his Polish colleagues were attempting to smuggle the two men, most probably Jews, out of the hospital illegally.

Biermann had asked Paul on two separate occasions if he suspected Polish hospital staff of helping Jews to escape. "No, sir, certainly not, but if I do hear anything, I'll tell you about it," Paul had answered, mildly surprised by the question and thinking it unlikely that any members of the Jewish or Christian hospital staff would be involved in such dangerous undertakings. Now, however, he was not only curious about what Anatol and Hubert were doing, but also imagining a way out for Kurt.

As he trudged back up the stairs, Paul reminded himself that taking food and medicine to Kurt and his neighbours was at best a courageous effort on his part, and at worst a weak attempt to appease his conscience. He now thought, however, that his efforts were negligible compared to the Polish rescuers of entire Jewish families. News had spread to the hospital about four of Łódź' Christian residents, dubbed *traitors*, who'd been caught hiding Jews in their basements and attics. Apparently, their less-than-Christian neighbours had somehow found out and reported them to the Gestapo. Two days after their capture, the four accused men and their entire families were executed.

Paul had also learnt about a Catholic midwife, Stanisława Leszczyńska, who'd been caught during one of her hazardous trips to the ghetto to smuggle out babies and small children in laundry trolleys. Biermann had mentioned that the midwife had been deported to Auschwitz concentration camp and her sons to the stone quarries of Mauthausen. Occupied Poland, it seemed, was the only country where the Germans had decreed that any help given to Jews was punishable by death for the rescuer and the rescuer's family.

When he reached the staff room, he pushed his morbid thoughts aside. If he were lucky, he might find a hot cup of coffee and a piece of bread. He hadn't eaten for hours.

"Ah, Doctor Vogel. I was just thinking about you."

Startled, Paul spun around. Doctor Leszek Lewandowski, the indolent Jewish Polish doctor who was in overall charge of the medical staff, sat on a lounger behind the door, reading glasses perched on the end of his round, bobble-head nose. He was completely bald, but his upper lip still sported a white moustache, long enough at the ends to tickle his nostrils and thick enough to resemble straw when not groomed. His pristine white doctor's coat was hanging over the side of the couch, and to Paul's disgust, he wore his *I couldn't care less* expression, which was usually reserved for his patients.

Paul had, when he'd first arrived, excused the man for his lack of leadership and enthusiasm. He'd presumed their brief, stilted conversations were because the Pole didn't have a great command of German or hated Germans as much as his staff members. But he'd been overgenerous; Lewandowski was dedicated to doing as little as possible for his fellow Jews.

"You were looking for me, Doctor Lewandowski? What did you want?" Paul finally asked.

"Kriminaldirektor Biermann has ordered me to supply him with a doctor from this hospital. Due to the nature of the task, you will go. Report to Alexanderhofstrasse in the ghetto at 08:00."

"My shift will be finished in less than two hours. You'll have to send someone else."

"No. The Kriminaldirektor specifically asked for you. You are the only German doctor in the hospital, are you not? I presume he wants you for that reason."

"What's going on in the ghetto?" Paul asked, filling his cup with coffee.

"You ask me that when no one will tell me anything? My position has been stripped from me since you came. I might as well be a piece of furniture in this room. All I've been told is a few thousand people are being deported from the ghetto. If you ask me, it's the best news I've heard in weeks. Thinning out the herd in this place will make our jobs significantly easier." Lewandowski scratched his head and yawned. "Ach, I really don't know how we're supposed to cope with such large numbers of people coming in week after week, month after month. Seems to me the Reich is using Łódź as Europe's Jewish dustbin…" He yawned again. "Think about it, if they're going to die of hunger in the ghetto anyway, shouldn't they just be left alone to do it quietly in the tenements? What's the point of sending them to us, eh? They're squeezing our resources, and most of them die anyway." He shrugged, "And now, deportations – what do you think, Doctor Vogel?"

Paul thought the man, although fluent in German, was an arsehole, but sickening as he was, he seemed to have the ear of the German military command in Łódź.

Worried about Kurt, Paul asked, "Do you know who, or what ages or sexes are being deported? Do you know where they're being taken?"

"No. I know nothing other than what I've just told you – they'll probably take the children. They contribute the least to the ghetto."

Judith Weber and her sister, Hilde, came to Paul's mind. "Why do you hate Jews when you're one of them? What have they ever done to you?"

"I don't hate them, Doctor Vogel. I just wish they weren't causing all this palaver. Were it not for the ghetto, I wouldn't be treading water in this place and getting no thanks for my efforts. This hospital was very different before the war. We practised real medicine."

"Don't you worry *you* could be deported?"

Lewandowski looked horrified. "No. I'm important. I serve a purpose. The hospital wouldn't function properly without me. Why should I stick up for the Jews in the ghetto when I'm trying to prove my case is very different to theirs?"

The poor man, who also lived in the ghetto with every other Jew, had no idea how precarious his situation was. He was delusional, in denial of reality, Paul thought, with a modicum of pity. "Tell me, Doctor Lewandowski, why should you be treated any differently?"

"I'm not talking to you about that." Lewandowski scowled at Paul and heaved himself off the lounger. "Go do your job. I want five minutes to myself."

******

Paul thought about placing a call to Valentina to tell her he wasn't going home yet, but it was only 7am and he didn't want to wake her. When he left the hospital building, he checked his watch again; he had almost an hour to find Kurt, and unlike his other unplanned visits, he was confident of finding him at home. The Germans had a curfew in place until 08:00 for everyone except German military personnel, doctors, and the Jewish ghetto police, and Paul surmised that the ghetto's residents would be speculating about the reason for the recent order and already panicking.

On his way to the German tenement blocks, he passed through Alexanderhofstrasse where he'd been told to report at 08:00. Jewish policemen were already at work, placing desks and chairs in a row in the road and marshalling endless horse-drawn carts. Military trucks were also in situ, supported by SS squads. Notably absent, however, was the habitual stream of factory workers. They normally walked through this street on their way to the factories situated outside the ghetto's main gates.

No work would be done today. Doctor Lewandowski had remarked that it made sense for workplaces to remain closed until the deportations had been completed. But it also begged the question of how many workers would be expelled, and whether it would affect factory outputs. It was typical of the insufferable man to be concerned with profits and money rather than the fates of his fellow Jews.

As instructed, Paul carried his medical bag, but his rucksack, half-full of food and medicine for Kurt and the people he lived with, was slung over his shoulder. Paul had been siphoning goods from the hospital for days in anticipation of seeing Kurt during the forthcoming weekend. The meeting had been arranged ten days earlier, when they'd last spoken to each other.

After taking a cursory look over his shoulder, Paul entered Kurt's building and went up the three flights of stairs to the third-floor. He knocked on the door of flat number fifteen and it was answered within seconds by a young girl of about ten years old. "Hello," she said, recognising him from previous visits.

"Hello, Gertrude. Is Karl at home?" Paul asked.

Paul had never entered the flat, although he'd been invited in many times. The people living there didn't know his name or where he worked. They saw him as a German doctor who was helping them, but no one seemed inclined to ask questions. And that was how Paul wanted to keep it.

Kurt appeared, sleepy-eyed but dressed. His health had deteriorated significantly, Paul noted. His body had shrunk further; he was like a slowly deflating balloon. His cheekbones were becoming more prominent, making his lips and mouth look bigger, and his once bright blue eyes were now dull, red-rimmed, and sunken in their sockets.

"We need to talk," said Paul, handing Kurt the rucksack. "Hide that somewhere safe and then meet me downstairs?"

Kurt frowned but took the bag inside, closing the door behind him. Five minutes later, he joined Paul in the hollow behind the ground floor stairwell. They talked there sometimes, unseen but able to pop their heads out to observe who was coming and going in the building.

"Why are you here, Paul? What's happened?" Kurt whispered.

"At eight o'clock, the Gestapo is going to order all residents from this district to gather in Alexanderhofstrasse. They're deporting people ... thousands, Kurt. I came to warn you and your neighbours."

Kurt's face fell. "Christ, not again. Who's being expelled this time?"

"I don't know ... children, the elderly ... but it could be anyone who's too weak to work."

Kurt's jaw muscles twitched. "Is this why the factory is closed today?"

"I don't know. Perhaps. I've learnt not to ask questions," Paul answered.

"Yes, you've learnt a lot, Paul. Duty to the Reich always comes first. No need to ask questions, right?"

Paul shook his head, but then brought out an unopened pack of cigarettes from his pocket and gave it to Kurt with a wry smile. "At least I've learnt to always bring you these. Have you still got the Zippo lighter I gave you?"

"Yes, miraculously, I've hung onto it." Kurt opened the pack, jerked it upwards until a cigarette popped up and then stuck it between his lips. He lit it and closed his eyes as he drew on it. "What do you suggest I do, Paul? What do you want me to tell the people I live with?"

Paul hesitated, unsure if Kurt could do anything other than warn the residents of what was coming.

"You can't help me or them, can you?" Kurt sighed. "No. You can't. Go back to your hospital, and forget about me. You made your choice long ago."

Annoyed at Kurt's increasingly surly attitude, Paul snapped, "How many times are you going to tell me what you think of my choices? I'm doing my best for you. I can't wave a magic wand and get you released. Maybe if you had told my family you were a Jew using false papers, my father could have got you out of Germany."

Kurt said nothing.

"For God's sake, Kurt, what do you want me to do? Disobey my superiors? Stop coming here? Where would that get us? I hate this place. I wish I could get back to Germany or Paris or bloody Russia, but I'm stuck here, just like you..."

"No. No, Paul, you're nothing like me. I'm a prisoner who's going to die in this shit-hole. You're a free man consciously helping the Nazis to kill me. I had raw carrot leaves for my dinner last night. I have dreams of standing before the whole world telling the masses that we're being systematically starved to death. What we are suffering here is beyond human endurance." Kurt pushed his fingers through his thinning hair, then glared at Paul. "Thank God, I still have dreams. My imagination is all I have left, my only break from the horrors of my reality."

Kurt drew again on his cigarette then exhaled with a ragged breath. Tears gathered in his eyes, and as he wiped them away with the back of his hand, he uttered, "Sorry ... sorry, Paul, I'm not angry with you. God knows I appreciate everything you've done for me. But I can't take this. I've tried, but they're killing us and we all know it ... fuck ..."

Unable to continue, he drew on his cigarette and tapped his knuckles against the side of his head. "I keep seeing it ... over and over. I watched a man hang himself in the stairwell two days ago. I got to him just as his backside slipped off the banister. I tried to pull him up but sometimes I'm as weak as the babies I live with. I went down the stairs and looked up at him. His worry lines were still on his face, but I swear he looked relieved that it was all over."

"I didn't know…"

"They will kill themselves."

"Who?" Paul rushed out.

"People in here. The last time there were deportations more than a dozen families in the ghetto took their own lives – mothers, fathers, children, grandparents, old couples. They'd rather commit suicide together than be separated." Kurt exhaled, the blue smoke clouding his eyes. "No one ever comes back, Paul. We all know there won't be reunions further down the road. Deportation is like death – it's a permanent goodbye, and some people can't bear it."

"You don't know that," Paul said.

"Yes, I do. Grow up. Open your eyes."

Paul's lips trembled at the hopelessness of Kurt's predicament. "I'll get you out. I will, Kurt. I might have found a way."

Kurt's eyes brightened for a split second, and Paul saw the old, powerful, confident thirty-year-old Kurt Sommer.

"You must hold on, promise me, Kurt."

"I will if they don't deport me today. And even if they do, I'll go out fighting when they put me on a truck. I won't leave here for an even worse destination." Kurt's anger disintegrated as he switched gears again. "Forget about me for the moment, what can we do to stop them taking Gertrude and her brother Joachim?"

"Find me in Alexanderhofstrasse. Bring them to my desk. I'll give you all medical certificates ordering you to the hospital, or I'll quarantine your flat and its occupants, stating typhus symptoms. They won't want you on transports if you're sick, not if they're sending you to other work camps." Paul's voice broke. "Find me, Kurt … and don't do anything stupid."

Paul's words were drowned out by the sound of whistles and dogs barking. Then came the evacuation orders being issued by a man shouting through a megaphone.

"Every man, woman, and child must present themselves now in Alexanderhofstrasse. Report now! Bring your belongings and those of your children! Those who remain in their houses will be punished! *Raus! Raus! Beeilung! Macht schon und zieht euch eure Mäntel an!* Hurry up and put your coats on!" The orders went on and were repeated time and again in an ominous monotone until shots sounding like fire crackers drowned out the man's commands.

Both men panicked. Paul wondered how he could leave the building unseen, and Kurt worried about being caught breaking curfew as he rushed back up the stairs to give courage to his neighbours.

"Go," Paul urged. "Remember, come to me at the desk. I'll write the hospital orders before you even get to Alexanderhofstrasse. Good luck, Kurt."

Alone, Paul pulled in a huge breath. He had to move. On the stairs, children were crying and were being told to hush. Scuffles were erupting, and tempers were flaring with angry words and shouts over the children's weeping. And now in the mix came the dull thuds of German rifle butts banging on doors. Paul counted to ten and then left his hideout to join the residents' disorganised exit.

Once he got into the street, Paul picked up his pace. But before he'd got twenty metres, he was stopped by the SS.

"Herr Oberartz, what are you doing here?" said a short, vicious-looking SS officer.

"I've been here for almost an hour visiting a sick child. Bad timing, Scharführer. And now I really must go. I'm needed in Alexanderhofstrasse."

Paul, praying that the SS had more important things to do than interrogate one of their own, set off through the crowded streets towards the selection commission without waiting for the Scharführer's response. It was not yet eight o'clock.

Chapter Forty-Three

As he zig-zagged through the ghetto's congested streets towards Alexanderhofstrasse, Paul was struck by the paradox between the Jews' panic-stricken faces and their well-ordered procession towards their destination. Men, women and children, backs bent under the weight of their bundles, formed an endless line. This was not the first time the ghetto's residents had been given an order to congregate with their suitcases; did they already know it was pointless to resist?

Paul struggled to comprehend the submissiveness of the Jews. It was possible, he supposed, that families truly believed their children were going to a camp in the countryside, as had been suggested, or to farms where they'd get more food and lots of fresh air. But he scoffed at those ridiculous scenarios. He no longer believed the Nazis capable of any benevolence towards the Jews and suspected that today's deportees would be going to even more appalling conditions. Not yet a father, he couldn't conceive of lining up calmly and quietly. He could only imagine fighting to the death to keep his child safe.

German military trucks were parked every fifty metres or so with SS soldiers training rifles on the residents still making their way to Alexanderhofstrasse. The Jewish policemen marching on both sides of the lines were also carrying their suitcases, or those of others. Paul wondered if their names were on one of the lists for deportation. In this prison complex, political organisations continued to exist and even engage in strikes when rations were cut. A rich cultural life, including active theatres, concerts, and banned religious gatherings, were, according to Kurt, used to counter official attempts at dehumanisation. Yet, willpower and strength of mind could not halt the ubiquitous separations of Jewish families or save Jewish policemen who threatened their own people with batons – this was the Nazis' most egregious and powerful tool to further demoralise a race of hated people – a Jew was a Jew, and in that spirit, not even those who worked with the Gestapo were safe from expulsion.

Chaim Rumkowski, the Ghetto's Jewish self-styled *king* was talking to a Gestapo officer. Paul passed the two men, his contempt hidden behind a friendly nod to the Kriminalassistent. He'd only seen Rumkowski once before this morning. Whilst making a speech about rations and the state of the ghetto, he'd surveyed his surroundings like an emperor, sweeping his arm across the backdrop of carts carrying vegetables, and Paul's hospital colleagues transporting a stretcher-bound woman. "Look, the streets are devoid of beggars, and only the faecal workers hauling away people's waste are out roaming. Everyone is happy, everyone is safe. We are very organised, are we not?"

The delusional narcissist had depicted the walled area not as a dilapidated ghetto, but as a leafy, productive commune. Kurt had claimed that the man's overbearing autocracy, including his periodic crackdowns, had resulted in the failure of Jewish attempts to smuggle food and arms into the ghetto. The Nazi clown, as Kurt often called him, had also been misleading his fellow Jews into believing that productivity would ensure survival, and his motto, *work is life,* rang hollow to everyone but himself. Paul suspected that one of the reasons Kurt had remained mentally strong was because he constantly dreamt of killing the Nazi-loving Rumkowski and his bootlickers.

The Gestapo monitoring the residents' progress pressed the Jews to keep going with friendly words and expressions. They wore strange grins on their faces, as though they'd been expressly planted there for the occasion to trick the Jews. "Come along, old mother, not far to go now," a Gestapo officer told a stooped, white-haired Jewish woman. "We'll get you to a nicer place than this before you know it." Paul quickened his pace, his clenched fists itching to punch the man's lying mouth.

At the corner of Alexanderhofstrasse, a woman with a child in her arms barged into Paul as she ran in the opposite direction to the crowd. Almost at his destination, he stopped walking and turned to watch the young woman weave left, right, left, and finally cross the road towards the entrance to a three-storey building. She tried the handle of a shop door, but found it locked and moved on to the next, but that too wouldn't open.

An SS Untersturmführer brushed Paul's arm as he rushed by. He seemed determined to get to the young woman who had run past Paul, as though she were the most important person in the crowded streets. The SS officer shouted when the woman and child reached another doorway, "Halt! Halt!" But then he surprised Paul by backing off to stand some metres away from her, as though he were waiting for something else to happen.

Paul gasped in recognition. The Untersturmführer was Gert Wolff, the young officer he'd shared cake with on the train, the man he'd promised to meet for a beer and a good night out. Hell would grow a conscience before he socialised with the Nazi scum, who was now looking up at a window.

Paul turned his attention back to the woman, who was trying desperately to open the door of an abandoned clothing store. Every fibre of his being wanted to help her and her child to hide, but powerless, or perhaps too cowardly to act, he silently urged her on.

The crowd started at the deafening noise of machinegun fire. Across the street, blood and grey matter spurted from the back of the woman's head and small of her back. She arched her back, dropped her child, then crushed it when she fell directly on top of it.

Near Paul, terrified screams erupted from the people crouched on the ground. Those who had still been walking, bunched closer together as the machinegun continued to spray bullets at the shop door.

Paul gawped in horror at the woman, her blood, and the window glass covering her. Dazed, he shifted his gaze to a third-floor window of a building opposite the clothing shop where the dead woman lay and saw the machinegun barrel poking through the open window. *Show your face, you cold-blooded murderer!*

Gert, joined now by two SS Stormtroopers, went to the corpses. He rolled the mother onto her back and then bent to examine the toddler who'd lain dead beneath her.

One of the Stormtroopers began dragging the young woman's body along the pavement by her hair. The other man lifted the dead toddler by one leg and followed his colleague to the corner of the street where they both disappeared. Gert holstered his weapon and trailed behind his soldiers. Outraged and disgusted, Paul quickened his steps to Alexanderhofstrasse, his rage in full display.

******

Paul sat at a desk next to a Gestapo Kriminalassistent, wondering what he was supposed to be doing; he'd been given no instructions at all. He clasped his recently-redeemed stethoscope in both hands and observed the man next to him, checking off the names of elderly people being sent to his desk. Paul had not yet seen Kurt or his neighbours, nor had he examined a single patient. And the children, he'd noted, were being shepherded to a specific staging point regardless of possible health concerns.

"Go to that truck over there, old father. You're going somewhere nice," the Kriminalassistent was telling an old man without even looking at him.

Paul shoved Kurt's and his neighbours' hospital admission orders in his pocket and got to his feet. *To hell with sitting here doing nothing,* he thought. Kurt was somewhere in the crowded street. The priority was to get him away from the area before it was too late to stop his deportation.

"Where do you think you're going, Doctor?" the fresh-faced Kriminalassistent demanded. "You need to stay at your post. Once Herr Kriminaldirektor Biermann gives us the order to process this last batch, you'll be examining naked Kikes as they run around and around in circles to the sound of Bach. It's amusing, but it's done for a very good reason, so you must pay attention."

"You don't give orders to me. Look at my epaulettes. I'm an Oberartz, not a Schütze. Remember that," Paul retorted. "I'm going to stretch my legs. Don't worry, I'll be back before your circus begins."

With a forced smile, the Kriminalassistent said, "Maybe I didn't make myself clear, sir. You see, those who are already being loaded onto the trucks were chosen for deportation regardless of their health. That's why you didn't need to examine them. Please, sit down, Doctor. Let me show you what we're doing here."

"I'll stand."

The Gestapo man slid a foolscap piece of paper to Paul. "Look at this list. Those I've already processed are at the top – see? They're either very old, disabled, very young, or women whose partners have already been deported for criminal or uncooperative behaviour, or are in the ghetto's prison. In the next batch, we've got to find out if the people who are left are sick or too weak to work. They're clever, Oberartz, got devious little minds, these Jews. They pretend to be strong and useful when they're really at death's door. That's why we get them to run around a bit with their parts out."

When the Kriminalassistent called for an elderly couple to approach, Paul reluctantly sat down again.

A man shouting through a voice-horn in German was asking people for their cooperation. Paul stared at the white-haired, stocky Rumkowski, and as always wondered yet again how some Jews could work for the Gestapo with such treacherous dedication.

Children were being lifted onto trucks. "It won't be long now," the Kriminalassistent said, nudging Paul's arm as if it were a great game.

Paul continued to watch the deportation procedure on the truck nearest to him. Children, the old, disabled, and women already in the back were being ordered to lie down flat in tight rows. Once in their positions, more people were lifted on and ordered to lie on top of those already there. And eventually, when the truck was loaded with seven layers of people, it set off.

In disbelief at the horror he was witnessing, Paul muttered, "My God … my God … what is this? What the fuck is happening here?"

"Keep your thoughts to yourself, sir," the Kriminalassistent snapped, his eyes following the truck down the crowded street. "We've got twenty thousand people to get through in the next couple of days, and we need as much space as we can get on our trucks, that should be obvious. This is not the only street we're using to stage evacuations. There's two more, on Goldschmiedegasse and Tizianstrasse. And in case you hadn't noticed, we're processing mostly German Jews here."

"I've already worked that out for myself," Paul retorted. "What I don't understand is why the people on that truck are being suffocated before they even leave this place. If they're going to work on farms or be taken to another facility, shouldn't your priority be to look after them, especially the children?"

The Kriminalassistent's lip curled. "You've no idea where they're going, have you?"

"No. Tell me," Paul demanded

"Not now, Doctor, we need to get on. I want this batch finished before Kriminaldirektor Biermann gets here. He's finicky about timing and getting things done right. You don't want to ask *him* too many questions, know what I mean?"

Paul felt physically sick as Gestapo guards on another truck pushed children onto their backs. A girl was screaming for her mother as she was hauled up by the arms. It was young Gertrude, the little girl who lived with Kurt. Inconsolable, she screamed again for her mama as she was pushed down by the soldier's baton.

"This is outrageous." Paul's chair toppled over as he leapt to his feet, and blinded by rage, he rushed from the desk.

The Kriminalassistent had also risen, "Get back here, Doctor," he growled as he tried to catch Paul's sleeve.

Lost in the image of children being murdered, Paul spun around and punched the Kriminalassistent on the nose. Then he barged through the crowd towards the truck.

"Vogel – Vogel – halt, Doctor Vogel!"

Paul's stomach clenched, his memory snapping back to the Brandenburg gas chamber and the children being led by the hand into it. Panting with fury, he turned with glassy eyes to see his father-in-law standing behind him with a four-man entourage. He stopped breathing, alarmed to note that he, and not the children, was the centre of attention.

"Good morning, sir … Herr Kriminaldirektor … I was…" Paul struggled to regain his composure. "I was going to the truck over there to…"

"You left your post and punched my assistant, that's what you were doing," Biermann cut him off.

Lost for words, Paul looked at the truck still filling up with more children. Their parents were howling, pushing against the Jewish policemen to get to their offspring and being beaten back with batons.

Paul closed in on Biermann, and hissed in his ear, "You have to stop this. For the love of God, this is monstrous. You're killing children."

Biermann glared at Paul, grabbed his elbow and frogmarched him back to the desk.

"If you were not married to my daughter, I'd be putting you on a charge. You're insolent … undisciplined … a disgrace to your uniform. I'm warning you, Vogel, if you don't respect the important work we're doing here, I will keep my daughter away from you and have you sent to Russia with your brother. He'll show you how to serve the Reich." He then addressed the Kriminalassistent. "Tell me what happened."

Paul perceived Biermann's threats as tawdry bluster, and he was relieved to note that only a few SS were still gawking while his father-in-law questioned the Gestapo assistant.

In hindsight, Paul's intentions had been instinctive. He'd not given any thought to the ramifications that might follow his actions. Only now, calming down, did he realise how close he'd come to ending his future in the Wehrmacht. The truth was, had Biermann not appeared when he did, he, the idiot Vogel, would have fought every guard to get to the children, and might now be facing arrest and possible internment in a prison camp. His lack of self-control scared him.

Paul saw that the truck was loaded and ready to leave. It also struck him that the children's fates had never been in his hands, despite his determination to impede the truck's departure. Every Jew being put on the transports was being taken to his or her death. Paul didn't know where or how the Gestapo or SS would kill them, but after witnessing mass suffocation on the trucks, it was apparent that the Jews' destination was to a grave or an oven, and there was not a damn thing he could do about it.

Biermann was issuing orders to the bloodied Kriminalassistent. Paul, observing them from behind his chair at the desk, concluded that when men reached their limits of tolerance they also marked a turning point in their lives. He'd exhausted his forbearance and excuses for taking part in mass exterminations, but ramming his opinions down the Gestapo's throat was not the way to save people. No, to achieve that he'd have to be much more discrete, and shrewder, than his father-in-law and his subordinates.

"I apologise for my outburst, sir." Paul bowed his head when Biermann returned. "It was uncalled for. I was wrong."

"Your apology is unacceptable, Vogel. You and I need to have a talk. It's long overdue. When you've finished here, meet me at Radegast Train Station." Then Biermann flicked his eyes to his assistant. "Start the last phase. I want this over by this afternoon. And explain to Oberartz Vogel, in detail, what's required of him."

Chapter Forty-Four

"Direktor Biermann looks after his own. You haven't heard the last of this, Oberartz Vogel, not by a long shot." The Kriminalassistent glared at Paul.

Paul continued to throw his medical instruments into his leather bag.

"You hear me, Doctor Vogel? You're finished. I'm Gestapo, and you punched me. Doesn't matter if you're the Kriminaldirektor's son-in-law or Herr Himmler's fucking brother, you're going to get dragged over the coals."

"Punching you in the face was the only decent thing I did all morning. Christ, do you never shut up?" Paul mumbled. "I hope our paths never cross again."

"They probably won't. You'll end up in the Chelmno camp with the Jews. Your kind always get their comeuppance."

"My kind?"

"Yes, traitors to the Third Reich."

"Don't be ridiculous. Say that again and I'll have *you* up on a charge." Paul was desperate to get away from the obnoxious Nazi, but he had not heard the name Chelmno before, or if he had he couldn't remember it. "What goes on at Chelmno?"

The street was almost deserted. The trucks and carts with luggage had been loaded and sent on their way, and the remaining ghetto residents had scarpered as soon as they'd been ordered to clear the street. Nonetheless, the young Gestapo Kriminalassistent glanced around him before putting his index finger to his throat and drawing it from ear to ear. "Gas vans. That's all I'll say."

Paul threw his bag over his shoulder and headed to his meeting with Biermann, mumbled phrases looping through his mind like a mantra. *"Let me not wander in the shadow of evil that consumes my soul and leaves me blind ... give me strength to fight the evildoers so that I may not tumble into their pit of sin ... let me not wander in the shadow of death..."* He didn't know where the words came from, but he couldn't stop repeating them.

He had already tumbled into a pit of sin. He was mired in human cruelty on an unimaginable scale, and now he was praying for absolution? After Brandenburg, he'd felt *forgiven,* but not this time. God didn't absolve atrocities like these, not even for those who prayed all day and flagellated their backs. If He did, He wasn't a good God.

A large crowd of deportees was gathered at the station. The station's name, *Radegast,* was painted in black against a white background on the roof. Its letters could be read from the road, a foreboding portent to those who saw it. In one hundred years, people would connect this inconsequential little station with the annihilation of human beings who had been born Jewish in a Nazi world. Paul wondered if Europe would be ruled by the Nazi Party in a hundred years. What a horrifying thought.

Instead of going straight to the building, Paul searched for Kurt on the crowded platform. He hadn't appeared in Alexandehofstrasse with the neighbours whose children had been taken, nor had he been on any of the loaded trucks. It now seemed likely that he'd found a hiding place and had left his companions to deal with their own fates, although that didn't sound like the loyal Kurt Paul knew.

As he pushed through the throng of people, countless unanswerable questions were thrown at him, making him regret he'd taken this route. Armed SS with their German Shepherd dogs, Gestapo, and ghetto police lined the narrow platform from one end to the other, but he was like a magnet because he had no rifle, was carrying a briefcase, and wore medical epaulettes.

To confirm what the Kriminalassistent had told him, Paul stopped to ask a Gestapo officer where the people were going.

"They're eventually going to Chelmno, Herr Oberartz, but not all the way on this train. They will transfer to a narrow-gauge railroad at Kolo."

Minutes later, a small boy tugged at Paul's trousers and asked, "Where are we going?" An indignant woman demanded, "Where is this train taking us?" An old man blocking his path, enquired, "Herr Doctor, will we be coming back? I've left my daughter and son-in-law behind." A crying woman, begged, "Please, may I wait for my husband?" Now that he had answers to their questions, he shut his mouth, shrugged people off and barged through the frightened mass to the building.

Before he could reach the door, the loaded train left the station with a loud whistle and steam shooting from its smokestack. As wagon after wagon trundled past, Paul caught glimpses of terrified faces at the barred windows, and as he turned from them, he saw hundreds more people cramming the platform. He was witnessing the end of the civilised world as he knew it.

"I'm here to see Kriminaldirektor Biermann," Paul informed the two rifle-wielding Gestapo guards outside the stationmaster's building.

"Is he expecting you?"

"Yes. I'm Oberartz Vogel."

"One moment, Doctor."

Almost immediately Paul was escorted inside and told to knock on the second door on the left. As he waited for an answer, a piece of his father's wisdom came back to him. *'Never show your feelings, or frown, or narrow your eyes when dealing with an adversary. Leave emotions to women.'* It was a tall order given his feelings today, but a necessary one if he were to be forgiven for his public outburst in Alexanderhofstrasse.

Biermann sat behind a desk writing in a ledger. He clearly knew Paul was standing before him but was content to let him wait.

The Kriminaldirektor's face was scarlet, as though every blood vessel in his head had burst. His chest was heaving, and his forehead was beaded with sweat, but even though his hands were shaking, he maintained his sangfroid.

"Are you all right, sir?" Paul asked, thinking of Valentina for the first time that day.

"I'm fine."

"It's been a difficult morning. Shall I come back later?"

"No, you will not come back later. You will stand there and convince me why I shouldn't throw you in Radegast Prison."

Biermann finally tossed his pen on the desk and scowled at Paul. "What the hell did you think you were going to achieve with that stunt of yours? Well? What do you have to say for yourself?"

Although Paul was exhausted, adrenalin was still coursing through his body. *Did his father-in-law really want the truth? All right, he'd get it.* "I was trying to stop the guards from suffocating children on the trucks. Had I managed to get to the vehicle, I would have fought the Gestapo, SS, and anyone else who'd got in my way."

Paul, spurred on by Biermann's silence, put his closed fists on the edge of the desk and leant across it. "I am a doctor, not a cold-blooded murderer. You sit there asking me what I was playing at when you knowingly made me complicit in mass executions? It is you, sir, not I, who is a disgrace to the uniform."

"Ach, for God's sake, don't be so damned melodramatic." Biermann sniggered in Paul's face. "You sound like your father used to when he disapproved of the Party's policies. You're getting more like him every day."

"Don't be *dramatic?*" Paul shouted. "I examined hundreds of people this morning. I put my stethoscope to their chests, looked at their teeth as though they were horses, and ran my fingers through old women's hair looking for lice and scabs. I did precisely what was set down in the manual your subordinate threw in my face, and I completed my tasks without complaint. And in not one single case, not one, did I see anyone deserving of deportation to the Chelmno extermination camp. Yes, Herr Direktor, I know what that place is, so it begs the question why you had me examining the health and well-being of those condemned people in the first place!"

Biermann's eyes narrowed, his face reddening further.

"That callous Gestapo assistant of yours was quite happy to tell me about the gas vans waiting for those people outside. So, who's being dishonest here? Is it you, the Wehrmacht, or me?"

Biermann's lips pursed. He began to rise but then slumped back into his chair, as though in pain. "For the sake of my Valentina, I'll give you this final warning … if you know what's good for you, you'll stop now and keep any further disapproval to yourself. We had a total of five doctors in the ghetto carrying out examinations this morning, and you were the only one to punch one of my men in the face. What does that say about *you?*"

Paul shrugged. "It says I was angrier about what was happening than they were. And with respect to my fellow physicians, what they do, or don't do, is not my concern. Every man must judge his actions by his own conscience." And that,

Paul thought, was throwing every one of his father's pearls of wisdom out the window.

Stuck for an appropriate response, Biermann began rubbing his left arm. His Valentina was in a fragile state, only a couple of months or so to her due date. She meant the world to him, and she was the only reason his cocky son-in-law had not been charged with assaulting a Gestapo officer and having Jewish sympathies.

"You've been using my protection to flout the rules. You assume you can be belligerent because you have a father-in-law who'll safeguard you. You've got a pair of balls on you, I'll give you that, Vogel, but it's time they were snipped. You've misjudged my indulgence."

Biermann paused to take a sip of water, then he wiped his brow with the back of his hand. "I've been sitting here for an hour wondering what to say to you. Your little flare-up this morning went largely unnoticed, but only because I stopped you from making the biggest mistake of your life. I won't help you again – that was the last time."

Paul, his face almost as red as his father-in-law's, leant further across the desk, forcing the Direktor to push his chair back. "I asked for your daughter's hand, not your help, sir," Paul said. "And I demand respect for the uniform I am wearing. I should have been informed of the deportees' destination. I have earned that professional courtesy."

Biermann hesitated. He needed to calm down. Vogel was giving him a severe attack of indigestion. "Did it ever occur to you that we are doing this – all this – for the good of the Fatherland?"

"No, it didn't, not once." Paul strode to the window overlooking the platform. "How can *this* possibly benefit Germany? Don't use the German people to excuse Nazi crimes.

They'd be horrified, utterly disgusted to learn that the Reich was exterminating their fellow citizens..."

"We're not exterminating *real* Germans," Biermann slammed his fist on the desk. "They're Jews! No better than a plague of locusts who've been feeding off us for years." He wanted the meeting to be over but hadn't yet decided how to punish his son-in-law without upsetting Valentina. This was a futile debate, one that neither would win. Paul, like his father, Dieter, could not be swayed or manipulated.

As he swallowed the rest of his water, Biermann noticed, really noticed for the first time how much Paul resembled his father in looks and character. It hurt. Dieter's stab in the back was a permanent source of pain.

"If a Wehrmacht soldier is not a good Nazi, he is also not a patriotic soldier. Therefore, he is a traitor," he muttered, as a wave of dizziness overwhelmed him.

Paul retorted, "You're calling me a traitor?"

"Not exactly. Perhaps that was too strong a word, but as we're being honest, you should know I regret introducing you to my daughter. She deserves better than you."

Paul stayed at the window, his eyes drawn to the appalling scene outside. He turned, his face full of hurt. "I'm sorry you feel that way. I love your daughter very much, and I will protect her with my life."

Biermann rubbed his chest. He felt as if a stone were stuck in his lungs. He could hardly breathe. He needed to lie down. "Do you know who *is* dishonest?" He asked the rhetorical question, and then continued before giving Paul time to respond. "Kurt Sommer is – Karl Ellerich, the Jew, the liar, the British spy. He is guilty of every fault possible in a person's character. Oh, for the love of God, wipe that innocent look off your face. You know what I'm talking about. You've been taking contraband to the Jew on a regular basis. I've been having you followed for weeks. Your own wife knows you've been stealing food and medicines to give to Sommer. She's disgusted with you – appalled."

Paul's face fell.

"And before you say another word, I also know you were at his building this morning."

Paul shrugged. "To be fair, sir, we both knew I was never going to obey your order not to see Kurt. My only question is why did you forbid me in the first place?"

Biermann lit a cigarette, then found that he was too breathless to smoke it. He stubbed it in the ashtray and felt another pain shoot up his arm. Paul, his quiet, unassuming son-in-law, was oozing confidence when he should be shitting like a terrified dog. "As I said, Sommer lied to you. Not only is your father alive, he's also a traitor to Germany."

Paul blanched. "What ... what did you say? You're implying that my father is alive ... he didn't die?"

"That's precisely what I'm implying, and if Kurt Sommer would only cooperate, I'd be able to prove it."

Paul eyes filled with tears, and he stammered, "Why would Kurt not tell me? Why did you not tell me? This is wonderful news ... just wonderful."

"I think you missed the part about your father being a traitor." Biermann clutched his chest as a sharp pain hit him.

"Never! My father was many things, but that? No, I don't believe it."

Biermann was annoyed with himself. He'd planned to keep this revelation from Paul a while longer, wanting to hit the boy with Dieter's treachery, and the news that Wilmot Vogel was missing in action at the same time. Not that he wanted anything more to do with the youngest Vogel. If he was dead, he was dead. Tough luck.

"Paul, I know it's hard to believe, but I have the evidence to back up my accusations. There's a lot you don't know about your father, but Kurt Sommer does. I showed you the files we had on him, but what I didn't say was that he collaborated with your father against the Third Reich."

Paul frowned, "No … no. You're wrong."

Biermann, although enjoying this small victory, was still disappointed with his lack of progress with Sommer. He'd underestimated the Jew's resolve. He wasn't going to break his silence or take Paul into his confidence despite the Gestapo stalking him daily and encouraging him to talk about Dieter with a few kicks and punches to his body. That morning, like many other mornings, Sommer had been detained outside his tenement building and taken to the Gestapo headquarters. There, in front of Biermann, he'd been beaten to within an inch of his life, but he hadn't uttered a word about Dieter or the artworks. The man was made of steel, and Biermann was fed up of tormenting the pig and getting nowhere. Maybe telling Paul was the right move to bring it all out into the open?

He flinched as a piercing stab shot up his arm. "I'm telling you the truth, Paul. Your father is alive, and your friend Kurt knows where he went after he left Germany. You should be angry with him for not telling you, not me."

Paul wiped his eyes, then seemed to straighten in the chair as though embarrassed by his show of emotion. "Why should Kurt say a damn thing to me? You've just accused him and my father of being traitors to their country – you, who's known my father for over two decades – I want proof of your allegations, and your evidence that he's still alive."

Biermann clenched his fists as he was hit by another wave of pain pressing down on his chest. "You're an impudent louse, Vogel. I have … I have compelling evidence, but you … you, not me, will get the corroboration from Kurt Sommer. You have three days…"

"And then?"

"Then I'll execute him as a spy and have you sent to Dachau as the son of a traitor. You can follow in your brother Wilmot's footsteps."

"You wouldn't do that to Valentina."

"Yes, I would. She understands that I do what I do for Germany. But whether she understands, or even loves you anymore, I really can't say."

Biermann struggled to his feet, intending to walk around the desk to face Paul. His hand flew to his chest, and as he staggered forwards more stabbing pains shot up his arm and squeezed his throat shut. "Paul … help me … can't breathe," he uttered as his legs gave way.

Chapter Forty-Five

Paul felt the full weight of shame on his shoulders while sitting in the back of a sequestered truck with his father-in-law. He'd noticed that Biermann was struggling to hold the conversation together in the station master's office, but he'd done nothing about it.

"Are you, all right?" he'd asked a couple of times, suspecting that he wasn't well at all. He'd *seen* the symptoms: the rubbing of the left arm, a hand at the throat, the kneading of the chest as though it were tight. But his affection for his father-in-law had disintegrated, and in the truth, part of him wished the man dead.

At Hospital Number 4, Paul shoved aside his bias and reported Biermann's condition to the Jewish doctor in charge of emergency admissions that day. "He's got severe chest pain, well past the angina pectoris stage. This is a full-blown MI – myocardial infarction. He hasn't regained consciousness."

"Did he stop breathing," the doctor asked.

"No," Paul answered, and added, "I'll see that his wife and daughter are informed. If you have any news, I'll be in the doctor's staff room on the third floor." Paul took one more look at Biermann, then gratefully left the hospital staff to their jobs. He'd get involved, but only if he were asked. He wanted nothing to do with Biermann's treatment.

When Biermann's car arrived at the hospital, Paul had instructed its driver to collect Olga and then to go to his own flat to collect Valentina. Then he'd telephoned Olga, saying that her husband had been taken ill, was in the hospital, and that his driver was coming to collect her. Between her sobs, she'd asked, "What's the matter with my Freddie?" but Paul had been non-committal telling her that he and the duty doctor would speak to her when she got there.

In the doctor's staff room, Paul lay down on the couch and was instantly reminded of the last part of his conversation with Biermann. *I have evidence that your father is alive.*

Alive – he didn't die in the explosion? He was a traitor? His father was a Nazi. How could he also be a traitor to Germany?

Paul was overjoyed at the possibility but also frustrated that Biermann hadn't given any more details. How did his father manage to survive a massive explosion? If he was alive, was he in England with the family? What proof did Biermann have? This was incredibly hard to take in. The only thing Paul understood was Kurt's silence. He didn't like it, but he appreciated the man's loyalty and reticence. It was apparent that Biermann didn't have enough evidence to prove his theory of treachery, spying, or anything else without Kurt's confession.

Paul's thoughts wound back to his visit to Spandau Prison. When he'd spoken to Kurt, his father-in-law had been in the room directing the very short conversation. Had Biermann known that Dieter might be alive even then, and if that were true, was the confession he wanted from Kurt more about Dieter Vogel than Kurt Sommer's past?

Paul's heart was racing. He was dead on his feet, but his turbulent mind was filled with too many disorderly notions to rest. The image of Biermann dying downstairs crossed his mind every so often, but he wasn't the least bit upset about that possibility.

Fifteen minutes later, it was not the telephone telling him his wife and mother-in-law had arrived that woke Paul from a light sleep, but Anatol and Hubert, the two Polish Christian doctors who had smuggled Jews out of the hospital some nights earlier.

Respectful to their sleeping colleague, the men padded softly to the small mobile electric cooker where the coffee and teapots sat. Paul observed them through half-closed eyes and wondered if they'd managed to smuggle any Jews out of the ghetto before deportations had begun that morning. Did they have Jewish children hiding in the basements of their houses, or had the executions of another two Polish Christians who'd helped Jews a week earlier halted their covert operations? The idea of saving just one Jew excited him, especially if that Jew was Kurt.

"Do you want some tea, Doctor Vogel?" Anatol, the younger of the two doctors asked in German as Paul stirred.

"Yes, please." Paul sat up and yawned.

"We thought you'd gone home," Hubert remarked.

Paul got up from the couch, went to the door, locked it, and then turned to face his colleagues. He was groggy, but fully committed to what he was about to say. This was not a spur-of-the-moment decision, but one that had been swirling in his subconscious for days. "I know you're smuggling Jews out of the hospital and hiding them somewhere in Łódź," he said, leaning against the door.

Anatol and Hubert stared at Paul with stony silence, which lasted until Paul snapped, "Come on, you two. I know you speak and understand German fluently, otherwise you wouldn't be working in Hospital Number 4. You're rescuing Jews, and I want to know how you're doing it."

Hubert shoved his hands into his coat pockets and responded in German, "You should get some sleep. You're talking nonsense. We're not involved in smuggling or rescuing anyone. We read the newspapers. People are being hanged for helping Jews. Do we look stupid to you?"

Paul's forthright approach to the subject was beginning to wane. The men standing passively before him were clearly not going to come clean with a Wehrmacht officer unless he incriminated himself. "I saw you with two Jewish patients on the stairs. One was called Abraham, the other, I don't know. But I do know you were taking them out of the hospital through the mortuary illegally."

"That's a lie. You didn't see anything of the kind," said Anatol, turning back to the tea cups.

Hubert, the elder of the two, gripped the kitchen counter. His face was grey, and his panicked eyes were flicking backwards and forwards from Paul to Anatol. "Why are you doing this to us?" he whispered.

Paul walked to the sideboard next to the cooker and lowered his voice. "Let me start again, Hubert. I saw you and Anatol with the Jews, and I heard your plans. Granted my Polish isn't fluent, but it's good enough to determine that you were taking them to somebody's house. Anatol, you told Abraham it was not the first time you'd done it."

Anatol made for the door, but Paul blocked his path. "I'm not going to report either of you. I want your help."

Hubert was taken aback, but Anatol remained sceptic.

"We told you, we're not involved in any rescues. Now, if you don't mind, I need to get back to work," Anatol hissed.

The three men paused to listen to the heavy footsteps in the hallway outside. Paul put his finger to his lips, Hubert cocked his head, now more curious than scared.

Paul continued to block the door. He had crossed a line and was in too deep to take back what he'd just said. Plunged into a conspiracy that could see him blackmailed or arrested, he surged ahead regardless of the danger. "Hear me out," he said, moving away from the door. "My father-in-law is Gestapo Kriminaldirektor Freidrich Biermann. He's in charge of ghetto operations…"

"We know who he is," Anatol butted in.

"Then you'll also know that my wife is expecting our first child."

"And?"

"And I could lose everything by asking you to help me."

When the men didn't respond, Paul spread his arms. "Look, I know how this must look to you, but had I wanted to get you into trouble, I would have reported you to the Gestapo last week. I certainly wouldn't be standing here offering to help you and asking you to do something for me in return. Will you listen to what I have to say?"

Hubert seemed to relax, but his young colleague still looked far from convinced.

"Is this a loyalty test? Some sick Nazi trick to get us to confess to something illegal?" Anatol asked.

"No, and it's not a trap either. I swear on my mother's life, it's the truth." Paul sat on the couch, freeing the exit for Anatol and Hubert. Short of getting on his knees, he had done all he could to persuade them.

Hubert sat on a hard chair opposite Paul, as though waiting for another revelation.

Anatol made to leave, gripping the door handle with one hand while making a fist with the other. "I'm warning you, Doctor Vogel, if you tell anyone you saw us helping patients escape from the hospital, we'll deny it. We're not defenceless Jews. We have rights. We also have records of every patient we have treated in this hospital since the day you arrived. None have gone missing or left here illegally with or without an escort." Anatol released the door handle and took a step forward. "You are making a big mistake."

"Doctor Vogel, why on earth should we believe a word you're saying?" Hubert asked in a more mollifying tone. "You're not our friend. We hate Nazis and their Führer. We hate that you're occupying our country, that you have come in here and taken over our well-ordered hospital and the keys to our pharmacy..."

"Stop ... Hubert, please stop." Paul panicked. He'd done this all wrong, not that he thought there was an ideal way to suggest committing treason. "Please, wait, both of you. I don't expect you to trust me straight away, but I haven't jumped blindly into this. I've been thinking about approaching you for days, wondering how I was going to talk to you without making you feel threatened. Clearly, I have failed, but I need your help and it's so damn important to me, I'll beg if I have to."

Paul laid his cards on the table. "I understand this must be hard for you to believe, but that is precisely why I'd be an asset to your rescue missions ... operations ... whatever you call them. Yes, I'm a German, but I also hate the Nazis, and I'm not one of them."

"Then why are you here?" Anatol droned.

"Orders – I'm in the Wehrmacht – but being in the German army is not my priority. I have more personal concerns, the highest being my friend who is imprisoned in this ghetto."

Anatol's eyes widened. "Is your friend a Jew?"

"Yes."

"Why do you want to help him?" Hubert asked.

"Karl Ellerich, also known as Kurt Sommer, is a man I respect and love. He is family. I'm committed to this course of action..."

"Hypothetically, what is this course of action?"

Paul took a deep breath and then exhaled. "I'd like to offer you a collaborative arrangement. I'll help you get Jews out of the ghetto, and in return, you will find a safe hiding place for my friend. Between the three of us, I have the best access to the districts inside the walled area. I can bring patients here whenever I want because of my uniform and my relationship with the Gestapo Direktor. The Gestapo and SS trust me, and the Jewish Police are used to seeing me wandering about the place and wouldn't dare question me. I will also promise you much needed medicine, which has thus far been denied you. I can't guarantee I'll be able to get my hands on enough for all the Jewish patients in our wards, but I will do my very best..."

"Hypothetically speaking again, "Anatol interrupted, "if you think you have the means to get Jews out, why would you need our help with your friend?"

"It's simple. You have the hiding places, the routes out of the city, and the contacts in Łódź. It's not enough for me to get him out ... he has to have somewhere to go ... be looked after."

"And your friend, is he a German or a Pole?" Anatol asked.

"He's a German Jew. He worked for my father for years using a false name and religion. To be honest, after the deportations this morning, I don't even know if he's still *in* the ghetto. But if he is, he's in grave danger. He doesn't have much time."

Paul's eyes pleaded. "Hubert, Anatol, please? The Gestapo are going to kill him."

"Go on, we're listening," said Hubert.

"Thank you. As I said, I'll do whatever it takes to free him. I'll follow your guidance, and I won't ask you who else is involved or where you hide the people you save. And if you think I am lying to you, or I'm a threat to your operations, take me to the back of the building now and kill me."

Paul now played his last cards, treading a dangerous path by sharing German secrets. "Do you know where the ghetto deportees are being sent today?" he asked, flicking his eyes from Hubert to Anatol.

"No. We weren't told," Anatol answered.

"I take it you do?" Hubert asked.

Paul felt his eyes prickle as the horror of the day struck him again. "The Jews are being transported to a camp in Chelmno. The people who left this morning … the children, the elderly, the young men and women who were on Rumkowski's blacklist, are probably dead by now or will be within hours. Chelmno is a death camp that operates gas vans to wipe out not only the Jews I mentioned, but eventually, all Jews in the ghetto." Paul gulped. "You didn't know just how important your rescues are, did you?"

The men looked stunned, and Paul, well past the point of no return, continued. "There will be more deportations, more people going to their deaths in Chelmno. This is just the beginning."

The atmosphere in the room changed. Hubert covered his face with his hands, his elbows balancing on his knees, his shoulders heaving.

Anatol cursed. "They can't do this…"

"I didn't get these details from an official source, but I have it on good authority that up to a hundred Jews are being gassed at a time. And soon it won't matter to the Nazis if a person is old or useless, or too young to work in their factories. They won't even care if they're non-Jews. They'll go after dissident clergy, Roma, and even Christian traitors. The Gestapo and SS are getting their orders directly from Himmler's office in Berlin, and I believe he eventually means to annihilate the Jewish race in Europe, and any other ethnic or nonconforming groups he sees as a threat to the Nazi Party."

The two Poles were silent, but their expressions revealed their thoughts. Paul, impatient for their decision, snapped, "For God's sake! If I wanted to trap you, I wouldn't be telling you these filthy secrets, or about my friend, Karl, which you can now hold over my head. I can help you – can you help me?"

He rested his head on the back of the couch. He'd said enough. If he were reading Anatol and Hubert the wrong way and they were not involved with a cell of Poles hiding Jews, they'd report him, and he'd be arrested and executed. That was how high the stakes were. He'd lied to them, but only once; he hadn't planned this meeting, as he'd claimed, but, enraged after the day he'd had, he'd jumped into it damning the consequences. He wondered what Max might say right now? He, who saw himself as the brother with gumption and a thirst for adventure and who perceived his twin to be a tame replica … what would he say?

Anatol finally reacted, dropping into the only free chair and shaking his head. "If you're lying to us, Hubert and I are both dead…"

"And if you report me, so am I." Paul heard footsteps outside in the corridor and someone knocked on the door. Anatol leapt to his feet to open it.

"Yes, nurse?"

"I have a message for Doctor Vogel."

"What is it?" Paul got up.

"Your wife is downstairs. She's asking for you."

"Thank you, I'll be down shortly." Paul closed the door and addressed the two men. "Consider what I've said, but don't take too long." As he turned the door knob, he added, "With or without you, I am going to get my friend out of this hellhole."

Chapter Forty-Six

Paul found Valentina and Olga in a waiting room talking to Doctor Abersztejn, the doctor treating Biermann.

"Ah, Doctor Vogel, I was just telling your wife and Frau Biermann that we might not have been able to save the Kriminaldirektor had it not been for your quick actions at the train station."

"Where have you been? You left Papa alone," Valentina cried.

"I'm sorry darling. I had to see a patient upstairs," Paul apologised.

"But who could be more important than my father? Really, Paul, I do wonder about your priorities sometimes."

In a rare show of defiance, Paul ignored his wife's last comment and asked the doctor, "Will he make a full recovery?"

"We hope so. No guarantees, of course, but we try to remain optimistic. He's reasonably stable at present, and as I told Frau Biermann and your wife, the next forty-eight hours will be crucial."

"When can he come home?" asked Olga, apparently not understanding the severity of her husband's condition.

"As I said, Frau Biermann, we're hopeful, but even if he shows signs of improvement, he'll be hospitalised for a further two or three weeks," the doctor replied.

There it was, the standard spiel to family members, meant to give comfort. Paul planted a smile on his face and took Valentina's hand. "Can we see him, Doctor?"

"Not yet. He needs rest."

"Can you explain the Kriminaldirektor's treatment plan to Frau Biermann and my wife? Understanding what you're doing might put their minds at rest."

The doctor nodded but continued to address Paul. "We're extremely fortunate to have an electrocardiograph here and we're going to do another ECG in a day or so to check whether the earlier disturbances of his heart's rhythm are still occurring. He's on oxygen to ensure he's getting an adequate flow to his heart, and based on our initial ECG, he is already starting to regain a better heart rhythm. The sphygmomanometer readings show his blood pressure has improved, we are commencing a medication regime of nitroglycerin for his angina pain, and we're also administering digitalis to slow his heart rate. And as you know, Doctor Vogel, he'll be on it for the rest of his life."

Finally, the doctor addressed Olga, who was still crying. "We can't give any promises at this early stage, Frau Biermann. You must be patient."

Paul tried to console Olga, who had slumped in a chair weeping into her white lace handkerchief. "Did you hear that, Frau Biermann? It can be fixed."

"No. I don't want to know … I can't take this. I need … I want to go home."

"I'll take you home."

"No. I want to go home to Berlin with Freddie. I don't like this place. We should never have come to Poland."

"Mother and I have had a terrible time of it," Valentina explained, wrapping her arm around her mother's shoulders. "We spent all day listening to gunfire and people shouting and screaming in that ghetto. Were the inmates rioting?"

"I don't know…" Paul shook his head, noting her use of the word, *inmates.*

"Well, if they were, it's not fair to my papa. He works hard to keep those Jews safe, and their nonsense today is probably the reason he took ill. Isn't that right, Doctor?"

"Well … erm … I think it could have been a number of things," the middle-aged doctor stuttered. "If you'll excuse me, I'll just go and check on the patient."

Olga, still sniffling, seemed to be calming down. "We must all give our utmost for Germany, even your father, dear. Don't you agree, Paul?"

"Yes." Paul kissed Valentina's forehead and squeezed her hand. "Darling, let me take you and your mother home. There's nothing we can do for your father now except wait."

"You're not going to stay with Papa?" Valentina was appalled. "Tell me you'll stay?"

"I suppose I could sleep in the staff room, but I'd rather go home to my own bed."

"No, you can't leave. What if he wakes up and no one's there?" Valentina rolled her eyes as though the very idea were preposterous. "I'll go to Mother's house. You can telephone us if there's any change in his condition."

"I'm off duty now after a very trying day. If I don't get proper rest I won't be any good to anyone," Paul snapped.

"Oh, you can be selfish at times. Please, stay here, there's a good boy."

After Valentina gave him a peck on his cheek, Paul watched the two women get into their waiting car. For the first time since meeting her, he'd wanted Valentina out of his sight. This *good boy* had something much more important to do than sit by Biermann's bed. To hell with him, and to hell with her!

Darkness was falling, and it was cold and drizzly with thunderclaps coming in from the east. The ghetto was still under curfew, but Paul had commandeered a horse-drawn ambulance cart and still had Kurt's hospital admission order in his pocket; he was confident that the ghetto's police force would let him pass should he be stopped and questioned.

"We have to cross over," Paul told Tomasz, the driver, as he manoeuvred the horse and transport across the road to the entrance to the German Jews' tenement blocks. Paul recalled seeing a couple of motorised ambulances when he'd first arrived in the city, but the Jews were now deprived of such comforts, as were the doctors and orderlies transporting the patients.

Paul was in high spirits, a strange phenomenon for him. He felt in control, confident, and very relieved. For the first time in weeks, the weight of Biermann's scrutiny and threats had been lifted. He looked over his shoulder; a habit as automatic as breathing. Were Biermann's men following him even though their commanding officer was lying in a hospital bed? Probably, but they wouldn't be given access to their boss until his doctor permitted visitors, which gave him possibly a week or two to sort Kurt out.

"… Doctor … Doctor Vogel. Which block is it?"

"Sorry, Tomasz, I was miles away." Paul pointed to a building. "This one here. The patient is on the third floor."

"I might have known," Tomasz complained. "I've been here four times today already. Fifteen people were shot and killed by the SS and Gestapo, and an entire family committed suicide on the fifth floor of another tenement block. I've had enough going up and down stairs, carrying bodies – those poor children. I wouldn't say this to any other German, but you're a kind man, sir, and I trust you…"

"Don't trust anyone," Paul cut in. "Don't talk to me or any other German about how you feel. Do you understand me?"

"Yes. But I wanted to…"

Paul sighed. "Shut up, please. I'm trying to think." Fifteen people had been shot that day. *Fifteen?* He'd seen one incident, the mother and child, but fifteen? And how many were in the family that took their own lives? How did they do it? Regretting telling Tomasz to shut up, he asked, "How did the family die?"

"The four children and the mother had broken necks, and the father had slit his throat, or someone else had done it for him. They were lying on a double bed, all six of them, three at the top and three at the bottom. It shook me, Doctor."

Kurt shot into Paul's mind. He panicked but then relaxed as he recalled Biermann's order that he obtain Kurt's confession within three days. That meant Kurt must be alive. If he didn't truly believe that, he wouldn't have taken the ambulance through the ghetto in the dark.

"Wait here until I come down for you. No point lugging your stretcher up three flights of stairs until I see what condition my patient is in," Paul said at the building's entrance.

An elderly man whom Paul had never seen before opened the flat's door and then stepped back hurriedly.

"I'm here for Karl Ellerich," Paul said softly. "Ask him to come to the door, please?"

The door remained open and Paul caught a glimpse of the flat's interior. A woman was lying on a blanket on the floor in the square hallway. She was covered by her coat and facing the wall, either fast asleep or ignoring his presence. The door to another room was ajar. A woman slicing a potato sat on the floor next to a bowl, and behind her were Gertrude's parents weeping in each other's arms. Paul sensed the absence of the three children who'd lived there. He'd watched them leave on the back of trucks, either already dead by suffocation or going to their deaths in Chelmno.

It was as though their souls had been yanked out of the place, leaving behind this morbid, sorrowful atmosphere that would never brighten.

"Herr Doctor, I'm sorry to report that Herr Ellerich can't come to the door. He's very ill."

"Take me to him." Paul, breaking his own rule about not entering the flat, barged past the man into the hallway. "Where is he?"

The bedroom floor was bare but rolled up blankets and pillows were stacked against the wall. Kurt was lying on one of the beds; the other was occupied by a young couple who got up as soon as Paul walked in.

"I'd like to speak to the patient alone." Paul dismissed the couple.

The extent of Kurt's injuries made Paul gasp as the terrible irony confronted him. "I came here to take you to the hospital using a false admission order, but it seems I have a genuine reason to admit you. Who did this to you, Kurt?"

"I'll give you one guess." Kurt tried to sit but gave up with a groan. His eyelids, swollen to twice their size, were impairing his sight. His speech was compromised because of a deep gash stretching across half his top lip. Matted hair was covered in blood at the crown, and dried, red streaks had streamed down his forehead to meet another deep cut above his left eye.

Paul sat on the edge of the bed. He was silent, afraid of sobbing if he opened his mouth. He lifted Kurt's bloodied shirt and spotted a football-sized bruise stretching from his side to his belly button.

Kurt winched, "Careful ... I think my ribs ... might be broken."

"This is Biermann's handiwork, isn't it?" Paul finally asked.

"Yes … he told his puppets to smash water glasses over my head." Kurt grimaced again. "Got upset when one didn't break … took three goes … I have a hard head, apparently."

Paul swallowed his disgust and set his lips into a hard line as he examined the bruised areas. "This is brutal, even for Biermann. It's not the first time he's beaten you, is it?" he added, noticing the yellowing bruises on Kurt's chest.

Paul pulled Kurt's shirt down and then stood up. He saw himself as a gentle man, not prone to violence, but he was kicking himself for not letting Biermann die on the floor in the train station's office.

"Don't take me with you, Paul," Kurt mumbled. "Biermann will get to me no matter where I am. And I don't want you involved in this mess."

"I'm already in this mess up to my armpits, Kurt. Trust me, he won't be bothering you again. He has his own health problems, and you're never coming back to this ghetto. I'll bet my life on it."

Paul stared at Kurt's battered features. He opened his mouth, shut it, then asked the question that had been uppermost in his mind since leaving the train station. "Biermann told me my father is alive. Is this true?"

Kurt groaned as he tried to turn onto his side. "No. Your father is dead. He died in Berlin. Don't believe a word that pig told you."

Paul gulped back a sob. "I should have known better than to trust that lying bastard."

Chapter Forty-Seven

At the hospital, Paul accompanied the orderlies carrying Kurt on a stretcher to a ward on the second floor. As soon as Kurt was in bed, he dismissed the men and pulled the curtains around the bed for privacy. Aware that he was technically off-duty and should have handed Kurt over to the Jewish doctor in charge of the ward, he injected Kurt with the morphine he'd pilfered before going to the ghetto. Being the supervisory German doctor had its perks, one of which was the keys to the pharmacy. They had once been treasured by Leszek Lewandowski, the hospital director, but being Jewish, he'd been ordered to hand them over to the Wehrmacht's hospital representative, Paul, a man far junior to the Pole in terms of experience, standing and age.

Before leaving Kurt, Paul instructed the Jewish doctor not to go near the patient until his return. Paul planned to hand the case over to Anatol, which was against the rule of Christian doctors treating Jewish patients. *Sod the rule.* He wanted Anatol and a private room made available for Kurt, and he was no longer going to beg for anything. He was going to take what he needed from now on.

Anatol stood near the Sister's office and his eyes narrowed at Paul's approach. "Why are you still here? Don't you have a pregnant wife to go home to?"

Paul, having taken the first step in his plan, including giving a shaky promise to Kurt, was determined to bring Anatol onside. "I've just admitted Karl Ellerich with serious injuries to his head and torso. He was badly beaten, and I'd like you to examine him before I go to see my father-in-law."

"Karl Ellerich? Am I supposed to know him?" Anatol then seemed to recall the name from their earlier discussion. "Ah, yes," he whispered. "He's the Jew who was in danger. I can't treat him. You know the rules."

"To hell with them. I need you to assess him and get him into a private room where he won't be supervised. The Gestapo tortured him today just as I thought they would. He has extensive bruising to his abdomen, numerous head injuries, and broken ribs. He was in agony, so I administered morphine, but no sulfa drugs yet. Will you help, please?"

"Where did you get morphine? We were ordered to stop giving it to Jews weeks ago."

Paul whispered. "I told you, I can help you save lives. Now, will *you* help me before the Gestapo finish him off?"

The two men strode towards Kurt's ward, but Anatol's evident nervousness was a concern. Paul placed his hand on the Pole's arm, halting him abruptly. "Wait, Anatol, I need to be honest with you. I was going to bring Karl here using a false admission order. It's been in my pocket all day. I intended to keep him here under false pretences until you and Hubert gave me your answer..."

"You're taking a hell of a risk, Doctor, and now you want me to get involved in some illegal scheme. I've told you before, I am not a Jew. I have my rights." He hissed, jerking his arm away.

"And I have my friend to consider."

Paul suspected that threats would only push the man further away. Anatol didn't trust him but was intrigued enough to examine Kurt, and that was a step in the right direction. "Anatol, I'm not doing anything wrong, and neither are you. I had nothing to do with the beating he got this morning. In fact, I was looking for him at the deportation site to give him the admission slip. Not seeing him in Alexanderhofstrasse is the reason I went in search of him."

Again, Paul placed his hand on Anatol's arm against his better judgement, and begged, "Please … please. Kurt will die if you don't help him."

Anatol looked unimpressed as he shrugged Paul's hand away and walked on. "I'll evaluate the patient, Doctor Vogel, that's all I'll say."

Anatol examined Kurt's injuries while a nurse took notes. He started with the head wounds and then gently prodded his abdomen while Kurt looked up at him, glassy-eyed.

"I'm worried about internal bleeding," Paul remarked.

"I agree." When Anatol had finished he sent the nurse to fetch an orderly with a trolley. "Say it's urgent, nurse, and while you're there, call the radiologist in from off-duty and tell him I'll be down in a minute."

The nurse raised her eyebrows. "But this is Doctor Bernstein's patient, Doctor…"

"Just do it. I'll speak to Doctor Bernstein … and not a word to anyone about it, do you understand?"

Kurt, relaxed under the morphine, was conscious enough to stammer, "Did you mean what you said about not going back to the ghetto? Did you mean it, Paul … Paul, did you?"

"Yes, every word, Kurt. I told you I'd find you a way out." Paul glanced at Anatol.

Anatol hung his stethoscope around his neck, then ordered Paul to leave the ward.

"I'll be outside," Paul said without objecting.

Kurt searched Anatol's face. "I have nothing to say."

"I only want to ask you a couple of questions about your relationship with Doctor Vogel? Is that all right?" Anatol asked.

Kurt nodded.

"How long have you known him?"

"Long enough …years. He's dedicated to medicine and he loves his family. He's a good man, but he's … I'm afraid he's going to do … he might do something even more stupid here than he did in Germany."

Kurt, drifting off, muttered, "Protect Paul, Doctor. He should have got out."

Anatol shook Kurt's shoulder. "Not yet. Who did this to you?"

"Eh … who? The great man of course, the Kriminaldirektor and his thugs." Kurt chuckled. "Shh … don't tell him I called him great."

After pulling a blanket up to Kurt's shoulders, Anatol went into the corridor.

"Well?" Paul asked.

"The first thing he needs before I even start treating him is the private room you suggested. He's too vocal for his own good. I'll clear out the storeroom on my ward and put a sign on the door. I'll give him the tag of having a suspected contagious disease. That will keep that coward Lewandowski away from the entire floor. Fortunately, or unfortunately, depending how one looks at it, I don't have any patients. Christians don't want to come here anymore, and who can blame them? I can see Hubert and myself being out of jobs soon, but that conversation is for another day. How much morphine did you give him?"

"Thirty milligrams. Correct for his less than seventy kilograms of bodyweight. Enough to ease his pain." Paul shrugged. "I might have been a bit heavy-handed. I'll leave a vial with you. He'll need more in the morning."

While waiting for the orderly to collect Kurt, Paul and Anatol discussed the patient's treatment. They had a couple of options but agreed that both were dependent on the X-ray results.

Halfway through a conversation about how they were planning to keep Kurt's presence a secret from Doctor Lewandowski, Anatol's hand went into his coat pocket. "I hope to God I'm doing the right thing," he said, pulling a folded piece of paper out and handing it to Paul. "Come alone to this address at nine o'clock on Thursday evening. The shifts change that day and the three of us will be off-duty at the same time – barring emergencies. My wife will make dinner and after we've eaten, Hubert and I will listen to you. I can't promise anything, Paul, but we will listen."

Paul's hopes soared. "Thank you, Anatol, you won't regret it."

"That remains to be seen. In the meantime, don't *you* make promises to your friend in there. You might not be able to keep them. Now, go home. I will take care of him."

Paul, reluctant to leave, repeated, "Don't let anyone near him, especially the Gestapo."

"I think Doctor Lewandowski might have something to say about that. You don't want to arouse his suspicion. He resents you being here." Anatol started to walk away, but then spun around. "By the way, Hubert is now treating your father-in-law downstairs. Kriminaldirektor Biermann refused to have a Jewish physician. When you see Hubert, don't mention your friend to him, not while he's treating a Gestapo officer. And Doctor Vogel, one other thing…"

"Yes?"

"Don't come back up here for at least the next two days. If you do, you'll draw unwanted attention to yourself and to Karl. When I finish, my nurse will take over his care until my return tomorrow. I trust her."

"I'm very grateful, Anatol."

"You should be. I am now taking major risks for you. I hope you keep your end of the bargain."

"I will, and more."

Paul went to the Aryan ward and found Biermann propped up in bed, dressed in a pair of hospital-issue striped pyjamas, the lower half of his face hidden under a mask attached to an oxygen cylinder.

Biermann removed the mask from his face, and asked, "Sort these damn pillows out for me, will you?"

"I'm glad to see you're feeling a bit better, sir," Paul said, plumping the pillows and placing them anew behind his father-in-law's head.

"I've been told I've got to rest for at least a month, but I won't put up with half that time in bed. Mark my words, I'll be back on my feet within a week or two."

"I don't think you will," Paul said with his doctor's hat on. "You've had a heart attack…"

"I know what I had." He wheezed. "But don't you think you're off the hook just because I'm in here."

"You concentrate on getting better, sir." Paul scowled, furious about everything that had happened that day, both at work and personally. One minute he'd been told his father was alive, then no more than a couple of hours later, Kurt had denied it. Who was telling the truth? It was too much. What kind of man played with another man's mind by lying about something like that?

"Did you hear me, Vogel?" Biermann asked.

"Sorry, sir. What were you saying?"

"I was saying, I'll feel a lot better when you bring me Kurt Sommer's confession. Three days, Paul. That's all you've got."

Biermann was becoming breathless and closed his eyes. Paul lifted the mask onto his father-in-law's face then made himself as comfortable as he could. What to do next? It was Sunday, and the meeting with Anatol and Hubert wasn't until the following Thursday evening. A lot could happen to Kurt in those four days.

He looked out the side ward door leading to the Sister's station and hallway beyond; no one was milling about. He rose, closed the door and then returned to the hard chair by the bed. He wouldn't shed any tears for Biermann should he die, and he wouldn't feel a gram of guilt for hoping he would. As a doctor, he'd buried his Hippocratic Oath at Brandenburg. The age-old pledge, spoken by the greatest medical minds since the age of the Greeks, had become a wishy-washy promise that German doctors in occupied Europe often ignored – more often, they were under orders that were contrary to its philosophy. He included himself in that group of medical professionals; shame on him.

He knew every word of the Oath, and its prayer to its mythical witnesses: Apollo the Physician, Asclepius, Hygieia, Panaceia, and all the gods and goddesses. It was a simple, comprehensive agreement in which doctors stated that they'd apply all known medical and ethical measures for the benefit of the sick according to one's ability and judgement, and more pointedly, to keep them from harm and injustice. Paul, having broken his oath time and again, often contemplated whether he still deserved the title of physician.

He listened to the hissing sound from the oxygen cylinder and felt an overwhelming urge to rip the mask off Biermann's face and interrogate him; instead, he got up, double-checked the door was closed and no one was about, and then gently lifted the mask. "I'm sorry to wake you, but I can't stop thinking about my father."

"Eh – eh? We'll talk in the morning." Biermann yawned, then seemed to change his mind. "What – well, what about him?"

Paul sat close to Biermann on the edge of the bed. "You said before you took ill that my father was alive, and a traitor. That's a very serious accusation to make and I think I deserve an explanation."

Biermann's expression soured again. "Not yet, you don't. I'll tell you when I have everything I need."

"Yes, I understand, but the problem with that is I don't see how I can get Kurt Sommer to confess if I don't know what I'm asking him to confess to."

Biermann glared.

"You used the word *treason* against your dearest friend – my father. I am grieving his loss, so if what you say is true, give me proof."

"He *was* my closest friend, and now he is the traitor who betrayed his country," Biermann spat. "He lied and connived behind my back, and I was the fool who gave him information on my investigations as I would to my closest confidant. I trusted him implicitly, and when I thought he'd died, I did everything in my power to help your mother, you, and Wilmot. His betrayal stings like a septic wound."

Paul, losing his patience, roughly replaced the mask over Biermann's mouth. Still no proof. He was getting tired of his father-in-law's repeated rhetoric of hurt, betrayal, and self-pity. "That's it, sir, relax your breathing – in, out – in, out."

When he'd pulled the mask down to the edge of his chin once more, Biermann muttered in a tired voice, "I am not asking you to help me. I am ordering you to get the information I need against your father and his accomplice, Kurt Sommers. My power stretches all the way to the Reich Security Office in Berlin, Paul, and if you don't do as I ask, I will see you prosecuted as a co-conspirator, along with your father and Wilmot. And when I do, you will be saying goodbye to your wife." Biermann wheezed. "Put the mask on properly, then leave … go on … get out."

The Vogels

Chapter Forty-Eight

Max Vogel and Romek Gabula

Somewhere in the North Sea
3 April 1942

The Grimsby fishing trawler carrying Max, Romek, a Royal
Navy lieutenant, and two RN ratings shadowed the minesweeper
until it reached the pre-arranged coordinates in the North Sea.
There, after Max had confirmed by radio that the naval vessel was
heading back to shore, he ordered the lieutenant to bring the
trawler to a full stop.

Max swept the horizon through his binoculars from the
trawler's port side, saw nothing, and then went to the starboard
deck to repeat his observations. They had reached their
destination two hours ahead of time and had no reason to think the
U-boat, being in enemy waters, would appear until the designated
hour.

The sea, while having a light swell, was reasonably calm this
spring night. The boat was not being tossed about or hit by too
much spray, giving the men good visibility with clear skies and a
full moon. More importantly, the lieutenant was confident he
could maintain the boat's position and control its drift.

Despite the comparative calm, Romek proved to be a bad
sailor, vomiting twice over the side of the boat while groaning
that he hated England. Max, needing the Pole to be in good form,
had taken him into the cramped cabin where the former continued
to moan about his misery from a bench seat that rocked like a
hammock.

"Never again – don't ever ask me to get on a boat again – you hear me, Max? Never."

Max chuckled at Romek's screwed-up face and his arms clutching his stomach. "Well, well, well, the great Romek Gabula has a vulnerability after all, and here's me thinking you were invincible."

"Shut up," Romek said, throwing up again in the fire bucket at his feet.

The trawler's skipper, a naval lieutenant who for the purposes of the mission went by his Christian name of Patrick, poked his head into the cabin, and said, "Flashes – sixty metres off our port side, sir. The conning tower breached the surface a few minutes ago."

"At last. Before you go, Patrick, don't let me hear you say *sir* again until this is over." Max eyed Romek lying half on and half off the narrow bench seat. "Get up, Romek. I need you now."

The sailors were leaning against the side of the boat near the stern where a pile of nets lay. Max sauntered to them, then stood with his back to the port side. "There's a German naval officer on that sub over there who has probably had us in his sights since the moment the boat surfaced. The Krauts will also have spotters sweeping the sea and sky ready to dive at the first sign of threat from us or elsewhere. Play your parts well, and if the German speaks to you, use your Irish slang but don't overact. He's an intelligence officer and will sniff out a lie from a hundred feet."

When Romek appeared, Max handed him the binoculars. "Take a look. You're in charge now." Then he addressed the lieutenant, "Do you have the automatic rifle and pistols at the ready?"

"They're behind the nets."

"Do not use them unless I give you the distress signal we discussed, or I'm dead, in which case you have my permission to shoot the Nazi buggers." The signal in question, removing his tweed flat-cap and scratching his head, was a simple but highly visible act that both Romek and the lieutenant would be able to spot. Max wasn't carrying his semi-automatic pistol, but he was confident that should there be a disaster he and his men would have the element of surprise on their side. Heller had decided against giving Romek a weapon, but Max had informed his boss that Romek would refuse to take part in what could be a dangerous mission without being armed. Heller had relented at the last minute, but he'd not been happy about it.

The dinghy's outline grew larger without the need for binoculars. With his last chance to give instructions, Max reminded the lieutenant, "Remember, if you see this going south, get on the radio to Coastal Forces for the Motor-Torpedo-Boats immediately and give the order to the MTB skippers to blow that sub out of the water. We're going into the unknown, Patrick. Romek and I might not have time or opportunity to signal you, but I trust you'll use your initiative?"

"Yes, I will. You can count on me, Horace."

Max smiled. "That will be all. Good luck, gentlemen."

"Well? What do you see?" Max asked Romek when he joined him on the mid-port side.

"Three figures in the dinghy," said Romek, lowering the binoculars. Then he looked again, this time past the transfer boat. "There she is," he said spotting the grey outline of a submarine's conning tower.

"We have one shot at this, Romek," Max said solemnly. "Don't cock it up. And for God's sake, don't let your tongue run away with you."

"I know, I know. Get as much information as we can out of him and say as little as possible. Find out what his intentions are for you and his explosives, and make sure he leaves here a contented man. Jesus, Max, I feel like throwing up. Get off my back, will you?" Romek grumbled, rolling his eyes.

Five minutes later, Romek leant over the port side and called out to Matador as the rubber dinghy came alongside. "Welcome to England!"

The German sailor in the dinghy threw a line to Romek.

"Got it. Come aboard." Romek shouted as he wound the rope around a jam-cleat.

Max studied the interaction between the first German who was climbing onto the trawler's deck and Romek, who now stood grinning like an excited boy seeing a long-lost school chum.

"Great to see you, my friend, *Señor Matador,*" Romek said in German and Spanish, his arms wide in welcome.

"I'm happy we could do this, Cicero. But we will not meet again at sea. It's far too dangerous for missions like these. I am, as the English say, on tenterhooks," Matador said, shaking Romek's hand.

"Seems like all the seas in the world are overcrowded with German ships, the British Navy, the Japanese, and now the Americans. But we take our chances for the sake of duty all the same," Romek responded, patting Matador's arm and waving towards Max. "Well, here is Horace, as requested. He was delighted to hear you wanted to meet him in person."

Max shook Matador's hand. "Sure, and it's nice to meet you, sir," he said in his natural London accent with a slight touch of an Irish brogue.

"This is my associate." Matador introduced the other German who climbed nimbly onto the deck.

Max eyed the man, so far unnamed. He was much younger than Matador and appeared jumpy as his eyes swept the trawler and the British sailors, who were observing the scene with interest from the stern area.

"Perhaps those fishermen could help my associate bring the contraband onboard?" Matador asked Romek.

"Is it what I think it is?"

"Of course. Delivered as promised."

Romek peered down at the dinghy, then he gestured to the British sailors to come to mid-port. "You men – see those blocks of wood in the dinghy? I want them stowed below. Help our guest – and handle the wood with care," he instructed the three men.

"Horace, your explosives are inside the hollowed-out blocks," Matador told Max in German.

Max cocked his head to the side in response, then looked to Romek for help.

"He said the explosives are hidden in the wood … inside the wood," Romek translated into English.

Max grinned and tipped his flat-cap. "Thank you very much, sir. An' I'll be puttin' them to good use, to be sure."

"He's raring to go," Romek added in German for good measure.

For a while, Matador and Romek spoke about the new technology that Matador had brought. Matador began the conversation in German but then switched to English, forcing Max to converse with him directly.

"Have you used this new photographic device before?" Matador asked.

Max turned the tiny camera in his hand. "Yes, I'm familiar with it. It won't be a problem at all."

"Will you excuse us for a moment, Horace?" Matador gestured to Romek to follow him to the bow.

Max and the unnamed German, whom Max presumed was an Abwehr agent, stood together in uncomfortable silence. The Royal Navy men had stacked the blocks of wood below and were now returning to the fantail where they'd been ordered to remain. They wouldn't be able to hear a thing, but they could monitor everything from there, and if necessary, get to their weapons lodged behind the nets in seconds.

Max gazed at the submarine, too distant to spot men on its deck, but just visible enough to see the outline of its conning tower. His plan was simple, on paper, but it all depended on Matador being predictable. As soon as he got back on board the sub, he'd probably send a coded message to the Abwehr in Berlin, confirming that the meeting had been successful, before diving and returning to … wherever. Or maybe the U-boat captain would pre-empt Matador and transmit success upon seeing the Germans leaving the trawler?

The lieutenant had been ordered to instruct the skippers of the two Royal Navy MTBs to move in for a strike as soon as he saw Matador departing the fishing boat. The torpedo boats were positioned out of visual contact; one to the north and one to the south. Both were in possession of the sub's coordinates, and the time they would need to prepare and strike had been calculated. The Germans' rubber dinghy would have to master the swells on its way back to the sub, giving the MTBs time to begin their attack run. Max assumed that the U-boat captain would expect to ping a British naval vessel at some point during their waiting period. After all, they were in British seas. The question was: what might he do if he felt truly threatened?

Max was also mindful that the Germans would go radio silent as soon as they began going under, and thus, the last thing Berlin would hear from Matador was that the mission had gone without a hitch. War was unpredictable, of course, as were the actions of men, so he only had his instinct and what the Royal Navy Intelligence branch would do were they in the Germans' position.

Max peered again at the British sailors, now sitting on the pile of nets that concealed their weapons. Behind him, at the bow, snippets of Matador and Romek's conversation in German wafted to him. He couldn't catch every word but had a good idea of the subject matter.

"… although they claim to hate the British as much as Horace does," Romek was saying, "I'm not taking the chance of them going to the authorities when they get ashore…"

"… double crossers would report seeing us," Matador was agreeing.

Max strained to hear more, but he only managed to pick up the tail end of the conversation with Romek insisting, "… despite being bribed with the promise of money for using their trawler for the night, the only way to make sure they keep their mouths shut is to put them down."

Matador's response was indistinguishable, but Romek was nodding, "Yes. I'll kill the three of them before the trawler reaches harbour."

"Come here, Horace," Romek shouted to Max in English.

Max joined the two men and, scowling with impatience, asked Romek, "What's goin' on 'ere? We'll be 'avin' the British Navy spottin' us if we don't wrap this up soon. I don't want to get killed 'afore I get the chance to blow something up. C'mon, we need to be leavin' right now. This is givin' me the bleedin' shits."

"Don't worry, Horace. We are quite safe for the moment," Matador said in English, as though he were Poseidon in control of the war-torn seas. "Cicero and I were discussing you. We want to give you the best possible chance to succeed, so I put it to Cicero that you should come with me to Berlin to train with the Abwehr in sabotage expertise. *Gut … ja?*"

Max looked surprised but hid his alarm. Unpredictability had reared its ugly head. "No. Not *gut* at all. I can't do that. I appreciate your offer, sir, but sure, you must know I'm a married man. I can't just up and leave my wife and my job at the docks without a bit of notice. She'll be onto the police in a jiffy."

Matador gestured to his associate to join the group, as Max considered the possibility of being whisked away to Berlin. It would be a great opportunity to spy on the Abwehr, but not for him, not with his face and background. Those two things could blow him out the proverbial water; he could be recognised as Dieter Vogel's son or mistaken for Paul. Neither scenario bore thinking about. He looked at the two Germans, whose stern expressions suggested it was not a request that he go, but a demand.

"No, no, it's not possible. I want to help you, God knows I do, but like I said, I can't just up sticks and disappear on me wife." Max gave Romek and the lieutenant the agreed-upon distress signal by removing his flat cap and scratching his head. Out of the corner of his eye, he saw Patrick casually get to his feet, stretch, and then disappear below, hopefully, to contact the torpedo boats. Romek then slipped his hand into his coat pocket.

"No, not tonight – tell you what, I'll get in touch wid ya through your man, here," Max suggested, gesturing towards Romek. "I mean, cooperating wid ya in England is one thing, but going to Germany? Well …it's not what I 'ad in mind."

Matador wagged his index finger in Max's face. "Ah, this is awkward – dear, dear. Now, I'm wondering about your commitment, Horace."

"I am committed, otherwise I wouldn't be in the bloody North Sea freezing me balls off and committin' treason."

"You said he would do whatever it takes," Romek snapped at Matador, surprising Max. "He'd better not be a double agent."

Romek then went a step further by getting his gun out of his pocket and pointing it in Max's face. "Why are you not happy about this offer? Is it because you're not taking this seriously? Are you a British spy?"

"Get that gun away from me bloody face or bejesus, I'll ram it up your arse and fire it out your mouth!" Max growled at Romek.

"Now, now, put your gun away, Cicero," Matador told Romek in German. "No need for violence. If Horace doesn't come with us, he can't be trusted, it's as simple as that."

"You do what you have to, but my gun is staying where it is," Romek insisted.

Max, his eye on Romek, felt his sleeve being tugged and turned sharply to Matador. "I don't like being touched," he grumbled.

"And I don't like the thought of going back to Berlin without what I came for," Matador said, his voice placating as he removed his hand. "Will you disappoint me, Horace? Can I trust you, or must our association end before we've even started?"

Max felt heat spread from his neck to his face. *Go with him or die,* was what Matador was saying. With no way to untangle himself from the Abwehr officer's web, Max tried to play for time. Thus far, only Romek's gun was visible, leading Max to believe that Matador fully trusted him and didn't see *Horace* as a serious threat, at least not yet.

Max chuckled, "This carry-on doesn't bode well for our future understandin', does it? But sure, all right … all right, I'll go wid ya. Jesus, Mother, and Joseph, if I'd a known, I'd have brought me toothbrush and pyjamas."

Romek lowered his weapon but didn't return it to his coat pocket. The sailors near the stern kept their eyes on Max, waiting for a signal to intervene directly. Because of this turn of events, Max now worried that Matador and his associate might kill the British sailors to make sure they didn't reach Grimsby alive, despite Romek's earlier promise to dispose of them. Yes, the Germans seemed to have confidence in Romek, but Matador was proving to be an unpredictable character who might just be hiding a semi-automatic weapon of his own under the ample folds of his coat.

"Then it's decided, Horace," Matador said, a cheerful smile on his face. "You understand why I insist, don't you?"

"I suppose you want to confirm I'm loyal and not be tryin' to get one over on ya," Max said. "You can trust me, sir, I'm all for the Nazis giving it to the British. But you could have asked me in a nicer way. I only met this Polish git day before yesterday, and I didn't like him shoving his bloody gun in me face. Seems to me you need to teach 'im some bleedin' manners."

Matador appeared amused before giving Romek a farewell handshake. "We'll have *ein glas Mistela* the next time we meet. Perhaps it will be in some street in London after our successful invasion," he told Romek. "We'll have fun, a good time like our soldiers in Paris are having."

"I'll look forward to that." Romek gestured to Max with his pistol. "Good luck with this one. I need to start using the new technology you gave me as soon as possible. I've got a good brain, but I don't get along with all this modern equipment business, so send him back to me quickly."

"*Ja, selbstverständlich!* Of course. He's one of the reasons I came here in person … a bird in the hand, as the English say. He will be a … Ah, ja. Ein gut egg, when he returns."

Matador gestured to the rope ladder. "Down you go then, Horace. Cicero will look after your explosives, and he'll keep his eye on your wife until you return – ach, why so glum? This is a good thing, nein?"

"Keep your mitts off my explosives," Max told Romek as he put his first leg over the side and onto the rung of the ladder to the dinghy. *Germany? Not bloody likely.* Time had run out, and so had easy solutions.

Chapter Forty-Nine

Max, the first man to disembark the trawler, swung his leg over the port side and put his foot on the top rung of the ladder. Out of the corner of his eye, he noted that the lieutenant had not returned. The two sailors were still lounging on the nets, and Romek was continuing to say goodbye to Matador.

As he climbed into the rubber dinghy, Max plotted escape scenarios in his head. A lot could go wrong. Much of his plan depended on the actions of others; the lieutenant having sent the order to sink the sub, Romek not choosing tonight to take his revenge on him for being Klara's lover, and himself, having the luck to sort this mess out whilst remaining in one piece. He nodded to the young German sailor seated between the oars, relieved that the man wasn't armed, at least not visibly, and then he sat on one of the three blown-up seats that ran the width of the vessel and watched Matador come aboard.

Max trained his eyes on Romek's handler, looking for signs or gestures he might be sending to the U-boat officer in the coning tower, who was probably watching everything that was happening on and around the trawler. His subject appeared relaxed as he sat in the forward seat, behind the German sailor but facing Max.

"Have you ever tried *Rostbratwurst,* Horace?" Matador asked over the sailor's shoulder.

"You wot'? No. Can't say I 'ave, sir," Max answered.

"You will enjoy it. It is a sausage, you know."

"Is that right?"

"Made from finely minced pork and beef. Usually we grill it and serve it with sweet German mustard and crusty bread – quite delicious."

"I'll look forward to that," Max said.

"Ach, you will enjoy many things the Fatherland has to offer," Matador was still rambling on like a German tourist guide.

The unnamed associate got into the dinghy and then caught the line that Romek threw down. Once the man was seated next to Max, Matador gave the order to the German sailor to start rowing towards the U-boat.

Max looked up at Romek, removed his cap and ran his fingers through his hair. Romek tipped his cap as a farewell gesture, but also returning Max's signal.

As the dinghy began to move off, Matador spoke to his man in rapid German about the captain of the sub. Max listened intently, but he was also facing the trawler and keeping his eyes on the deck for the sign that would launch his escape. He needed a sign; the timing had to be perfect or near as damn to it if he were to stand a chance. For the first time that night, he admitted to being terrified.

"... he has been instructed to dive as soon as we are secure on board."

Finally, the associate spoke, "Will he be able to alert Berlin that the meeting was a success before we go under?"

"I presume he has already done so."

Max caught a glimpse of glinting metal emanating from Romek's figure. *It was time.* Beneath his feet, the dinghy lurched as it met a swell. The water looked freezing cold. If he went in, he'd have about three minutes, tops, before his body went into shock.

"Don't be nervous, Horace. Submarines are quite safe," Matador said.

Max nodded, whilst placing a hand on the lip of the dinghy, which was now bucking as it met another gentle roller. "Sure, I'm looking forward to a ride in that thing." Petrified, but also resolved to escape, Max sucked in his breath, half-rose, and then did a backward flip into the icy sea.

Within seconds, the freezing water bit into Max's skin through his heavy clothing that pulled him downwards at an alarming speed. Disorientated and spiralling blind, his situation was compounded by the muffled sound of shells from the British Bren light machinegun; the British were spraying the dinghy and its occupants with bullets.

He was almost out of oxygen, his limbs were cramping, and as he thrashed his way upwards, he felt as though he were hauling a two-ton anchor with him.

His body shuddered as it intuitively gulped for air. He looked up, his eyes widening, as he saw Paul's face. His brother's expression was grim, and disapproving eyes glared downwards. With a final spurt of energy, Max kicked upwards and broke the surface.

As he sucked in the icy air, he was greeted by an almighty explosion, and the U-boat erupted in a ball of flames. He wheezed, rasped for breath, and swallowed water already being laced with oil from the sinking submarine. The torpedo had snapped it in two, the screech and shriek of twisting metal accompanying the aft and fore sections to their graves.

Max turned full circle. The dinghy had completely disappeared along with the three Germans. The trawler was moving quickly towards him, and two shadows seemed to be flying in the air. The icy drink had robbed his body of all feeling, and his oxygen deprived brain was seeing flying spectral figures. Overcome by exhaustion and hit by the stricken sub's wake, Max's head slipped beneath the surface and met the dark abyss once again.

******

When Max awoke, he was lying on his side on the trawler's deck vomiting the North Sea out of his lungs. Deaf, apart from the ringing in his ears, he pulled his knees up to his chest to cough and heave, breathe, then heave again. His chest burned, and salt water stung his throat. That he'd managed to get from beneath the waves to the trawler's deck was a miracle by anyone's standards, albeit *how* remained a mystery. He rubbed the salt from his eyes, the faces of the Germans as he went over the dinghy's side and the U-boat's fireball imprinted on his retinas.

After more vomiting and coughing, he rolled onto his back and surveyed his surroundings. A bright moon in a cloud-covered slate-grey sky welcomed him back to full consciousness, and at a nudge to his ribs he turned to see Romek sitting beside him. The Pole was soaking wet and appeared unusually shaken.

Max sat up, held his nostrils closed and blew to clear his ears. He croaked at Romek, "What the hell happened?"

"I saved you from drowning." Romek hawked and spat phlegm. "Me and one of the sailors went in to get you as soon as we disposed of the Krauts."

"Thank God, you didn't hit me."

"We aimed at the dinghy, not you," Romek grunted.

Max noticed a sodden RN rating with a blanket wrapped around his shoulders. "Thank you ... both of you," he wheezed again.

"We need to get you into the cabin to heat you up, sir," the dry sailor said

The trawler's engine was grinding and spluttering as it hit maximum knots in the rising swell. The English coastline was still a faint line, but they were approaching it as fast as they could whilst retracing their outward route.

Below, Max undressed and threw his wet clothes in a pile. He put on dry trousers and an old frayed fisherman's pullover and then slumped into the bench seat in the cabin. "Jesus, that was close," he muttered.

The seaman handed Max a flask with brandy in it. "Drink this, sir."

"Perks of almost drowning? What's your name?" Max asked the lad.

"Archie – Archie O'Sullivan, sir. That was a hell of a stunt you pulled out there, if you don't mind me saying so."

Max chuckled. "Some might consider it a stupid stunt. But I wasn't planning to go down with that U-boat. Are you in the medical branch?"

"No, sir, but I was in medical school before I signed up. I hope to transfer to a hospital ship."

"Good for you..." Max coughed, then rubbed his burning throat.

"I suggest you don't talk much for a while."

Max pointed to his throat. "Good idea. I'll let the brandy calm this down."

"Is there anything else I can do for you?"

"Yes. Give me fifteen minutes alone, then send Romek to me," Max answered.

After taking a few more sips of brandy, Max sat at the radio station and began to transmit Protocol B, then he waited patiently for a response. This message was going directly to Charlie and Heller at MI6, and both men would know exactly what to do when they received the coded phrases.

When *Roger – received* came back a couple of minutes later, Max went to the bench seat, sat down, and put his feet up.

Romek entered the cabin, already undressed with a grey blanket wrapped around his naked body. His lips were blue, but he looked happier than he'd been for a long time and even gave Max a friendly smile. "Now, I'm satisfied. Finally, I'm doing something productive. This is what I call contributing to the war effort."

"It didn't go completely as planned," Max said hoarsely with a wry smile, "but it was as near as damn it, when you consider I might have been on my way to Berlin or the seabed, by now."

While Romek was dressing in dry clothes, he said, "I've lost my handler. What now, Max?"

"I sent Protocol B to Charlie. We won't know for a while whether the Abwehr believe the message."

"Which was?"

"Simple. The Germans turned up at the rendezvous site. The meeting went well, and Horace had returned to the submarine with Matador when the U-boat apparently hit a mine and exploded. You don't know what happened to the sub's crew, but you'd like instructions on how to proceed in the event of Matador's untimely demise."

"You sent all that in a message?"

"No," Max responded with a grin. "I sent a pre-arranged coded message, known as Protocol B, to instruct Charlie to trigger the text I've just related to you." Max was worried that the cock-up might be much bigger than he wanted to admit to Romek. "The next few days will be crucial."

"You mean if they contact me, I'm still in, and if they don't believe it, they'll be gunning for me and may even kill my family in Warsaw?"

"Something like that," Max said with reluctant honesty. "I'm sorry, Romek, but everything depends on whether or not the sub's captain transmitted it had been a successful mission before his boat was torpedoed. From what I overheard on the dinghy, my best guess is he did."

A little while later, Max and Romek stood at the trawler's bow as she entered Grimsby harbour. Max's chest felt tight, but he'd already decided to get the first available train back to London.

He glanced at Romek, who looked troubled. Max surmised that his old friend was thinking about his family, but at this point he couldn't say anything that might alleviate his concerns.

The meeting had not gone to plan, Max thought again, but it had been a win for the British. The Germans had not read the atmosphere correctly and were too trusting of Romek and Horace to anticipate such an outcome. But it had been a close call, a difficult mission that could have dire consequences for other British double agents.

Max studied Romek, who was staring at the black outline of the harbour wall with an unfathomable expression. "No point dwelling on it, Romek…"

"You should have gone with them," Romek retorted. "What I wouldn't have given for the chance to see the Nazis' seat of power in Berlin. You could have brought back a bucket load of intelligence on factories and armament depos."

"I disagree. It would have been a very bad idea." Max had no intention of telling Romek why it would have been a disastrous plan; about his twin brother or any other member of his family. They were off limits, like many subjects between them.

Taken by surprise by Matador's order that he go to Berlin, Max had given Romek the distress signal to let him know it was a no-go. Romek's instincts had been spot-on, on two occasions: the first being when he'd pulled his gun out, and the second when he'd signalled to Max in the dinghy with the glinting metal, which had been a shiny new florin coin. Claiming he didn't trust *Horace* had been a gutsy move and precisely the right thing to do. His unscripted actions had been flawlessly executed despite the tiresome personal issues between them. And, Max thought, more importantly, Romek had jumped into the drink to save his life.

"Look on the bright side, Romek. We now have one less German U-boat to worry about. This is a huge win. C'mon, let's have a mug of tea before we get in."

"I hate your English tea. It's like boiled piss," Romek said, nonetheless following Max to the cabin.

Max hugged his warm cup – the British solution to all things, his mother always said. She was right in this case. It was certainly hitting the right spot.

Romek, sitting opposite, tapped his fingers against his tin coffee mug while staring fixedly at Max. "You could have died, flipping into that freezing water like that."

"But I didn't, thanks to you and the sailor."

"Did I do well, Major?" Romek grunted.

"Yes, you did. We should talk about what happens when we get back to London…"

"Blah, blah, blah, not now. Whatever you want to tell me can wait until we get back to the house. I need fresh air. I'm going back up on deck."

Max let Romek go without objection. He closed his eyes, his need to sleep immense. But then he remembered the envelope Heller had given him and got up to find it in his wet trouser pocket. *'Don't read it until you get back from the mission, that's an order,'* Heller had said. Well, the U-boat was gone and with it the operation. End of Mission.

He looked at the envelope with *Max* handwritten on it. The paper was soaking, so he carefully peeled the envelope away from the one-page letter inside. At least the paper was in one piece.

The ink had run into a few words, but they were still legible. He laid the page flat then read the smudged lines.

From Major Bernie Blackthorn. Classified
To Jonathan Heller
cc Major Vogel.

Excerpt of report from agent .... Report dated, March 7th, 1942.

Upon our arrival in ... we were informed by the leader of the ... that Klara Gabula had accidentally been killed. We were shown the grave and I later confirmed her death to the appropriate section in London.

During our stay, I overheard a conversation between two Frenchmen, during which they contradicted the cause of agent Gabula's death. Subsequently, agent ... and I secretly exhumed the body to find a gunshot wound to the corpse's temple. It is, therefore, most likely that Gabula was murdered by ... or someone in his group.

In order not to disrupt our alliance, we did not reveal our discovery to the person or persons we believe were involved in the murder ... please advise.

Max read it twice more. Tears of rage smarted his eyes. He was so furious, his fingers trembled as they made a clumsy attempt to fold the piece of paper and replace it inside the envelope. As shocked as he was, he couldn't admit to being surprised by the terrible news. Darek, now with SOE, had once mentioned that Duguay did not forgive errors. The Pole had gone as far as to say he was scared stiff of the Frenchman. All names, places, and groups in the message had been redacted, but it was evident that the agents were referring to the Communist Partisans, Duguay, and the farm where Paul had been held.

A wave of bile rose in Max's throat and then spewed from his mouth before he could get to the fire bucket. He wiped his lips with the back of his shaking hand, feeling more disgusted with the part he'd played in Klara's death than the puke now staining his fresh clothes.

Chapter Fifty

Max Vogel

After attending a meeting with the Twenty Committee and representatives from MI5 about Max's semi-successful or semi-failed mission, Max and Heller retreated to his office with their tails between their legs and glasses of Scotch in their hands. The top brass had thrown Romek's double agent status into disarray, and Heller was fuming.

"I knew it. I bloody knew someone would take Romek off me," Heller said, tossing his whisky down his throat and then refilling his glass.

"It was only a matter of time before MI5 claimed him, Jonathan. And to be fair, the running of double agents based in Britain doesn't fall within MI6's brief anymore."

"I despise these brusque changes. There's too many of us, Max. If you ask me, the authorities have gone completely overboard in their organisational zeal. Every damn week the Twenty Committee is fighting with MI6, MI5, and the B1A subcommittee over one agent or other, not to mention those secretive, think they know-it-all people in the Wireless Board sticking their noses in. This is Churchill's fault … sweeping into office and amassing Intelligence Services like a kid in a bloody sweet shop."

"I disagree. We have the Prime Minister to thank for SOE *and* the Twenty Committee. The German's can't touch our extensive intelligence apparatus, and it's all down to Mr Churchill's perseverance. We have to move with the times, Jonathan."

"Oh, I'm all for moving with the times, Max. It's the speed and direction we're taking that's got my hackles up. You wait and see, Romek will probably go to MI5, then SOE will get him or he'll eventually end up being smuggled into Poland to the Polish Free Army. It's like a damn game of chess."

Heller went into a desk drawer, brought out an antique brass match striker and vesta holder in the shape of a boot, and a fat half-smoked cigar. He struck a match, then took his time lighting the cigar whilst peering at Max through the smoke, "It's a pity you had to kill Matador," he eventually said.

Max disagreed. He was irritable because of his superiors' unwillingness to give any credit to the men who'd performed admirably on the trawler. Thus far, he'd kept his temper in check, but he was coming perilously close to losing it now with Heller. "Would you have preferred it if had I gone with him to the U-boat?"

"I would have preferred it had you refused to get off the trawler. Look at you, you're no good to me sneezing and blowing your nose every two minutes. You could have got yourself killed."

"Is that all you can say? It would have been better, Max, if you'd been blown up on a German U-boat, or better still, had the Germans shot you for *not* getting on the dinghy … bloody charming."

"Watch it, Max."

Max swallowed the remains of his Scotch and his retort, then slammed his empty glass on the table. "You weren't there, Jonathan. Had you been, you'd have seen that Romek and I did the same as you or any other agent would have done. The Twenty Committee agreed with our actions, as did MI5, apart from that upstart who looked about twelve. You seem to be the only other bugger who disapproves with how we handled it."

Heller got up, cigar still stuck between his fingers, and crossed to a filing cabinet. He opened a drawer, took something out, and then slammed the drawer closed. When he came back, he tossed an envelope on the table. "Forget the mission for now. We might have bigger things to worry about than Romek's cover being blown. While you and he were away, Mrs Mullins intercepted this letter when it was delivered to the house."

Max took the letter out of the envelope and raised a questioning eyebrow when he saw a white twenty-pound note in its fold, stamped *S&Co.* "What the devil has Selfridges department store got to do with Romek? Do we know who sent it?"

"We traced the note back to a woman named Likla Nowak. She's a Polish national, and records show she purchased the note."

"Has she been questioned?"

"No, but we know where she lives. MI5 are keeping her under surveillance, hoping she'll lead them to an answer. Has Romek ever mentioned her to you?"

"No, never heard of her." Max turned the rare note in his fingers. "Romek is a lot of things, Jonathan, but he's not duping us. He'll have an answer for this."

"I'm not convinced. The money is going to him for a specific reason. She didn't send him this out of the goodness of her heart."

Max shrugged. "Maybe the Poles are wooing him for information about what we're up to?"

"Bribing him, more like. I don't give a damn if the Poles *are* our allies, if Romek's double crossing us he'll be punished, and so will the Poles."

Max was uneasy about Romek and national security being mentioned in the same sentence, but he was unwilling to get drawn into a game of supposition. "Why do you still have the letter?"

"Because you're going to reseal it and hand it back to Mrs Mullins, who will, at some point, tell Romek it's just arrived for him. Then we'll wait to see if he tells you about the money or makes a move in another direction."

"If he does, I'll be ready." Max eyed Heller as he topped up their glasses.

Heller was swaying in his chair, partly because he hadn't left the building since the North Sea mission began and was dog tired, but also because he was drinking the whisky like water.

Max, forgetting about their little spat, smiled to himself. He was in the same boat. If he had another Scotch, he wouldn't have the legs to make it to a bomb shelter if the sirens went off. Oh, to hell with it, he thought, accepting the refill. If MI5 were taking Romek off MI6, then he, the always-available-for-any-job Max Vogel, would be given a new case or mission. His life was about to change again, but at that moment he was officially off-duty. He deserved a night off.

"What are you going to do about Duguay?"

"You read it then?" Heller stubbed his cigar out.

"Yes. You can't let him get away with murder. He's got to be brought to justice."

"We need him, Max. So, he *can* get away with it, for the moment."

"Can I speak freely, sir?"

"You're drinking my Scotch, aren't you?"

"All right, then the first thing I want you to know is I'm glad to be getting away from Romek. The man saved my life, yes, but our relationship is no longer conducive to business."

"Oh? Why do you say that?" Heller asked, his tumbler half way to his lips.

"It's a long story." Max swallowed uncomfortably. "I did a shitty thing to him by having an affair with his wife. We carried on for almost three years, and I finally came clean to Romek a few days before the mission."

Heller wore a grim expression. "Does he know she's dead?"

"No."

"That's something, I suppose."

"Is that all you have to say?"

"No. It's about time you owned up to it. Bernie Blackthorn and I knew about your affair months ago."

"How could you possibly know? I never told a soul."

"You didn't need to. You lost control during Klara's debriefing, remember? It was evident you were emotionally involved when you tried to strangle her." Heller leant forward in his chair. "Blackthorn and I agreed not to come after you, or her, because you were never going to work together again…"

"I thought I was going to Poland with her?" Max interrupted.

"No, Max, that was never going to happen. I suggested to Blackthorn that you be side-lined in that basement until we could figure out what to do with you."

"You did that?"

"No, Blackthorn did. I only suggested it. You, your brother, Paul, Klara Gabula, and your father's situation made you both an asset and a problem. You're lucky we didn't dismiss you from the intelligence services altogether."

Max had always accepted that he'd been morally and professionally wrong to pursue Klara. But he had truly loved her. Maybe the alcohol was getting to him now, but he was quite prepared to declare that he'd do it all again given the same choice. There was no better feeling in the world than mutual desire between a man and woman. He was beginning to feel a strong pull towards Judith Weber, and although she was nothing like Klara in character or looks, she was getting under his skin.

"I'm sorry," Max said, despite his inner bravado. "To be honest, I feel as guilty as sin for her murder. I suppose I deserved that."

"Ah, Max, don't be so hard on yourself. You were irresponsible. You stabbed Romek in the back, but what's done cannot be undone. You didn't kill her. She asked for Paris, and she got it. That wasn't on you or me."

Heller released a long sigh, pursing his lips and making a soft rattling sound. "This damn war. I don't know about you, but I'm sick of seeing death and destruction and getting bad news. We all deserve a bit of happiness, Max, even when the world is tumbling down about our ears."

Max delved into his jacket pocket, then remembered he'd left the letter about Klara's death in his wet jacket at home. "If there is to be justice for her, promise me I can dish it out when the time comes."

"Oh, don't you worry, we'll get our revenge. Klara was one of our own, and she was deliberately murdered … but, no, sorry …I won't promise you anything, not when I've got half a bottle of Scotch inside me."

"Our day will come. To Klara." Max made a toast, echoing Heller's sentiments.

Max pondered whether he should tell Heller about his feelings for Judith; he didn't want to repeat the mistake of keeping his relationship a secret. In his job, there was no room for skeletons in an agent's cupboard, especially when they involved relationships that might become security risks. But these thoughts were pushed aside when there was a knock on the door and Charlie entered.

"Come in Charlie, but if it's work you've got in your hand, take it to Major Barrett. I'm off home now. Join us for a Scotch if you've finished your shift," Heller said.

"Sir, I have bad news from the Burmese front…"

"What's going on there?" Max asked, being out of that loop.

Charlie hesitated, as he shared *a look* with Heller.

"Tell him," Heller said.

"Japanese bombers dropped incendiary bombs on Mandalay on Monday," Charlie began. "This created a firestorm across the whole city. Reports are still coming in, but our men on the ground think that maybe three-fifths of the wooden houses have been destroyed, including the former homes of the Burmese kings."

"Casualties?" Heller asked in a sober voice.

"We don't know yet but based on population numbers, they'll probably be in the thousands."

"Who sent the transmission?" Max asked.

"The Royal Air Force," Charlie answered. "The city is devastated. They say it's stinking with the stench of dead bodies…"

"Let me see that," Heller demanded.

When Charlie handed the two-page report to him, Heller read in silence until he shared aloud a piece with Max. *"… brick, plaster and twisted tin roofing is strewn across every street. Buzzards and carrion crows are wheeling above the dead bodies that are lying on the streets and bobbing like rotten apples in the moat surrounding the fort. That and a few temple stones are the only places untouched. And to make things worse, the firefighting equipment was destroyed in the strike.*"

Max, thinking about British involvement, asked, "How many troops do we have over there, Charlie?"

"We've got around seven thousand British forces propped up by a Chinese expeditionary force. They're trying to hold the north of the country."

"True, but the Japanese also seem to have been reinforced by at least two divisions. Let me read on," Heller said, then read the next page aloud:

The Allies are facing growing numbers of Burmese insurgents and the civil administration has broken down in the areas they still hold. With our forces cut off from almost all supply sources, the Allied commanders have decided to evacuate from Burma.

When Charlie left after declining a whisky, Heller locked his desk drawers, and put on his coat. "I've had enough. A rotten end to a rotten day. I'm going home."

After hearing the terrible news about the Burmese death toll, Max's thoughts turned to his family. "I don't suppose we could ask Romeo in Berlin to find out who's on the casualty lists from the Russian campaigns?"

"Your brother, Wilmot?" Heller buttoned his coat and then stuck his hands in the pockets.

"Yes," Max replied.

"As soon as you see to this business with Romek, go to Bletchley. Take a couple of sick days off before you're reassigned."

"Will you contact Romeo on my behalf about Paul and Wilmot?"

"I'll see what I can do."

Max got up but was reluctant to leave. He was persona non grata with Bernie Blackthorn at SOE until he returned to that fold, and Heller was the only person who might be able to give him an answer to another nagging question.

"Jonathan, where is Frank?"

"Out of the country."

"Is that all you're going to give me?"

"Yes. Goodnight, Max – go find a nice warm woman to dance with – have a good time for once."

Max grinned. There was only one woman he was interested in, and he was going to see her soon in Bletchley.

Chapter Fifty-One

Wilmot Vogel

The Mannerheim Line, Finland
April 1942

Wilmot got out of the bathtub in the ablutions hall and padded naked to the mirror that stretched from one end of the wall to the other. Below the glass was a row of tiny sinks, so small that a grown man's two hands could barely fit inside them. He pondered the question, yes or no, looked at his reflection sideways, straight on, tilted his chin, lowered it, and then asked Haupt for his opinion, "Shave it or leave it?"

Haupt who was already shaving, cocked his head to the side. "If you want to be as good looking as me, you should take it off or at least trim it."

Wilmot grinned. Twenty-nine-year-old Haupt, with his large green eyes, coal-coloured hair, greying at the temples, and strong square jaw, *was* a good-looking man. He hadn't noticed the captain's looks before, for all prisoners were ugly when emaciated and sick with malnutrition. He looked like a completely different person from the one who'd jumped off the train with him.

"I'll trim it, but I'm keeping the beard. It'll keep my face warm," Wilmot decided, peering into the mirror. "Jesus, I look like my older brothers, Max and Paul, only I'm a darker version, and better-looking."

Wilmot had spent almost two weeks in hospital in the Finnish occupied city of Viipuri. He was still pitifully thin, having not yet restored his lost body fat, and he'd also suffered the loss of two toes to frostbite; the middle one on his left foot and his pinkie toe on his right one. He'd been very lucky not to have lost fingers, feet, nose or ears, the Finnish doctor had told him.

Wilmot, although grieving for the appendages, thought he'd been even more fortunate not to have felt pain or seen how bad his feet were becoming. They'd been sore for weeks, then they'd gone completely numb. Only when a nurse had removed his socks here in Viipuri – they had been on his feet inside his boots for five months – did he notice the damage; stinking, gangrenous, with greenish-black decayed tissue resulting from a loss of blood flow. No wonder he'd felt nothing; the toes had been rotten and dead. And as for the smell, well, he'd got used to the rancid pong of men, including his own.

Wilmot and Haupt's beds were next to each other in the ward. The hospital rules stated that officers and enlisted men be cared for in separate sections of the hospital, but Haupt had insisted they weren't out of the woods yet and that keeping them together was necessary to ensure they recovered both mentally and physically.

The two men had spent many nights reminiscing about their journey, the wolf attack, and Jurgen's passing. They knew just about everything there was to know about each other's lives and had even shared their triumphs and failures in war.

After being discharged, a nurse had brought Haupt and Wilmot two fresh uniforms, including coats, scarves, hats and gloves, forwarded from Viipuri's German command. Wilmot stroked the material of his new Schütze trousers and jacket, loath to put them on. He'd had enough of war and killing, the stench of death, and the thousands of corpses he'd seen with their limbs and backsides jutting out of endless snow.

"You'll have to call me sir or Hauptmann from now on, Willie," Haupt said, as he clipped his Hauptmann's epaulettes onto his jacket's shoulders.

Willie joked, "Up yours, Haupt. You'll have to pay me before I ever salute your wolf-shitting arse."

After dressing, Wilmot sat on the edge of the bed and eyed the hard, leather boots that were guaranteed to pinch toes when new. He was dreading pulling them on his feet. Apart from the pain which would subside with time, he'd walked barefoot as though he had ten toes, and for some strange reason still felt an itch where the amputated ones used to be. He picked up a boot, looked at it with disgust, and then threw it back on the floor.

"Let me help you," Haupt said, breaking into Wilmot's gloomy thoughts. "I know what you're thinking, Willie, but what you're going through is a perfectly natural reaction for a man who's suffered an amputation. You got off lightly. You could have lost your leg."

"Fuck off, Haupt. You have no idea what reaction I'm having. It didn't happen to you, did it?"

"C'mon, you won't even notice the difference."

"They weren't your bloody toes!" Wilmot glared again at the boots, picked them up, and tentatively pushed his feet into them, one at a time.

He was wearing bandages under his socks and the boots felt tight, but as he walked up and down the ward he was pleasantly surprised not to feel anything abnormal, not even a slight limp. He grinned, his humour returning. "Right, shall we get out of here and face our future, *Hauptmann* Albrecht?"

Haupt sighed. "I can't wait to see my wife and babies, Willie. This is what I've been living for, this moment, when we're told we're going home."

"Me, too. Just think, this time tomorrow we could be on a supply plane to Berlin." Wilmot grinned, but then remembered he had no one to go home to.

Wilmot entered the hospital director's office fifteen minutes after Haupt had gone in. Worried about his feet, he cautiously came to attention and stretched out his arm in a salute to the Wehrmacht Major. "Heil Hitler!"

The Major returned the salute and then looked Wilmot over. "Schütze Vogel, I am Major von Kühn. Hauptmann Albrecht has told me you're a courageous soldier, said you have nerves of steel. Well, I have good news for you, young man … you have been awarded the Iron Cross Second Class for continuous bravery before the enemy."

"Thank you … thank you, Major." Wilmot's eyes welled up. He was a hero, albeit for second class acts of heroism, as the award stated, but it was a good enough medal to be going on with … *him, a bloody hero!*

"Yes, I know, I know, Schütze Vogel, it's a great honour. You're not the first soldier to get emotional," von Kühn said, as though he'd seen this reaction a hundred times before.

Wilmot nodded. Emotional? He felt like a face-slapped eight-year-old drowning in tears; anything but a brave combat soldier. His dream had come true. This moment defined him; he was a hero with an Iron Cross, not an SS failure from Dachau prison camp or an insignificant soldat who'd never received a battle commendation – if only his father were alive to hear about this – and Max and Paul; he'd love to see their faces when that beautiful cross was pinned on him.

"Sit," said the Major, pointing to the chair next to Haupt.

Wilmot wiped his eyes, sniffed, then sat as ordered. He glanced at Haupt's profile and was shocked to see his face white and lips set in a tight, angry line.

"What an incredible journey you two have had, quite extraordinary," von Kühn said from behind his desk.

"Sir, may I ask a question?" Wilmot asked.

"Of course, Schütze, this is why you're here."

Wilmot glanced again at Haupt, who was still looking unhappy about something. "I was wondering … and the Hauptmann was as well … we were wondering why the Russians might have been taking us further north instead of west to their fortified areas? It seems to me, now that I'm free and I know where I am, that they were deliberately bringing us closer to the battlefront at the Finnish lines. And given that they had five-hundred German prisoners of war in their custody, it seems odd … it just seemed very odd to us."

"It would indeed," the Major replied, then paused. "That's because you didn't witness the Russian attacks on the Finns in the February skirmishes. My guess is they were taking you to the Russian ammunition depot not far from their front lines. Our long-range reconnaissance patrols reported seeing the construction of a new Russian base dangerously close to the Mannerheim Line. I imagine they were planning to use their prisoners as labourers. We know their troops were thinly spread on the ground, that's why they couldn't break through the Finnish defences."

He paused again. "Hmm, you two have been very fortunate. We blew up that ammunition depot and the surrounding area during the fighting. We flattened the place, and unfortunately, any German prisoners who'd been there would almost certainly have been killed."

Wilmot, thinking about the friends, officers, and strangers they'd left on the train, said. "If only more of our men had listened to Haupt and me. We tried to persuade them to jump off that train with us, but they kept saying it was safer to stay…"

"I told you, you shouldn't think like that," Haupt blurted out. "If everyone on that cattle wagon had jumped, very few would have survived the journey. We couldn't find enough food for the three of us, so imagine eighty men living in that forest, most of whom were at death's door before we even got on the train." Haupt shifted his gaze to the Major and apologised, "Forgive me, Herr Major. Unlike Schütze Vogel, I see no right or wrong in leaving our men behind. We tried to look after Schütze … his name was Jürgen … but the lad was too weak to combat the cold. We did our best."

"Sir, might I ask another question?" Wilmot said, still pondering over what was wrong with Haupt.

"Ask away," von Kühn answered.

"I was wondering if our families were informed that we were missing in action?"

"Ah, yes, I've looked into that." Shifting his attention to Haupt, he said, "Hauptmann Albrecht, your family was notified some months ago of your supposed death or capture. I've written to them personally to give them the good news that you've been found alive and well."

"Thank you, Herr Major," Haupt said.

With an altogether less confident expression, von Kühn said, "Getting in touch with your family was more difficult, Vogel. Your next of kin is Kriminaldirektor Freidrich Biermann of the Gestapo, correct?"

Heat spread from Wilmot's neck to his face. Talking about his family was painful and for that reason, he had named the

Kriminaldirektor as his first contact should anything untoward happen to him. "Yes, Herr Major. My father died last year, and my mother returned to England, her country of birth."

"I see."

"The Kriminaldirektor is a close family friend. He offered to support me should I ... well, should I need anything. Does this mean he knew I was missing and now also knows I've been found?"

"Yes, to the first part. According to our records, he was informed in December that you were missing, presumed dead. But when I wrote to him at the Reich Security Office in Berlin to give him the good news of your survival, I received a reply saying he'd been posted to Poland. As you know, our military postal service, as good as it is, can often take quite some time to deliver letters in certain parts of occupied Europe. Ach, don't be glum, Vogel. I'm certain the Gestapo forwarded the letter to Litzmannstadt, so be patient. You'll get a reply, eventually."

Then von Kühn picked up a gold lighter and held it in the palm of his hand. "I got this off a dead Russian commander on the Mannerheim Line in the last week of February. It's a nice keepsake – look, it even has his initials on it."

He offered a cigarette to Haupt who refused. "What about you Schütze Vogel?"

"Thank you, sir. I will have one," Wilmot said.

"You haven't had one for months, so why are you bothering now?" Haupt tutted.

The Major held out the pack, "Keep the whole pack, Vogel. If you don't deserve them, who does?" He then unfolded a map and spread it out on the desk. "Come closer. I want to show you our progress."

Haupt and Wilmot moved to the desk. Willie looked at the map, his heart racing, his hopes for a return to Berlin disintegrating by the second. No wonder Haupt was looking dismayed; he'd probably received the bad news already. He must be devastated.

In the spring of last year, Finland and Germany came to an understanding that Finland would assist Germany in any war against the Soviet Union," von Kühn began. "Because of those discussions, eighty-thousand German troops crossed from Norway into Finland at Petsamo – here. Now, although most of our troops are in northern Finland in the Lapland area, we also have units concentrated on the Finnish side of the Mannerheim Line. These units, along with the Finnish forces, were instrumental in holding back the Russian Army's most recent attack on the Karelian Isthmus. As successful as they were, however, German and Finnish troops are in dire need of more combat-hardened men. The Finns have so far lost about twenty-five thousand men to the Russians on the lines, hence our ongoing support – do you both understand how vital it is that you remain here?"

The Major oozed enthusiasm, seemingly unaware of his audience's dismay. "You are both going to be based in Viipuri, but you can expect to join the front lines for reconnaissance duties when required. Look." Von Kühn drew his finger down a black line on the map. "The line runs from the coast of the Gulf of Finland in the west, through Summa to the Vuoksi River and ends at Taipale in the east. The area around Summa is the most heavily fortified because it has proved to be the most vulnerable to attack."

He paused, then raised his head. "You'll find that both Finnish and Soviet propaganda have considerably exaggerated the extent of the line's fortifications. Don't get me wrong, the Finnish troops did a marvellous job turning the pristine landscape around the line into a charnel house for the unprepared, underfed, and initially overwhelmed Soviet troops. They used its myth to improve national morale, and our spies are reporting that the Russians are overstating its strength as the reason for their troops' slow progress against Finnish defences."

The Major shrugged. "The truth is, the majority of the Mannerheim Line is nothing like the French Maginot Line or others like it, with huge bunkers and lines of dragon's teeth. The Finns have built defensive positions using the natural terrain, like fallen trees and boulders, but with some success, I might add."

"Are there no bunkers, sir?" asked Wilmot who was enjoying the easy conversation with the Major despite the bitter news he and Haupt were receiving in drips and drabs.

"Yes, but the bunkers along this line are mostly small and thinly spread out and they have hardly any artillery…"

"We're not getting leave in Germany, Willie. It's all been for nothing," Haupt uttered, his watery eyes round.

The Major, annoyed at being interrupted in full flow, gave a sharp rebuke. "I understand this is not what you wanted to hear, Hauptmann, but as I said, we're stretched thinly on the ground. The war is lasting longer than we anticipated, and it seems this country is short of manpower. Many of Finland's older generation of soldiers have already been released from active service to return to farming and industry and such like, and I need all the men I can get my hands on." He stared at Haupt, daring him to argue. "I assure you, Viipuri will be a much more comfortable base compared to the Leningrad suburbs or anywhere else in Russia."

"Thank you, sir," Haupt said.

"Thank you, sir," said Wilmot, wondering if he'd live to see the day his Iron Cross got pinned on him.

Chapter Fifty-Two

A Finnish soldier with a pack reindeer struggling on slippery ice passed Wilmot, Haupt, and their German guide as they neared Viipuri's military barracks. Two Finnish tanks marked with swastikas stood on the corner of the busy street, and next to them, a mechanic was doing something or other to a propeller-driven snowmobile. It was a bustling, albeit damaged city that had opened its gates to hundreds of Finnish refugees from the surrounding provinces.

The ground was covered in slush and snow, and Wilmot, shading his eyes with his hands in the blinding white light, peered at four separate wooden fences running parallel to each other along the length of the thoroughfare. He trudged on in his snug new boots while observing people standing within the *lanes* between the fencing. As he got closer to the area, he saw that they were not fences at all, but rows of wooden grave markers.

"This is a hell of a strange place to put a graveyard. Who are they for?" Wilmot asked their Schütze escort.

"They're memorials. The people here call them the graves of the Cathedral's heroes. The Finns recaptured the city from the Russkies in August last year, and during the battle the Finnish locals took the area surrounding the church. They maintained that the enemy wanted to destroy it, but personally, I think it's Finnish propaganda. I was here, and I can assure you, the Russian forces didn't seem interested in destroying the buildings. They wanted the city, not its ruins."

The Schütze paused, then said in a softer voice, "If any army was burning places, it was the Finns themselves. They didn't want to leave anything intact for the Russians." He shrugged. "Ach, what does it matter? Every city needs inspirational heroes. Let the Finns believe what they want to believe."

"This might not be as bad as we think, Haupt," Wilmot said, eyeing a bar on the other side of the busy road. "That place is open – and look, there's a restaurant – I'm not saying it will have food in it, but you must admit, this is the most civilised place we've been in for over a year."

Haupt didn't respond.

Wilmot asked the Schütze, "What's your name?"

"Otto Krause. Yours?"

"I'm Willie Vogel."

"And yours, Herr Hauptmann?" Otto shot a sideways glance at Haupt but didn't get an answer.

Who would want to talk to Haupt today with his face like a bull dog, and him grunting and groaning every time he opened his mouth? He was distraught about not getting leave to see his wife and family, but he'd been in the army long enough to know that leave was a luxury very few soldiers got.

"What do the likes of us Germans do around here?" Wilmot asked the much-friendlier Otto.

"Not much. We play cards, drink beer when we're off duty, go to a dance they hold on a Thursday night, and watch the football matches they put on every couple of weeks or so between us and the Finns."

"Did you hear that, Haupt? They've got a dance on once a week," but Wilmot was met with a stony, disinterested glare.

"There are some nice women here, but they're stuck up," Otto continued. "The Finns don't seem to like us very much. I don't know why, considering we're allies and have their backs."

"Is there still fighting in the city?"

"Not much … nothing to speak of. No, nothing since last August. I'm in awe of how these Finns tackled the Soviets. I spent time at the Mannerheim front last winter. The Soviet riflemen kept coming at us, but they were like a bunch of suicidal nitwits the way they floundered through the deep snow in sub-zero temperatures. Half of them froze to death before they even fired a shot." He grinned. "*Half* might be a bit of an exaggeration, but imagine, Willie, the Finns and Germans being outnumbered ten to one and still managing to push the Soviets back.

"The Russian tanks and their crews took a hammering from us as well. We were lobbing Molotov cocktails at them, one after the other, non-stop. I don't know what Herr Major told you, but we don't have nearly enough weaponry on the Mannerheim, even after taking what we've captured from the Russkies. I suppose taking down the Russian bear is too expensive for the little Arctic fox, so they use what they have on hand." He chuckled, "Some people call that incendiary device a poor man's grenade, but Molly worked like a charm for us. I loved tossing those and watching the Russkies erupt in flames. Ach, well, at least we were keeping the enemy warm."

Otto then took another quick look around to see if anyone was listening. "The Finns love a good story. The latest myth is that Soviet paratroopers are so desperate to get across our lines, they're jumping from airplanes without parachutes, hoping that a snowbank will cushion their fall. Some Finnish soldiers believe it's true … stupid buggers."

The barracks used by the Finnish Army in Viipuri looked more like two expensive residential buildings, with elaborate entrances and wrought-iron balconies on some of the previously privately-owned apartments.

Wilmot and Haupt separated when they reached the front of a smart burgundy-coloured building that housed officers and command offices.

"We don't report until tomorrow. Do you want to see the sights tonight?" Wilmot asked Haupt. "We could maybe have dinner? They gave us money, and it's been a long time since we did anything like that."

"No, I'll be mixing with other officers now, Schütze Vogel. You know the Wehrmacht loves its protocols. Goodbye. Have a good evening."

Wilmot's chin dropped as Haupt walked away. "I suppose I should have expected that. Seems he's already forgotten everything we've been through together," he mumbled to Otto.

Wilmot's dormitory housed thirty men. Fifteen beds on opposite sides of the long room had lockers at each side, and an ablutions hall through the door at the far end. When Wilmot was shown his bunk, he realised he had nothing to put in his locker, not so much as a tin of toothpaste powder or shaving soap.

"I'll go with you to a restaurant if you want, Willie, and I'll tell a couple of my friends you're coming? We want to hear your stories. You and Herr Hauptmann are famous," Otto said.

Wilmot looked longingly at his bunk: the blankets, a pillow and the window shutters behind it keeping out the light. It was now midday, the dormitory was empty apart from two men asleep on their bunks, and Wilmot was desperate to remove his boots and free his feet. He was also physically exhausted, proving what he already knew to be true; he was still very weak and unprepared for duty.

Otto, waiting for an answer to his invitation said, "You'll enjoy it."

"All right, Otto. I'm going to have a sleep right now, but how about I meet you downstairs at seven o'clock this evening."

Rough hands were dragging Wilmot along the ground. He tried to fight his assailant off but was struck on the side of his head with a pistol butt. He was going to be executed. The pile of German soldiers lay on the ground beside the train tracks and he was about to join them. Gripped by insurmountable terror, he screamed at the top of his lungs and was struck again…

"… Willie, wake up …. Willie, open your eyes!"

Wilmot's eyes flew open. He gasped and swallowed air as if he'd been drowning. Where was he? "What is it … what's going on?"

Otto's ashen face looked down at Wilmot, his lower lip trembling.

"What is it?" Wilmot sat up.

"You have to come with me to the officer's block."

"Why?"

"It's your Hauptmann – you've been ordered to come – right now, Willie."

When he reached the officer's building, Wilmot was escorted to the first floor by a Gestapo Kriminalinspektor. The man said nothing as they walked up the stairs, and he remained silent even as he ushered Wilmot into a sparsely-furnished room.

Wilmot was met by a stern-faced Oberartz – the doctor, two orderlies, and a stretcher standing upright against the wall. Without words being uttered, with no body or blood to look at,

Wilmot instinctively knew the reason for his presence; Haupt was in trouble. "Where is he, sir?" he asked the Oberartz.

"Come with me."

In the corridor, Wilmot saw a growing number of officers congregating outside the ablutions-hall. "Go back to your quarters. You will be questioned later," the Inspektor barked at the men.

Wilmot was taken to a row of toilet stalls. He halted halfway along, looked down and saw a crimson lake beneath his boots. His mind went blank, forgetting every other person around him, as he fell to his knees in an ever-widening pool of blood surrounding his friend.

Haupt lay on the floor with his long legs inside the toilet stall and his torso in the passageway. Deep gashes ran from both wrists up the inside of his forearms to his elbows. His body was soaked in a blanket of dark blood. Some had run off him like a river to a grate in the floor. Wilmot, on his knees, shuffled closer to Haupt, saturating his new uniform trousers in blood as he slid across the tiles.

In one of Haupt's open palms sat a single, bloodied razor blade, and in the other a picture of his wife and children.

Wilmot wept like a baby. Then he slumped with his back against the wall, stroking Haupt's head and sobbing, "Stupid bugger … why … what did you have to do that for, Haupt … Haupt … why?"

The Inspektor pulled Wilmot to his feet. "Hold yourself together, man." He held a bloodied note inches from Wilmot's tearstained face. "Do you know what this means?"

Wilmot couldn't read a word. His eyes were blurred with tears, his thoughts chasing the past then broken by the present. Haupt jumping fearlessly out of the train's window and falling face first in the snow. His stories about his children on nights when they huddled together like lovers. The prayer he'd said at Jürgen's pathetic burial site where his semi-naked body lay bare to the elements because they couldn't dig a hole. His shame when he'd opened-up about his time in the SS Einsatzgruppen death squads – and his bloodied face as he ate raw wolf like a ravenous caveman.

A strange thought popped uninvited into Wilmot's mind. Haupt could have hung himself or put a bullet in his head, but instead he'd drained his body of blood. Had he wanted to make a statement; an apology for the innocent blood he'd spilled? Or was slitting his wrists an act of rage against Viipuri's German Command? *Wipe away my blood. This is your fault.* All this blood. Haupt's face turning grey – blue lips – eyes with misty pupils staring at nothing…

"Answer me, Schütze Vogel – what does it mean – the note?"

Wilmot shook his head and looked at the stained piece of paper:

No medal. My men.

"Well? Does that note explain to you why Hauptmann Albrecht might have taken his own life?"

Wilmot stared at the words, and another memory surfaced. One night in the forest, Haupt had wept and prayed for forgiveness for leaving the men behind on the train. He had cursed himself for cowardice and for deserting the soldiers in his charge. In the darkness, he had aired the self-disgust he'd previously hidden so well – was that dereliction of duty? If it had been in Haupt's mind, was it enough to make him commit suicide? Or was it the disappointment at not being able to go home that had tipped him over the edge? Probably the latter.

Wilmot studied Haupt's clean shaven, peaceful face, as he searched for answers. Nothing came to him but his own growing anger and disgust, but to appease the Inspektor, he said, "I'm betting it was because of the guilt he felt for leaving our fellow prisoners on the train. As I told Herr Major this morning, we tried to convince them to come with us, but in a wagon carrying almost ninety men, only a handful, including Haupt and I, were willing to jump out of the window. And of that handful, I think some were shot in the back as they ran, two we never met up with in the forest, and one died. Or, you know what, maybe he hated himself for being in the Nazi death squads that roamed the Baltics and Russia executing Jewish men, women and children."

"Are you saying that Hauptmann Albrecht committed suicide because he escaped, and his men didn't? Is that why his note says *no medal*?" the Inspektor asked, ignoring Wilmot's mention of Haupt's job as a Jew killer.

Wilmot's eyes welled up as his loss became evermore real. "Haupt was a deeply private man who rarely complained about the freezing cold, or our starvation. He made jokes when we were at our lowest ebb and ate a wolf when its body was still warm. He didn't talk much about himself apart from his desire to go home. How am I supposed to know why he ended his life?"

"You will do your duty and think harder," the Kriminalinspektor snapped.

Wilmot, angry, in part on Haupt's behalf, faced the cold-blooded men looking for clinical answers when he had none to give. The Inspektor and everyone standing around him were ignorant pigs.

"Do my duty? Look at me ... look at me! Do I look like a soldier who's fit for battle or for any other sort of duty? I can't walk half a kilometre without having to lie down afterwards. I have nightmares about my days in captivity that are so real I think I'm still living them. Sometimes, I can't even think straight enough to put one foot in front of another. I was tortured in body and mind and starved to the point where I dreamt of eating my fellow prisoners!"

Wilmot's temper, kept in check for so long under the Russian yoke, exploded out of him now. "Every minute of every day, I thought I was going to be sliced open. Do you know the Russians have a game? It's called ... who shall we kill today? Do you know what's it's like to think you're going to be next to get a bullet in the head, or your throat slashed for the Russians' amusement? Or how much effort it took just to stay alive in the freezing cold? Or what it feels like to watch a comrade fall dead at your feet, and other men walking over the body as though he were a bump in the road? No, you don't. You know fuck all!"

Wilmot's heart was breaking. He covered his face with his trembling hands, soaked with Haupt's blood, and sobbed, "Hauptmann Albrecht needed his wife's loving arms and a few days of good food and his own bed, that's all he wanted ... the dream that kept him alive ... all he needed to get back on his feet. But he didn't get it, did he? No. He got another front line because you lot don't give a shit about anything or anyone apart from your beloved Führer and his vision for the world. You're a disgrace, leaving him lying here like a piece of meat, asking for reasons so you can complete your paperwork. He's worth ten of you – all of you!"

He staggered, swaying with exhaustion in the now silent ablutions hall. Outside in the corridor, curious officers murmured amongst themselves. Wilmot went to the door and let loose again. "This is what you get for fighting for the Fatherland. This is all the thanks you can hope to receive!"

Still holding onto the door frame, Wilmot glared at the shocked Inspektor. He was in a world of trouble, yet he didn't feel like apologising to the morons who were *still* standing in blood beside Haupt's body, demanding answers as to why he might have done it, and not asking a single question about who he'd been as a man.

"May I be dismissed, Herr Kriminalinspektor?" Wilmot uttered, half expecting to be arrested for his insolence.

The white-haired Gestapo man with small round spectacles perched on the tip of his nose frowned but then surprised Wilmot with a soft response. "I will send someone to find you tomorrow morning, Schütze Vogel. He will escort you to the Gestapo office on Krasnoflotskaya Ul Street. I will also see to it that you have two weeks' leave, here in Viipuri, starting right now. All I ask is that before you resume your duties, you write a report on how you found Hauptmann Albrecht's mental state in the days running up to his suicide. It could help his family to understand. Go, you are dismissed – and Schütze, well done for escaping the Russians."

Chapter Fifty-Three

Paul Vogel

Lodz, Poland.
April 1942

Freddie Biermann was still in bed in the ward's side room five days after his heart attack. Doctor Lewandowski was afraid to transfer him to the Christian or Wehrmacht hospitals because of the risk of making his already serious condition worse, as well as the punishment he'd receive if anything should happen to such a senior Gestapo figure en route. He had, however, removed all Jewish patients from Biermann's floor, and had procured Christian cleaners and nurses with German family ties from other hospitals. Lewandowski had remarked to Paul, that this, he hoped, would appease the Kriminaldirektor's Aryan sensibilities.

Every hospital resource they had was at Biermann's disposal and, thus far, he'd received the best medicine available. Dissatisfied, however, with Anatol's depressing prognosis, and worried about a shortage of drugs in the city, Biermann had requested that a senior German physician come from Warsaw to examine him. Two days later, an Oberfeldarzt Lieutenant Colonel arrived with added supplies of the vascular dilator, glyceryl trinitrate, and the foxglove extract, digitalis, to control heart rate irregularities, plus a bucketful of bad news about his patient's medical prospects.

In Biermann's room, Paul discretely observed his parents-in-law. Olga filled up her husband's water glass. He smiled at her,

511

and then she kissed his forehead. He patted her hand and sat forwards as she lifted the glass to his lips, and after taking tiny sips, he said, "Thank you, my darling." That they were devoted to each other was indisputable, Paul thought, but it was also apparent that Biermann hadn't shared his work secrets with his wife, or the true state of his health.

Ignored in the doorway, Paul wondered whether Biermann had told Olga about the senior physician's recommendations. Before leaving for Warsaw that morning, the Oberfeldarzt had informed Biermann that even after three or four weeks in hospital, he would still have a long road towards *some level* of recovery. The doctor had finished his visit by advising Biermann to retire immediately from the Gestapo, but Biermann had vehemently refused, endangering his heart further with his outrage.

Paul weighed up the risk he was about to take against leaving Kurt to die in the hands of the Gestapo. After spending days pondering over his ambitious plan, he still maintained that helping Kurt and others like him to escape far outweighed the hazard one mighty act of treason might bring. Not even for Valentina would he deny his conscience. He imagined telling her and was horrified when he pictured her reporting him to her father. He often wondered nowadays if he and she had anything in common other than Biermann.

Paul pushed those thoughts to the kerb and focused on Kurt's situation. Biermann had mentioned Kurt's name only once since his heart attack. On that occasion, he'd reminded Paul that he was going to follow through with his threats should Kurt not be forthcoming with a full confession about Dieter's treachery and whereabouts. And in what must have been a mindless error, he had also mentioned the missing Vogel art collection, confirming that Kurt's suspicions had been justified; Biermann was being pushed to retire early on a low pension, and given Germany's economic condition, would love to get his hands on some very expensive masterpieces. Paul had noticed during his short stay in Berlin and Dresden that the walls in both the Vogel houses were bare, but he'd assumed at the time that his mother had disposed of the paintings after his father's death.

Conscious that his knees were knocking when he stepped into the room, Paul headed for the iron railing at the bottom of Biermann's bed. "Good evening, sir. I have some news for you ... Kurt Sommer is critically ill upstairs in this hospital."

"Critically ill?" Biermann asked, glancing at his wife.

"Paul, are you talking about Kurt, your father's driver ... that nice man who used to love my cakes?" Olga asked.

"Yes, Frau Biermann..."

"That's right, him," Biermann cut in, and smiled at his wife. "Why don't you go home dear? Put your feet up. You must be exhausted with all this coming and going."

Olga, ignoring her husband, asked, "But why is Dieter's driver in Poland?"

"He's a Jew, Frau Biermann. You didn't know that?" Paul said.

Biermann shot daggers at Paul, then smiled at his wife. "If you're determined to stay, dear, give me five minutes alone with Paul, will you?"

Olga raised her neatly-plucked eyebrows at her husband then got up and left, promising to return after she had taken a short walk.

Paul closed the door behind her.

"If you ever mention Kurt Sommer in front of my wife again, there will be hell to pay. What are you playing at?"

"I'm sorry, sir. I assumed you'd already mentioned Kurt to Frau Biermann. I didn't know it was a secret."

"He's in this hospital, you say? Why?"

Paul raised a quizzical eyebrow. "Why? The Gestapo brutalised him in your offices on the day of the deportations. I assumed you directed that action."

Biermann's breathing was accelerating, his fists clenched on the bed cover.

"His injuries are considered fatal. He's hanging on, but the doctor treating him is not hopeful. He could die at any moment." Paul shook his head. "Forgive me … I don't know what I was thinking. I knew Frau Biermann was very fond of Kurt."

Biermann's eyes narrowed, but Paul stood his ground and kept his gaze steady. "I suppose you won't need to kill him now. You might have already done it."

Paul turned on his heel and left the room, revelling in his small victory. His father-in-law wouldn't dare take a dying man from his hospital bed for further interrogation, especially now that Olga knew about Kurt's condition. She would, of course, tell Valentina, who'd also been fond of Kurt, and if there was one honest thing about Biermann, it was his craving for respect from the two women in his life.

Paul realised that the Gestapo hadn't heard about Kurt's hospital admission. Biermann, starved of visitors other than family members, had been cut off from his supply of information, and that lack of access to current affairs had allowed Kurt the time to recover. Of course, telling Biermann that Kurt was in the hospital was a risk, Paul admitted, but he was hoping that his upcoming meeting with Anatol and Hubert would permanently remove Kurt from the Gestapo's grasp before the week was over.

"Is that you finished for the evening, Doctor Vogel?" a Gestapo guard, placed there for Biermann's protection, asked Paul as he hurried to the hospital's main entrance.

"Yes, that's it for another day," Paul answered with a casual wave.

"It's great news about the Kriminaldirektor getting better, isn't it?" the man shouted after Paul.

I was hoping he'd die, Paul wanted to shout back.

Paul looked at the address and directions written on Anatol's note as he stood under the first street gaslight outside the ghetto. It wasn't far, but it would involve a tram ride and decent walk afterwards.

"Let me know when we are in Feilenstrasse, please – it used to be called Popiela," Paul instructed the tram conductor when it left the station.

"It will be our fourth stop," the conductor retorted with a grumpy voice without looking at Paul. No need to ask where he stood on the occupation, Paul thought.

Anatol's house, a detached villa, was in a quiet cul-de-sac two streets from the tram stop. Paul, with his crude map, had found the house easily because of Anatol's drawing of a gate with the letters EG soldered into the iron. The house had once belonged to an affluent Jewish family, and Anatol had once commented that he'd purchased it cheaply after the Jews had been removed – it never ceased to amaze Paul how one man's misfortune became another's gift, or how easily the gifted person accepted such benevolence as a God-given right.

An attractive young woman took Paul's coat, and then ushered him into the living room. Three men were present: Anatol, Hubert, and a third man who got up from the couch and turned to face Paul.

Paul gasped, flicking his eyes from Anatol to Hubert until they settled again on the third man.

Gert Wolff, the half-Polish SS Untersturmführer Paul had met on the train to Łódź smiled, "Hello, Paul."

Paul backed away, but the woman who'd taken his coat locked the door before he could reach it. His breath caught in his throat, his heart pounding in his chest. He'd walked into a trap; he was more livid than afraid.

"I didn't expect to see you here, Gert. What a pleasant surprise." Paul said with a nervous smile. He hadn't done anything to incriminate himself, yet. Anatol and Hubert were Poles, he was a German; therefore, Gert would believe his word over the that of the Polish men. "I didn't know you were acquainted with my hospital colleagues."

"Sit down, Paul. I'm not going to bite you," Gert grinned. "We're all friends here."

"Friends?"

Anatol spoke up. "Yes. Gert is one of us. He helps in ways you couldn't imagine. Do sit, Paul. You look like a stuffed dummy. Sit, let's get down to business."

"I'm not sitting anywhere until he tells me why he's here?" said Paul, his eyes narrowing at the nonchalant Gert, relaxed and appearing amused at Paul's discomfort. "Last time I saw you, you were chasing a woman with a baby on the day of the deportations."

"Yes, that's right," Gert acknowledged. "I was trying to get to her before the sniper took his shot. Unfortunately, I saw him in the window preparing to fire and had to back off."

Gert moved towards Paul with a genuine smile. "Look, I was just as surprised to hear about your request as you are to see me here. Ever since Hubert told me about you, I've been keeping tabs on your movements. I saw you in the ghetto with the orderly and ambulance cart. I watched you go into the tenement block, and then come out some time later with your friend, the Jew that Anatol and Hubert had mentioned to me. I wanted to be sure you weren't trying to trick us, and to be honest, I'm still not convinced by your motives."

"We told Gert we trusted you," Anatol said.

"And if they trust you, that's good enough for me. For now," Gert added.

Paul relaxed, although his pulse was still racing. He was shocked at seeing Gert, but trust had to go both ways, didn't it? If not, he might as well leave now.

Once Paul had taken his seat, the woman opened the door and left the room.

Paul wondered what might have happened had he made for the locked door. "Your wife, I presume?" he asked Anatol.

"Yes. Vanda."

"All right, I'm listening."

Anatol glanced at Gert who nodded and said, "Good, but before we begin, we need to set a few ground rules. We have no reason to doubt your sincerity, Paul. However, in the event of a double-cross on your end that results in our arrests, we will hand over a dossier containing proof of your own treasonous acts against the Third Reich. From this moment on, we are inextricably linked. If we go down, you go down with us. Is this acceptable to you?"

Paul gulped then nodded. "Yes. That's fair enough."

For an hour, the three Poles talked candidly about their operations, how they executed their rescues and what precautions they took. Paul had noted early in the discussion that they were steering clear of mentioning other Polish networks within the city and surrounding areas. He assumed the different cells might cooperate with each other, but it was clear that they were sharing only the vaguest of information about them, which was smart; if he knew nothing about these other units, he wouldn't be able to give the Gestapo information on them should he ever be interrogated.

What dismayed Paul the most was the growing threat to the rescuers' efforts, not from the Gestapo or SS, but from Jews.

"…we find it hard to believe as well, Paul, but Chaim Rumkowski is an autocrat." Anatol continued to elaborate on the Jewish menace against escapees. "His ghetto currency prevents people from smuggling food into the ghetto because the Jews no longer have real currency to barter with outside the walls. He makes sure his opponents are on the expulsion lists and reports those he feels are a threat to his position or are trying to subvert his rules."

Gert added, "He also testifies against people he's caught trying to escape even though he knows they will be executed."

"Anatol and Gert are hard on Rumkowski, but he brings a measure of stability and jobs to the Jews." Hubert puffed away at his pipe. "And we all know that were it not for the productivity of the factories contributing to the war effort, the ghetto would have no purpose and might even be shut down. And where do you think the Jews would go then, eh?" Hubert was much older than the other two men, and seemed to prefer listening to speaking, but Paul surmised nothing went on without his approval.

"My uncle is too soft on Rumkowski," Gert spat, "the old rat wouldn't hesitate to report any of us in this room."

Surprised, Paul stared up at Gert. "Hubert is your uncle?"

Gert chuckled. "My mother's brother."

Paul continued to listen to talk of the Jews acting on behalf of the Gestapo and SS. He had long since questioned Rumkowski's motives for siding with the Nazis, and asked, "What does this Jew get out of supporting the Gestapo?"

"He gets to live a little longer," Gert said. "He sees the successful escapes of fellow Jews as his failure and worries that he'll have his authority taken from him. Without his position, he's an old, fit-for-nothing Jew with his name on the top of the deportation lists."

Anatol added, "We're as wary of him as we are of the Kriminaldirektor, your father-in-law."

"I wouldn't worry too much about him," Paul said. "With his health as it is, he's on his way out."

Anatol nodded, "To be honest, it's a miracle he's still alive."

"Hah, it's bad luck if you ask me," Hubert grunted.

Vanda returned with black tea for everyone. She then sat on the arm of Anatol's chair.

Paul looked at the wall clock and realised he'd been there for almost two hours and that dinner wasn't coming. "I meant every word I said about wanting to help you," he said to Hubert, "but my biggest concern now is Kurt ... Karl ... I'm sorry, I can't get used to that name. I don't know how much Anatol told you about him, Gert, but he's running out of time."

"Anatol and Gert have come up with a plan. Listen to them," Hubert said, then grew quiet.

"We have safe houses dotted around the city, and despite the ongoing threat of execution should we be caught, our network continues to grow," Anatol began.

"But removing patients from the hospital to our safe houses has become more dangerous because of the Schupo guards at the ghetto's exit," Gert added. "They didn't used to look in the back of ambulance carts or under the sheeting covering the corpses until Biermann arrived in Łódź."

Paul, becoming more disheartened by the second, was wracking his brain for a way to get Kurt out, even as Anatol and Gert seemed to be closing every conceivable avenue. "How do you get people out if not in a cart going through the checkpoint?"

"We rarely do now. We concentrate on helping those we can, like the Jews who have been in hiding in the un-walled parts of the city."

"I have SS clearance to remove live patients from the hospital to our SS immigration headquarters outside the ghetto," Gert said. "But even I can't transport Jews without the proper paperwork."

Paul shifted his gaze from the fireplace and directed it at Gert. "As I told Anatol, Kurt is known to the Gestapo. It's a wonder that they haven't found him in that hospital storeroom yet. I can't ask you to risk…"

"Listen, Paul," Anatol interrupted. "Gert will not be involved in Kurt's rescue until after we get him out of the ghetto gates in a coffin."

Paul's eyes widened in confusion. "Jews don't get coffins."

"That's right, and that's why we're going to have his dead body transferred to the mortuary for research. The pathologist will take samples under the pretext of Kurt having died of an unknown, probable communicable disease such as smallpox, which would put the fear of God into the Germans. But of course, it will not be Kurt's corpse."

Hubert added, "It's the only time we get access to coffins."

"The head of the hospital pathology department is a friend of Hubert's. He often takes Jewish cadavers illegally for medical research for the ongoing education of junior doctors, and given that your father-in-law is out of action, we will have the time for us to get Kurt to a safe location from the public mortuary whilst taking another body already there to be buried in his place."

Hubert, packing his pipe with tobacco, said, "Even if Biermann finds out and sends one of his Kriminalassistents to the mortuary to confirm the body is Kurt's, he'll be too late. I'll make sure the anonymous cadaver is disposed of within an hour of Kurt's arrival at the mortuary."

"You can do that?" said Paul. "When will you do it?"

"Tonight," Gert answered. "But you've got to be as far away from the hospital as possible when we take him. I suggest you spend time with your wife."

"That's a novel idea. We'll go home to my apartment if I can tear her away from her mother's house." Paul had a lot of questions buzzing around his mind. Kurt's rescue plan seemed complicated, but he felt they had told him all he needed to know regarding the ins and outs of the escape, and it was time for him to leave. They had a job to do, and Valentina was expecting him at the Biermann's house.

He rose from the couch, relieved and excited about what he'd heard. "I have a lot more questions, but as time goes on I'll become more familiar with the finer details of your operations."

"Don't get carried away, Paul," Hubert warned. "This is a dangerous path you're taking, and only we four know what you're getting yourself into. Tell nobody, trust no one. This is how we survive."

"We will also be asking you favours, and we don't expect you to refuse us." Anatol slipped in.

"Yes … yes, of course. I'm grateful to you for trusting me. Will you … I presume you'll let me know where you've taken Kurt?"

The room grew quiet. "No," Hubert said with an emphatic shake of his head. "That's a detail we won't share. I hope you've said your goodbyes to him. You won't be seeing him again for a while. If you do, we will all have failed."

Chapter Fifty-Four

Kurt and Paul

"How are you feeling, Kurt?" Anatol asked, as he closed the storeroom door behind him.

"Better, Doctor. I'm not sure if it's day or night in here – what is the time?"

"Just after three."

Kurt, anxious about why the doctor was at his bedside during the night shift when doctors usually worked office hours, looked at the closed door and then back to the man who was filling a hypodermic syringe from a glass vial. "What are you doing with that needle? What's in it?"

Anatol squirted liquid from the tip of the needle and then replaced the vial in his pocket.

Kurt tried to sit up, but fell back, too weak to get up on his own. "Have you come to kill me? Is this how you do it here?"

Anatol put the syringe on the bedside table and smiled. "No, Kurt, I'm not going to kill you. I'm here to save your life. Paul Vogel has sent me to get you out of here, but to do that I need to give you an injection, a mixture of Atropa belladonna combined with morphine. It's a strong sedative that will make you sleep through your entire rescue. The Atropa belladonna and morphine are the nearest medications that we know of that can preserve life but mimic the symptoms of death. You will have dilated pupils and depressed respiration, which will get you through the briefest of inspections, which is all we need."

Alarmed, but desperate to believe Anatol, Kurt looked again at the needle. "Get me out of where … the hospital, the ghetto? Where are you taking me? How will you do it?"

"I'm taking you somewhere safe. As for your second question … how I'm going to do it? That doesn't concern you. All you need to know is you're in good hands. Paul trusts me, and you should, too."

Anatol sat on the edge of the bed. "Do you want the chance to live, Kurt?"

Kurt swallowed. *Yes, he wanted to live, of course! But he also wanted to know what the man was going to do.*

"Kurt, do you want to escape? If so, I must inject you now. Time is not on our side."

"And where will I wake up?"

"If we're successful, you'll be in the basement of a house, lying on a bed, and that is where you will stay until the Germans leave Poland. You might be cooped up there for months or moved somewhere else. The Gestapo might find you, in which case you'll be executed along with your hosts. This is your choice. I won't put you under or move you without your consent."

In hiding for years, or death in the ghetto or some concentration camp? Kurt mused. It didn't seem like much of a choice, but one outcome was infinitely better than the other. "I'll take my chances with you. Can I speak to Paul before you put me under?"

"No. Not until we think it's safe for him to come to you."

"I understand." Kurt had seen this doctor talking with Paul on a few occasions. Paul had mentioned that the man was a good friend and trustworthy, which he'd thought strange, because Paul didn't trust anyone.

Anatol placed his hand on Kurt's shoulder. "I don't have much time to do this. You either trust me or you don't, in which case I'll say goodnight and we will forget this conversation ever..."

"No. Please, Doctor, get me out of here. I won't ask you what or who is involved." Kurt, still in pain with three broken ribs, choked back a sob as his emotions flooded him with a potent blend of hope and fear. For months, he'd dreamt of freedom while believing he'd never attain it. If the price of life was a dark, dismal basement, he'd take it. He'd suffer every discomfort and months of loneliness to be free of the Gestapo, the squalor of the ghetto, and an eventual gas chamber.

Kurt sighed and relaxed. His eyes followed Anatol as he picked up the needle. "Thank you," he croaked when the needle found a vein.

"Freedom, Kurt, is worth every risk," Anatol said. "Without it, we are barely human..."

******

It wasn't pain that bothered Kurt the most but the bleariness preventing him from opening his eyes. His head, arms and legs felt trapped under a great weight. He tried to sit up, but waves of nausea swirled in the pit of his stomach and up his throat. His ribs still hurt, stabbing like daggers, and he had to concentrate on taking shorter breaths than was usual. He felt strangely relaxed, as though untethered to the world around him, yet questions were beginning to nag him. Whatever had happened, wherever he was, he seemed to be alive, but without any memory of what had occurred.

"Open your eyes … Kurt, open your eyes."

Kurt moaned. Someone was pinching his earlobes and tapping his cheek. "Get off," he groaned.

"Open your eyes…"

Shut up, Kurt wanted to say, as his face was slapped again.

Now his body was being pulled up the bed until he was in a sitting position with his head resting against a pillow. He tried again to open his eyes, this time managing to keep his eyelids up. Doctor Anatol sat on the edge of the bed, and standing behind him was a woman holding a glass of water.

"You … Anatol?" Kurt murmured.

"Yes. It's me," Anatol grinned. "You're safe, Kurt. We got you out."

Tears welled in Kurt's eyes, whether from relief or the drugs in his system, it mattered not. Unfettered emotions going back years poured down his face. He couldn't stop weeping, and being weak, sounded like a cat meowing.

Anatol, appearing deeply affected by Kurt's reaction, said, "You're safe now, you're safe. It's over." He stood up, giving way to the woman beside him. She sat on the edge of the bed, put the glass to Kurt's lips, and spoke to Kurt in Polish.

Kurt, trying desperately to focus on the woman's gold cross and chain, began to drift off until those annoying fingers tapped his cheek again. "Let me sleep…"

"Not yet. Take a sip of water, Kurt, just a few sips," Anatol urged. "It will help wash the drugs out of your system."

After he'd drunk some more water, but not as much as he would have liked, Kurt became alert enough to focus on his surroundings. Anatol and the woman stood close to the bed. At the bottom of the bed was a wall, and on either side of the bed, more walls, one of which had a door – he was in a tiny box.

"Where am I?" Kurt croaked.

"You're in my house, in a blocked off corner of the basement. This is my wife, Vanda."

"Hello … I'm sorry for sleeping…"

"Oh, don't apologise," said Anatol sitting on the edge of the bed again. "I gave you anaesthetics. I had to give you a heavy dose of morphine to make sure you didn't become conscious during the rescue.

"Is that why I feel sick?"

"Probably. They can have nasty side effects. There's a bowl beside you on the bed if you need it. You're going to feel groggy for a while."

Anatol indicated the tiny space. "It's not much, but it's all we have to offer for now. The main basement is behind those walls. This portion is concealed on the other side by my junk cupboards. Should the Gestapo or SS conduct a search here – and there's no reason why they should – they should not notice this small area. Not unless they tear the place apart. We'll keep you safe, and as time goes on and we become more confident, you can sit in the basement. We have an old armchair you can use, and books in German to read. I'll bring you the odd newspaper, although they are not always easy to find, and when you're feeling better you can come upstairs and eat with us, even listen to the radio."

Kurt coughed and drank some more water. He was feeling more like himself, but with consciousness came worries. "Biermann will be looking for me. He's a stubborn man, and he won't believe I'm dead until he sees my corpse. You and your wife could be in grave danger."

"Don't worry about him. He's very ill. He had a serious heart attack and though he hasn't been told, he's not expected to recover fully. He could have another one at any moment."

Kurt was elated. "Do you think he'll die?"

"He might do us all that favour."

God, please kill the bastard, Kurt thought. "Does Paul know where I am?"

"No, and I'm not going to tell him, for his sake and ours."

"I understand. I don't know how to thank you – I have nothing…"

Vanda poured water from a jug into the glass which she set on the vegetable crate beside the bed.

"Vanda will bring you some soup later, but you should sleep now."

Kurt's eyes teared up again. "Doctor, I don't expect you to understand this, especially when I'm not looking or feeling my best. You see, for as long as I can remember, my life has been an endless battle for survival … now I'm… it has purpose again. Not yet, but when I regain my strength, I'd like to fight the Nazis. Is there any way you know of to get me out of the city?"

Anatol chuckled. "We'll talk about that some other time – and, yes, I do understand. Sleep now."

Alone with his thoughts of freedom and battles to come, Kurt let out a contented sigh, then drifted off, his tears still wet on his cheeks.

******

"You're back," Biermann grumbled when Paul entered his hospital room. "I've had a horrible night. Is Valentina with you?"

"No, she was looking a little peaky this morning, so I told her to rest."

"This damn heart attack of mine isn't good for her or the baby. It's a bloody nuisance for everyone concerned. It couldn't have come at a worse time."

"Frau Biermann will be here soon," Paul said. "I thought I'd catch you alone before she arrived. I didn't think you'd want her to hear the news that Kurt Sommer died during the night. His internal injuries were too serious to treat."

Biermann's face turned purple and he clicked his tongue. "Hmm. Unfortunate. Not good news. You let me down, Paul … let yourself down."

"With respect, sir, I didn't beat Kurt to death. You and your Gestapo did."

Biermann frowned. "Where's Sommer's body?"

Hubert had personally instructed the sympathetic pathologist dealing with the corpses at the public mortuary to incinerate the cadaver of a ghetto Jew while recording the dead man's name as Karl Ellerich. Biermann's investigation was over, Paul thought, and that meant he was safe, politically, at least. His father-in-law was a lying, vicious piece of shit. Hopefully, his obsession with Dieter Vogel's paintings would fester and give him another heart attack to finish him off.

"I don't know where Kurt's body went. I was at home with Valentina last night. I found out about his death this morning. Three others died as well but they were also insignificant Jews. I'm sorry, but I didn't think to ask the nurse where their bodies were taken. I presume they were incinerated if contagious or buried in the Jewish cemetery pits," Paul answered with a mournful expression.

"I want to see Karl Ellerich's corpse. I won't be tricked again … not again."

Paul shrugged, "I'll make enquires, but the chances of his remains being intact are slim."

"Even so, you will try. Bring what's left of him here to me."

Biermann was tired, but Paul was beginning to wonder if he might have also lost oxygen to his brain. He shook his head and muttered, "You want me to bring a corpse to your bedside? Are you mad?"

"No, not mad … diligent. I don't trust you, Paul. When did you see him last?"

"Yesterday evening. And I told you then he wasn't expected to live through the night."

"Did he say anything to you?"

"Apart from he didn't want to die, no."

Paul rose from the chair, throwing Biermann a defiant glare as he crossed to the other side of the bed. There, he poured water from the jug into an empty glass, and then handed it to his father-in-law. He'd suffered enough questions from the old bugger and didn't need to tolerate them anymore.

"Sir, may I speak to you as a son-in-law who cares about you?" Paul asked in a more affectionate tone.

Biermann's skin was tinged grey, his lips still blueish with oxygen deprivation, but his eyes hadn't lost their superior arrogance. "If you're going to tell me to give up on my investigation, don't bother. I've sent word to Manfred Krüger, my Inspektor. He's familiar with your father's case … and with Hauptmann August Leitner's murder."

Paul's eyes widened in genuine surprise. "Leitner? Murder? What murder? He died in a car crash."

"No … don't think so, and neither does Hans Rudolf … remember him?" Biermann sat up straighter and took a deep breath through his oxygen mask before pulling it down to the edge of his chin again. It was on, off, on, off, depending on whether he listened or spoke.

"I had a chat with the Inspektor before leaving Berlin," Biermann continued. "He had some interesting theories to share about Leitner and you, and about the day the Hauptmann died. Kriminalinspektor Krüger will interview you about Leitner and Karl Ellerich when he gets here. Given my inability to work at present, I will direct him from this bed – I'm sorry, Paul, but I cannot let family connections interfere with these cases. You must understand."

Paul's jaw tightened, as he felt himself falling back into the Gestapo hole he'd just climbed out of. He clenched his fists, furious that his heart was beating a tattoo in his chest. Biermann, even at death's door, continued to have the upper hand.

"Why are you doing this to me ... to yourself? You're going to have another attack if you get worked up about a tragic accident that happened almost two years ago. It's a closed case ... and the ... the fixation you have with my father has already cost Kurt his life. Will you have it cost your daughter her marriage?"

Paul paused to catch his breath. "What are you trying to achieve? You're chasing ghosts that no longer have any bearing on your life or that of your family. No one cares about Dieter Vogel anymore. For Christ's sake, let it go..."

"How dare..."

"Yes, I dare!" Paul panted, fuming now and careering out of control. He glanced at the pillow behind his father-in-law's head and wished he had the balls to crush the life out of the man.

Biermann's hands trembled as he pulled at the oxygen mask, clicking his tongue again and again like an annoying tick. He gestured to the door, waving Paul off with his habitual dismissal. "I have my reasons, and I will pursue your father for as long as I live and breathe, using any means at my disposal. I will win, Paul. I always win. Now, get out and don't come back until you have what I asked for. I want to see the Jew's body, or at the very least a photograph of the corpse … and I expect an apology from you."

Paul turned at the door. He would never come back to this room while Biermann was in the bed. "I pity you. You have everything a man could ever want … a family that loves you, and a new addition about to be born … a miraculous recovery from a heart attack that would have killed healthier men than you, and the chance to retire and get out of this war…"

"I'll have everything I want when you cooperate with me, and I see your father hanging for his crimes…"

"I'm doing nothing for you. And you will not threaten me again."

"I am Gestapo!"

Paul's chest heaved with anger as he approached the bed again. "You might be a Gestapo Kriminaldirektor with a long reach, but I also have connections in Berlin. My father met some very important people in his professional life, men of higher standing than you. They came to our houses, they ate my mother's food and bought us kids presents. Try … dare to come after me with your Inspektors and Assistents, and I will set an even bigger pack of wolves on you. You, *Father-in-law*, will rue the day you smeared my father's good name and desecrated his grave. Now, for your daughter's sake, let this be the end of it." Paul turned on his heal and slammed the door behind him.

Chapter Fifty-Five

Max Vogel

London, April 1942

Since their return from Grimsby, Max had given Romek plenty of opportunities to mention the letter with the rare twenty-pound note that Mrs Mullins had given him the minute he'd walked in the front door. Max had informed Romek that guards were no longer needed to monitor his movements, and he was to stand down from all intelligence-related business until Charlie at MI6 heard back from the Abwehr. And in the case of not hearing back at all, he was to be considered *burnt* and would be transferred to another British Intelligence section.

Their mission now, Max had also informed Mrs Mullins, was to find out why the Pole had been given such a large sum of money. To do this, Romek needed to believe he had the space to contact his female benefactor without MI6 constraints on him. The reality of the situation, however, was that even more agents were involved in around-the-clock surveillance on the Pole, with Max being kept in the loop as to Romek's whereabouts every time he left the house.

Max, who was still recovering from a bad cold, was reading a book in the living room. It was mid-afternoon on the sixth day of the current operation, and the gentle April showers had become thunderstorms with a downpour that had been hammering the streets all day.

Someone was moving on the stairs. Even if one tiptoed, the squeaking sound of uncarpeted wood alerted those in the living-room and kitchen. Max was dozing off with his heavy novel, *The Story of My Experiments with Truth,* by Mahatma Gandhi, resting on his chest. He jumped at the noise, leapt off the sofa, and went into the hallway.

"Where are you going, Romek? It's pouring down out there," Max asked from the living-room doorway.

Romek opened the front door with one arm already in his coat sleeve. "I like the rain, and where I'm going has nothing to do with you. Heller has let me off the hook, remember?"

"You're not going out in that, are you love?" asked Mrs Mullins appearing in the narrow passageway. "You'll catch pneumonia. It's raining cats and dogs!"

Romek cocked his head to the side and looked puzzled, "Well, Mrs Mullins, as long as a cat or dog doesn't land on me, I'll be all right. I'm going to the library. I won't be long," said Romek going outside, and closing the door behind him.

Max waited a few seconds, then went to the living-room window where he watched Romek hurry along the street in the direction of the underground station; the library was two streets farther on from there, as was Camden market and the shops.

"Do you think he's going to the library?" Mrs Mullins asked Max.

"No. He picked up two books yesterday," Max replied.

Mrs Mullins said, "It's been six days since I gave him the envelope, Max, and he hasn't said a word about it. Despite his moods, I find him a rather nice chap. I'd hate to think he was double-crossing us."

Max agreed. Agents knew their number one rule was to alert their handlers when anything out of the ordinary happened or if they met anyone not directly involved in their cases. Romek's silence on the letter and money was troubling.

"Mike and Tom are tailing him. If Romek so much as goes into a pub or café they'll telephone me. Don't worry. If he contacts anyone, we'll know.

"Well, I hope you get to him before he does anything silly. He can be slippery, our Romek."

"As can I."

The telephone rang fifteen minutes later, and Max instinctively knew the operation was a go. This was confirmed when Tom explained that Romek had met with a young woman in a bed and breakfast establishment called Rochester's in Camden High Street. Tom had observed Romek and the female speaking to an elderly man at the reception desk before disappearing up a flight of stairs, presumably leading to a bedroom.

Mrs Mullins helped Max on with his coat.

"Thank you. I hope this doesn't become violent, Mrs M. I'll lose if there's a punch up. I'm still not feeling great," Max grinned.

"That's why you have Tom and Mike at your back. If you ask me, you should be on leave recovering from that cold, not here babysitting Romek."

Max ran to the garden gate, closed it behind him, and made for the opposite end of the street to the one Romek had headed for. His car and driver were parked out of sight, just around the corner.

"Let's go, quick as you can, Stan," Max said, diving out of the rain into the passenger seat. "We're going to the Rochester Bed and Breakfast. It's on Camden High Street near the market."

Stan put his foot down. "I might not be able to park outside because it's market day, sir," he said as he pulled into the traffic.

"Get as close as you can."

Tom opened the passenger door for Max as the car came to a stop outside the Bed and Breakfast. Mike was also there, and he was moving along a flower shop van so that Max's car could park. Very few vehicles were on the road nowadays, but market stalls and people selling bomb-damaged goods on wooden handcarts had overflowed from the High Street and were blocking adjacent roads.

Inside the three-storey Bed and Breakfast, Max ordered Tom to watch the entrance for anyone else going in or coming out while he spoke to the owner of the establishment.

"A man and women arrived about fifteen minutes ago. My friend standing at the door used your telephone just after they went upstairs…"

"That's right, 'e seemed to be in a bit of an 'urry. It's all legal 'ere. I got me papers to prove it," the man interrupted.

"You're not in any trouble," Max assured him. "I just want you to tell me which room the couple went to?"

"Who are you?"

"I'm with the government and this is very important – which room?"

The man, his eyes flicking from Max to Mike and finally to Tom, responded with a grimace, "Oh, Gawd, I 'ope I'm not gettin' into any funny business 'ere."

Max extended his hand, palm up, "The spare key?"

"Now, I don't know about that…?"

"Give me the key, or I'll have you arrested for obstructing an on-going investigation."

"I don't bleedin' know … comings and goings … strange men and women dolled up," the owner grumbled, as he took a key off a hook behind him. "Up those five steps to the mezzanine floor.

Room two, you can't miss it. The number's 'anging upside down – screw loose."

As Max walked up the stairs with Mike behind him, he resolved to go easy on Romek. It was possible, he thought, that this was nothing more than a romantic dalliance between Romek and the woman who had sent him money. It might not be a great mystery but a very simple one, easily solved. For the first time that day, he felt as though he were the one doing wrong, an interloper in what might be a private party. Nonetheless, when he reached the door, he turned the key in the lock and walked in without knocking.

"Shit – shit, Romek! Go downstairs, Mike. Make sure we have the right room."

Max flicked his eyes around the empty bedroom. The bed was made, the window wide open with rain coming in. Max crossed to it, stuck his head out and looked down. It was an easy jump onto the tarpaulin of the full horse-drawn dustcart parked directly below. Even without it, an agile man and woman could have made it.

An envelope sat on the bedside table with *Max* written on it. Max picked it up and ripped it open. *Goodbye, predictable Max – bye, bye.*

"This is definitely the room, sir, and I checked with Tom, no one has left the building."

"At least not through the front door," Max said, scrunching the letter in his closed fist. "Nice one, Romek. Very nice."

******

When Max arrived at Heller's office, soaking wet and fuming, Heller didn't look the least bit surprised to see him. Stony-faced behind his desk, Heller gestured Max to sit, and then immediately picked up a two-page letter with the Polish Government in Exile's official stamp.

"It seems Romek has been busy. This arrived an hour ago with Captain Kaczka. I never did like that man with his heroic limp and leery smile. I should have expected this, I suppose," Heller said, still clutching the letter.

"You said he brought this an hour ago? That's about the same time I was racing around Camden looking for Romek."

"Well, more fool you."

Max let the sarcasm go, sensing he was in more trouble than Romek. "I take it the Poles had something to do with Romek's disappearance; if that's what's happening here?"

"Before you read the letter, you should know that I'm not going to take Romek to task over this. Because of our recent botched mission, as the Twenty Committee see it now, they have decided to let Romek go, but take the necessary action against the Poles. This has caused a severe loss of trust between our two governments, and it will have to be resolved."

Max, not taking in the part about the Poles, grumbled, "Is this a joke? After getting this far with Romek, we're now going to let him walk out on us just because he doesn't want to play anymore?"

"We didn't get anywhere with him, Max," Heller retorted. "Romek and the Poles have been planning his defection for weeks ... since day one ... read it for yourself."

Max read the letter from top to bottom, but then went back to the highlighted paragraphs. The duplicity in them stung him to the quick.

Romek's family, of which there are seven surviving members in Poland, were removed from Warsaw and subsequently relocated with the Free Polish Army for their own protection. This was after an operation which lasted weeks and involved numerous Polish Free Fighters in situ. Only Romek's grandmother and great uncle chose to remain in their home, and they were arrested by the Gestapo three days ago and are presumed to be dead or incarcerated.

Max's head shot up as that sank in. "Does this mean what I think it does?"

"Yes. Given that the Abwehr have not sent a single transmission to Romek since the North Sea fiasco, we must presume they found the loss of their U-boat and agents suspicious. Romek is finished, and unless we want to give him a new identity and put him back in the field as a subagent, we might as well let him go."

"What about the woman, Nowak, who sent him the money?" Max cocked his head.

"She works for the Poles. I presume Romek was going to disappear and use the money she sent him to hole up somewhere until our Captain Kaczka got him out of the country using Polish resources. Or he might just have been toying with us for the fun of it. We might have scuttled their plans by intercepting the letter and then whisking Romek off to Grimsby, but the truth is, and it's in the letter, Romek probably schemed to make his family safe and then bugger off to join the Polish Free Army from the word go. There's no great mystery here, Max. His stunt this morning was to humiliate you. We've been triple-crossed, and that doesn't happen very often."

Max felt the irony. He'd trained Romek who'd apparently become a better spy than he could have hoped for. All of Romek's visits to the library, his cups of tea in the local café, and his walks in Camden had probably entailed contact in some form or other with other Poles. They would have been brief encounters; a handshake and the passing of a note, a nod of confirmation for a meeting, a fleeting, coded conversation with someone in the library, a note inside a book?

"What now for Romek?" Max asked.

"Nothing, as far as we are concerned. We don't want to throw him in jail, and if he's not going to cooperate with us, the Poles might as well put him to good use in Poland." Heller grunted, "It could have been worse, I suppose. He might have been working for the Krauts instead of the Poles. I persuaded Captain Kaczka to bring Romek in. We'll debrief him and then let him go."

Heller leant across his desk. "It would be better for all concerned if you weren't included in the meetings, Max. Leave this to us now."

Max frowned. "I've let you down."

"You let yourself down by giving Romek a reason to hate you. Go to Bletchley, get your health sorted out. I need you back here in five days. You'll have new orders to come back to. A posting out of the country."

"Where this time?" Max asked, still coming to terms with his last assignment being abruptly terminated.

"I'll come to see you in Bletchley over the weekend. I have business with your father, and I believe we have a birthday party to go to. We'll discuss your new posting then."

Max was desperate to know where he was being sent, but he sensed that Heller had finished with him for the time being and didn't want to rock an already shaky boat. It had been a tense meeting, and he was certain that many of the details surrounding Romek's defection had been left out of the conversation because he was no longer considered to be trustworthy.

"I'll see you in Bletchley, then," Max said, getting to his feet.

"Max, before you go … I will be telling Romek about his wife's death when I see him, but not how she died. If you ever see him again, keep your mouth shut. I don't want any more cock-ups. You hear me?"

"Yes, I understand." Max swallowed. "Thank you, Jonathan. It'll be easier for him coming from you."

Heller dismissed Max with a wave of his hand, and the latter walked out of the office feeling two feet tall and two years old.

Chapter Fifty-Six

The Vogels

Bletchley Park, England

Max took Judith to the pub for a quick lunch, after their long country walk. She was beginning her afternoon shift at three o'clock and wouldn't be home until after midnight.

Max felt better than he had in months. His concerted effort to switch off the noise of war and to enjoy a more serene setting with those he loved had done him the world of good.

He was constantly thinking about his new posting, however, for Jonathan had mentioned it without using the word assignment. A posting was of a more permanent nature than a mission or operation, and Max was anxious; he had no idea where it might be or for what duration, and he'd not yet shared the news with his family.

Max caressed each of Judith's fingers as she studied the menu. With her, he'd found a peace that not even Klara had been able to provide during their most passionate encounters when obsession and desire had overruled his head and his heart.

Romek's betrayal had knocked Max for six. He'd arrived at his parents' house a conflicted man and with his confidence in the gutter. Judith had sensed his troubled mind, and without question or demand had lifted him up. She *was* his peace, a gentle soul, a safe harbour to shelter in when he felt himself floundering. He was in love with her. It was not a question; it was his truth, and it had come so very easily to him.

"I've had a wonderful time with you, Judith," he said.

"And we still have the weekend together." She smiled. "I was thinking, Max, if you want I could visit you in London. I'll be working with Mr Heller again soon."

He couldn't lie to her. To her, he would give only honesty for she deserved that and more. "If I could, I'd be with you every day, dearest, but I'll be going away again soon. It might be out of the country."

"You are?" Judith whispered. "Of course, you are. It's your duty. Take care of yourself – I couldn't bear it if…"

"Will you wait for me?" Max held her eyes. "Is that asking too much?"

Two small creases formed between Judith's eyebrows. "What does it mean to wait for you? Of course, I'll be here or in London."

He smiled at her naivety. She was not being coy, at least not deliberately; she just didn't understand his meaning. The previous day, they had kissed, cuddled, and had even lain naked on a rug in an old barn they'd found during a picnic; the only occasion the weather had allowed them a long outing in the fresh air. They hadn't made love, but caressing her, exploring her body and feeling her warmth against his bare skin had seemed more intimate and beautiful than anything he'd ever experienced before with a woman.

Max recalled a question Hannah had once asked their mother. His sister had been a teenager at the time, full of romantic ideas and dreams of men sweeping her off her feet. "Mama, when did you know you loved Papa?" Hannah had asked. Their mother's answer had been immediate. "The first time your father took me to dinner, I felt comfortable, settled, as though I'd known him all my life. It was as if an electric lightbulb had been switched on inside me. Everything seemed brighter, warmer. I felt safe, and for the first time I saw my reflection in another's eyes. You can't possibly understand, dear, but one day, you will. I promise."

Max had thought it a ridiculous feminine notion to believe that love could blossom in an instant, but their mother had aptly described how he felt now with Judith. Perhaps he had phrased the question wrongly? War didn't give love the luxury of subtlety.

"Judith, what I meant to say," he began, still holding her gaze, "was that I am falling in love with you, and when this terrible war is over, if I make it through, I would like to spend the rest of my life with you."

Judith's hand, still clutched in his, tensed. "I had no idea."

Max was startled at the confusion in her face. Was she angry, shocked or maybe afraid to say she didn't feel the same way about him? Had he gone too far, too soon? *Stupid idiot.* "Forgive me, Judith. This probably isn't the right time. I shouldn't have…"

"Oh, yes… yes, you should have," she pre-empted him, now with tears brimming. "Whenever I read your letter, I prayed I'd see your feelings in the words, but I didn't dare think you could love a woman like me – a Jewess."

"No. No, Judith, you must never see your religion as a detriment, not under any circumstances. You must know by now that most British people abhor fascism and racism in all its forms. There will always be bigots in this world, and those who fear the unusual, the different, the idealists. But, to me, you are Judith, intelligent, sweet, kind Judith, and one of the strongest people I've ever met. I can see you love me too, my darling, so let's not waste a moment more on small hurdles made large by the weak and the cowardly." Max took a sip of water from his glass, then cast all caution aside. "Will you marry me? Say yes, please … be my wife."

She nodded. Then nodded again uttering a tiny sob. "Yes, Max … yes, I will … oh, I wish I could thank Paul and your father right now for saving me. They brought me to you. I think I must be the luckiest woman alive."

******

Laura had made a beautiful birthday cake, despite the sugar and flour rationings. She'd bartered with other women in the village for the ingredients she'd needed to bake the sponge and make it rise. "You've outdone yourself," Dieter had remarked when he'd seen it.

It was midday, and Judith's birthday lunch was to begin at one o'clock. Judith, who had been working until the early hours of that morning, was still asleep, and Laura had ordered everyone in the house to keep as quiet as possible.

Hannah and baby Jack were also attending the party, but Hannah, worried that Jack's squeals would wake Judith up, had bundled her son in his pram and headed off on a long walk in the crisp air to tire the toddler out.

Dieter, Heller and Max huddled in Dieter's office. It was, in fact, called a third bedroom, albeit not big enough to house a bed. Dieter often retreated there to listen to his radio and read as many newspapers as he could lay his hands on. The news was often slow to go to press, meaning he usually learnt more about the latest developments through intelligence gathered at Bletchley Park before headlines for public consumption hit the stands. But despite the delays, he enjoyed certain journalists' perspectives on politics and the war.

Heller and Dieter were discussing the recent German strike on Malta. Valetta, the Maltese capital had been hit hard and its iconic Royal Opera House had been reduced to rubble. Max kept his eyes on Heller, hoping he'd finally tell him where he was being posted to. Unsure if this was Heller's way of compounding the rebukes he'd received in London, Max was erring on the side of caution. Far be it for him to interrupt his boss and Dieter Vogel. He supposed he should be honoured for being allowed to attend the intimate gathering in the first place.

Heller had talked about everything from the sinking of the American coastal steamer SS *David H. Atwater* by gunfire from a German submarine off the United States East Coast, to the newly released comedy film, *My Favourite Blonde*, starring Bob Hope and Madeleine Carroll. But he had not seen fit to put Max out of his misery, yet.

Max excused himself and went to the kitchen for some water to settle his nerves and curb his frustration.

Laura touched his arm. "Max, I've just woken Judith, so be a love and tell your father and Jonathan that I'd like them to be seated at the dining table in twenty-five minutes."

Max returned to the office where Heller and Dieter were in the middle of a discussion about Egypt. He leaned against the wall near to the door as the debate heated up and waited for the opportunity to relay his mother's message.

"We should never have committed to that second British intervention in February," Heller said. "What right did we have to compel King Farouk to accept al-Naḥḥās as his prime minister? The monarch will get his revenge on us, you wait and see, Dieter."

"I thought it a necessary evil to stick our noses in," Dieter disagreed. "And the Wafd party's overwhelming success in the general election last month proves that the British took the right action. At least we'll have better cooperation with this new government."

"It's not looking good over there," Heller shook his head. General Rommel's *Deutsches Afrikakorps* are revelling in their advances. Between you and me, we're being out-fought every inch of the way. If the Germans keep going, they'll push us out of Cairo altogether."

As though seeing Max for the first time that day, Heller then asked Dieter, "May I have five minutes alone with Max before lunch?"

"Mother wants us seated in twenty minutes, Father," said Max.

"I'll go and give her a hand, shall I? Don't be long, you two."

After Dieter had left and closed the door behind him, Heller seemed to relax. "I'm sorry, Max. I wanted to tell you earlier, but you'll need to keep this under your hat for now, I'm afraid. I'm sending you to Cairo, but you'll also cover our Libya operations. I suspect it will be a long stint."

Max's heart raced. Give him a posting anywhere in Europe and he'd take it in his stride. He possessed the tools for the western front: languages, familiarity with terrain and culture, an in-depth knowledge of battle lines and strategies, clandestine networks and habits of both the Germans and the Resistance. But Egypt and Libya? Those countries and their inner workings were a mystery to him.

"Egypt? I'll admit that never crossed my mind," he said, calmer than he felt.

"Well, it'll be front and centre in your mind now. I'm giving you a week to get up to speed with the intelligence we have to date. We've lost two agents over there in the past six months. We think there's at least one mole in our camp, if not more. Egypt's turned into a damned hotbed for spies. I need my best over there."

Max eyebrows shot up.

"Oh, don't look at me like that. You know how highly I think of you. You're hot-headed and impulsive, Max, but despite your failings, you're still my best agent."

"Thank you, sir. When do I leave?"

"We'll get you kitted out and ready to go next Sunday, and in the meantime, this news must remain top secret."

"What am I to tell my parents?"

"That you're going off to war and you'll write to them, the same as every other young man does, I suppose. Max, I haven't forgotten what you went through with your brother Paul. Wondering if a loved one is still alive must be excruciating. I'll have a quiet word in your father's ear at the appropriate time, all right?"

Max felt a swell of love as he looked around the dining table. Mother giggling after Father had whispered something in her ear. Heller, rattling baby Jack's toy clown with bells on its hat, and making him giggle, and Hannah, a lost look clouding her pretty features, no doubt thinking about Frank and wherever he might be.

He gazed across the table at Judith's eyes, those wonderful dark orbs. Then on an impulse he tapped his coffee spoon against his water glass and rose. "Everyone, I have an announcement to make."

Heller's eyes widened, but Max shook his head. "No Jonathan, nothing to do with work or war. What I'm going to share is infinitely more personal and much more pleasant." He smiled at Judith, then at his parents, and finally at Hannah, who slid her gaze to Judith, perhaps with some feminine sixth sense.

"Come on, Max, don't keep us in suspense," said Dieter with a sparkle in his eye.

"I've bought a birthday present for Judith, and I wanted to give it to her at this table where she and I are surrounded by the people we love." He went into his pocket and retrieved a little blue velvet box. When he opened it, a gold ring of sapphires set around a diamond glinted in the light. "Judith, will you do me the honour of accepting this token of love, with the promise of becoming my wife?"

Laura squealed, startling Heller and Dieter who were staring with their mouths open.

"I knew it. I knew it would happen. I just knew it!" Laura jumped from her chair and raced to Judith's side, embracing her with kisses to both cheeks.

Dieter, with a much more subdued reaction, asked, "How and when did this have time to flourish?"

"When you weren't looking apparently, Papa," said Hannah, her eyes swimming.

"It seems none of us were looking," Heller said, with a surprised but congratulatory nod at Max.

"Well, what do you say, Judith? Do you think you can control my boy?" Dieter asked.

"No, not control." She giggled as she gazed at the ring Max was placing on her finger. "But I *will* love and cherish him always."

Chapter Fifty-Seven

Wilmot Vogel

Viipuri, Finland,
The Mannerheim Line
June 1942

Wilmot was thrown into action against the Russians as soon as he arrived on the Mannerheim Line at the beginning of May. The area surrounding the Syväri River, situated close to the Finnish-Russian border, had been mercilessly besieged. The three Soviet corps, encompassing large formations of KV-1 tanks, had breached the Finnish defences in April, and Wilmot had caught the beginning of the Finns and Germans' counterattack using four divisions of tanks from the remnants of the third and sixth *Panssari Komppania.*

Wilmot, sitting on the supply wagon next to Klaus, the driver, breathed the sweet air now free from the taste and stink of fuel, gun powder, and cordite from the Flak 88mm antitank guns that had clogged it for almost a month.

"I can't believe how warm it is. I didn't think I'd ever feel heat on my face again," Wilmot remarked to Klaus.

"Don't get carried away, Willie, it's only sixteen degrees."

"Hah, you should have felt what I did in the Russian forests when I was on the run … then you'd know what cold really feels like."

"You might be right. Ach, I suppose I've been spoilt being with the Finns. They're mostly outdoorsmen, and the cold doesn't bother them because they know how to tackle it. When I was with them in January on reconnaissance patrols they seemed to take the weather in their stride. Mind you, they do build good snow caves and dugouts, much warmer than we ever managed when I was with an all-German unit. To be honest, I think the cold weather is one of the reasons they've been successful against the Russkies. The Finns' tactics of using the heavily forested terrain to bottleneck the enemy with their vastly superior numbers has really worked. They've turned this countryside into a graveyard for unprepared Soviet troops.

"The Finns certainly seem to be motivated to fight," Wilmot remarked. "It's beautiful here." It was stunning but, although he'd never share his melancholic musings, he also sensed loneliness in every bush and rock standing in solitary splendour. They somehow reflected his own feelings of isolation.

The dramatic vista was interrupted by ugly wooden watchtowers like alien beings planted on foreign hills, squat stone bunkers, sad-looking raped tree trunks, and barbed wire fencing that distorted the otherwise perfect landscape.

The Finns had closed potential traffic and attack pathways with myriad anti-tank ditches and the circular defence lines made from square-pyramidal fortifications of reinforced concrete – the hedgehogs and dragon's teeth. These were supported by a complex system of ditches and barbed wire runs that protected the anti-tank barriers against sappers, bridge-layer tanks, and engineer teams. It had made a lot of sense to Wilmot, for the Russians were forced to attack trenches as they had in The Great War, without armoured forces or direct fire support and at a terrible cost to life.

"You know, Klaus, I've only fired my rifle once since getting here. Remember when that Soviet unit managed to sneak behind our lines? I'll be glad to get back to full duties. I've been quite happy sitting on this wagon, but I'm ready to fight now. I'm fit."

"You've been fattened up like a Christmas turkey, despite the rest of us feeling half-starved all the time," Klaus giggled like a girl, as he was apt to do. "I like your stories, Willie, we all do. You're a celebrity around here with your Russian prisoner of war tales, and the promise of an Iron Cross, not to mention losing your toes."

It was not for extraordinary feats that he was admired, Willie admitted to himself. It was his ability to turn his horrendous experiences into a humorous adventure saga. Only when he closed his eyes at night did he relive the savagery and suffering of his imprisonment and subsequent escape.

As they neared a Finnish fortified bunker, Wilmot noticed more changes in the landscape.

"Look, Klaus, the ice has gone. The rivers are running again … and I never noticed those brown rocks before…"

"That's because everything was white."

"Ach, it's beautiful."

"You sound like an old woman."

"I know …maybe …I suppose it's because I never thought I'd live to see anything like this again."

Wilmot suspected that his new-found appreciation for the land, and life in general, was due to his many brushes with death and his erstwhile belief that he wouldn't survive to see another spring or summer. His renewed optimism had lifted him out of the black hole of despair that had undoubtedly finished Haupt off. But in a strange twist of fate, it had also turned his grief to resentment. Wilmot rarely mentioned the Hauptmann to anyone. He'd been inconsolable for days after his friend's suicide, but now he was disappointed with the man who'd tried so very hard to survive only to throw his life away when he'd attained victory. Every day Wilmot thought, *Look, Haupt, look at what you're missing.*

Upon arrival at the friendly bunker, the unit of ten Finns and four Germans were given six-hours to eat and sleep before taking over line guard duties, allowing those men already in the bunker to go on reconnaissance. Wilmot helped Klaus unload the wagon and then went inside the tiny stone fortress that was their respite area. Floor mattresses and a wood-burning stove looked inviting; however, he noted that the place had no weaponry and armaments of any kind.

"We might as well put a welcome mat out for the Russians, Klaus. I can't see us holding back the Red Army with rifles," Wilmot remarked.

"Don't worry, Willie. This bunker hasn't seen action since February. I'll be quite happy to spend the rest of the war here. This is where I do all my writing."

"What writing?"

"You know, letters to my family, a bit of poetry."

Since his meeting with Major von Kühn in Viipuri, Wilmot hadn't thought to write to Kriminaldirektor Biermann. He'd presumed, wrongly it seemed, that the major would at some point hear back from Biermann. "To be honest, Klaus, I'm a bit disappointed not to have received a single letter from anyone since last year," he said, a little down in the mouth. "Kriminaldirektor Biermann – you know, the man I told you about – he hasn't replied to Major von Kühn in Viipuri, or at least he hadn't before we went on patrol. I was hoping he would inform my brother, Paul, and then Paul could maybe find a way to let my mother know I'm all right."

The lanky, freckled-faced, Klaus, looked puzzled. "Why don't you write to your mother in Berlin? That's where you're from, isn't it? The postal service picks up our letters once a week from Viipuri aerodrome, and they deliver mail whenever a plane comes in..."

Wilmot's face reddened. Keeping secrets and lying wasn't easy when one was apt to forget what the secret and lie was about. Luckily, Wilmot didn't need to say anything further on the matter, for a booming voice outside shouted for him.

"Schütze Vogel! Get out here – now!"

Outside, Wilmot was met by two German Panzergrenadiers getting out of a Soviet BA-6 armoured vehicle, which had been acquired after one of the recent failed Russian advances.

One of the grenadiers said, "We're here for you, Vogel. Get your gear together."

"What's going on?" Wilmot questioned his unit's Obergefreiter.

"You're going back to Viipuri. It must be urgent if they sent a tank for you."

"We have to leave now," one of the Grenadiers said. "We've been ordered to hand you over to a transport unit further up the line. They'll give you a lift to Viipuri. You'll be sleeping in the city tonight, lucky bugger."

Wilmot grinned. Joy spread through him, tears poured down his cheeks. "My God, at last, they're sending me home on leave."

"No, they're not. As far as we know, you'll be leaving Viipuri tomorrow afternoon to come back here. They just want to see you for a short time. God knows why, but there it is, get a move on." The Grenadier handed Wilmot his orders.

Wilmot, anxious rather than excited, strode towards the tank. "I'm ready to go now. My gear is already on my back in my rucksack."

The men in Wilmot's unit gathered around, patting him on the shoulders and back as he climbed into the armoured vehicle.

"Well done, Willie. Don't forget to pin your Iron Cross to your camouflage uniform before you come back. We all want to see it on you," Klaus told him.

Of course, Wilmot thought, *he was going to get his medal.*

In the armoured car, Wilmot looked at his orders which had been scribbled quickly on a piece of paper, and read, *08.00 at the Viipuri aerodrome. Wear dress uniform.* "Dress uniform?" he muttered. He didn't have one. He was carrying a toothbrush, a tin of tooth powder, and a fresh pair of long johns. The last item had been a must. When he'd been with the Russians, he'd shat himself, and that feeling of walking about with hard shite rubbing against his arse had disgusted him and made his backside raw. He'd been forced to keep them on, stinking like a sewer for almost a month. Never again, he'd thought, when he'd eventually removed the johns despite the sub-zero temperatures.

Alarmed by the vehicle's accelerated speed that was causing it to skid, Wilmot began to imagine more sinister reasons for his orders. He was to testify to a military court about Haupt's and Jürgen's deaths? He was to write yet another report about the Russians' military intentions, based on his time with them? He was in trouble for opening his big mouth about something or other, which he was prone to do, but on this occasion couldn't remember doing? *Be at the aerodrome at 08.00,* but he wasn't getting on an aircraft, according to the driver. So, what was it all about?

"Can either of you tell me why I'm going to Viipuri?" he asked. "You seem to be in a hell of a hurry to get me to wherever we're going. Am I in trouble?"

"We don't know anything," the driver shouted over his shoulder. "They'll probably tell you what's going on when we get you to the base."

"I wouldn't worry about it, Schütze. If you had done something wrong, they'd have sent us with a pair of handcuffs."

"Alright. That's comforting." Wilmot sighed.

Chapter Fifty-Eight

Viipuri, Finland
June 3rd, 1942

As soon as he arrived in the city's military barracks, Wilmot contacted Otto Krause, the man who'd guided Haupt and him through Viipuri's streets weeks earlier. He was determined to go out, get drunk, perhaps talk to a woman, and even kiss one if he were lucky. Not since Poland had he socialised with the opposite sex, albeit without having been allowed to touch any of them. He'd almost forgotten what it was to have a good time, and thanks to Otto kindly offering to take him to a club, he was looking forward to the evening ahead.

Outside the restaurant bar, Otto gripped Wilmot's jacket sleeve, stopping him from going in. "Just remember, Willie, the Finns aren't always friendly towards us. I don't know why they dislike us, but sometimes they deliberately start a brawl when they've had a few drinks. And don't ask me why, but our *Feldgendarms* usually take the Finns' side."

"What's our military police doing in Viipuri?"

"There's been a spate of German desertions, and they've been sent to get them back. They've executed two of the daft runaways already. Point is, don't lose your temper. Walk away from a fight, even if they insult your mother, and run like hell if you see the Feldgendarms coming into the bar. You've got your medal ceremony tomorrow, and you don't want to cock that up."

"Okay, Mama. Understood," Wilmot grinned.

When Wilmot entered the club, his mind reeled to his early days in the SS when getting drunk and rowdy was a common, almost required, off-duty pastime. The air was blue with smoke and the smell of tobacco, beer, and perfume. It was packed with Finnish and German troops in uniform and women dressed to the nines with red painted lips and beautifully coiffed hair.

"Nice, eh?" Otto shouted in Wilmot's ear.

"I'm in bloody heaven, Otto!" Wilmot shouted back.

They squeezed into chairs at a large round table where eight men were already seated, some with women perched on their laps. Wilmot smiled at a particularly lovely cigarette girl who was passing through the tables with her display tray of the new *Milde Sorte* and the more familiar *Atikah* cigarettes. On closer inspection, he counted only a couple of packs of German cigarettes, the rest were Russian *cardboard* lookalikes called *makhorka*.

Otto gestured to the cigarette girl with a wave of his hand, and when she got to the table he asked for four loose makhorkas.

Willie grimaced, his mind going back to his captivity. "Have you had those before, Otto? They're bloody disgusting."

"The German ones are too expensive. Only officers can afford them." Otto picked up a makhorka and waved it in front of Wilmot. "Someone's making a fortune taking these from dead Russians." He picked up three more, then paid the girl who smiled sweetly at Wilmot before leaving.

A memory of the Russian guards smoking the makhorkas flashed through Wilmot's mind. They flattened the ends by pinching the tubes to make them easier to hold, and when they'd finished smoking them, they'd spit great gobs of rancid phlegm on the ground.

At the sound of an American accent, Wilmot ogled the man sitting next to him. He was wearing a Finnish army uniform and was talking to the man seated on the other side of him.

As though sensing Wilmot's curiosity, the man turned and snapped, "What are you looking at, ya ugly Kraut?"

Wilmot kept his gaze steady. The American, in his mid-twenties with black hair and dark, almost black eyes, was much taller than the others at the table but thin as a rake. And he'd had more than enough beer, judging by the way he was cursing and rocking in his chair.

"Sorry, I didn't expect to hear English being spoken, even less so with an American accent," Wilmot responded in perfect English.

"Where did you learn to speak like that?" the American asked, surprised.

Wilmot extended his hand, and after some hesitation the man shook it. "I spent a lot of my youth in England. I've got some distant relatives there … haven't seen them in years. I'm Wilmot. You're from America, I take it?"

"Louisiana, been there since I was four years old – my family is originally from Helsinki. Name's Aleksi Koivisto. Call me Alek."

Wilmot felt a tap on his shoulder; Otto had bought the drinks and laid a tall glass of beer on the table next to Willie.

"I got you this," Otto said, eyeing the Americans.

"Where's yours?" Wilmot asked.

"At the bar. I've met some friends. I'll be back in a while."

Wilmot took long slugs of beer; it was cold and bitter but just what he needed. Then he turned back to Alek. "How come you're in the Finnish Army?"

"I wanted to kill Bolsheviks. I might have grown up in America, but this is my country, and these are my people. It's a long story, but to cut it short … back in 'forty, I read about the huge number of casualties from this area. I don't mind tellin' you, I got as mad as a bluebottle in August. One day, I was in New Orleans at work in my pa's garage, taking a break and reading the newspaper, and I just got up off my behind, packed a bag, said goodbye to the folks, and got myself on a ship, then another ship, trains, and God knows what else. Eventually I entered Finland through Norway, much like you Krauts did."

"So, you've been here for two years?" Wilmot asked.

"Yep, and a bit. I'm not the only American here, either," Alek said, pointing to the two men next to him. "See those two guys? They're Jewish Finns from Brooklyn, New York."

Wilmot's eyes widened. "You're Jews?"

"Yeah." Alek leant back in his chair. "You got a problem with that?"

Wilmot lifted both hands. "No. Not me, my friend."

Knowing what he did about the German policies on Jews, Wilmot wondered why Jewish foreigners would want to set foot in this part of the world.

"See, now, you Nazis are all the same when it comes to Jews. You really can't stand us, can you?" said Alek, taking an angry swig of his beer.

"Why do you say that?" Wilmot asked, eager to learn how much Alek knew about the Nazi persecution of the Jews.

"Why? It's kinda' obvious. All the newspapers are talking about the Jewish refugee situation in Europe. I reckon if they're all trying to escape Germany and other countries your lot have occupied, it's because nothing good is happening to 'em. I heard tell that Jews are being murdered by your Nazi buddies."

Wilmot's stomach twisted as he recalled the Russian guards going down a line of German prisoners and shooting them in the heads while shouting, *'That's for a Jew! That's for a Jew! And that's for a Jew!'* as they went along. He'd seen plenty of Russian soldiers kill Kikes; they didn't give a shit about their Jews' wellbeing, but they seemed to find them a good excuse to murder defenceless German prisoners.

Wilmot finished his beer and tried to calm his thoughts; he had little control of his mouth once he got going, and tonight was not the night to get on the wrong side of anyone. "You shouldn't say things like that unless you're sure of your facts. Maybe you should hush up before you get yourself into trouble."

Alek leant in, nose to nose with Wilmot, and growled, "I don't need facts, Kraut. Everyone knows you're throwing Jews into refugee camps and treating them like pigs. Well, here's a news flash for you … Finnish Jews don't get persecuted. We're respected, so you can forget about pissing us off in *this* country."

"For God's sake, what's wrong with you? If you hate Germans so much, why are you fighting with us?" Wilmot retorted.

The man sitting beside Alek leant across, his eyes round with beer. "Do you really think Finns wanted to ally themselves with your precious Adolf? No, no, boy, we're only sittin' here today because we need food and fuel and arms from Germany. That's the only goddamn reason." With that, he and Alek promptly turned their backs on Wilmot.

Wilmot pushed his chair back and lurched to his feet, the beer already affecting his brain. He wanted to find Otto; he was there to have a good time, not to defend his country against Americans who were now the enemy of the German people everywhere else but Finland, it seemed.

He looked down at the Americans whose loud, boorish voices irritated him. Unable to stop himself, he poked Alek's shoulder. "Why don't you lot join your own army? Go on, put your money where your mouth is and fight us Krauts like men on the battlefield."

He walked away before he could do any more damage and found Otto at the bar talking to a short, surly-looking man with his arm around a young woman in a floral dress.

After Wilmot had bought Otto a beer and swigged half of his own, he began to calm down. The soft, melodic voice of the singer soothed his angry soul, and eyeing pretty women took his mind of the recent altercation.

Seconds later, for no apparent reason, the dour-faced man landed a vicious punch to Otto's nose. He reeled back, blood dribbling down his face, then staggered into Wilmot whose beer glass went flying, the contents landing squarely on the front of the woman's dress.

All hell broke loose. The woman shrieked but Wilmot could do nothing for her as a punch from nowhere caught him on his cheekbone, followed by a right hook that crunched his jaw. He howled with pain and staggered backwards into people before skidding on his backside across the wooden dance floor.

Above Wilmot, Otto was body-punching a man in a Finnish uniform. Two other men were also throwing punches at each other, and women were screaming and running for cover.

Wilmot heaved himself to his feet, about to join the fray until some unseen strongman pinned his arms behind his back and frogmarched him outside.

Dropped unceremoniously to the cold, wet pavement, Wilmot howled when his bony buttocks hit the ground. Dazed, he raised his eyes and squinted up at the American, Alek, and his two tipsy, giggling buddies.

"Bloody hell, Alek, what was that for?" Wilmot said, getting warily to his feet.

"Like I said, Nazis are trouble every time. But you know what, Kraut, you don't seem like a bad fella. I figured I should get you out of there before you got yourself into a whole world of trouble. If I was you, I'd hightail it out before your military police fellas get here and whip your ass to jail. I'm bettin' most of them folks in there will be up on a charge or arrested before the night is over."

Wilmot brushed himself down, glad that he hadn't gone out in the dress uniform he'd borrowed for the ceremony the next day. He shook Alek's hand just as the Finnish police and two German Feldgendarms arrived in a military jeep.

"Thank you, Alek. I owe you."

"Yes, you do," Alek grinned. "Nice meeting you, Willie. Good luck. Don't you be getting' yourself into any more trouble."

Alone in the street adjacent to the barracks, Wilmot perched on a shop window ledge and gently prodded his swollen jaw. People were strange; he'd never understand them, he thought. He'd liked that Alek, and he'd had a great time. Pity it had ended abruptly and with only one and a half beers in him.

******

At 07:00 the next morning, Wilmot left for Viipuri's military airbase on a crowded truck carrying German soldiers. When they arrived, the concourse was packed with both German and Finnish servicemen who were forming into platoons. A rare gathering of high-ranking officers up to the echelon of generals were also on-site and huddled together near the air strip. Every so often, they broke off their discussion to look up at the sky as if waiting for a plane to land.

A military band was playing the *Westerwaldlied, Song of the Western forest.* Wilmot felt a surge of emotion; it was a marching song he and his platoon mates used to sing when they were on one of their gruelling hikes in Russia. *Oh, you lovely Westerwald! Over your heights the wind ...* funny, he couldn't remember the rest of it. It had gone, like his dead comrades.

Stunned by the massive turnout, he stood open-mouthed beside the truck, his eyes darting in every direction.

"Name and rank?" a gruff voice asked Wilmot.

"Schütze Wilmot Vogel, Herr Stabsfeldwebel. Heil Hitler!" Wilmot's insides were churning while the master sergeant checked his list.

"Form up with that lot over there." The Stabsfeldwebel pointed to four lines of men.

Wilmot reported to the Leutnant in charge of a German infantrymen platoon, repeating his name and rank, and adding his serial number.

"Very well, Schütze. Form up in the front row." The Leutnant ticked off his name.

The band began to play again as a brand new Focke-Wulf Pw 200 Condor aircraft came into land. It taxied and came to a complete stop a mere fifty metres from where Wilmot stood, but because the sun was shining in his eyes, he couldn't see who was disembarking the plane by its forward steps.

The platoon was ordered to come to attention. Wilmot's heart was thumping with pride as the band began to play the German national anthem, but loud as it was, he also heard the man standing next to him gasp and pull himself up even straighter than his ramrod position of attention.

Out of the corner of his eye, Wilmot saw the Führer – Adolf Hitler – striding across the runway in conversation with Finnish Field Marshal, Baron Carl Gustaf Mannerheim.

It's a dream. It must be a dream. It's too good to be true. Wilmot tried to wrap his head around what he was witnessing. Adolf Hitler was not only in Finland, he was now only fifteen metres away from the platoons.

Many times, Wilmot had been to rallies in Berlin where Hitler had appeared on a dais, so very far away he'd looked no bigger than a pin, and his voice had been like a whispered echo through a scratchy sound system. Yet here, now, Schütze Wilmot Vogel, was watching the great man in his brown Führer und Reichskanzler uniform walking across the airfield towards him.

Wilmot was very close to the action. He could see the Iron Cross pinned on Hitler's jacket; it was sparkling as though someone had just polished it. His coal black moustache was perfectly trimmed, and his face, although just as it appeared in photographs, was heavily wrinkled with a stark pallor. He looked human, as human as every other man there, but he wasn't like anyone else. *He was the Führer!* And there was a possibility, Wilmot thought, a real possibility that Germany's leader, would come closer and might even say something to someone in the front line of the platoon. He hoped he'd be close enough to hear.

Wilmot held his breath. His heart was banging so loudly under his ribs he thought the soldier next to him would hear it; but perhaps his too was pounding.

Hitler approached Wilmot's platoon, leaving Field Marshal Mannerheim to watch from a distance. The Leutnant saluted the

Führer with a snap of his arm and a click of his jackboots. Then the father of Germany walked past the first three men until he came to stand before Wilmot.

"Schutze Vogel, step forward," the Leutnant commanded.

Wilmot, his legs like pliant rubber, took a step forwards and stood proudly. He couldn't see Hitler's face, being a good twenty-five centimetres taller than his leader and with his eyes front, but eventually, he heard that unique, unmistakable voice.

"Schütze Vogel, you're a brave man," Adolf Hitler said.

Wilmot, his eyes smarting with emotion, said, "Thank you, Mein Führer." Then he dared to return his leader's gaze in a moment that would be forever etched in his mind and seared into his heart.

"I knew your father, Dieter. Not personally, you understand, but as a loyal member of the Party. He was a good Nazi and a great benefactor. My condolences. He will be missed."

"Thank you, Mein Führer."

The Leutnant held out a black velvet tray with the Iron Cross Second Class medal on it. The Führer pinned the medal on Wilmot's jacket at chest height just as the flash of a camera went off. Wilmot instinctively bowed his head, then saluted, "Heil Hitler!" Then the Führer walked off to another platoon.

"Congratulations, Schütze Vogel," Major von Kühn said, appearing in front of the platoon from the right with two Hauptmanns standing behind him. "You are promoted forthwith to Obergefreiter, by order of the Führer."

Wilmot was weak at the knees. Random thoughts tumbled through his mind as he stood to attention for a further fifteen minutes while Herr Hitler inspected the troops. He was now a Senior Lance Corporal. Him, Willie Vogel, no longer the grunt in military rankings. He'd shot up – *not just one rank, but about four.* He had just spoken to Adolf Hitler, an achievement neither of his brothers nor anyone else he knew back home would ever be able to beat. The Führer had known the Vogel name. He didn't just pretend to know it, he'd said, Dieter. This, Wilmot thought, was his finest hour, one that would live with him until the day he died and was buried – with his Iron Cross stuck to his chest.

Chapter Fifty-Nine

Paul Vogel

Łódź, Poland
June 4th, 1942

It had been two months since Biermann's heart attack which, according to the most renowned German senior physician available in Poland, should have killed him. Paul still believed that death was knocking at Biermann's door and could take him at any time, but every morning his father-in-law insisted he was feeling stronger. Maybe he was staying positive for his wife's benefit or because he truly thought his health was improving, Paul mused, but eventually the Biermann family would have to face the medical facts and deal with them.

Paul wasn't happy about lying to Biermann about his prognosis, but he had agreed with all the doctors who'd treated his father-in-law that it was important to maintain an optimistic outlook, not so much for Biermann's sake, but for Olga's, and, of course, Valentina's. She was nearing the end of her pregnancy, and as far as Paul was concerned, Biermann could die the day after she gave birth, but preferably not before.

Before arriving at the Biermanns' front door, Paul got out the key his mother-in-law had given him from his trouser pocket and peered through the dining-room window. Biermann, Valentina, and another man in a Gestapo uniform were already seated at the table. Valentina had mentioned that morning that her father had invited a friend from Berlin to dinner, and she'd reminded Paul numerous times not to be late.

"Ah, come in my boy, come in. We were waiting for you," Biermann said, as Paul entered the dining-room.

"I'm sorry I'm late," Paul said, as he bent to kiss Valentina's forehead.

The stranger got up and extended his hand. "Kriminaldirektor Biermann has told me a lot about you, Paul. It's good to meet you in person."

Paul's relationship with his father-in-law was now purely a farcical display of niceties created for Valentina and Olga's benefit, but they only thinly veiled the contempt both men felt for each other. "It's nice to meet you, Kriminalinspektor." Paul smiled at the good-looking young man.

"This is my colleague and good friend of … how many years, Manfred?" Biermann said.

"Six, sir."

"Six years, eh? Where does time go? Paul let me properly present Kriminalinspektor Manfred Krüger. He arrived from Berlin this morning."

"Are you planning to stay in Łódź for a while, Herr Kriminalinspektor, or is this a short visit?" Paul asked.

"I am relieving Kriminaldirektor Biermann, so I presume this will be an extended stay in *Litzmannstadt,*" he said, accentuating the German name.

Surprised he had not been told about this appointment, or that his father-in-law was leaving, Paul sat down next to Valentina and gave her a tender smile. Life was going to become even more difficult with a younger and more energetic Gestapo officer breathing down his neck.

"I hear you're kept busy at the hospital?" Krüger said, interrupting Paul's thoughts.

"Yes, all four hospitals are extremely busy, but desperately short of medical supplies…"

"Our armed forces need medical equipment and medicines far more than civilians do, and as for the Jews … well, I don't know why they're getting medicines at all." Biermann cut Paul off. "You'll have to make do … no point complaining about it."

"I know that, sir, and we *do* make do. But I'm a doctor, and my job is to care for the sick. To be honest, I sometimes think the Jews who are ill would be better served if they were looked after by family members in their ghetto homes."

"That's not a bad idea," Krüger mused. "It would certainly save money."

Paul raised an eyebrow. The Kriminalinspector apparently hadn't recognised the sarcasm.

Valentina rolled her eyes, a sign of impatience that Paul had come to know well.

"Darling, can we *please* not talk about your job at the table?" she snapped. "I'm feeling squeamish enough without having to hear about Jews dying every time you come home. I do wish they'd all just go away."

Olga appeared from the kitchen carrying a platter of pork. "Good, you're here, Paul," she said, leaving again with the promise of boiled potatoes.

Paul focused on his plate, disappointed again with his wife. He was tired of hearing her speak negatively about the Jews; she possessed not one iota of sympathy. "They probably wish they could go away as well, darling," he said when Olga reappeared with the potatoes and took her seat beside her husband. "I'm sure they'd much rather go back to their own countries than live in a ghetto with curfews and shortages." Paul picked up his knife and fork and began cutting the meat.

"Oh, really, Paul, how can you say that? I get angry thinking about how much it must be costing to feed them, when real Germans are forced to endure measly rations."

"Forget about the Jews, darling," Olga said. "We don't need to worry about them anymore, do we…?"

"Now, dear, I was going to tell Paul after dinner," Biermann interrupted.

"Tell me what?" Paul asked, flicking his eyes from Biermann to Krüger and then to Olga. "What have I missed?"

Krüger dug his knife into his potatoes, keeping his blond head lowered as he ate. Olga stared at her daughter, while Biermann beamed.

Paul tensed. "For God's sake, what is it?"

"We're leaving for Germany tomorrow morning," Biermann said. "I am being recalled to Berlin where a rather pleasant desk job awaits me at the Reich Security offices."

"I've never been happy here, Paul, you know that," Olga added hurriedly.

Paul wasn't surprised, but he was dismayed at their bad timing. Taking Valentina's hand to comfort her, he said, "I'm surprised you're leaving now. Valentina could do with your support, what with me being at the hospital every day. It would mean the world to her if you could stay here until the baby's born."

Valentina pulled her hand from Paul's grasp as though his fingers were scalding hot. "I'm going with them, Paul."

They were waiting for him to respond, but Paul's throat had closed, and he couldn't swallow or breathe. He reached for his glass and forced himself to take a sip of wine, and then another. Even Krüger, a man he'd only met five minutes earlier and who had no right to hear this private family conversation, seemed to be enjoying the moment. Valentina was leaving him. *What the hell was he supposed to say?*

He turned his back on Biermann and Krüger and faced Valentina. "Darling, you haven't thought this through. You're due in less than two weeks … it's far too dangerous for you to travel. I can't permit…"

"She'll be in a first-class carriage and quite safe with us," Biermann butted in. "I've spoken to the senior physician who visited me from Warsaw, and he has assured me that my daughter will be fine. She wants her child to be born in Germany, not Poland. Do you find that so very hard to understand?"

"Will you give me a minute to discuss this with my wife?" Paul retorted, his eyes boring into Valentina's. "Dearest, listen to me. We were given the opportunity to live together in married quarters in a foreign posting. Do you know how rare that is? If you leave, you'll be taking my unborn child with you, and when he or she is born you might not be able to return to me."

"She knows how fortunate she was to live with you here, but your apartment has nothing to do with the Wehrmacht or your posting," Biermann piped up again. "I've been paying for it out of my own pocket so that you and Valentina could be together, and her mother and I could have her close to us. And it has cost me a small fortune, I might add."

Paul was dumbstruck, and unable to find a dignified response.

Biermann smirked. "That's right, Paul. When we leave tomorrow, you will have to vacate your lodgings and go into barracks. I suggest you start packing tonight."

Paul finally turned to Biermann, his eyes brimming with hatred. It had always seemed strange to him that an officer of his low rank should have the luxury of living with his wife in married quarters, but before leaving Berlin, Biermann had assured him that he'd taken care of everything regarding their move to Łódź. He'd even gone so far as to say he'd signed the Wehrmacht Accommodation application forms on Paul's behalf.

"You deliberately manipulated me into this posting using your daughter as bait," Paul said, no longer caring about showing respect for his father-in-law or behaving like a good son-in-law for the benefit of Biermann's newly arrived Gestapo dog. "You lied through your teeth to me, to my wife, and to yours."

"Now, that's enough of that. I demand respect for the Kriminaldirektor!" Krüger growled.

"Shut up, Inspektor. This is a family matter. It has nothing to do with you." Paul stretched out his hand to Valentina. "Darling, let's talk about this in private."

Valentina lowered her eyes, unable or unwilling, to look at her husband.

"Valentina, listen to me. I can afford to pay for the apartment, or this house if you'd prefer to stay here? I can even afford to employ a nurse to live with us until well after the baby's born and you're back on your feet. I have money – don't leave, please. Think about what you're going back to – the Allies are bombing Berlin. The attacks are more frequent now. You and the baby will be much safer here…"

"Stop it, you're scaring me. I want to go home." Valentina sniffed. "I'd never forgive myself if anything were to happen to Papa and I wasn't with him."

"What about me? I want to see my son or daughter being born. Is this what *you* want, or have your parents persuaded you?"

"No. I want to go. I'm sorry, Paul, but I hate it here. And Papa's right, I want our child to be born in Berlin with Mama and Papa to help me through it. Please understand, I got such a terrible fright when Papa became ill, and I can't … I won't have the baby in this horrible country, and with all those thousands of Jews who could riot or go mad and take over the city. Can't you think about me for a change? You work every day, and I'd be so very lonely without my parents' company."

"But we're a family ... you and I, and our baby. We've come this far ... darling, please, don't make me miss my baby's birth."

"Paul, won't you try to understand her point of view? She's made her decision. Please don't badger her." Olga sobbed as she clutched her husband's hand. "You're upsetting everyone."

Biermann scowled and picked up his fork, his other hand still held captive by Olga's. "Let's eat before this lovely dinner gets cold. Come on, Paul. Valentina has made her decision, and I won't have you bullying her into changing her mind."

Paul leapt to his feet, knocking his chair back and throwing his napkin on the table. He was furious, humiliated and felt as though the woman he loved had just slapped him publicly across the face. *Love?* He wasn't sure what that word meant to Valentina. She certainly didn't have anything like the feelings he had for her. "If you're leaving in the morning, will you at least come home to the apartment with me now? We can have one last night together, can't we?"

Valentina began to cry, using her napkin as a handkerchief. "Papa's driver helped me to pack this morning, and I ... well, I just don't want to go back there ... sit down, Paul. I'm very upset, and you're spoiling the night for our guest."

With his pride and marriage in tatters, Paul leant down and kissed Valentina's cheek. Unable to suffer Biermann's smugness and his sidekick's amusement, he backed away from the table. "What time is your train tomorrow?" he asked Valentina.

"Nine o'clock. Where are you going?"

"I'm going home. I have a very early start at the hospital, but I'll come to wave you off at the station…"

"This is preposterous! How dare you walk out on your wife and us and this wonderful dinner. Sit down, Vogel!" Biermann barked.

"Freddie, please don't excite yourself," Olga cried.

"Blame him if anything happens to me." Biermann coughed.

At the door, Paul gave Valentina a long, hard stare before saying, "You're leaving me. You understand that?"

She nodded.

"All right. I'll see you tomorrow before you depart." Defeated, Paul mustered what little pride he had left, raised himself to his full height, clicked his heals together, and gave those at the table a shallow bow of his head. "Enjoy your meal. Goodnight."

Chapter Sixty

On his way to the apartment, Paul had little trouble justifying deserting his wife on the eve of her departure. He had no excuse, he knew that, but his pain had been too much to bear. The indelible stamp of humiliation, made complete under his father-in-law and Inspektor Krüger's barely concealed sniggers, would never wash off him. Any remnants of respect, mutual trust, and loyalty between he and the Biermann family had disintegrated, and it would never be retrieved. Valentina had chosen. She had elected to leave him and return to Berlin despite the ongoing Allied air raids on the German capital and her pregnancy almost at term. He was the outsider, the last consideration in all her decisions.

He closed the door behind him and cast his eyes around the almost empty apartment: a bedroom, a living area, a kitchen and a bathroom. The place looked abandoned. Valentina's feminine touches were gone: the ornaments and flowers, home-made cushion covers, bedspread, curtains to match, and her clothes. His heart pounded erratically. All gone: the baby's crib, towels, nappies, and the bits and pieces lovingly gathered for the infant's arrival had been removed. All, but the residual fragrance of baby talc remained; Valentina loved to sprinkle the powder on her body, and that reminder pained him more than anything else.

He picked up a red presentation box containing the gift his father-in-law had given him upon his arrival in Poland; a 1936 bottle of Glen Grant. At least Valentina had left that.

On the kitchen counter, he found a brown paper bag. He put the bottle into it and then headed to the front door. He didn't need this empty nest; he needed a friend.

When Paul arrived at Anatol's villa – it was not the first time he'd turned up without an invitation – he suspected he was going to interrupt his friends' dinner. It had been a gruelling day at the hospital with multiple cases of influenza being reported in the ghetto, and Anatol, who'd left the hospital five minutes before Paul, had remarked that he was going straight home to his wife.

As Paul predicted, Anatol and Vanda were finishing their evening meal. Anatol invited Paul to sit at the table whilst Vanda fetched two long tubular glasses for the Scotch. Upon hearing that Paul hadn't eaten anything since that morning, she then brought a plateful of chicken pieces and a potato.

"Like everyone else, we don't have much, Paul, but chickens we have. Had," she said with a heavy sigh.

Anatol poured the whisky into the glasses, and then he and Vanda remained silent as Paul related his rotten evening at the Biermanns'.

"What will you do, Paul?" Anatol asked.

"What can I do? Valentina has made her feelings clear." Paul clasped his expensive whisky in both hands and took a sip. He'd been candid. Without hesitation, he had aired feelings about his wife that he, thus far, had held very close to his chest. Trust had grown between him and Anatol, and Paul was grateful for the shoulder to cry on. The least he could do was be completely honest. "So, there you have it. I can't see a way forward."

Paul picked at the chicken, forgetting his awful situation for the moment. "Thank you. This is just what I needed. Do you have your own chickens, Vanda?" he asked.

She frowned. "I had twenty, but the SS confiscated eighteen last week. After we suck the bones of this one, we'll be down to one – it's not even producing eggs anymore, poor thing. I think it must be lonely – I don't even want to eat it."

Anatol stroked his wife's hand. "She was very fond of her chicken coop, Paul. We have a large garden at the back of the property that no one can see from the street. Vanda used to give the eggs and chickens to neighbours and family, and those who are helping to hide Jews."

"I had roosters, hens laying eggs, and others producing chicks. I can't imagine who told the SS we had poultry. I was very careful not to broadcast their presence to anyone."

"To be fair, darling, they did make a racket," Anatol said.

"I know, but why would someone want to tell the Germans about them when I went out of my way to feed the neighbours? Oh, well, it doesn't matter who it was, I suppose. I was lucky to hold onto them for as long as I did, considering the Germans take whatever they want." She got up, smiling though clearly upset. "I'll leave you two to talk. I have ironing to do."

After pouring two more whiskies, Anatol said, "Tell me more about this new Gestapo Inspektor."

Paul tensed. He was still furious, and even more so now that he'd got the disastrous Biermann's last supper off his chest and a whisky in him. "He's cocky, as you'd expect from a Kriminalinspektor. He and Biermann seemed close … I mean very friendly. I wouldn't be surprised to discover that the new man is every bit as nasty as Biermann but with more energy. I'm worried, Anatol. I think you should warn the others that Krüger means business."

Anatol poured water from a jug into an empty glass. "I'll certainly mention him to Hubert and Gert, but as long as we keep our noses clean and continue to use the systems we already have in place, we should be all right. It's you who should be concerned. If your father-in-law's malevolence is as bad as you say, the new Kriminalinspector will be keeping a close eye on what you're doing. It might be better if you continue to pilfer drugs for us when you can, but don't take part in any rescues."

"You're right. I understand." It upset Paul that he couldn't contribute more to the network. "I'll try and do more pilfering in the future." He grinned.

Anatol sighed and smacked his lips. "Ah, I never thought I'd taste a Scotch as good as this again."

Paul chuckled. "I find it hard to believe that my father-in-law once liked me enough to give it to me."

Anatol's smile died. "I'm sorry, Paul, very sorry about your wife leaving. But, maybe it's for the best, eh?"

"Yes. Maybe it is." On the tram journey there, Paul had considered that with Valentina out of the picture, he'd have more freedom to help what he now, secretly, called the Polish Resistance. "With her gone, I'll be moving into the barracks. It will have its challenges and drawbacks, of course. The Wehrmacht loves its inspections, and as an officer I'd feel compelled to socialise in the officers' mess, but it could work..."

"... in our favour?" Anatol mused.

"Hmm, yes, I suppose it could. Officers love to gossip. It might help us."

"Paul, I have to ask this," Anatol said. "I trust you, I do, but this has been on my mind since you got here. Blame the whisky, whatever, but ... you see, I don't understand why people like you and Gert are still serving in the Wehrmacht when you both detest what you're being ordered to do. Why not run – fight the Nazis? That's what I would do – how can you want to...?"

"… you don't understand how it works, and you certainly don't know me well enough to judge," Paul retorted, then instantly regretted it. "I'm sorry, Anatol. You're not the first person to ask." Paul took a slug of Scotch. "I have a twin brother. His name is Max – we're identical – and I mean identical in every way."

Anatol's eyes widened in surprise. "Well, that is something I didn't know about you."

Paul felt liberated just saying Max's name. Too afraid to mention him to Valentina and Biermann, who had made Max the unclean, the outlawed before Paul had married into the Biermann family, he now felt his eyes welling up with emotion.

Anatol had relaxed, his look now strangely sympathetic as though he sensed Paul's pain before he'd even mentioned his earlier troubles. "What's really bothering you?" he asked while pouring Paul two-fingers of neat whisky.

"Max is an officer in the British army."

"Dear God, how did that happen?"

"It's a long story. Let's just say my family is complicated, and of mixed blood."

"You have British in your family?"

Paul chuckled at Anatol's gaping mouth. "Yes, on my mother's side. Max was always for the British, never for Hitler or his Nazis. I suppose the question you asked hit a raw nerve because it's the same question he's asked me many times. But what he and you don't seem to understand and should, is that I have family in Germany, an uncle, aunt, cousins, and more importantly, a younger brother serving in Russia. If I were to run, not only would my family be punished, I would also lose my wife and unborn child."

"It seems to me you have already lost your wife."

Paul flinched at that cold, hard truth. "Yes, you might be right."

In the silence that followed, Paul pondered over how big a threat the new Kriminalinspektor might be, especially now that Valentina was leaving Poland and had apparently been brainwashed by her father. Whilst Paul was confident the Gestapo had no evidence of any wrongdoing against him, he was also aware that the secret police were very good at fabricating charges. Now convinced that Biermann wanted the Vogel art collection, he tried to imagine how Krüger would go about getting the information he and Biermann needed, now that their star witness, Kurt Sommer was *dead.*

The new Inspektor would chase his own tail, as Biermann had in the last few weeks, Paul deduced. Maybe he shouldn't be afraid of Krüger, after all, or maybe the whisky was relaxing him a little too much, and he was missing something.

"Anatol, I should be getting home," Paul said with a yawn. "I need to pack, but before I go, I was wondering if it might be possible for me to visit Kurt one day?"

"We've been through this, Paul…"

"I know, I know, and I appreciate the need for secrecy, but I'd love to see him with my own eyes … you know, have a chat with him … it will put my mind at rest. If it makes you feel easier, you could blindfold me on the journey to wherever he's living. I don't even have to see the faces of the people who are hiding him."

"No. I've told you how he is. He's well, getting stronger, and living with Poles in a house somewhere in the city. That's all I will tell you. Please, don't ask me again." Anatol gave Paul another sympathetic look. "I understand you a bit more now, Paul. We have a hard road ahead of us, but you can and will play a role, as will Gert, and perhaps one day soon, Kurt as well. We have big plans, a new war to fight, and these plans will revolutionise what we are doing here."

Paul, his interest piqued, hesitated at the door. Anatol handed him the remains of the bottle of whisky in the paper bag, then gave Paul an affectionate pat on his shoulder. "Go home. We'll have time enough for business in the days ahead."

Paul got on the tram, his thoughts whirling. He was disappointed at not being able to visit Kurt. He was bereft, worried, and missing his family more than ever. But he was also coming to terms with Valentina's departure. Maybe, as Anatol had pointed out, it was for the best. She still loved him; it wasn't over. Their marriage was being put on hold as were many during this war, and he had probably overreacted. He would put his family back together when the war was won, and he went home to Berlin. He'd focus on those goals.

As he staggered slightly along the street where he lived with his bottle tucked in his jacket, his thoughts turned to Wilmot. Poor Willie, always the forgotten one. He'd write a long letter to his younger brother, and then he'd write another to Max, even though he would probably never send it. He wanted to make Max proud, and one day he would. Strange, he was no longer afraid, but excited. Anatol had said a new revolutionary war was coming, and he was not a man prone to exaggeration.

The Guardian of Secrets

Winner of the 2016 Outstanding Historical Book of the Year the IAN Awards
Silver Medal, 2015 Readers' Favourite Awards

Reviews

"It has been a long while since a book has pulled me in as much as this one did. Spanning generations and countries, we are taken through WW1, the Spanish Civil War and the build-up to WW2 and beyond, almost a century of history, culture and creed. From the green fields of Kent to the orange groves of Valencia, we go on a journey with Celia Merrill as she seeks to escape her abusive husband. I cannot begin to describe where this book takes us, for this review will then be pages long, but it is an emotional journey.

"The author clearly researched well. I was there for every bomb that fell and smelled the hot air filled with orange blossoms. This is so well written it did not feel as if I was reading; it felt as if I was there, in place and in time. Excellent work.
"This is a big book in every way; how wonderful to read something with depth and length. Guardian of Secrets deserves each of the five stars and I highly, highly recommend it."

About the Author

Jana Petken is a bestselling historical fiction novelist. She served in the British Royal Navy and during her service studied Naval Law and History.

After the Navy, she worked for British Airways and turned to writing after an accident on board an aircraft forced her to retire prematurely.

She is critically acclaimed as a gritty, hard-hitting author who produces bold, colourful characters and riveting storylines, and she has won numerous major international awards for her works.

For more about this book and any other Jana Petken novel:

Contact Jana Petken

Website: http://janapetkenauthor.com/
Blog: http://janapetkenauthor.com/blog/
Facebook: https://www.facebook.com/AuthorJanaPetken/
Twitter: https://twitter.com/AuthoJana
Pinterest: https://es.pinterest.com/janpetken/
Youtube: https://www.youtube.com/watch?v=gmrLECGgP8I
Goodreads: Jana Petken
Email: petkenj@gmail.com

Made in the USA
San Bernardino, CA
29 November 2018